"IS THIS ANOTHER CIVILIZATION TALKING TO EARTH?"
Letters began to form a string of words along the bottom third of Sam's screen.

"NAME DESIGNATE SAM"

Sam gasped. "My God, what is this?"

"FROM HIS SIG ATTAINED AT TAU CETI PLANET. MESSAGE RECEIVED AS FOLLOWS"

Sam's and Lisa's attention jumped from the computer screen to the receiver speaker as they heard static and then a human voice:

"So back to you in New Zealand, Mac. Again, the name here is Sam. I am six years old and I live in Pasadena, California. . . ."

Sam violently rolled his chair away from his equipment. He was ashen, his voice weak. "Lisa, my God. I sent that transmission in 1976. They know who I am. Maybe they know where I live. What do they want with me?"

SETI

FREDERICK FICHMAN

A ROC BOOK

ROC
Published by the Penguin Group
Penguin Books USA Inc., 375 Hudson Street,
New York, New York 10014, U.S.A.
Penguin Books Ltd, 27 Wrights Lane,
London W8 5TZ, England
Penguin Books Australia Ltd, Ringwood,
Victoria, Australia
Penguin Books Canada Ltd, 2801 John Street,
Markham, Ontario, Canada L3R 1B4
Penguin Books (N.Z.) Ltd, 182-190 Wairau Road,
Auckland 10, New Zealand

Penguin Books Ltd, Registered Offices:
Harmondsworth, Middlesex, England

First published by Roc, an imprint of New American Library, a division of
Penguin Books USA Inc.

First Printing, November, 1990
10 9 8 7 6 5 4 3 2 1

The Search Begins

All had not agreed on the wisdom of the program, but the program had been initiated.

Eighteen common-sized asteroids had been placed in position so that the entire quadrant would be covered. The asteroids were precisely carved and secured together. Linking multiplex duplicators were implanted and focused toward the main collector. Analysis and computation were performed by tuned wide-spectrum analyzers.

At first the received signals were random and disjointed. Their content made no sense. Finally, image formation had been completed, but the content again made no sense. Library images had been compiled and studied; still no sense could be made of the content. Trying to think like the aliens who had sent them did not make it easier to decipher their meaning.

The decision was made to concentrate on audio signals containing voice component only to break down the psychology of what had been sent. Not as much data needed to be analyzed; more valuable were the message and the sounds made by the alien voices.

Then, there was an amazing happenstance. While old data was being cleansed, a lower-frequency emission was detected, recorded, then analyzed automatically, systematically. The signal was clear and precise due to the voice qualities of the alien sending it.

Subsequently, the specific radio source was considered an element of a general-radio-frequency planetary beacon drifting in the mass radio confusion of naturally occurring background noise. The radio source was from a planetesimal 3.617 parsecs away, from a quite ordinary sector of the galaxy orbiting a quite ordinary star. The position was third plantesimal from that star, its distance ninety-two million miles.

Some time later, correlation with a future event directed attention to this transmission. The connection would be explored and considered. Perhaps the time was now right to take advantage of the signal and tangent planetesimal recovery.

CHAPTER 1

He could barely see over the desktop, but three thick Los Angeles phone books helped. His small hands were just strong enough to twist the stubborn frequency knob. But six-year-old Sam Alexander could copy Morse code at twenty-two words per minute, in his head, and no one his age in the United States held an Extra Class FCC Amateur Radio License. He was a radio-communications prodigy.

It was very early in the morning, and Sam was sitting at an old battered desk cluttered with amateur-radio receivers and transmitters and associated equipment. Pilot lights and power-indication bulbs of various colors glowed and winked as Sam's tiny voice was amplified and transmitted from a tall vertical antenna just outside his window in the backyard of his modest Pasadena home.

He was still dressed in his pajamas, his feet covered by a pair of old floppy socks.

The morning sun was blasting through an aluminum sliding window just to the right of his desk. It flooded the room with bright light that penetrated every square millimeter. But it could have been the dark of night; Sam was concentrating on the awkwardly accented English voice being transmitted from Yugoslavia, halfway around the world.

Most boys his age had posters of sports stars or movie favorites plastered over their walls. Sam's walls were covered with QSL contact cards from around the world. Artwork and photographs blended into a collage of colored images from the most remote parts of the Earth. The entire wall behind his bed was covered with a wallpaper world map. Sam had stuck small red pins in every country he had contacted either by voice or Morse code. He had 128 pins on that map so far. He was waiting for his father to buy another box of pins so he could stick in eighteen more.

Most boys his age knew where the nearest toy store or movie house was located. Sam knew the locations of the Seychelles, Sumatra, Western Samoa and Belize. Although English was the preferred language on the voice frequencies, passing pleasantries in German or Spanish or French was not difficult for Sam.

Sam said his 73s—his goodbyes—to Stephan in Zadar, situated on the Adriatic coastline. His voice carried through the Shure 444 microphone and into his Swan transceiver. The electrical signal was modulated and amplified further as it sped through the Heathkit linear amplifier. It moved out of the house through the coaxial cable to the eighteen-foot-long, ground-mounted vertical antenna. At the speed of light, 186,000 miles per second, it shot off the antenna and angled toward the ionosphere. The signal, for the most part, reflected back toward Earth. The process was repeated till some of the electrons passed the amateur antenna of YU2RST in Yugoslavia.

But not all the signal was reflected back to Earth. A small number of electrons were headed on a journey and into deep space.

Sam flipped the power switch to the off position and turned to look at the map of the world. Yugoslavia seemed to stand out in particular detail. He knew it was difficult to contact that country; not many ham-radio operators were allowed on the air there.

He swung back around and grabbed a pencil. He began to scribble into his radio log the frequency, time as described in Greenwich Mean Time, Stephan's call sign, and Stephan's city. Then he put the pencil down, and a broad smile crept across his sweet face. His dark hair almost covered his clear brown-green eyes. He was excited, and he wanted to tell his father.

Sam swung his feet to the edge of the chair and hopped off. He padded to the narrow doorway, then stopped as he sniffed the smell of bacon, suddenly permeating the house. He could hear his mother banging pots and talking back to the voice of the ingenuous talk-show host on her small kitchen radio.

On his route to the kitchen, Sam stepped into his father's combination office and ham shack. Now as many QSL cards or maps covered the walls, but here was just as much, if not more, amateur-radio gear of every type and description. The room was the same size as Sam's, but the lighting was more indirect. One wall was filled to capacity with books, mostly scientific; subjects ranged from astronomy to physics but were mostly radio-wave propagation and microwave radio astronomy.

Congratulatory plaques from various scientific organizations were situated next to achievement letters and awards from the Jet Propulsion Laboratory. One picture showed Sam's father, Peter, sitting in the small cockpit of an old Cessna 150 two-seat aircraft. Another picture was of Peter and another man standing next to a large steel-frame, dirty-gray radio telescope.

Peter Alexander, hunched down in an overstuffed chair, was engrossed in the morning paper; he didn't hear Sam until the little boy had bounced into his lap. Peter was startled but pleased to see Sam. Sam greeted his father with a big yawn and curled up in his father's lap into a small ball of love and warmth. Peter took off his glasses, gave Sam a hug, and kissed him on the forehead.

"Good morning, Sammy," Peter said softly.

Sam seemed sleepy again, although he had been up for an hour working with his ham-radio gear. He replied to his father with a small grunt, then snuggled farther down into Peter's lap.

Peter folded his paper and tossed it onto the nearby equipment desk.

He looked down at Sam. "Hey."

Sam closed his eyes and looked very nearly asleep.

Peter moved a bit to look Sam in the face. "Hey, sleepy-head, I heard you on this morning. Any interesting countries you contacted? I got into Canada and Mexico. Whatddya think of that?"

"That's nice." Sam yawned. "I worked . . . uh, let's see."

Peter waited for the answer. Then he shook Sam very gently. "Hey, c'mon. Who did you work this morning? Please tell me. I'm really interested. Tell me?"

"OK," Sam said, as he opened his eyes. "Lessee . . . I talked to Antarctica last night, and . . . and I talked with stations in West Germany and Yugoslavia this morning.

"The foreign DX was really coming in good, Dad," he added with sweet innocence.

"You did it to me again."

"Sorry, Dad. I just got lucky."

Peter hugged Sam again. "Hey, that's OK. Someone in the family has gotta rack up those countries."

"Yeah, I guess. But at least they let you try for those alien planets at work. Can I help you with that sometime?"

"Someday. Someday."

Sam snuggled again into the warmth of his father's arms.

Sam adored his father and loved his mother dearly. They were special, not like other parents. His were the best parents in the world. He was proud of his father's radio-astronomy work at JPL, although he didn't understand it. He loved his mother's cooking and admired her ability to throw a baseball, although he did wish she threw the ball a little harder and straighter.

"I'll tell ya what you can help me with," Peter said.

"What? Tell me."

" 'member what I promised last month?"

Sam sat up quickly, his eyes wide open. "This morning? Are we going this morning?"

Peter playfully grabbed his son's stomach. "While you were in your room talking to the world, I was in the garage packing and getting ready."

Sam jumped up in excitement and landed on his feet. "Oh, boy! The desert!"

The incline of the blazing-hot sand dune was approximately twenty-six degrees, but the large black desert beetle had no problem scampering to the top. The low-angled afternoon sun glistened on its shiny carapace. The gentle tapping of its feet mixed with the soft whine of the wind. The sky was deep azure; the sand was blanched bone-white by the relentless sun.

The insect crested the dune, then stopped, frozen in position. It flinched as the silence was shattered by the deafening roar of an unmuffled VW engine. Sailing over its tapered head, roaring over its jet-black body was a 150-horsepower sand-rail dune buggy.

The cherry-red vehicle threw its two occupants to one side, then the other, as it raced down the dune. The beetle disappeared under the sand, looking for shelter from the noise and vibration.

The dune buggy continued up, over, and around the undulating dunes that stretched out for miles ahead. In every direction, all that could be seen were the dunes. Occasionally a motorcycle or all-terrain vehicle would jump over the horizon, then plunge into the sand valleys. Now and then, a screaming military jet would maneuver overhead, making another run and pass at the target range miles away. But it was the roars and screams of the dune buggies that dominated what was heard on those dunes.

To the north, the dark-brown chocolate mountains and the seemingly endless stretch of the Mojave Desert. To the west, more desert and the farming town of Brawley. To the southwest, the Mexican border and the border town of Calexico. To the southeast, the Arizona border and Yuma.

The Sand Hills were one of two favorite spots in the California desert where enthusiasts pushed themselves and their machines against the 37.5-degree-incline dune limit, the scorching heat, and the unstoppable intrusion of sand. The sand that provided the perfect footing for the twelve-inch-wide paddle tires was also the enemy of carburetors and the possibility of a good night's sleep. Sand collected in carburetor eject tubes and human ear canals with equal ease.

The red buggy roared away from the still-buried beetle, kicking up rooster tails of sand in its wake. It crossed over the lip of one dune, made a dizzying run several times around a tight sand bowl, launched into the air again, then jolted to the top of a 400-foot incline. It moved farther away, the engine noise becoming fainter, as the sun touched the top of the dunes in the west. The temperature and the wind began to drop as night approached.

Sam put his hands behind his head as he stretched out on a small blanket, perched on the precipice of a flattened dune. Thirty feet away, Peter struggled to loosen a screw in the carburetor assembly; he readjusted the flashlight to move it closer to his work. The red dune buggy had turned black in the darkness.

Peter put down the screwdriver and looked around at the dunes. Far in the distance, he heard the roar of engines and saw the pinpoint dots of hundreds of headlights of other dune buggies trying their luck on Competition Hill. Peter tightened his windbreaker. He looked over at his son.

"Sam, have you zipped up your jacket?"

Sam stared up at the dome of sky, filled with stars, galaxies, supernovas, pulsars, quasars . . . planets. He replied weakly, "Yes, Dad."

"That's all I need to do—bring you home sick. Your mother would kill both of us." Peter turned his attention again to the carburetor.

As Sam looked up, he tried to delineate the solar system. He saw the steady glow of Jupiter; that was easy. He could almost see the small bumps on either side of Saturn. The rings? Was that Saturn? He didn't think that any other planets were in the sky at the moment. There, the Orion nebula; the gas has a greenish tint. Right?

The silence of a meteorite encountering the Earth's atmosphere belied its brilliance as it arched overhead.

"Ooooohhh! Did you see that?" Sam asked.

"What?" Peter replied.

Sam, continuing to watch the night sky, didn't answer. Then he rolled onto one elbow. The roaring of the distant dune buggies grew louder as several tried to scale the steep Competition Hill and be first to make it to the top. Bragging rights would be important around the desert campground fires that night.

Away from the hill, Sam could see single buggies bouncing up and over smaller, more manageable hills, moving in absolute silence. Their million-candlepower halogen headlamps were dots of light against the featureless blackness of the desert mounds below Sam's vantage point.

Rolling over on his back again, Sam looked up at the sky. He concentrated on the artwork above.

"Dad?"

Peter, who finally had taken the carburetor apart, meticulously began to remove sand from the slender blower tubes.

"Dad?"

"Yes, son, what is it?"

"How many stars are in the sky?"

Without looking up, Peter replied, "More than you could possibly imagine."

Sam seriously considered the answer and continued to stare at the sky.

"Dad?"

The questions never stopped, Peter thought. He didn't mind but was amazed at how they were an integral part of his son's personality.

"Yes, son, what is it now?"

"How many of those stars have planets around them? You know, like the Earth is around our star, the Sun."

Peter stopped his tedious work and looked over at Sam. "More than even both of us could possibly imagine."

Sam was very proud of himself and very pleased with the answer. He smiled and nodded. "Good. I hope so."

Below and beyond, the concentrated dune-buggy lights laced through the plane near Competition Hill. Scattered much farther away, tiny lights crawled across the desert floor almost to the horizon. Sparkling above the horizon were the tiny lights of distant suns—of stars millions of miles away in space and millions of years ago in time. It was difficult at certain moments to differentiate where the horizon ended and the sky began; they blended together without demarcation. It was difficult to separate the battery-driven lights of the dune buggies and the nuclear-force-driven light generated by the stars. It was all one tapestry.

CHAPTER 2

11.8 Light Years Later

The city of Escondido, California, was inland and north of San Diego. The sight line to the east was dramatically enhanced by the piercing, rugged, barren mountains of the Anza-Borrego Desert State Park.

Twenty thousand or so people lived in that city, which was the gateway to the Anza-Borrego Desert and the Mojave Desert beyond. Escondido was sprinkled with mini-malls, business-technology parks, and stretches of single-family-housing units that resembled the color of the hills just to the east.

The Alexander family ran a successful auto garage just off the main east–west highway, Route 78. That state highway ran eastward toward the mountain community of Julian, climbed over the hump, then dropped into the desolation of the desert. The Alexanders had the last fully stocked garage and competent cadre of mechanics the intrepid motorist would encounter before challenging the searing desert heat and the freezing nighttime temperatures.

The main Alexander house, a two-story Cape Cod with a detached three-car garage, was situated just off the road a few hundred yards away. Above the garage, seventeen-year-old Sam Alexander lived alone in a large window-lined guest room complete with full bath and mini-kitchen. His Aunt Marion and Uncle Stu lived in the main house with Sam's five-year-old twin cousins, Cindy and Mindy, and his nineteen-year-old cousin Sara.

Throughout the evening, Sam was on the roof of the

garage. The flat roof was topped by a redwood deck to prevent Sam's feet from punching a hole through the ceiling. Access to the roof was through a trap door that Sam had designed and cut himself. Two twelve-foot-diameter satellite dishes dominated the space; an amateur-radio antenna farm studded the remaining area. Aluminum tubing and cables ran in various directions in seeming disarray. Sam knew the function and operational parameters of every antenna part.

Shafts of light from Sam's trouble lamp danced around the roof and at the base of one particular dish. Sam grunted and groaned as he tried to tighten the remaining loose bolt near the bottom joint of the azimuth motor and the short-stub tower mounting. Finally securing the two-inch nut, Sam tossed the ratchet socket wrench aside. He stood up, took a deep breath, and looked up and around at his antenna farm. He pulled one of his Aunt Marion's dishtowels from his back pocket and wiped his hands. Zipping up his leather bomber jacket, he examined the cable line as it entered the room below through a six-inch conduit. He stepped back to the edge of the roof and gazed upward at the starfield. The lights of Escondido blocked the fainter stars.

Sam's cherubic face had changed since his fifth birthday. It was longer, and its expression was somewhat sadder. His eyes were still large, clear, and bright. His curiosity and intelligence were often mixed with thoughts of the past and apprehension about the future. No matter how bright he was—or eccentric, as most of his classmates saw him—he was still saddled with the emotional and biological changes of a teenager. Wanting to fit in while not being held back was a difficult dilemma for him. His interests were not at all typical of his high-school classmates, and those interests dominated his time and energy.

His grades were above average but not superior. They could have been, but his limited time was funneled into one area, into the astronomical brass ring: finding a signal from an extraterrestrial civilization. "Finding alien radio signals'' sounded foolish and impossible to everyone except Sam.

In the past several years he had applied his computer and radio skills toward his goal. He knew quite well the work that had been done up to that point. Frank Drake's '60s project, Ozma, and his Cyclops had only been a start in a field from which most astronomers shied away.

To those astronomers, the field was more a sociological fad and popular-interest movement than true scientific exploration. It was the meat for science-fiction writers or speculative documentaries that might appear on ''Nova'' on PBS.

Still, Congress had seen fit to explore the possibilities, providing minimal funding for NASA's SETI (Search for Extraterrestrial Intelligence) program. Radio-telescope time would be squeezed into an already tight schedule, and new radio-spectrum analyzers and computer programs would be developed. Scientists would study a limited number of stars capable of sustaining life on circling planets and only a widely scattered set of frequencies.

Sam had always believed—along with amateur radio-telescope enthusiasts, amateur-radio operators (450,000 in the United States), and computer/radio hackers—the possibility of a private citizen's being the first human to detect intelligent communication from a distant planet. NASA scientists and university astronomers would admit only in private the distinct possibility that a private citizen might be the first. Of course, when funding was requested, that possibility was never publicly uttered.

It was the belief that he would be the first that kept Sam continuing to explore. But more than that, it was the desire to continue his father's work in that area at NASA and JPL that made him press on. It seemed natural to Sam; it was essential to Sam. For him, it was an obsession. He was compelled to explore at an explosive time in his life, when he was growing, changing, and discovering the rest of his environment.

Marion pushed open the kitchen door and continued to wipe dry a large skillet as she looked up at the roof. She still looked like a teenager in her jeans and bulky sweater. Now, however, she was perturbed at her nephew.

"Sam, are you still up there?" Marion shouted.

Sam turned and stepped toward the railing. "Yes, Aunt Marion," he said sheepishly.

"You have a school day tomorrow, so finish what you're doing up there."

She stared at Sam as he turned away, looking at his dish, then back at his aunt. She waited patiently for a reply.

"Now?" he asked.

Her hands, one holding a dishtowel and the other grasping the skillet, rested on her hips. Sam knew what that meant.

"Yes, now," she said sternly. She then went into the house.

Sam turned back to his satellite dishes and shook one of the concave fiberglass bowls gently, trying to inch it toward some alignment. Then, leaning back against the railing, he pulled a small hand-held transceiver off his belt, flipped several microminiature switches, and punched in numbers on the pad. A quiet beep accompanied each numerical insertion. He tightened the stubby "rubber duck" antenna and pulled the microphone–speaker up to his mouth.

"W . . . A . . . 6 . . . J . . . E . . . R, this is K . . . 6 . . . Z . . . D . . . Q. Efrim, are you there?"

Sam's friend Efrim was sitting up in bed. Surrounded by a scattered conglomeration of comic books, he was catching up on some light reading. Efrim rolled his chunky body toward his nightstand and picked up his handheld transceiver. It was a different make and design from Sam's, but the function was similar.

As Efrim began to talk, he also began to pick his nose. This foul habit was seldom seen except at night or when Efrim dropped his guard.

"J . . . E . . . R. So I'm busy. What's up?"

Efrim pulled his radio away from his face and rested it on his lap. He looked over at a small desk cluttered with amateur-radio equipment, much less sophisticated than Sam's. This made Efrim extremely jealous. He never dropped his guard about that.

Sam's compressed voice rattled the speaker of Efrim's radio. "My SETI dish, that's what. I finally fixed the motor tracker for the dish. Ya wanna come over and listen with me some more? Have you heard Mitch or Rollo on tonight?"

Efrim looked at the green digital clock prominently placed on his equipment desk.

"Haven't heard either, and Mom won't let me. It's too late. You're gonna have to listen for the little green men yourself."

Sam stepped a few short paces toward a ragged-looking chaise lounge. He adjusted the back to a more vertical position and swung his body carefully into the chaise.

"OK, K . . . 6 . . . Z . . . D . . . Q, clear. See ya in school tomorrow. Go back to pickin'. And don't hit any blood vessels; you'll bleed to death."

"Ha, ha. Very funny. J . . . E . . . R, clear," Efrim replied quickly. There was a short burst of squelch, and Sam's radio was quiet.

Sam flipped the power switch to off and let the radio rest on his stomach. One hand was behind his head as he looked up at the moonless night sky. Turning slightly to his right he watched the wind rustle the tops of several nearby Mexican Fan palm trees. He loved to hear the gentle swishing of the fronds. That sound was as much California as the pungent smell of the chaparral wafting down from the nearby hillside.

The sound, sight, and smell of the warm California night relaxed him, then lulled him toward sleep. His eyes grew heavy; his grip on the hand-held transceiver grew weak. Sam slipped into sleep as above and around him, the thin aluminum tubing swayed with the ebb and flow of the breeze.

The streets and neighborhood around Sam's roof and the Alexander house were quiet. Most families were settled in and beginning to sleep for the night. Dogs had stopped barking, and air traffic overhead was now sparse.

But at that moment—not unlike any other moment since

March 1899, when Guglielmo Marconi sent the first wireless-radio message across the English Channel—radio-frequency signals saturated the atmosphere. That part of the electromagnetic spectrum was always alive with activity. At any moment at any location, a radio signal of some sort could be detected, amplified, and turned into sound waves with the proper equipment. And those signals, at wavelengths that penetrated the ionosphere, flew away from Earth at the speed of light. The Earth became a radio-frequency lighthouse beginning at the turn of the twentieth century.

As Sam sank deeper and deeper into sleep, those terrestrial radio signals were all around him. His forest of antennas was at attention, ready to catch the stray electron flows that drifted by. But it was one of the satellite-dish antennas, activated twenty-four hours a day, seven days a week, that detected an unusual extraterrestrial electron flow.

The focus point of Sam's Alpha satellite dish captured the signal and guided it through the low-noise amplifier and toward the connecting coaxial cable. The signal traveled at the speed of light through the cable and through the antenna-signal amplification equipment in his room.

The signal sped through several other pieces of equipment—receivers, amplifiers, spectrum analyzers, a small black box marked "META" in orange letters—then into Sam's Compaq 386 computer with its enhanced 80387 math coprocessor chip.

At that moment, two events simultaneously occurred. A raspy white noise spilled out of a small speaker mounted on an amplifier crammed with switches and meters. And buried deep in the white noise, a moderately pitched warbling tone grew steadily louder.

Accompanying this sound, a multicolored graph quickly formed on a color monitor resting on top of the computer. With various axes plotted and detailed, a thin green line stretched across the screen. But in the middle of the line a narrow but steep spike formed, dominating the graph. The pyramid-shaped spike continued up to almost the top of the screen. The graph flickered as the signal strength and the sound of the white noise and tone component dropped; then the signal strength came back to its original level.

The whirring of a nearby computer disk drive added to the noise. The graph suddenly moved up and was squeezed as a message began to scroll across the bottom of the screen.

The desolate northern Mojave Desert was home to the coyote, the rattlesnake, and the sensitive listening post known as the Goldstone Deep Space Tracking Network. A gigantic 230-foot parabolic dish antenna system sat in a natural bowl-shaped location that protected it from Earth-generated radio interference. At the base of the large dish, a cluster of support buildings housed the man-power and equipment needed to receive the faint radio signals and send them on their way to NASA and JPL for interpretation.

The monitoring engineer was not at his location as the primary computer screen abruptly cleared an endlessly moving line of data. There was a pause, then a graph appeared . . . a solid line with only the slightest hint of a pyramidal spike. An almost inaudible raspy white noise and a modulated warbling tone emanated from a speaker somewhere in the control room.

Sam's radio telescope wasn't the only telescope receiving the strange signal that night.

CHAPTER 3

"Sam, you're running late. Breakfast is ready. C'mon.''

Dark became light. Silence became sound. Comfort became discomfort.

Aunt Marion's voice rattled through Sam's head like rolling thunder. He opened his eyes as the first blast of morning sunlight smashed into his face. He sat up quickly to face an exceptionally bright morning.

Sam looked through half-lidded eyes and found himself still lying on the chaise lounge on the roof. He could have cared less about his antennas or anything else at that moment. His mouth was bitter, his joints were stiff, and he was soaked with dew.

He stood up slowly and almost tumbled back into the chaise. He bent over to stretch. He reached up to the deep blue morning sky to stretch again. He yawned and slowly made his way to the trap door leading into his room.

Sam descended the wooden ladder and closed the trap door. He hopped down the final step and landed in the middle of the room. He rubbed his head and slipped off his jacket as he walked toward his wall of equipment.

Stretching from one side of the huge open room to the other was a combination workbench and equipment stack that Sam had constructed. Directly behind the equipment was a floor-to-ceiling window facing east, toward the clearly visible desert hills.

Dominating the equipment stack was a bank of computer monitors and associated computer equipment. To the side were at least eight radio receivers and amplifiers of all makes and models.

Overhead, the large feed-through conduit opened up into the room. A tangled mass of cables splayed in every direction like spaghetti. Clocks of various sizes and display formats gave time in Sidereal, UTC, Pacific, Eastern, and twenty-four-hour formats. Pegboards held electronic tools and supplies for every conceivable purpose. Work lamps hung from the ceiling and were clamped onto the heavy desktop.

The remainder of the room was sparsely furnished with bedroom basics: a bed, dresser, and mirror. Next to Sam's bed was a nightstand; on it, a black-and-white picture of Sam's parents standing next to a small Cessna airplane. A general-coverage shortwave receiver switched on, and the rhythmic time-tone of WWV could be heard. The monotone recorded voice of the time station jarred Sam into full consciousness. ". . . at the tone, fifteen hours nine minutes, coordinated universal time."

Sam glanced at his watch. "Oh, shit," he said softly.

Another general-coverage shortwave receiver switched on. ". . . and that's the summary of the news. . . . You're listening to the world service of the BBC. We now look at . . ."

Sam reached for the volume knob and turned it down. He was late and didn't give a damn what the announcer with the stiff British accent wanted to look at.

Sam stepped into the bathroom as still another piece of equipment switched on. It was an ordinary television set. The screen filled with the images of a morning talk show. Three middle-aged women were sitting between a beautiful hostess and an even more beautiful host. Sam could hear the audio through intermittent flows of sink water and flushing toilet water.

". . . OK, we're back now on 'A.M. San Diego,' where this morning, now twelve minutes after the hour . . ."

"Oh, shit!" Sam screamed through a mouthful of toothpaste.

". . . with three interesting and frightened ladies who

say they were abducted, or at least think they were abducted, by UFOs . . .''

Sam turned into a wild man as he flew through the bathroom door and toward his dresser. He tore off his pants and shirt and slipped on fresh clothing, all the while stumbling, occasionally cursing at a button that wouldn't button or a jeans snap that wouldn't snap.

''. . . Going on with you, Mrs. Webster. You say that you were then carried or placed on the examining table inside the craft, correct?'' the host asked in serious tones. Mrs. Webster, distracted by memory, sniffed once as she continued her tale.

Sam glanced at the monitor as he put on a dry pair of Reebok sneakers and started to collect his books from the workbench.

''. . . It was horrible, just horrible. First the long needle in my stomach like a huge shot. And then one of them stuck a device at the base of my skull.'' Mrs. Webster began to cry, then sob. ''A horrible purple flash filled my head and eyes.''

Mrs. Webster became nearly hysterical. This caught Sam's emotionless attention. He held onto one of his books as he stared at the television. ''I begged them to stop. Oh, God, please. Sweet Jesus, make them stop.''

Sam smirked. ''OK, lady, If Jesus won't, I will.'' He punched in the power switch. The screen went blank, and the hysterical crying ceased.

Sam grabbed his notebook and started to turn to the door, then took a quick step toward the dot-matrix printer. He ripped off the protruding sheet, folded it quickly, and stuffed it into his shirt pocket. He was in such a hurry that he failed to see the frozen graph with the dominating spike still in full view on his dedicated SETI computer monitor. He rushed out the door and bounded down the attached staircase.

Aunt Marion pushed aside the condiment tray on the kitchen table to make room for a plate of scrambled eggs. Stu, a somewhat squat man with a benign, quiet personality, was engrossed in the sports section of the morning paper. He ignored his twin blond daughters, Cindy and

Mindy, as they squealed and laughed loudly. Slender, cute Sara was carefully reading the product-description panel on a cereal box. She occasionally ate a spoonful of nondescript brown flakes.

"Mom," Sara said. "Listen to this. Do you know that there are 250 milligrams of sodium in this cereal and damn near one cup of sugar in this shit?"

Stu looked up from his newspaper. "Sara, please watch your language."

The twins were delighted. "Yeah, it sounds like crap," Cindy added.

Both little girls burst into laughter.

"Ladies," Marion pleaded as she loaded the dishwasher.

Cindy and Mindy then grabbed the milk carton at the same instant.

"Mine."

"Mine."

"Mine!" Cindy screamed.

"It's mine, damn it!" Mindy shouted back.

Stu looked up. Marion reached over the girls' heads, grabbed the milk, and sat at the table. She poured a bit into her empty glass.

"Now it's mine," she said, glaring at them both. Then she whispered to Mindy, "And watch your mouth, young lady."

Sam opened the outside door and walked in quickly.

"Good morning. I hear everything is normal."

Marion watched Sam as he grabbed a piece of toast and started to walk out of the kitchen and into the dining room.

"Hi, everybody. Bye, everybody," Sam said quickly.

"Sam?" Marion asked.

Sam stopped near the door, then stuck his head around the corner. "Yes, Aunt Marion," Sam said sheepishly.

Marion stared straight into Sam's eyes, smiling slightly. "You did it again, didn't you?"

"Uh."

"You fell asleep on the roof, right?"

"Uh. Gotta go, Aunt Marion. I'm late."

Sam disappeared through the front door. The family sat quietly as they heard a crash of books and a scattering of papers.

''Shit!'' Sam screamed.

Cindy turned to Stu and, in an innocent voice, said, ''See, Daddy, Sammy does it too.''

''Eat,'' Marion shot back.

Sam ran from the house and jumped into his four-wheel-drive Jeep Cherokee. The roof of his vehicle was crammed with antennas. Between the driver's and passenger's seats, mobile and portable radios were stacked six deep. Switches and meters lined a section of the dashboard. Sam had done some major radio-equipment installation.

He deactivated the alarm system and sped away from the quiet suburban street.

Weaving in and out of heavy traffic, Sam turned up the volume on his amplified cassette radio. The rock group Def Leppard could be heard a block away, mixed with the monotonous beeps and tones of the WWV radio time signal.

The school parking lot was quiet as Sam found one remaining parking spot in the rear. He was late again. He knew it. The excuse would have to be good this time. He tried to think of one as he set the alarm system.

As Sam walked quickly toward the school entrance, he suddenly remembered the piece of computer paper he had stuffed into his pocket. He pulled it out and read it quickly. He saw the graph. He looked at the text below it.

Sam froze in his tracks as he read the message that would change mankind's concept of itself and its place in the universe. It would be the most important message that man on this planet had ever received—and there he was, Sam Alexander, late for his first-period biology class.

He read the message again and looked at the graph. Was this a mistake? Or, this time, was it for real?

The hair on the back of his neck rose. He felt the chill of goose bumps all over his body.

"A SIGNAL OF UNKNOWN ORIGIN HAS BEEN DETECTED. PLEASE NOTIFY CONTROL OPERATOR IMMEDIATELY . . . A SIGNAL OF UNKNOWN ORIGIN HAS BEEN DETECTED. PLEASE NOTIFY CONTROL OPERATOR IMMEDIATELY . . . A SIGNAL OF UNKNOWN ORIGIN . . ."

CHAPTER 4

Why was it, Sam wondered, that his Reeboks squeaked loudly only when he was trying to sneak down the empty hallway of Los Robles High School? He tried to lighten his step as he passed the administration office and walked toward the next hallway.

He passed row upon on row of beige steel lockers and heard teachers calling off roll or describing something that they thought was humorous or exciting on television the previous night. Sam looked straight ahead as he tried to step quickly rather than walk, thumping all the way. He imagined for an instant that he had the ability to float smoothly and gently above the splattered vinyl asbestos-tile floor. It would be wonderful to sail just millimeters above the surface, in perfect control of pitch, yaw, and roll movements.

But the sound of his biology teacher's voice brought him back to reality. He must have been a hundred feet—although it seemed a thousand—from the double doors of the biology auditorium and lab. He slowed as he approached the door. Five feet, two feet, then finally one foot from the door, he stopped short. He looked at his watch. 8:45 A.M. He was thirty minutes late, and for the third time this school year. The session was just two months old. This time he was really in for it.

Perhaps this time he could slink in. His teacher, Mr. Timmerman, was so engrossed in his own universe when he was lecturing that he barely noticed any movement ten feet beyond his thick glasses. Sam put his eye close to the crack in the door. He watched the middle-aged, bespectacled man with disheveled hair turn away from the classroom and toward the blackboard. This was his chance.

As he reached for the door, a near catastrophe occurred. His thick biology text was on its way down to the floor and a certain loud crash. But Sam's quick reflexes saved what would have been the definitive announcement that Sam Alexander had arrived.

Sam opened the door and stepped in. He held the door as it closed behind him. Turning toward the class, he sensed that all eyes were riveted on him. Most of his thirty or thirty-five classmates then turned away just as quickly.

Sam looked toward the blackboard. Timmerman was still engaged. He tiptoed down the aisle and concentrated on grabbing the remaining open seat in the middle of the class. He thought it best to approach from the rear.

At the back of the class, he passed the "punks." Instead of the typical laid-back Southern California dress, black leather and black jeans with well-worn rock-band T-shirts was the standard punk issue.

One of the most menacing-looking punks, Dozier, grabbed Sam's arm. Sam didn't resist as he stopped dead, his route blocked by Dozier's leg. Dozier looked Sam up and down, spending most of his observation time on Sam's wild Hawaiian shirt. Dozier pulled Sam closer.

"Hey, man, that's a truly rad shirt you got on there," Dozier whispered.

"Thanks. I appreciate that from such an illustrious fashion critic as yourself," Sam replied.

He pulled his arm away sharply and quickly reached his chair. He looked across the room. A redheaded, green-eyed beauty gave him a big smile. Sam paused and gave her a nod.

Timmerman, scribbling and diagramming madly at the blackboard, droned on. "It is at this point that the starch compounds are transformed into usable energy by the ATP . . ."

Sam slid into his chair. Without turning, Timmerman

asked, "And just what might that new substance be, Samuel?"

Timmerman turned quickly on his heels and leaned against his combination lab table and lecturn.

Sam sank into his chair, his books still in his lap. He turned white; he seemed lost. Looking around the room, he saw the smiles, heard the snickers, and felt the general pleasure that his classmates were having at his expense. He squirmed under Timmerman's gaze. He looked toward the cute red-haired girl, Lisa Marie. Her head was down. Suddenly she looked sympathetically toward Sam.

He heard the snickering and the whispering and felt the eyes on him again. My God, he thought, the cruelty of kids his age. His thoughts slowed his response to his now-approaching teacher.

"What was that, Mr. Timmerman?" Sam asked plaintively.

There were a few more chuckles. Sam heard Dozier chortle, "Duh, where am I, coach? Did we win?" to two greasy friends nearby.

Timmerman stopped midway from the front of the classroom and looked over at Dozier. "Mr. Dozier, at least Mr. Alexander is passing this course, as opposed to you, just on the edge of failing this course."

Dozier glared at Timmerman. He did not like to be embarrassed or humiliated in front of his peers. This time, their snickering was directed at Dozier.

Timmerman looked down at Sam. "ATP transforms . . . ." He gestured to Sam to finish the sentence.

"Uh . . . uh . . . ATP transforms starch to . . . uh . . . sugar."

Sensing the victory of the forces of good over evil, his classmates began to cheer and shout approval. Timmerman held up his hands. "OK, silence. Let's have it calm in here while I talk to Sam."

Sam apprehensively stared at his teacher.

"Sam, that's correct. Now just one more simple question. You're late, again. What is your creative excuse this time?"

Sam looked into Timmerman's eyes. The truth was definitely necessary here. In a nanosecond, he determined that his teacher would receive any carefully concocted scenario with unmitigated scorn. "In other words, Sam," he said to himself, "no bullshit." No matter how incredible or how ridiculous his explanation would be to his teacher and classmates, Sam would tell the truth. His face sagged.

"If I told you, Mr. Timmerman, you wouldn't believe me. You'd think I was nuts."

The greaser next to Dozier shook his head and snorted, "C'mon, man. Let's hear it."

Timmerman looked at the greaser, then back at Sam. "Try me."

Sam took a deep breath and sat up in his chair. "Well, I had to check my SETI experiment. Sorta a form of biology, like exobiology."

Timmerman looked as though he were genuinely interested. He folded his arms and cocked his head, waiting for more information.

"Really? Tell us all about it . . . in twenty-five words or less. What does 'SETI' mean?"

Sam became slightly excited at the prospect of telling a near-intellectual equal about his search and experiment. He started to answer, but stopped briefly to scan the room. All eyes were on him now. Nervousness started to creep in again.

"It . . . uh . . . is an acronym. It stands for 'Search for Extraterrestrial Intelligence.' "

The room broke out in laughter. Only one classmate didn't laugh—the red-haired girl. She just stared at Sam.

Sam heard a few catcalls, a few accusations of "nerd." That was a misnomer, however. He was too good-looking (or "cute," as many of the girls secretly thought) to be called a nerd. His dress sometimes was different or strange. But he didn't carry a plastic protector in his shirt pocket; he didn't have caked-on dirt around his ears or neck; he didn't plaster his hair down with cooking oil; and he didn't walk like a chicken. His build was better than those of most of his fellow males. What set him apart were his intelligence and his quiet personality.

Many of the young females he was in class with were attracted by his air of mystery, the power of his mind, and his firm build.

Now, however, his biology classmates were laughing at him, not with him.

Timmerman said, "Quiet, class. Most of you don't even know where Senegal is located, let alone Saturn—or Sirius, the brightest star in the night sky. Sam, please explain further."

"I'm looking for radio signals from other intelligent civilizations."

There were more chuckles. But interest, on the other hand, was rising.

The greaser leaned over to Dozier and whispered for everyone to hear, "Man, this dude's a poser."

Timmerman stepped toward the greaser. "Mr. Craig, please just shut up."

The frustrated teacher turned and walked back to his podium. "Enough of this, Alexander. No more tardiness . . . alien civilizations or no."

Craig leaned toward Sam. "Hey, man, that excuse was shred. Extremely shred." Sam didn't acknowledge the vacuous comment.

"I wonder why," Mitch said.

Efrim took another gigantic bite of his dripping peanut-butter-and-jelly sandwich.

"I wonder why we don't have an indoor cafeteria."

Rollo answered, "Because the school people don't have the money to build one, dummy."

Efrim, squat and rotund. Rollo, skinny and truly nerdish. Mitch, smaller and shorter than Rollo. They sat under a long canopy covering two dozen weather-beaten picnic tables in the schoolyard adjacent to the administration building. Around them, students chatted or laughed and stared at one another, making derisive remarks about teachers, schoolwork, or other students. Occasionally, a basketball flew into the crowded eating area and landed in someone's pudding or applesauce. A loud "Fuck" or "Shit" would be heard, and if the kid who threw the ball was smaller than the kid who got it, a fight would start.

Money had a great deal to do with why Sam's three friends, also amateur-radio operators, were sitting outside on picnic tables instead of in a large multipurpose cafeteria. But it wasn't the total explanation.

In Kansas City, where winter temperatures sometimes went down to twenty degrees below zero, with winds of forty to fifty miles per hour, it would be difficult to eat lunch outside without it freezing instantly or blowing into a nearby snowdrift. But in Southern California, especially in the temperate part of the state, lunch could be eaten outside in September or December or February. And if it rained, the canopy would provide protection. At Sam's school, students could purchase hot food at the "hog trough" window, but experience had shown that eating the daily hot meal at Los Robles was taking one's life into one's hands. The nearby landfill was thought by the students to be the source of the food served. The unique odor was thought to be toxic-waste by-products.

Sam walked toward his group's table with a disgusted look on his face. He threw his backpack on the table with a thud and plopped down next to his best buddy, Efrim, who didn't miss a beat. He just kept on eating.

"Hey, Samyo. What's up?" Efrim asked, his question filtered through a wad of bread, peanut butter, and jelly.

Sam opened his backpack and pulled out an empty, squashed lunch sack. He threw it in the middle of the table. His three friends stopped eating.

"Uh-oh," Rollo whispered.

"Again," Mitch said.

"Yup," Sam answered quietly.

Efrim stopped eating. A worried look crept across his face. "Ya know, I gotta feeling someone doesn't like us."

Sam looked around the table. "My locker has been hit twice. Rollo, yours once. Mitch, how many times?"

"Four. No, five times."

Sam put his hand on Efrim's shoulder. "And you, good buddy. Is it twelve now, or ten?"

"No. Actually, twenty-two."

Sam looked around the schoolyard. "Yeah, I thought there was a *T* in there somewhere."

Rollo leaned forward and said, excitedly, "Listen, we have to fight these bastards. Why don't we rig up a step-up transformer and a solenoid switch? We wrap up our lunches with aluminum foil, wire it to a transformer and a nine-volt battery, and . . . *zap*. Someone grabs it, and they get a couple of thousand volts."

"Only a couple of milliamps. We don't wanna kill omeone," Mitch said quickly.

Even more quickly, Efrim added, "Yeah, sure, butt faces. And what happens if Mr. Rollins or Timmerman or that weasel face Miss Gooch goes snoopin' around on a surprise locker check?"

Sam turned to Efrim. "We'll all get had.'Cause they'll know only the freaks in the ham-radio and computer club could rig something up like that."

They went back to eating. Thinking. Scheming. Trying to design and rig an untraceable alarm/punishment system for use against the enemy. Mitch looked over at Sam.

"Hey, Sam," Mitch asked, reaching into his lunch bag, "ya want a banana?" Mitch held up a mushy brown banana that had seen better days. "My mom always gives me one. She says it'll keep my potassium up and keep me regular."

Efrim laughed. "Will it keep your dick up, too?"

Rollo suddenly looked at Mitch and scooted several inches away. "You got diarrhea."

"No, anal-vapor breath." Mitch shoved the banana in Rollo's face. "It's for constipation, not diarrhea."

Efrim dropped his sandwich. "You guys, *please*. I'm trying to eat."

Mitch said, "Shit, motormouth, nothing ever stops you from eating."

Sam swung his legs under the table, leaned on his elbows, and whispered, "The hell with eating." Efrim gave Sam a dirty look.

Sam said quietly, "Listen, fellow electron and DX

chasers, I think I may have hit the mother lode last night with my SETI search.''

Efrim completely ignored Sam. ''I wonder who is doing this to us, guys. Why is my locker being hit more than yours?''

Mitch and Rollo, however, leaned toward Sam. Sam tried to ignore Efrim.

''I pulled out the data from an overnight stop-search alarm message,'' Sam said. Then he opened his backpack and pulled out the crumpled computer printout generated by his SETI computer.

Efrim looked straight ahead, his expression turning from contemplation to fear. Color drained from his face.

Sam continued, as he pointed to the pronounced spike jutting upward on the graph, ''If you look at the intensity of the spike in comparison to the background noise along this line of . . .''

Efrim held up his hand and said weakly, ''I think I know who smashed your lunch, Samyo.''

Sam was about to give Efrim a shot in the arm with his swift fist for interrupting an explanation about the first indication of radio signals sent by an extraterrestrial civilization. But when he looked past Efrim, he saw that he would have to deal with a more immediate, pressing problem.

Looming over and ever closer to the four friends were the punk Dozier and his unkempt tough-guy friend, the less-than-brilliant Craig.

''Man, those two look like they stepped out of MTV's Headbangers Ball,'' Rollo whispered.

Dozier sat down next to Efrim and gave him a toothy, evil grin. ''Hey, butter butt, what's happening?'' Then he glared at Rollo. ''What was that, pal? MTV what?''

Clearly intimidated, Rollo whispered again, ''I was asking if anyone watched the Headbangers Ball on MTV last night.''

Craig roared with laughter. ''Wow, these dudes listen to heavy metal. Heavy-duty shit, man.''

Dozier grinned again and looked at Sam. The smile turned into a sneer. ''Yeah, yeah, yeah.'' The last word trailed off as Dozier looked at the computer printout. Then he grabbed it.

Sam's face turned red. "Hey, Dozier," he protested. He started to move, but Craig held him firmly in place.

"Siddown, geek."

Efrim, Rollo, and Mitch squirmed. A small crowd began to move toward the confrontation. As usual, trouble invariably switched on an unspoken communications link among students, telling them that a fight was about to begin.

Sam's face was flushed with anger as his three scared, stunned friends waited for the first blow to be thrown.

"Hey, pal, we just wanna talk," Dozier said.

Dozier squinted at the graph. He turned it upside down, then sideways.

"What is this shit, anyway?"

"It's a graph for Rollins's science class," Sam said sharply.

Craig leaned closer to Sam. "Hey, man, why you wanna take that science shit for? Why don't you get into something useful, like woodworking? Man, I made a great pen holder for my dad. That sonofabitch is so tough, my old man uses it to prop up the air conditioner he's got in his garage workshop."

Dozier tossed the chart back to Sam. Sam stuffed it into his backpack.

Dozier looked directly at Efrim. Efrim's body quivered with fear. The sweet taste of the peanut butter had turned into the coppery taste of panic, fear, and terror. Mission accomplished, Dozier turned back to Sam.

"Why so uptight, Alexander? I just wanna congratulate you on that most bitchin' excuse you gave to Timmerman this morning."

Craig chimed in, "Radical, man. Can I talk to these space dudes you're talkin' to?"

Sam turned and looked up at Craig. He replied coldly, "I haven't found 'em yet, so there's no one to talk to."

Dozier shook his finger. "Don't be lyin' with me, man."

Craig put his hand on his hips. "Hey, man, the guy's

a poser. It was just a bullshit excuse. There ain't no space people.''

Sam sat silently, staring up at Craig. Then he turned back to Dozier. Dozier stared back. Timmerman had made Dozier look foolish in front of the class, and Dozier blamed Sam.

Dozier stood up and stretched. "Well, buddy," he said, putting his arm around Craig, "Timmerman believed, so what the hell. More power to the guy.'' He gave Sam a hard slap on the back.

Sam stiffened. Under the table, he began to ball his hand into a fist. He had to use all his willpower to keep from jumping up and popping Dozier in the mouth. Sam knew that with his tardiness record, getting into a fight now would not be a good idea, so he held himself back.

Efrim looked up and softly asked Dozier, "You want some of my sandwich?''

Dozier stretched, yawned, and rubbed his stomach. He stepped up to Sam and looked into Sam's eyes. "No thanks, I already ate.''

Craig turned away from the table and grabbed Dozier's arm. "C'mon, man. Let's split. Enough of this shit.''

Dozier followed, but not before making a last remark. "See you burly dudes later.''

Sam and his friends watched the punks walk away.

Terrified, Efrim looked at Mitch. "For a while there, I thought we were dead meat.''

Mitch answered, "Not with four of us sitting here, dipdoofus.''

Sam watched Dozier and Craig melt into the mass of milling students. Efrim turned to Sam and held his sandwich up to his friend's face.

"Samyo, ya want some of my sandwich?''

Sam turned and stared blankly at Efrim.

CHAPTER 5

The repeat sequence would be initiated with the rise in signal level and quantity received from the planetesimal beacon. This orbiting beacon had been confirmed as the point from which the signals were being broadcast at random trajectories. Spectral analysis had confirmed that the source was not gaseous and that nuclear consumption of gas and other material was not taking place. It was not, then, a star, brown, black, white, orange, blue, opaque, translucent, or transparent.

Because of the position of the receiving equipment beyond the orbit of the beacon's satellite, this expansion of data seemed to occur on the dark side of the terminator from a heavy-mass solid planetary material on the planetesimal.

The transmission, therefore, would be adjusted and formed to coincide with signals being received. The mode would become congruent.

The message transmitted would be perfunctory.

Command . . . begin . . . NOW!!

The message, carrier, and transversion packet signal was on its way to Earth.

CHAPTER 6

Sam shoveled the food into his mouth as if he hadn't eaten all day. He hadn't. His cousins, Uncle Stu, and Aunt Marion gave Sam their full quiet attention as he attacked his dinner in the family dining room. Aunt Marion had always insisted that Sam be part of the family and that all members of the family would eat dinner at the same time. Tonight, at a modest setting, Sam was gorging on brisket, potatoes, cooked carrots, and string beans.

"Sam, didn't you eat the lunch I packed for you?" Marion asked.

Sam slowed for a moment, and looked up. "No. I mean, yes, but I'm still starved."

The family ate quietly.

Cousin Sara put down her fork and took a deep breath. She rested her elbows on the table and studied Sam.

"Sam, tell everybody what you told me today."

Sam didn't look up or miss a bite of his meal. Marion continued to cut a tough piece of meat and waited for an answer from Sam.

"C'mon, Sam. It's interesting, even for a cluck like me who doesn't know anything about what you're doing."

Cindy giggled at her older sister.

Mindy asked, "What's a cluck?"

Sara, sitting at an angle from Sam, grabbed his arm.

"C'mon. Tell everybody."

Sam pulled his arm away and shrugged off the question.

Stu looked up from his plate. When his deep voice rolled across the table it was calm and steady and reassuring. Sam's uncle never showed anger; he kept to himself. He was not effusive with his children, Marion, or Sam. He could laugh loudly, but generally he was quiet. He moved and talked slowly. But there was always that baseline strength and authority.

"Son, why don't you tell us? We're interested," Stu said.

Mindy quickly followed in her high, penetrating voice. "Yeah, Sammy, tell us 'bout your sparement."

Sara corrected, "Experiment."

Marion looked at Sam out of the corner of her eye. "You're spending too much time with that, Sam. Your schoolwork is going to suffer."

"I have to do it, Aunt Marion. I just have . . . to do it," he answered quietly.

Sam put down his fork and knife and glanced around the table, then directly at Stu. As he began to speak, he seemed more confident. His voice grew in strength. He was talking about something he loved to do.

"This morning, as I was leaving for school—quickly— I looked at the computer, then later at a printout I took with me to school. The printouts and the computer indicated that I picked up something last night on my Alpha microwave dish. A signal. An alien signal, maybe. From space, from an extraterrestrial source or maybe . . . civilization. I'm not sure of the exact source point, but . . ."

Cindy and Mindy immediately began to howl with laughter. Sam's lips pursed, and his face turned red with anger.

"Quiet, you two! Let's hear what Sam has to say!" Marion shouted. Her efforts to quiet the twins were unsuccessful.

Stu gave his girls a hard stare, but they didn't notice. They were hysterical with laughter.

Sara shouted at them, "Will you two shut up?"

Sam pushed back his chair hard. He stalked out of the room.

Cindy squealed, "Sammy's searching for alien monsters with green, slimy, hairy bodies, and smelly, too."

Stu grabbed her arm. "That's enough," he said firmly. Cindy stopped laughing for a moment, then began to scream with delight again.

Stu grabbed his napkin and laid it gently next to his plate, then looked across the table at Marion. "I'll talk to the boy," he said.

As Stu shuffled toward the living room, he took a deep breath and went over in his mind what he would tell Sam. Stu knew that Sam was intelligent and sometimes highstrung. He still was his guardian, but he was not his father. Sam never reminded him of that, but they both knew it. But firmness, quiet firmness, was Stu's best weapon, he figured.

As he took his final steps into the living room he looked down at Sam, who was stretched out in front of the television, flipping through the channels, pressing the remote control, and staring blankly at the screen. He finally found a program that interested him on the independent television station in San Diego. Sam saw the familiar characters of Mr. Spock, Captain Kirk, and Dr. "Bones" McCoy. McCoy was trying to teach Spock about some human emotion that Spock didn't understand and that McCoy believed Spock needed in order to survive.

Stu stopped for a moment and looked into Sam's face. "My God, he looks so much like Peter," he thought.

Stu still had difficulty reconciling the loss of his brother and his beloved sister-in-law, Ann. At that moment, he missed his brother even more than ever. And the pain and loss and yearning were emotions that Stu knew Sam was experiencing, too.

Stu and Peter Alexander were much alike when they were growing up near San Diego. They both loved to work with their hands, to experiment. Stu was more mechanical; he loved cars and contraptions. Peter loved electronics and the outdoors; he would spend hours in the crystalline air of the desert. Stu remembered how excited Peter was about the lack of light pollution then, and how he later decried the growing light-contamination problems that nearby Mount Palomar was experiencing.

"How many years now?" Stu wondered. "Two or four since Peter and Ann were lost? No, maybe it was fall of 1984. The Olympics. Did that . . . no, it was later."

Stu suddenly returned to reality. He had to stop thinking; self-indulgence was foolish when a pained Sam was sitting in front of him. But for a moment it was warm and soothing to think of his beloved brother and of the barefoot days, Nehi sodas, and hot summer days near the cool turquoise ocean in La Jolla.

He slowly turned the corner by the couch and eased down next to Sam. Sam didn't move. He just stared at the screen, emotionless.

Stu slowly, gently reached over to the remote control and turned down the volume of the television set. Sam didn't resist. He wanted to listen to the timbre of his uncle's soothing voice.

"Sam, may I sit with you for a moment?"

"Yeah . . . I guess so."

"Ya know, Sam, ever since your mom and dad were lost over the Pacific in their plane, we've thought of you as our son. We've tried to treat you like you were our son. We love you and care for you like you were our son." Stu put his large hand tenderly on Sam's shoulder. "Do you know, Sam, how much we care about you?"

Sam turned toward Stu, and his eyes began to glisten. He was trying hard to stay strong, to be tough. It was something he had developed, something he thought he must do to protect himself. "I know, Uncle Stu, I know."

"We've allowed you a great deal of freedom in the process. We've allowed you to use your folks' insurance as you see fit, because we feel you're smart enough and old enough to know what to do. We love you, Sam, and just hope you feel the same way about us."

"I do; I really do," Sam said. He turned away. "It's just that I'm constantly being teased by Cindy and Mindy about my work. It's bad enough that I have to hear about it at school and from other people."

"They are just two rambunctious little girls. Listen,

Sam,'' Stu said, grasping his nephew's shoulder a bit harder, ''just have a little more patience with them—and us. Try to control that short-fuse temper of yours.''

Sam sighed. ''I'll try, Uncle Stu. I really will.''

''We only want what's best, what your parents would have wanted for you.''

''I hope I know what that is.''

''Well, you'll have to come to terms with that. But don't try to rush it. Don't push yourself or us. Don't try . . .''

Sam's concentration began to fade. He drifted. The television audio seemed to increase. The ''Star Trek'' theme overpowered everything else he heard, even what Uncle Stu was trying to tell him. ''What was he saying? Was I suppose to answer?'' he thought.

''Un-unh,'' he told Stu.

Sam turned his head and looked through the front picture window. The sky was black. Then he looked toward the garage and his second-story living quarters. His eye followed the line of the garage upward to the flat roof. He could see the outline of his two small parabolic satellite dishes. He stared at the Alpha dish.

Uncle Stu continued to speak. Sam heard the ''Star Trek'' theme again.

Sam squinted as he stared at the dish. It looked larger, as though he had the ability to adjust his field of vision. It was like watching a movie, seeing a slow, steady zoom in. He began to hear the raspy white noise and the embedded warbling tone.

Stu was speaking. What was he saying?

The tone, the warbling tone, continued.

CHAPTER 7

Sam's bedroom was alive with radio noise, the steady clicking of the radio time-clock WWV, and the hissing of the TV set and off-frequency radio receivers. The bank of equipment was lighted by tiny green, blue, red, and orange bulbs. Every light in the room was switched on. One green phosphorus computer monitor and a color monitor displayed the SETI graph, now blank, while a larger color monitor displayed a panoply of three-dimensional shapes.

Sam loved to see those random shapes change, move, and rotate. He used various sophisticated, high-resolution graphics programs just for fun, just for the visual titillation.

The power consumption in the room was pushing the limits, straining the house's wiring and the red-hot circuit breakers. But here in his room, with all his equipment, he was in control. At his fingertips were sophisticated pieces of equipment that he directed and managed.

He was hunched over his black and orange META box. The cover was off. As he tweaked and turned several internal potentiometers, he was happy and focused on the work he was doing. He looked up at the clock and put down the plastic "diddle stick" adjusting tool.

"C'mon, Efrim. Where the hell are you?" he muttered.

Sam rolled his chair to the bank of radios and picked up one of the microphones.

44

"W . . . A . . . 6 . . . J . . . E . . . R, this is K . . . 6 . . . Z . . . D . . . Q."

Sam put down the mike. The silence of his two-meter amateur radio was broken. ". . . Z . . . D . . . Q, this is J . . . E . . . R . . . what? Where are you?"

"Pulling up in front of your house," Efrim replied.

"What took you so long?"

"I had to talk my ass off to get out after nine P.M., Sam. *Capiche?*"

"I understand, but it's less than an hour before we could be getting something."

"Gimme a break, will ya? It's lucky I'm even here. It's a school night, ya know."

Sam took a long, deep breath, then leaned back in his chair. He tried to calm down and slow his blood pressure. "How 'bout Mitch and Rollo? Are they gonna make it?"

"You gotta be joking, man."

Sam leaned forward with a big smile on his face. "Hey, bub, what are you ratchet-jawing with me for? Why don't you just come in, if you're in front of the house?"

"Because you keep asking me questions a mile a minute, that's why. Holy shit, Sam."

"That's a no-no," Sam chuckled. "Cursing is not allowed on the air."

"Will you stop busting my chops? W . . . A . . . 6 . . . J . . . E . . . R, clear and coming in."

"K . . . 6 . . . Z . . . D . . . Q, clear and Q . . . R . . . T," Sam said.

He hung the microphone on a nearby hook and turned off the radio. He reached over to his main SETI receiver and turned the volume higher. All he could hear was a steady sheet of background noise; nothing broke that stream. He turned the volume even higher. He stared at the speaker, straining to hear something. Hoping to hear something. Praying that he would hear something.

Instead, all he heard was Efrim's heavy footsteps coming up the stairs. They stopped. Sam heard Efrim's heavy pounding on the door. Then, in a cheerful and high-pitched, playful voice, Sam asked, "Yes? Who is it, please?"

"It's the Arrowhead water man. Open up the fucking door, Sam. I gotta piss bad."

"It's open, dear," Sam said, laughing.

Efrim burst in, breathing heavily from the long trip up the stairs. He was sweating profusely and had a look of desperation on his face. Sam knew this look. Efrim was desperate much of the time, in constant need of fulfilling his demanding creature comforts.

Efrim took two steps into the room and slammed the door behind him.

"I gotta pee real bad. I need a Pepsi even worse. And what's to eat?"

Efrim was stretched out on Sam's bed, watching a nearby television monitor. The picture was scrambled, but Efrim didn't seem to mind; watching the Erotica cable channel and just listening to the audio was good enough for him. A large open bag of Fritos lay on his stomach, and two empty Pepsi cans were at his side.

"Hey, Samyo."

Sam was busy pounding commands into his computer and scrolling through data on the screen. He glanced at the digital readout on his main SETI receiver.

"Hey, Samyo, we really have to wire up a black box for Erotica. I'd like to see what's going on."

Sam answered, clearly distracted, "Use your imagination."

"I wanna see the real thing."

"Well, Efrim, go to the Embarcadero in San Diego or Hollywood Boulevard up north, and you'll get what you want—and maybe what you don't want. What penicillin can't kill."

Sam concentrated on the SETI receiver. It was constructed of several parts: power supply, preamplifier, detector circuitry, and signal amplifiers. It was mounted on a floor-to-ceiling standard nineteen-inch equipment rack. A thick bundle of wire spewed out from the rear of the rack in every possible direction. The most important connection, however, was the RG-58U cable that went through the META black box, then into the Compaq 386 computer.

Sam was completely in his element, flitting from one piece of equipment to another. He occasionally stopped to ponder an equipment or adjustment problem. He would mumble to himself. Then a light bulb would go off in his head, and he would determine a solution to the perplexing problem of the moment.

Sam turned and looked quizzically at Efrim. "Efrim, the signal strength from that sector of the sky is down from last night. I'm not hearing nearly the level of the background noise I should be hearing."

He stood up and pushed away from the long, home-made plywood desk that stretched from wall to wall. Sam began to pace. He nervously looked at the row of digital clocks. Only ten minutes remained before the return of the signal, Sam hoped.

"Efrim, it's almost oh-eight hundred. I gotta find out what's going on. Will you help me and stop eating chips and watching that crap?"

A look of understanding suddenly crossed his face. He looked at the scrambled monitor and heard the moans and groans broadcast by the Erotica channel. He grabbed Efrim's leg. "Efrim, what transponder and satellite is this crap on?"

"I dunno. I just turned your B dish. I knew you were using A, so . . ."

Sam raced over to the Beta controller and looked at the digital readout. "Westar five, transponder ten."

He pulled down the ladder from the trap door and scrambled up to the roof. He didn't have to look very long to find the problem.

Sam tumbled back into his room. When he hit the floor, he rolled on his back, then popped back up. He lunged for the satellite-dish control panel he had constructed and pushed the positioning switches for the Beta dish. Efrim sat up quickly, sending Fritos flying in every direction. His television monitor suddenly went blank. Snow buried the Erotica channel. The loud hiss of blank audio filled the room.

"Hey! I was watching that stuff," Efrim protested.

"That *stuff* was interfering with the reception on Alpha."

Efrim stood up. "That isn't fair. It was just getting to the good part."

Sam finally released the control buttons and turned off Efrim's monitor. Then he put his hand on Efrim's shoulder and tried to be as polite as possible. "Just listen up, Efrim. The Beta dish was pointed at Westar five, transponder ten. Beta was pointed directly in the line of fire to Alpha. Beta's position was making it impossible for Alpha to detect . . ."—he turned toward his row of clocks—". . . what may be coming in in three minutes. Ergo, a man and a woman screwing each other on the Erotica cable channel was about to block the most important transmission ever received in the history of man on this planet, in the four billion years this planet has been in existence."

Efrim closed his eyes and tilted his head to one side as Sam hopped back into his chair and turned up the volume on the SETI receiver. It sounded more alive. Sam and Efrim could hear more volume and static pulses.

"Jeez. OK, OK, I'm sorry. Forgive me. Kick my ass. Don't let me use the bathroom. Stick a hot poker in my eye, spider in my pants. Force me to look at pimple-face, fat-ass, onion-breath Lilah Cummins. God forbid, don't feed me for a week. I'm sorry."

"Efrim, pull up a chair and relax. Start the tape deck recording. Drink another Pepsi and come over here to make notes while I control the computer and receiver."

Efrim dutifully did what he was told. He sat next to Sam. He rested his head on his hands and listened to the clear noise emanating from the speaker. Several seconds passed. Sam tapped several more commands into the computer. The computer-generated graph adjusted to center-screen, full-screen.

Efrim sighed. "Nothing. Absolutely nothing."

Sam concentrated on the screen. He turned up the receiver volume even more, near the threshold of pain, then looked up at the digital readout of the Alpha dish. "Same position; no change," he whispered to himself. Then, louder, he said, "Efrim, just be patient." Sam turned the volume back to a normal level.

"How can I be patient?" Efrim asked. "I gotta go home and go to sleep. It's past midnight, and my mom's gonna lower the boom. What if they're not on this frequency, or on at all tonight?"

"They'll be here. I'm gonna leave it right on fourteen-twenty megahertz, exactly where they were last night. Sometime soon." Sam looked at the digital clocks. It was one minute past the hour.

"I should be taking a nap or something else constructive and worthwhile."

"Like eating?"

"Yeah. I'm hungry." Efrim sat up and folded his arms. "Why am I here?"

"I wanna make sure someone else hears this besides me."

Efrim thought for a moment. "How do you know NASA or some other government types aren't listening for these guys?"

Sam stared at the monitor. The sampling of the signal was constant as the line across the graph was traced, then retraced, then retraced again, all in a matter of seconds. The line looked like it was sampling a heartbeat rate on a hospital monitor. The flat line with only a small occasional squiggle, however, determined that there was no life in this sampling.

Sam said, "I don't know what the government is doing. But if they are listening, they're listening to ten million other channels at this moment. Right here, on the radio frequency of water and hydrogen atoms, I seriously doubt it. It's too obvious for them. They'd rather be difficult and do things the hard way. It's too obvious. It's too obvious. They're not listening here. No one is but me."

"Well, it's obvious to me I wanna sleep. I'm not used to . . ."

The signal returned, first faintly, then loud and clear.

Sam was jolted, ramrod vertical, as though he'd been hit by a burst of electricity.

Efrim was stunned. His excitement began to build. "What's that, Sam? What?"

Sam turned slowly and smiled at his flabbergasted friend.

"Them."

Efrim leaned closer to the computer screen. Repeated over and over, retraced over and over, the erratic baseline graph and the pronounced jagged spike in the middle of that graph. The peak varied slightly with each retracing, as various data lines scrolled on the extreme left side of the frame. Graph-signal strength, attenuation, modulation-to-carrier ratio, Doppler shift.

"Them?" Efrim shouted. "Who are 'them'? Where are 'them'?"

"Bad English, Efrim," Sam said calmly. He punched in a new set of commands. "Don't let Mr. Eberle hear you talk like that, or you'll flunk out of English for sure."

Efrim looked down at Sam's hands, which were wildly manipulating the keyboard. The screen went blank momentarily. Efrim was freaked. "What are you doing?"

"I'm gonna see if we can go to text. I wanna try to let META translate this. If there *is* anything to translate, other than a fluctuating tone surrounded by an envelope of static. I hope I put in the right parameters for whatever we're picking up."

The raspy white noise with the warbling tone folded into the transmission was loud and clear. It had a recognizable rhythm and pacing. Certain phrases sounded familiar, regular. Perhaps the repeating patterns had some meaning, or maybe they were just repeating.

"I wonder if this is a beacon. Let's get some text, baby. C'mon, c'mon," Sam said.

Efrim was zeroed into the screen. "Are they talking to us?"

"I hope so, Efrim. Here we go."

The screen began to flash a jumbled combination of repeated letters and numbers. The central processing unit of the Compaq and Sam's META black box were talking to each other, running through endless combinations of deciphering codes and languages. The thousands of hours Sam had spent programming and designing his SETI radio and computer system were going to be either validated and vindicated or repudiated and rejected in several moments by the equipment he had come to know so intimately.

Sam grabbed the case containing the Compaq computer's guts. He squeezed it. He whispered to it. "C'mon, baby, give . . . give . . . give."

Efrim excitedly said, "Oh, shit, this is great. This can't be happening. This is fantastic. We'll be in *Astronomy* mag, or *Sky and Telescope* for sure. Hell, we may even make *National Geographic,* or maybe 'Nova' on PBS."

Sam ignored his friend as the screen continued to scroll nonsense and irrelevant text.

"Give, honey. Just give," Sam whispered to the computer.

It did. The signal continued to blast from the speaker. Then a series of beeps came from the computer and the screen went blank. In a split-second, the screen came back and began to scroll a message. Sam switched on the VCR and checked the running audio recorder, all in a split-second.

PLANETESIMAL EARTH******************
FROM PLANETOID IN CETUS******************
ACCEPT THIS HELLO PROGRAM**************
****
TO BE CONTINUED**************************

Sam and Efrim sat motionless and speechless. The backup hard-disk drive whirred softly for several seconds, then fell silent. The message repeated on the screen, then repeated again and again and again. The signal was strong and clear.

Efrim furrowed his brow. "Bullshit. I'm tellin' you, this is bullshit. 'To be continued.' What is this two-parter? Like 'The Menagerie' story on 'Star Trek'? Someone is playing with us. This is a terrestrial signal. It's coming from Earth."

Sam also was slightly perturbed, but more controlled.

"Who, Efrim? Look at where the antenna is pointed— into space. There are no satellites at that position."

Sam pulled out his satellite-position map from the small library of books on top of the computer and threw it at Efrim. "Alpha is pointing right at the constellation Cetus. I know where the hell it's pointed. I know, God damn it. There is nothing else on fourteen-twenty megahertz. That's an international treaty frequency. No one else is on fourteen-twenty."

Efrim was quieted by Sam's rage and excitement. He replied, "Till now."

CHAPTER 8

The average distance between the Earth and the Moon is 238,856 miles.

At a distance of 477,712 miles from the Earth a flat disk, several meters thick and 100 meters in diameter, held stationary. Between it and the Earth was the Moon. The black, velvety space beyond was filled with the steady light of distant stars.

Smooth concentric circles radiated from the center of the disk, which was surrounded by a faint magenta aura— the only color that could be seen, save for the deep azure of the atmosphere surrounding the Earth. The dark-brown outlines of the North American continent and part of the South American continent were barely discernible.

It was night on those two continents, but the dawn terminator could be seen creeping across the Atlantic Ocean. A new day was approaching for the people of the Western Hemisphere.

The magenta disk seemed to be suspended in place, as if it were painted in its present position. It was positioned so that the flat broad part of the disk was facing North America, particularly the Southwest. There were no markings or protuberances of any kind on the surface. Moving closer to the disk would have revealed nothing. Only until the space just underneath the protective skin of the disk was penetrated would a passing astronaut or cosmonaut hear any noise. In space, there is no atmosphere. Sound is not heard in a vacuum. But inside the shell of the satellite, environmental systems duplicated the atmosphere of its home planet. It was necessary to duplicate the atmosphere because of the design requirements of the transceiving equipment.

The interior construction was almost biological and visceral. The noise in the environmental shell of the satellite was raspy white noise bursting with a smooth warbling tone. *Sam's* raspy white noise. *Sam's* smooth warbling tone. *Sam's* hello program from Cetus.

CHAPTER 9

Three times per week, unless it was called for an urgent pickup and delivery, a special messenger service dispatched a vehicle from offices in Barstow to the Goldstone Deep Space Tracking Station thirty miles away. It was a drive through uncompromising, desolate desert, freezing in the winter and blazing-hot in the summer.

A computer printout, containing the faint blip received from deep space twenty-four hours before, had been stuffed into two separate packets. The original would be sent to JPL in Pasadena, and a copy would be sent back to NASA headquarters in Washington, D.C.

The Pasadena package reached its destination without incident. The Washington packet was misrouted. From Washington, it went on to Australia on the next available commercial jetliner.

As Sam continued to sleep soundly and the original Goldstone printout sat in the depository drop of the mailroom at JPL, the second printout was making its way to the second leg of NASA's Deep Space Network. Within hours it would arrive at the headquarters of the Deep Space Network in Canberra and be placed in the hands of personnel from the Australian Department of Science.

Visiting the facility at that moment was a delegation of scientists and technicians from the Soviet Union. They were part of a technical team that was inspecting the facility for the possible cooperation of the NASA Deep Space Network in providing downlink facilities for the

Soviets' unmanned Mars mission in the not-too-distant future.

The misrouted package from Goldstone, containing evidence of a very faint intelligent transmission detected at 1420 megahertz, would make for some lively and interesting conversation at lunch between the Australians and the Soviets.

CHAPTER 10

The embarrassment would have been too great, so Efrim kept the index finger of his right hand away from his nostril.

He continued his leisurely stroll among the adobe buildings of Los Robles High School toward his outdoor locker. All the lockers were outdoors. There were no interior hallways at Los Robles High. This bothered Efrim, who would much rather be surrounded by an artificial environment all the time. His comfort zone was very narrow and very structured. He hated to be either too cold or too hot.

When he visited his cousin Larry in St. Louis, Efrim spent a day at Larry's school. It was marvelous. The halls were wide, and not once did he have to venture into the Midwestern heat and humidity to go from one classroom to another. Of course, Efrim had visited in the spring. He failed to realize how cold it could get, and generally did get, in the dead of winter. He also didn't realize that Ruskin High School did not have air conditioning, unlike Los Robles. But that was the length of Efrim's view. He was not a long-vista thinker; he just worried about the moment. Perhaps that insulated him from any pain about the past or worry about the future.

Unlike his good friend Sam, Efrim had a very normal and quiet life. No fires of ambition burned in his belly. His parents were living and were not separated, and he thought he was blessed by being an only child. There were no big brothers to intimidate him or little sisters to annoy him. He liked the arrangement and received all the attention, all the time.

But Efrim was not callous. He was very sensitive to Sam and Sam's living arrangements, to Sam's having lost his parents and now having young twin girls continually yapping at his heels. He almost felt sorry for Sam. But Sam wouldn't let Efrim feel sorry for him. Whenever conversation turned to the past or to his parents, Sam would simply ignore the subject. In public, and especially with Efrim, Sam would resist being drawn into any conversation about the loss of his parents or the pain it caused him.

Efrim reached his locker and began fumbling with the combination lock. He turned the small black combination wheel first one way, then the other. This was the second year he'd had that locker, and Efrim still had trouble remembering the combination. He finally got the numbers set. But the locker was once again jammed. He shoved, pushed, and pounded on the flimsy metal door till it finally gave way. Efrim realized the commotion he was making and turned to see whether anyone was looking. He heaved a sigh of relief. It was still early, and the buses hadn't arrived.

Efrim pulled out the precious lunch his mother had made him that morning. He started to put it inside the locker, but stopped and looked around the grounds again. He looked at the nearest building, then turned toward the mammoth playing field, the fence, and the buses starting to pull onto the property from the service entrance hundreds of feet away. He shook his head and put his lunch back in his book pack, carefully placing it in the corner of the bag. This was one lunch that Efrim was determined would not be stolen. He sighed again, knowing that his lunch was safe and secure. Efrim was playing a game with whoever was going after his needed daily sustenance, and he was not going to lose. It was a matter of life or death.

Sam sat in his four-wheel-drive vehicle at an intersection just in front of the on ramp to the San Diego Freeway. He held the microphone of his two-meter mobile radio in his right hand as he looked down at the frequency. The red fluorescent numbers read 146.565 megahertz. Sam wondered where Efrim was. "Damn it, why isn't he listening? Where the hell is he?" After the previous exciting night, he wanted to get Efrim on the radio quickly.

Sam was displaying the typical impatience he had seen in so many other radio operators. They expected their gear to always work and the station operator to always be available. Sam had gotten used to the convenience of being able to raise someone quickly, effortlessly. He had taken for granted the system of repeaters and lightweight, easy-to-use handie-talkies, and he wanted to talk to Efrim *now*.

The traffic light held on a long red, and the rush-hour cross traffic at that busiest of intersections seemed endless. The morning crowd was impatient to jam onto the freeway and stream north toward Los Angeles or south to San Diego. Sam could hear a chorus of car radios tuned to FM rock stations or talk-radio stations and cassette tapes blasting out music of all flavors. He could also see some drivers entertaining themselves with interesting conversations.

Sam tapped his steering wheel nervously and wondered why people talked to themselves in their automobiles so often. He was amazed by the number of times he had seen people jabbering away, mouths fully open, or sometimes through clenched teeth. Perhaps it was a diversion from the grueling drive, or maybe these people were really talking to someone else in their heads. It was mostly older people, Sam thought, in their thirties and forties. Of course, he had seen kids his own age doing it, but they were mostly singing along with the lyrics of some song on their radios or CD players.

"Aha," he said. "That's the next piece of gear I'll put in here." He suddenly laughed out loud and looked to his left at another driver waiting next to him at the light. Had he seen Sam talking to himself?

The light changed. Sam steered his Jeep up the ramp

and past the sign that read "San Diego Freeway North . . . Los Angeles."

He put the microphone to his mouth as he looked at the merging traffic to his left. The jeep engine roared Sam into the flow of traffic. "W . . . A . . . 6 . . . J . . . E . . . R, this is K . . . 6 . . . Z . . . D . . . Q. Where are you, Efrim?"

Efrim was leaning against a tree, reading one of the most valuable comic books in his collection. He looked up occasionally and watched the buses unload at the far end of the campus. He was isolated enough near the perimeter of the school grounds that he could read in peace.

The comic book he was reading was a favorite. It was a Marvel Comics remake of the famous *Silver Surfer*. Anyone who knew about the subject matter knew that this was a hot book. The Silver Surfer stood proudly on a flaming asteroid as it hurtled through space. His strong physique, rippling muscles, and stern eyes were encased in silver. In his left hand he held his transportation system, a silver-coated surfboard shaped very much like an emery board. This board had five long grooves—purpose unknown other than looking good. Explosions surrounded this hero as he soared through the ether of space, conquering evil and rescuing damsels in distress, only to be denied their pleasures because of his gleaming coating.

Efrim studied the last page carefully. He could not hear Sam calling on the radio; his full concentration was on that climactic page. The Silver Surfer, larger than life, bold and strong, flew above the jagged mountain peaks of some desolate planet. Efrim smiled slightly as he looked at the Surfer. He wondered how he could ever get his own body to be as strong and trim as the Silver Surfer's.

Sam only wondered how much the Silver Surfer weighed, in ounces. He infuriated Efrim when he discussed the feasibility of melting the Silver Surfer down, making him into silver bars, and waiting for the price of silver to rise. Nothing angered Efrim more than hearing

Sam talk about his comic-book heroes in such an unemotional way. Sam loved to have fun with Efrim's colorful heroes and their implausible feats of bravery and fantasy.

Sam's muffled repeated calls could be barely heard on the receiver in Efrim's backpack. At last, Efrim turned the handie-talkie on for his early-morning daily contact with Sam. Efrim put the comic book on his lap and frowned as he thought about Sam's derision of his heroes.

Sam called again. Efrim moved back to reality and fumbled quickly for the push-to-talk switch. Sam called once again. The audio was forced through the tiny two-inch internal speaker. "Efrim, I know you're there," Sam said, exasperated.

Finally, Efrim reached the bottom of his stuffed book bag and grabbed his small radio. It squirted out of his hands, but he caught it in midair just before it crashed onto a nearby sidewalk. Efrim was more angry at Sam than at himself. He turned up the volume and pulled the speaker-microphone to his mouth.

"Damn it, Sam, you almost made me drop my radio!" Efrim shouted "I already had to replace one IF chip in this thing last month."

But Sam's steady voice, coming through the small speaker, calmed Efrim. "Take it easy. I've been calling you. Where were you?"

"I was reading *Silver Surfer.*"

"Not again. Man, you're gonna wear that thing out."

Efrim was excited again. He turned back to the last page and pulled the radio to his mouth again. "Sam, lemme just read you the last page again. It's really cool."

"Efrim, wait. I gotta tell you something."

Too late—Efrim was keying right over Sam's transmission. He'd thought that Sam was through talking. He always thought that whoever he was talking to was through as soon as he keyed down and transmitted. If Efrim was transmitting, everyone should be listening. Anyone who doubled with him, well, it was his fault.

"Sam, Sam, lemme just read this to you," Efrim said, pulling his knees to his chest. He furrowed his brow, concentrated on the comic-book dialogue, and pulled the radio even closer. "OK, here it is. The Surfer is zooming along, skimming the mountains, riding the air currents, see? He's filling the entire page. Here we go. He's above Earth, by the way, not in some hokey alien-type joint. OK, he's talking now. OK."

Efrim took a deep breath. His concentration was supreme and his voice dramatic. " 'Though the one I treasure most of all is forever denied me—though I'm sentenced to endure earthly confinement as a bird endures its cage—still, my heart is light, for I have been true to my destiny! I have bested a demon and brought new life to a world! I know not what tomorrow may bring.' " Efrim finished with a broad flourish. " 'But today, the Surfer soars.' "

Slowly, Efrim put the comic book on his lap. A wide grin was plastered on his face. "Now, I ask you. Is that cool, or what?" He finally released the transmit button.

Sam stared straight ahead at the fast-moving traffic, catatonic with disbelief that his friend was so taken with the Silver Surfer. He finally put the microphone to his mouth again. "Efrim, you've totally flipped out. You're taking this much too seriously."

Efrim's signal came back, but this time the signal started to break up. His voice was mixed with the sounds often described as "frying bacon," which occur when the distance between stations increases.

"I should hope so. Hey, Samyo, where are you? You only got five minutes to get here, and your signal is breaking up."

"I've been trying to tell you, Efrim, but you doubled with me. I'm just getting on the freeway. I'm going to JPL, Efrim. The Jet Propulsion Lab in La Canada-Flintridge. I wanna play the tape of the beacon or message or whatever it was we picked up last night. I know someone there. I wanna see what they think."

"Oh, baby, you've already missed a couple of days."

"Cover for me," Sam pleaded gently.

He waited for Efrim's usual quick-key response.

"Oh, man, I don't know . . . what . . . I say . . . to

Tim. . . ." The simplex signal was deteriorating badly as Sam moved farther away from Los Robles High School and from Escondido.

Sam raised his voice and pulled the microphone close again. "Efrim, I'm losing you. I'll call you when I get back today, after school. Cover for me, will ya? I'll stop by Fantasy Castle in Woodland Hills and pick up a new *The Thing and Daredevil* for you. K . . . 6 . . . Z . . . D . . . Q, clear."

Sam listened for a response. But now the distance between the two radios made further intelligible transmissions impossible. Sam reached down and turned off the squelch. All he heard was dead air. He turned off the radio and took a deep breath. He looked toward the horizon and thought again of the white raspy noise and the warbling tone. He glanced over at the passenger seat and focused on an innocuous-looking cassette tape sitting on his briefcase. It seemed so simple to Sam. The tape might as well have been Dokken or U2 or Van Halen. Instead, it contained a radio message from an extraterrestrial civilization trying to make contact with humans on the planet Earth.

CHAPTER 11

Oak Grove Drive passes La Canada High School and the emerald lawns of Oak Grove Park till it curves gracefully toward the Jet Propulsion Laboratory.

Sam slowed his vehicle as he approached the main gate more than a mile away. It was a reflex action. He turned off his radios, all of them. He slowed even more as he saw the top floors of several of the 132 buildings on JPL property. The warm, familiar feeling came over him again, the same feeling he'd had many times before when his father took him to work at JPL. It was as if he were approaching some great monument, Valhalla, a place of reverence and respect. Something great was happening in those buildings. Wondrous, glorious experiments were being manned and monitored by people who truly loved their work. More than just a corporate sense of loyalty, these people had almost a nationalistic sense of loyalty to JPL.

Those 5,400 engineers, scientists, and support personnel worked in an atmosphere of exploration and discovery, where any day could bring about the revelation of the secrets of the universe. Remote satellites that duplicated the senses of man reached out beyond the fringes of the solar system.

Images flashed through Sam's mind: the rushing digitized photographs of the Moon as Ranger crashed into the surface, shooting pictures before disintegrating; the rock-strewn desert vista of the Martian surface, and in the foreground, the frail, gleaming, white body of the

Viking lander; and, of course, the Voyager pictures taken on the grand tour of Jupiter, Saturn, and Uranus, the moons in the Saturnian orbit and the burning ring of stars in the Milky Way taken by the Infrared Astronomical Satellite. More images: the convoluted Uranian moon of Miranda and the faint signals, barely four watts, transmitted from those robots millions of miles away to the Earth's surface. He remembered hearing those signals in the great hall of Mission Control and Spacecraft Tracking.

Sam was coming back to those 176 acres, and it was as if he belonged. It had been several years since his last visit, but the memories were fresh and crisp.

He could barely see the nearby San Gabriel Mountains through the schmaze—the combination of smog and haze. To his left, the parking lot was full as JPL engineers and employees scurried to various buildings. To his right was the main entrance and the Information Center. He tried to see inside the visitor lobby. It looked crowded.

At the main gate, he slowed behind a telephone-company truck. The Pacific Bell installer or repairman pulled out his ID. Sam became nervous, knowing that he had no appointment, no ID, and no connection to JPL now in any way. He wondered whether he would be able to talk his way onto the grounds.

His stomach began to flutter; he could feel his heart rate increasing. He dried his palms on his jeans. Then he sat straight up as the telephone truck moved away. The guard held his infamous brown clipboard. Sam knew that his name was not on the visitor/vendor list.

The guard took one step from the gate and stared at Sam's van as he waved him forward. He looked at the front license plate on Sam's vehicle and scribbled the number on the clipboard list.

"Yessir. May I help you?"

Sam cleared his throat and tried to be as cool as possible. "Uh, yes, I'm here to see Mr. Richard Redden. My name is Sam Alexander." Sam anticipated the next question. "I have an appointment."

The guard looked at him, then stepped inside the shack.

He scanned the list of daily appointments for Sam's name and shook his head.

"No, I'm sorry, son. I don't see your name. What time was your appointment with the deputy director?"

Sam looked quickly at a digital clock on his dashboard. "Just about now. 10:30 A.M."

The guard put the appointment list down and turned to Sam's vehicle. Behind him, cars, vans, and trucks began to line up. The guard could see the impatience on the drivers' faces.

The almost completely gray-haired guard was getting grayer and more agitated. He grabbed a nearby wall phone.

"What's the extension up there?"

Sam smiled and shrugged. "I'm sorry, sir. I really can't remember." He pretended to be looking for a note. "I know I have it written somewhere."

The car behind Sam was idling quickly as the driver gunned the motor several times. The guard hung up the phone with a hard slam.

"OK, OK," the exasperated guard said. He pointed to the visitor parking section of the nearby lot. "You just park in the section marked for guests." He then pointed to the adjacent visitors center. "March over to the check-in desk and have them ring up Mr. Redden."

Sam was pulling away from the main gate even before the guard finished his sentence. He heaved a sigh of relief. At least he'd gotten past the gate. Getting onto the premises and through that swinging dutch door in the visitors center would be more difficult.

Sam's nervousness transformed into excitement as he approached the double glass doors of the visitors center. He looked at his reflection in the glass for a split-second before he opened the door. He was proud of his appearance. In his coat and tie, and carrying a leather briefcase, he looked older, looked as though he really did have an appointment with the deputy director of the Jet Propulsion Laboratory. Now if he could just get past the front desk and to Richard Redden, he was sure he would be listened to. He took a deep breath and opened the door.

The noise of a small milling crowd immediately increased Sam's excitement. He stood just inside the door and looked at the long reception desk in front of him. Behind the desk, a gallery of breathtaking photos from Voyager, Ranger, and Surveyor lined the wall. He looked around the room. Some of the other visitors were government types, he figured, judging by their dress and the briefcases they were carrying. At the far corner of the room near the end of the reception desk, a clump of senior citizens chattered away, laughing and ogling a huge photo montage of the Jupiter and Saturn moon systems.

A large and not-too-friendly-looking young receptionist was involved in an intense conversation with the leader of the San Clemente Senior Citizens Recreational Club. Sam gripped his briefcase, took a deep breath, and moved in slowly behind the group leader.

Sam listened closely as the frustrated receptionist tried to explain to the elderly gentleman why his tour would not begin for another hour. The time had been changed by the tour group, and the tour guide would not be available. Sam could hear the man grumbling about his tax dollars as he walked back to his group. The disappointed seniors groaned loudly as he tried to explain the snafu.

Sam didn't notice the eyes of the receptionist riveted on him as she waited impatiently for him to move forward. He jumped when he heard her voice. "Next," she said sharply.

Sam was frozen for a moment. Then he gained his composure and stepped forward. As he started to speak, his voice almost cracked, but he forced air through it. "Good morning. My name is Sam Alexander, and I would like to see Mr. Richard Redden."

The receptionist raised her eyebrows and shook her head slightly. She scanned Sam as he braced for the inevitable next question.

"Do you have an appointment?"

Sam hesitated. "No."

"Young man, why are you here today? Isn't this a school day for you?"

"Yes, it is, but I have to speak with Mr. Redden. It's very important."

"Are you a relative or friend?"

"Uh, no, I . . ."

"Does he know you and what this is about?"

"No."

The receptionist leaned even closer. Her voice softened. "Honey, why are you here?"

Sam gritted his teeth and moved back a step. He hated to be called "honey," and he didn't like to be patronized.

"I'm here to see Richard Redden."

Neither the receptionist nor Sam noticed Richard Redden escorting two uniformed Navy officers to the glass entry doors at that moment.

The receptionist sensed Sam's firmness and decided to respond in kind.

"Listen, sweetheart, you need an appointment to see the deputy director. Mr. Redden just cannot see people off the street."

Richard heard his name as he turned away from the departing officers. He approached the information counter. He looked at the young man arguing with the receptionist and saw that their conversation was not friendly. The boy looked familiar to Richard. Then he realized that the young man was a taller, older Sammy Alexander. He hadn't seen Peter's son in years, but the resemblance was unmistakable. He slowly approached Sam.

"I'm not just off the street," Sam said, his voice beginning to rise with his temper. "Just tell him Sam Alexander is here. My father, Peter Alexander, used to work here. I have some information on a SETI contact that . . ."

Sam stopped in midsentence and stared up at Richard Redden, a co-worker and not-so-close friend of his father. Richard's dull auburn hair had darkened even more and it was streaked with gray. The crow's feet, lines, and creases on his face were deeper, and his cold black eyes were even blacker and colder. He was ancient, according to Sam. What was he now? Sam thought to himself. Fifty? Maybe fifty-five? Richard was in fact fifty-three. He had a tall, slim, unmuscular build and was starting to show a spare tire around the waist. His distant, distracted look was still there, and his smile was still hard to detect. As Sam remembered, he rarely smiled. He was always too intense for Sam and his father. Richard had a reputation for wanting to move on something fast without considering the ramifications. At times he was quick-tempered. He lived alone and had no family.

A mathemetician by trade and training, Richard had moved from a lifetime military career into a career in experimental mathematics, where he could work alone, without supervision, without contact. The loner was now deputy director of JPL.

His years of service with JPL cemented his administration position. His sometimes-abrasive personality, combined with a sharp, cunning mind, was offensive to many people. But he was the organization's ramrod.

Sam often wondered how Richard Redden ever became deputy director. That should have been his father's next move. That would have been his father's next move. Well, Sam thought, at least someone his father worked with got the job. Sam only hoped that if he ever got to JPL, Richard would be gone by then. To Sam, Richard was just OK. Something fake surrounded the man, but Sam considered the man to just be strange. Some genius types were like that, he thought. And at that moment, he was the only contact at JPL Sam could approach with not-so-complete confidence. Tentative, uneasy confidence.

The receptionist looked up and saw Richard. She immediately sat at attention. "Mr. Redden, this young man . . ."

Richard smiled, slightly. He held up his hand and placed his other hand on Sam's shoulder. Sam turned toward him, reassured by the warm hand on his shoulder and the smile on Richard's face. He was glad to be rid of the receptionist.

"Mr. Redden, hi. I'm . . ."

"Sam, I know who you are."

Richard held out his hand. Sam shook it with vigor.

Richard continued. "Sam, I knew your father quite well while he was here at JPL. In fact, we worked together once."

Sam began to feel comfortable and at ease.

"I know—he told me about you and your work together on SETI. Which is why I'm here. I want to talk to you about something."

Richard looked at the receptionist. "Marty, sign him in with me."

She quickly handed Sam a stick-on visitor pass.

Richard and Sam moved from the confines of the stuffy visitors center and directly into the quadrangle of JPL. To his left, Sam saw the towering dark-blue administration building. He looked around at the beautifully landscaped, parklike quad, the bridge, and the building beyond. On top of several buildings he saw gleaming antennas and equipment. The sun was warm and the air was cool. Sam savored the moment.

Richard and Sam walked slowly toward the administration building. Richard enjoyed the break from the routine and the opportunity to get away from administrative battles. He looked carefully at Sam and became serious. He was intrigued by seeing Peter's boy after all the years that had gone by. He noticed Sam's contentment.

"I guess this is the first time you've been back since you lost your folks."

The comment abruptly changed Sam's mood. He stared up at Richard and squinted as the sun bore down on his face. He was almost offended by the curtness of Richard's approach.

"Yes, it's been quite a while," he said.

Richard sensed what he had done and put a reassuring hand on Sam's shoulder again. But it didn't feel as reassuring as before.

"I knew your folks for a long time," Richard said. "Although we weren't close, I was still shocked to hear about them."

Sam looked down at the ground. "Were you at their memorial service? I don't think I saw you there."

They approached the wide concrete stairway in front of the administration building, then walked up slowly.

"No, Sam, I'm afraid I couldn't make it. I was taking a tour of some facilities at Kwajalein Island in the Pacific." As sincerely as he could, he looked at Sam and added, "But you know my thoughts were with you then."

They continued up the staircase and into the lobby. A winding concrete-and-steel staircase was just to the right.

Richard pointed to the staircase. "C'mon, let's walk up this way to my office. I need the exercise. I'm not young and healthy like you," he said, chuckling.

Josephine had worked for Richard Redden for almost ten years, and she recognized the sound of his heavy, shuffling feet coming from the end of the hall. She also detected a smaller, more delicate step matched with Richard's.

Richard turned the corner; Sam followed closely behind. The outer office where Josephine screened all visitors and calls was sparsely furnished but fairly large. Her face lighted up as she saw Sam, and she paid more attention to the young visitor than to Richard. She was not as animated around Richard as she could have been. She had no strong emotional attachment to Richard and she liked to keep it that way. She was there for a job, and that was it. There were never any secretary–boss lunches, only the obligatory dozen roses on Secretaries' Day. Josephine had determined long ago that the flowers Richard sent arrived only because of the peer pressure of his fellow administrators.

Richard almost swept past Josephine, with Sam silently in tow. Sam smiled at Josephine. At the heavy wooden door of his office, Richard turned quickly.

"Josephine, this is Sam Alexander," he said.

Sam stepped up to her and held out his hand.

"Nice to meet you, ma'am."

"Sam, very nice to meet you," Josephine said.

"Sam is Peter Alexander's son. Remember him?"

Josephine was in her mid-fifties and had been with JPL

since 1969. She had known Sam's father but never knew anything about his family or personal life. But upon hearing that Sam was Peter's son, she flushed. Then a truly large smile crossed her face. She turned directly toward Sam and held both his hands.

"My goodness, Sam, then it is very nice to meet you."

"Thank you, Josephine."

Richard opened the door to his office and stepped in. Sunlight from the large window overlooking the quadrangle flooded the outer office.

Sam pulled away from Josephine.

Josephine winked at Sam. "I guess you better go. Maybe we can talk later."

"OK. Nice to meet you."

Sam looked over his shoulder at Josephine. She was pleasant, and he liked her. He sensed her compassion. She was someone who evidently knew his father; it was a connection with the past, a sincere and heartfelt connection. Sam hesitated for a moment, but he had business to conduct. He stepped into Richard's office.

As befitted the deputy director, Richard's office was large and well appointed. A simple oak desk dominated the room. It was set in front of an oak credenza filled with plastic and wooden models of spacecraft and rocket launchers. The credenza sat under the large window overlooking the quad. On the left-hand return of the desk, three thirteen-inch color monitors were encased in a single light-green cabinet. In front of the monitors was an extensive keyboard. The monitors were turned off.

Richard moved quickly to his position behind the desk, ready to hold court. He gestured for Sam to sit in front of him in one of the matching guest chairs.

Sam looked around the room as he sat. Behind him was a three-piece seating area with a couch, coffee table, and side chair. Lining the room were huge, brilliant color pictures from the successful Voyager missions and deep-space astrophotographs. On the wall next to Richard, Sam saw a row of black-and-white photographs. Richard was in every one, standing with politicians and scientific notables; a movie star or two was thrown in for flavor. Sam was intrigued by one photograph of Richard that obviously was taken at a cocktail party; everyone was holding a glass of liquid refreshment. Richard was standing between Arthur C. Clarke and Isaac Asimov, Sam's favorite science-fiction authors.

Then, of course, were the diplomas, mostly from California schools. Richard did not have a doctorate, but the citations and other important-looking pieces of parchment indicated that his professional background was mathematics and some geology. For a second, he wondered how anyone could leave the exciting, ever-changing world of mathematics and the study of geology to become an administrator. Was it for the money? Or the title?

"So, Sammy, what can I do for you?" Richard inquired.

Sam's head swung around. He was caught off guard for a moment by being called a name he didn't particularly like. But Richard was a stranger. He squirmed in his chair. He cleared his throat.

"Mr. Redden . . ."

Richard held up his hand and cocked his head. "Please, Sam, call me Richard. OK?"

"OK. Well, Richard, I hope you won't think I'm nuts or anything, but I think I've found a SETI signal."

Richard raised an eyebrow, smiled slightly, and leaned back in his chair.

Sam continued, "Ya see, I'm into ham radio and radio astronomy. I've converted some surplus dishes—microwave dishes—and built some specialized receiving equipment. And I built an interface device for my computer system that's a combination spectrum analyzer and cipher modulator–demodulator. I call it my secret black box. Actually, it's a black box with orange lettering called a Mega Channel Extraterrestrial Analyzer, or 'META,' for short."

"Isn't there . . . ?"

Sam responded quickly. "Yeah, I named it after that META that was put together at MIT by one of the professors there, I think. Anyway, I've found a way to compress bandwidth, speed up the signal search through bunch of frequencies, and also analyze and translate signals through various encryption and modulation possibilities. I built and burned some of the chips myself and used them in series and parallel with a bunch of IC chips I ordered through the mail.''

He took a deep breath. Richard was hanging onto every word. He had the man's attention.

"Shall I go on?''

"Please, please.''

"OK. Here we go.'' Sam took another deep breath. "The other night, and last night, my equipment picked up an anomalous signal. The first time I picked it up, it was recorded on computer disk. Last night I was able to record it on audiotape.'' He reached into his briefcase and pulled out a microcassette recorder. "I transferred it to a micro tape so I could play it for you.''

Richard leaned forward and rested his elbows on his desk. Sam put the recorder on Richard's desk.

"Ya wanna hear it?'' Sam asked.

Richard shrugged. "Sure. Why not?''

Sam pushed the play button. The raspy white noise and the warbling tone were audible, although constricted by the miniature speaker of the recorder.

Richard listened carefully. He turned his right ear closer to the speaker. He shook his head, then leaned back. He was finished listening. Sam caught the cue. He turned off the tape recorder.

"Sam, at what frequency did you record this at, and were you receiving in AM or FM or single sideband?''

"It really seems to be a form of radio teletype, simple radio teletype, and I got the signal right on the water hole. Right on the hydrogen line at fourteen-twenty megahertz.''

Richard stared at Sam, then smirked. "You know, of course, that that is almost too obvious.''

Sam reached into his briefcase and pulled out a manila folder. From the folder, he pulled a single sheet of computer-form paper. Richard reluctantly reached for it.

"And this is the plain text of the signal sent. It's simple

and unbelievable, I know, but this is what I received last night,'' Sam said.

Richard read the sheet, then put it on top of a red plastic file folder on his desk and studied Sam. There was a long silence between them. Sam was finished with what he had to say to Richard; now he waited for Richard to pick up the conversation. He longed to hear words such as ''what a momentous discovery,'' ''this is what we've been waiting for,'' ''this is quite a coup,'' ''we'll do anything we can to help you.'' But life was not that simple.

''Sam, have you talked to anyone about this?''

What a strange question to ask, Sam thought.

''No,'' he answered. Efrim crossed his mind, as well as Mitch and Rollo. But of what importance is that to Richard Redden?

Richard continued to consider what he had just heard. He swiveled toward the desk return and reached for the main power switch of the three color monitors. He then grabbed a copy of the *Los Angeles Times* from the credenza behind him. Sam couldn't understand what was happening. There he was, telling the deputy director of JPL about what might just be the greatest discovery in the history of mankind, and the man was turning on his televisions and reaching for a newspaper.

Richard fumbled through the paper until he located the View section.

''Sam, I wanna read you something,'' Richard said. ''Listen to this: 'Astronomers have announced the discovery of the most distant and galaxy ever known.' It says in the article that this group of astronomers at Johns Hopkins found a cluster of stars 15 billion light years away.'' He looked at Sam. ''That is long before the Earth was even formed.''

Richard looked back down at his paper. ''It says . . . oh, yeah, here . . . that the newly discovered galaxy, 4C41.17—isn't that romantic?—is far too faint to be seen by the eye, but emits a radio signal a billion times more powerful than the sun's radio signal, making it the most powerful radio galaxy we know of.''

Sam shrugged. "What's the point? I don't . . ."

"Sam, this is great news for SETI hunters. Here we have a galaxy with a large cluster of stars—or suns, if you will—on the fringes of the known universe, a galaxy that existed before our own Earth, Sun, and solar system, and even our own galaxy, the Milky Way, was formed. And it puts out a signal a billion times more powerful than the Sun. Are—or I should say, were—there planets surrounding those stars or suns 15 billion light years away?"

"But what's that got to do with me and my discovery?"

"It's got to do with these guys who've discovered a monster using unbelievably sophisticated equipment. I know what Pete Billings is doing there at Johns Hopkins."

Richard leaned back again. Time to give a lecture, he thought.

"Sam, we have a multimillion-dollar, ten-year program here at JPL and NASA to find, or at least search for, the possibility of extraterrestrial intelligence. Your father was a pioneer in this field with Frank Drake and Project Ozma, then Project Cyclops. But a lot has changed since then. It is much larger and much more complicated. Larger and more complicated than your single META and your home computer and a surplus satellite dish."

Sam's face sagged. He was being treated like a dumb kid who didn't know what he was doing or talking about. He sank down into his chair.

"We have the two huge 200-meter dishes at Goldstone and Canberra in Australia on line now, with the 1,000-foot monster at Arecibo, the world's largest radio telescope, hooked up and involved in the ongoing search," Richard continued. "We're using spectrum analyzers developed at Stanford that are able to discriminate among ten million discrete channels . . ."

Sam suddenly became wide-eyed. "I've got that capacity, but I needed only the most important channel to locate this signal."

That slowed but did not stop Richard. "We're looking at a range of frequencies between one and ten gigahertz, and the whole shebang is being run by the Life Sciences Division of the Office of Space Science and Applications at NASA HQ in Washington. I mean, we have some pretty heavy dudes, as you might put it, working on this, Sam."

Richard paused dramatically. He turned to his monitors and punched in a few commands. On one monitor, he brought up a high-resolution picture of the rings of Saturn; on another, the boiling atmospheric features of Jupiter; and on the third, a picture of the fractured surface of Miranada.

"Look at these images, Sam. They were taken by sturdy but fragile, tiny spacecraft hurtling at tremendous speeds past the giant planets in our solar system. And from millions of miles away, they sent back detailed pictures and other telemetry that has changed our notion of how the universe might have been formed and of the forces that are currently at play on these planetary bodies."

Richard's cadence and volume began to race and rise. "The point is that JPL and NASA have the experience, equipment, and manpower to run the SETI search far beyond the means of any single amateur-radio operator who has an interest in radio astronomy."

"Mr. Redden, some of the biggest and most important discoveries of mankind were not made by large government organizations or private corporations. They were made by single individuals."

Richard's mouth drooped a bit. He realized that he was pushing Sam too hard and not getting through. So he smiled and became open and friendly again.

"You know, Sam, after that long blowhard speech I just gave, you may just be right."

"I know," Sam replied.

"This signal of yours may be terrestrial in origin, or it may be a satellite passing overhead where your dish was pointed, or it may be a bit of unfamiliar space-generated, natural-source noise we haven't figured out yet. Or you may have picked up a signal from an alien civilization located in deep space. I just don't know; I really don't.

"So what do you want from me?" Richard asked. "I mean, how can I help you? Why have you come to me, and what can I do for you? I mean that in the most honest and sincere terms."

Sam shook his head. He didn't know what to think. Why was this guy talking so much?

"I'm sure," Sam said quietly, "that around here, you must have ways of verifying my discovery. Maybe you could check the authenticity of this signal and we could work together, or you could help me present this to the press or to some official scientific organization. If you were with me on this, they'd listen to both of us together more than they would to me alone. Then we could move on and try to figure out where the signal is coming from, who is sending it, what they really are saying, and what information on Earth we should send back to them."

"That sounds reasonable, Sam. Of course, the time and distance differences would make two-way conversation impossible. Do you have the original of that tape with you?"

Sam paused and considered his options. Slowly and reluctantly, he pulled out a full-size cassette tape. It was a copy; the original was safe in Sam's room at home.

"I need both tapes—your micro and the original cassette—so we can analyze the signal," Richard said. "Don't worry; they'll be safe with me."

Sam handed the tape to Richard.

"I'll talk this over with a few people," Richard said as he handed Sam a business card. "Give me your telephone number, and I'll get back to you in a short while."

Sam wrote his telephone number on a piece of note paper as Richard chatted amiably about the SETI search and Sam's potential discovery. Then Richard escorted him past a very pleasant Josephine, who said, "Come visit again soon." He walked away from Richard's office alone.

Richard stepped toward a large window and leaned against it. He watched Sam emerge from the lobby and walk toward the Visitor Center. Richard glanced at Sam's tapes and the printed text, which was still sitting on top of his red file. A "HOT" file. A file containing the data shipped to JPL from Goldstone. Data that matched, though not in signal strength and amplitude, the tapes he had just received from Sam.

Richard thought about the META black box Sam had constructed and about how he could get his hands on it—legally or illegally.

The parking lot was still packed, and Sam temporarily forgot where he had parked. That occupied his mind until he saw the antennas protruding from his Jeep Cherokee at the far end of the lot. He cursed the long walk, but all the way to his vehicle he considered his conversation with Richard and Richard's reaction. Had he done the right thing, going to Richard and giving him the tape? Sam shook off the uneasiness. He was too excited about his discovery.

CHAPTER 12

Genady Mirotshinov secured the top button of his bright-red down parka. He looked toward the north and tried to make out land, but it was difficult. Through the thick fog and heavy mist, he could scarcely make out his "fishing trawler" and the useless nets, harpoons, and other fishing paraphernalia. The only trophies that this boat prized itself on catching were a stray U.S. military in-the-clear message, telemetry from a coast-launched test missile, or radar search patterns from the dozen or so inland radar dishes scanning his home country. The only fish on board were those to be eaten by the officers and men of the *Provideniya*—which strangely, was also the name of a nearby town on the Bering Strait.

Captain Mirotshinov looked up. A gray blanket surrounded him, and he felt small, cold drops of drizzle on his face. He sipped his steaming, strong tea and continued to digest his black-bread-and-sausage breakfast. His eyes were heavy and thick from a night spent with a bottle of vodka. He shook his head and pledged once again to break the habit that made waking up in the morning so difficult.

He turned away from the ocean and tried not to concentrate on the uncomfortable position of his boat: longitude 155 degrees, 49 minutes, 11 seconds; latitude 58 degrees north, 14 minutes, 19 seconds. The *Provideniya* was south-southeast of the town of Seward, Alaska, and just beyond the territorial waters off Montagu Island in the Gulf of Alaska. He knew that the Americans knew he was there. He looked up at the forest of antennas stretching from one side of his ship to the other. The array of long-wire, yagi, and satellite-dish antennas that designated his ship a spy ship—no different, he often grumbled, from the American cruisers sailing in the Barents Sea off the coast of Mother Russia.

Mirotshinov put his tea mug on the rail and rubbed his callused, sea-worn hands. After thirty years at sea, the wet cold still bothered him, and his arthritis problem was growing. He would ask for a transfer when he returned to port. These extended missions were getting too difficult, and he hoped for a job opportunity in the naval attaché's Office of Intelligence in Havana. He looked back out at the unusually flat, gray sea and smiled at the thought of a warm white beach on the azure Caribbean Sea.

His thoughts were interrupted by the quick footsteps of Corporal Inaiyev, communications technician. Coatless and occasionally slipping on the wet wooden deck, Inaiyev trotted up to his captain, holding a half-cut sheet of yellow paper.

Mirotshinov looked at the excited corporal walking quickly toward him.

"Aleksi, you fool, where is your coat?"

Inaiyev suddenly realized that he was wearing nothing more than his duty uniform, without any coat to cut the chill. He saluted perfunctorily and handed the captain the note.

"Comrade captain, this radioteletype message was too urgent for me to waste time looking for my parka."

Mirotshinov reached for the note and at the same time searched for his glasses inside his parka.

"My young friend, never neglect your health and the dangers imposed by being at sea. You don't have your health, you don't have anything." Mirotshinov took a deep breath and began to read the note. "Perhaps, next time Moscow will . . ."

He suddenly lowered the paper and looked out to sea. Then he looked at the shivering corporal.

Squinting at the note again through his water-spotted glasses, he said, "You're in luck, corporal."

Inaiyev shivered. His teeth began to chatter as he asked, "How so, comrade captain?"

"Moscow has ordered us south." The captain looked at the corporal, then up toward the antennas.

Mirotshinov continued, "They want us south, off San Diego. Corporal, have Titov lay in a course immediately at top speed with these new coordinates." The captain handed the note to Inaiyev. "And tell the chief engineer I want to see him."

"Ye . . . yes . . . sir," Inaiyev stammered, still shivering.

Mirotshinov walked cautiously toward the forward ladder leading to the bridge. "Tell the engineer I want his spec books on the gimble motors and mountings for the twelve-meter dishes. Those idiots in Moscow want me to do some radio astronomy and point the damn dish up."

Inaiyev followed dutifully. "Yessss, comrade captain. . . . Comrade captain?"

Mirotshinov stopped, then turned. "Yes? What is it?"

"Your tea." Inaiyev pointed to the precariously situated cup. But as the two men watched, a small swell tipped the ship to port and the cup slid into the ocean.

"At least it will be warm near San Diego, comrade captain."

"Yes, it will be warm, my friend. Maybe even hot."

CHAPTER 13

It was no accident that the atmosphere of the Jet Propulsion Laboratory was very much like that of a college campus. The facility was, after all, an operating division of the California Institute of Technology. The surrounding hills and the inner and outer greenbelts made the operating plant a pleasant place to work. Beyond the exhilarating work that was being carried on by the hundreds of dedicated staff members, there was a camaraderie and purpose of mission that set JPL apart; the men and women of JPL loved the work they were doing and where they were doing it. Although the facilities were cramped at times, this was the threshold to space. This was where robot spacecraft were designed, tested, and controlled, and where their data were eventually digested.

Richard Redden's mind was not on the feeble signals being received at Spacecraft Mission Control as he walked out of the administration building very late in the afternoon. He walked briskly down the middle of the service road, up a slight incline, then past the Optical Communications Research Laboratory toward the far north end of the property. He was making his way to a cluster of low-rise buildings. His weekly round-trip walking tour usually took him in that direction, but never to the small lab tucked away in one of those buildings.

He reached the first one-story building and turned right, then walked quickly down a narrow sidewalk, his suit coat slung over one shoulder and a slim briefcase in his right hand.

The long afternoon shadows had made the area between the buildings a cool oasis. As Richard stepped through the door, he was chilled even more by the cold blast of air in Audio Processing. He was met by a cacophony of signals, bleeps, and blips emanating from the four-room suite of offices. Richard strode down a narrow hallway and into a laboratory crammed with audio expanders, compressors, tape and disk storage devices, computer terminals, and stacks of various size tapes, all crammed together helter-skelter.

A small, skinny, young technician had his hands on two audio potentiometers and was adjusting the level of a loud series of hissing tones mixed with other garbage audio. The technician didn't see or hear Richard walk into the room.

Richard set his briefcase on a chair and walked up to the involved technician. He reached into his pocket and pulled out the tape of the SETI contact Sam had recorded the previous night. The technician looked up, nodded, and held up one finger, indicating that Richard should be patient.

Richard wasn't. His demeanor was stern.

"Excuse me!" he shouted over the noise.

The technician turned down the volume. All that could be heard now was the quiet hum of several nearby recorders and the whoosh of the freezing air spilling from the overhead air-conditioning ducts.

"How are you today, Mr. Redden?" the technician asked cheerfully.

Richard threw the cassette down on the control panel, jammed with dials, lights, and switches, in front of the tech. "Tell me what this is," he said.

Richard grabbed his briefcase and waited impatiently for a response. The technician picked up the tape, then looked at the stack of tapes to his right, marked "Jupiter Approach." He shook his head.

"I'm sorry, but I'm in the middle of this project, Mr. Redden. I could get to it . . ."

"Now. Do this now. I want you to stop what you are doing and work on this tape. It is more important."

The technician was surprised by Richard's abruptness.

"I dunno. I was told . . ." he began.

"Forget it. This is more important, believe me."

The tech turned the tape over several times and scrutinized it carefully.

"What's so important? I mean, what's on here?"

"Supposedly radio teletype. Maybe 300 baud, I would guess, but I don't know. It sounds a great deal like very slow and very simple radio teletype. You tell me. Tell me what the hell is on here. What it says."

Richard turned and weaved around a freestanding multichannel one-inch recorder on his way toward the door.

"I'm in a hurry," he said over his shoulder as he went through the doorway.

"How'd you get it?" the technician called after him.

There was no reply.

"Who recorded it?" the technician shouted.

Over the idling noise of the technician's equipment, he heard Richard reply from the far end of the hallway.

"I did."

CHAPTER 14

The timing was perfect—4:30 P.M., not more than fifteen minutes after his regular arrival time from school. But as Sam pulled into the driveway and shut off the engine of his Jeep, he saw Aunt Marion stepping out the front door to greet him. That was not normal. Sam tried to flush his mind of Richard Redden, JPL, and his earth-shaking discovery. He would have to concentrate on dealing with his aunt. He knew by the look on her face that he was in trouble.

Sam pulled his book bag from the back seat and walked toward Marion, clearing his throat. Marion waited for him to approach. Her hands were on her hips now. That meant *big* trouble. Then she folded her arms. Even bigger trouble.

"I got a call from school today," she said caustically. "Make this a good one, Sam. Where have you been?"

He slouched, trying to gain courage to once again tell her the hard truth.

"Well, I didn't go to school."

"I know. So where were you?"

Sam rocked back and forth from one foot to the other.

"Would you believe LA?"

Marion's eyes widened. "Los Angeles? What were you doing in Los Angeles when you should have been in school?"

"I had somewhere to go."

"Where was that?"

"Pasadena. The Jet Propulsion Laboratory."

Marion stiffened. Questions flashed through her mind. Why did he go there? Did this have anything to do with his father?

"What? You're building a rocket now? Just listening for planets isn't enough? Are you planning a trip to Mars or Pluto with their help?"

"Maybe a little farther out than a planet in the solar system."

"Sam, you're going to have to pay more attention to your schoolwork and less attention to your wires, or space signals, or whatever you do up in your room. I'll pull the plug myself if I have to." She shook her finger at him. He didn't like that. His face tensed.

Marion realized that her finger-pointing wasn't appreciated and put her hand down.

"It's very important to me, Aunt Marion."

"I know, Sam. But I can't have the school calling me all the time, asking me where you are. Am I right?"

"You're right." Sam glanced toward the street and watched several cars pass the house. "I'll try to concentrate on my schoolwork more."

Marion put her hand in his. He liked the feeling. It was comforting and reassuring, and he desperately needed that at that moment.

"For me, Sam. Do your schoolwork for me."

Sam stuck his key into the lock of his room above the garage. He was alone again, in his domain, where he had absolute control. Closing the door behind him, he threw his book bag over his bed and toward his desk. But he missed. The heavy book bag slid across the desk and into a small bookcase. An entire row of reference books flew in all directions. Then the bookcase, top-heavy with the remaining books, tipped over and Sam's book bag fell onto the scattered reference books. The loud crash made Sam jump. His nerves were on edge. He was anxious and unsure about his morning trip, his aunt's pressure, and the sound of the signal constantly bouncing around his mind.

"Oh, God, what next?" Sam asked, exasperated.

The orange late-afternoon sun filtered in through a large window next to his long equipment stack. He approached the window and stared first at the passing traffic, then over the rooftops of the houses across the street. In the distance, he could see the faint outline of the foothills surrounding nearby Anza-Borrego Desert State Park. His lips curled upward and his tense face softened as he relaxed a bit. He closed his eyes. He began to weaken as the excitement of his visit and the long drive began to take their toll.

"A few minutes." He turned away from the window and stumbled to his bed. "I'll lie down just for a few minutes."

Sam sat on the edge of his bed and pulled off his shoes, his eyes already closed. He could still feel the warmth of the sun on his face as sleep crept up on him. He swung his legs over the side of the bed, stretched out, and nestled his head on his smelly foam-rubber pillow. As if he were falling in slow motion off a golden mountain into a velvet-blue abyss, he drifted deeper and deeper into sleep. His descent was slowed only momentarily by the pop and crack of the stucco exterior of the garage, expanding in the heat of the day. He then let go. Shadows lengthened. Light became dark. Only the sound of the signal remained on top of his consciousness.

It was known as the Candy Store. To amateur-radio operators, however, the treats were not pralines or truffles or buttercreams covered with thick, rich milk chocolate. It was the new radio equipment that excited the ham. The retail equipment store known as Henry Radio was crammed with sophisticated receivers, transmitters, meters, microphones, hand-held radios, computers, and accessories. While other people might spend hours in The Broadway or in Saks Fifth Avenue, hams could spend hours playing with the equipment and arguing about which rig was better for a particular application. The latest high-tech, state-of-the-art models lined the shelves and mockup ham workbenches. All the price tags listed sale prices.

Several rows of shelves contained hundreds of switches, plugs, and cables. Henry's had every conceivable switch or plug for the do-it-yourselfer.

Beyond the amateur-radio section were the latest television and audio components, displayed in their own electronic-gadgetry heaven.

Henry's was a store that, to the chagrin of the proprietors, at times had more lookers than buyers. It was part of the game. Amateur-radio operators were among the small group of consumers in the United States who carefully read the specification lists on equipment.

Richard Redden walked through the double doors and stopped just inside the store entrance. He scanned the room and the strange-looking group of people shopping there. He thought that in terms of appearance, dress, and manner, the clientele resembled the techies who populated JPL. Another group of dedicated-to-the-cause types.

He moved into the store, inspecting the carefully arranged equipment and the customers hunched over counters. Myriad radio noises ricocheted off the walls and reverberated through the room. To the untrained ear, it was just noise—confusing, meaningless radio noise. Richard paid no attention to the noise or to his surroundings.

A scrawny young salesman was stocking a nearby rack of cable fittings. Richard noticed his plastic shirt-pocket protector, with the logo of an electronic-components supplier emblazoned on the flap. He smirked at the sight and thought, "How typical."

The salesman looked up as Richard approached him. "Yes, sir. Can I help you find something?"

Richard looked around, then down at the young man. "Yeah. Where would I find a directory of ham radio operators? You know, with their addresses and phone numbers and such."

The salesman stood and pointed to the far corner of the store.

"Book rack third shelf over, on the bottom. It's called the *Amateur Radio Callbook*. It contains the names and calls and addresses, but not the phone . . ."

Richard had turned away before he could finish his sentence. "What a rude son of a bitch," the salesman thought.

Richard immediately saw the thick directory on the bottom shelf. He bent over and picked it up. Then he saw a problem. The directory was divided into call areas—zones numbered to correspond to different sections of the country. Richard looked over at a man who was thumbing through a computer-programming guide.

"Say, do you know what call area California is in?"

The man looked up, surprised. "Six. We're in call area six. Are you going for your novice ticket? Ya better know that before you take the test, buddy."

Richard ignored the man. He turned to the area-six section and thumbed through it until he found the page he needed. He ran his thumb along the line of names until he stopped on the listing he wanted: Sam Alexander, 6607 Mountain View Road, Escondido, K6ZDQ.

Richard looked over his shoulder, then gently tore the page containing Sam's name out of the book. He folded the sheet quickly and stuffed it in his pocket. And in a singsong voice, he said softly to himself, "I know where you live."

CHAPTER 15

Sam thought he heard his name being called, but he wasn't quite sure.

"Sam, c'mon! Last call for dinner!" Marion shouted.

Half-awake, groggy, Sam lifted his head off the pillow and looked out his window. It was dark, well into night. He glanced at his clock. 6:45.

Sam sat up and swung his leaden legs onto the floor. He yawned and stretched and stared at his equipment. No pilot lights were shining, other than the blinking power lamps of his SETI equipment cluster. The computer was silent. The monitor display was rock-steady. Nothing had been detected, and there were no deviations from the straight-line graph plots.

As Sam started to stand, his telephone rang. He fell back onto the bed and reached awkwardly for the phone on his nightstand.

"Hello," he said.

Sam listened, his eyes still closed. Suddenly, they popped open and he sat up in bed.

"What? Hello, Lisa. Yeah. Hi."

Below, Marion opened the kitchen window and yelled for Sam again. "This is it, Sam! No food unless you're down here in thirty seconds!" she shouted.

Sam turned his concentration away from Marion and back to the telephone conversation with the cute red-haired girl who always seemed to pay close attention to him. He paid attention to her as well.

"My aunt's calling me for dinner now. But I guess I

could . . . sure . . . Oh, fifteen—no, maybe thirty minutes. OK?''

He was now wide awake, refreshed, and excited. "OK. See ya in a bit.''

Sam jumped out of bed and ran to the door. As he opened it, he could see Marion moving around the kitchen sink. "Aunt Marion, I won't be eating here tonight," he called.

Lisa lived ten minutes away from the Alexander house. But what a difference ten minutes made. Her home was at the far edge of the boundary of the Los Robles High School district in the wealthier section of town. Sam wasn't sure what Mr. Marie did for a living, but he surmised that it was something that made the family a good hunk of change. As he drove down the dark street, he struggled to see the house numbers. He liked Lisa. She was smart and kind of cute, kind of friendly.

Sam pulled up to her well-lighted house and shut off the engine of his Jeep. He looked in the mirror one more time, reached into the glove compartment, and found a small bottle of spicy cologne. A dab or two, and he was ready.

By the time Sam approached Lisa's door, she had opened it. "OK, I'm ready. Let's go," she said.

Sam waited for Lisa to bound down two stairs from the front porch and join him in front of the house. They turned and walked silently to the curb.

"Boy, this is some surprise," Sam said. He opened the passenger door.

Lisa stepped inside and sat. She was wearing a pair of white jeans and a thin, loose-fitting aquamarine shirt. Her red hair bounced off the top of her collar. Sam thought she looked fantastic. She had a small frame and blazing green eyes. And her smile—when it flashed, Sam could feel his legs grow weak. He noticed how soft and feminine her hands looked, and it didn't take much for him to notice that she had well-formed, moderate-size breasts. She smelled good, looked good, and felt good when she brushed against him on her way into the passenger seat.

"Let's go," Sam said cheerfully. He closed the door and walked around to the other side of his Jeep. He took a deep breath and exhaled rapidly. "Wow."

Sam got in, started the Jeep, and fastened his seat belt. He stared at Lisa for a moment. He had always liked what he had seen at school. But now he was captivated.

"This is a surprise," Sam said again.

"Yeah. I thought maybe a pizza and a little help from you on my math homework would mix nicely," she replied demurely.

"Absolutely." Sam continued to stare into those big green eyes.

"From what I've heard in class, I think you might know more about calculus than I do."

"I don't know about that."

"I do."

Sam put the transmission into drive. "Ready?"

She nodded.

Sam drove a little bit more slowly and with straighter posture than normal. A few awkward silent moments went by.

"Why don't we have some tunes? Turn on the radio," Sam said.

Lisa looked down at the dashboard, then at the stack of radios to her left. All of them were on, and the frequency displays glowed in various shades of brown, green, yellow, and red. She was confused and had no idea which radio dial she should turn.

"Which one?"

The pizza had long been cleared from the table. Lisa stared out the window next to the booth, watching the traffic and the twinkling lights along the street in front of the Pizza Hut. She was either bored or just enjoying being with him. Sam was sure it was the latter. It was. He pretended to be drinking his Coke as he watched Lisa out of the corner of his eye.

A young waitress in a gingham shirt and jeans stepped to the table and pulled out her check-order book.

"So, guys, any dessert tonight?"

Lisa turned and smiled. "No, thanks. Not for me."

Sam replied in kind. "No, I don't think for me, either. Maybe another Coke."

He looked at Lisa. She shook her head.

"OK." The waitress left. As she did, their eyes locked. Lisa cocked her head and crinkled her brow.

"You know, of course, we didn't do much math tonight," she said.

"I wouldn't have done much math tonight anyway. I tell ya what—we can carefully compute the bill when the waitress brings it over."

"Sam, tonight is the most I've ever heard you talk. I mean, in class you don't say much. You're usually hanging around your friends, huh?"

Sam twirled his straw in his drink. "I guess I do. But I've noticed you around in school, in class." He chuckled. "I guess I just haven't had the guts to say hello."

"Or call me on the phone?"

"Or call you on the phone," Sam replied quickly. "But I'm glad you did."

Several more seconds of silence passed. Sam thought there was nothing wrong with that. Chattering away like a magpie didn't seem appropriate at the moment. Silence was preferable; just being with Lisa now and enjoying her presence was enough.

"Sam," Lisa said, "that was a creative line you gave Timmerman the other day."

He turned serious. Lisa noticed. Uh-oh, she thought. Mistake.

"It was no line, Lisa. It was the truth."

Lisa leaned forward, her gaze riveted on Sam's face. He sensed her interest.

"Really? Tell me about it."

She was truly interested in what he was doing. Unbelievable. Fantastic, Sam thought.

"Aw, c'mon, you wouldn't find it that interesting."

"How the hell do you know that? Maybe I would. I

mean, you find it interesting and important enough to miss school. Right?''

''So you noticed I wasn't in class today?''

''Yeah, I did. So did Timmerman.''

Sam's face dropped a bit. ''I know. My aunt said the school called.''

Lisa seemed confused. ''Your aunt. Why . . .''

''I live with my aunt and uncle.''

Lisa thought for an instant and decided not to explore that question.

''So tell me more.''

Sam looked away, then back at Lisa. He tried to think of a clever, clear way to explain what he was doing and why he was doing it so that Lisa wouldn't think he was a geek, nerd, or worse. He reached over to the corner of the table and grabbed the salt shaker. He took off the cap and poured the salt in a neat pile in the middle of the table. Lisa watched him, confusion in her expression.

''What on earth are you doing, Sam?''

Sam didn't answer. He flattened his hand and pressed down on the pile of salt, then rotated his hand counterclockwise. He repeated the procedure several times as he shaped and widened the concentric circles of salt into a spiral. Then he used both hands to enlarge the spiral even more.

''Sam,'' Lisa said, trying to penetrate Sam's concentration.

He finally finished and looked up at Lisa again. ''OK. Ready?''

She shrugged.

''Let's pretend this is the Milky Way, our galaxy.''

Lisa blocked out all restaurant noise and distraction. To her, this was starting to sound interesting. Again, Sam sensed that interest. He was somewhat astonished, but felt for the first time that there was a soulmate sitting in front of him, someone who might truly be interested in his driving passion.

''Let's further pretend that each of these grains of salt is a star or sun in the Milky Way,'' he continued. ''Let's say there are 400 billion grains of stars down here. And some of them may have planets like ours, rotating around an estimated ten thousand or so suns. Planets or planetary disk material, depending upon the age of that sun or solar system. And for argument's sake, let's further say that some of those planets may have intelligent advanced civilizations.''

Sam took a deep breath. "Now, a guy named Frank Drake, a scientist who's been in the field of astronomy, trying to find these planets with intelligent advanced civilizations, has come up with an equation to determine and make an educated, estimated guess on how many exist. Using an abbreviated version of that equation, let's just say that of those 400 billion stars in our own Milky Way galaxy, there is just one star with planets that contain advanced civilizations, although planetary disk material has recently been discovered rotating around distant stars.''

"Civilizations with people like us?" Lisa asked.

"Or similar." He spoke more quietly and with more intensity. "Lisa, the point is that there may be 100 *billion* salt shakers or galaxies like this. That's ten *billion trillion* stars in all. The odds are tremendous that planets around a small percentage of stars may send out radio or TV signals like we do. The electromagnetic spectrum that includes light and sound frequencies is common throughout the universe.''

Sam took a deep breath and leaned forward, his elbows and arms now in the salt. "Lisa, I wanna be the first human ever to receive a signal from one of those radio or TV broadcasts from a race of beings, intelligent beings, outside our solar system, beyond Jupiter and Saturn and Neptune.''

"Sam, don't you think that maybe the government space people are doing the same thing?" Lisa asked suspiciously.

Sam sat up again. He had considered that question many times, and he knew the answer. "They have multimillion channel receivers and huge dishes and large budgets, but they aren't concentrating on the frequencies

I am, and they don't have the special circuitry I've designed just for this purpose.''

He paused for a moment. "You think I'm nuts?''

"No. I think you're cute.''

He laughed. Then froze. His beeper began to beep wildly, the rapid emergency signal repeating over and over. Sam lifted it from his belt buckle and looked at it before recycling the switch. Lisa was surprised.

"What's that all about?''

Sam leaned across the table and kissed Lisa on the mouth.

"I have a beep-alarm system tied into my SETI equipment. Let's go *NOW*. The stars are calling us.''

Sam's fingers rested on the keyboard of his computer. He tapped a command into the central processing unit, and the graph structure on the monitor changed. The volume was on his main SETI receiver turned up high. Tape recorders turned and disk-drive systems whirred quietly and intermittently as data was downloaded and saved. The room lights were turned off; Sam sat in the glow of green, yellow, and red light-emitting diodes. On the monitor, a message repeated and scrolled again and again:

MESSAGE TO FOLLOW . . . EXTRATERRES-TRIAL ORIGIN . . .

Lisa moved close to Sam and put her arm around his shoulder as she stared at the screen.

"What's happening?'' she asked.

Sam turned and looked into Lisa's eyes. Her face was no more than six inches away.

"Something wonderful,'' he said softly.

Sam closed his eyes and moved slowly to her lips. They kissed gently. They pulled away slowly.

"I agree.'' This time Lisa leaned toward Sam. They kissed again.

The computer alarm beeped, and Sam turned his attention toward his equipment again. He tapped in more commands. The original graph with the straight baseline continued to be retraced—this time, however, with a sharp spike. The message remained the same:

MESSAGE TO FOLLOW . . . MESSAGE TO FOLLOW.

"They're sending the same message over and over. Repeating it constantly," Sam said.

"Who are 'they'?"

"Good question."

"Where are they?"

Sam reached up to a nearby bookshelf and pulled down a large star-chart book—in which he had used a pair of his undershorts as a marker. He threw them down and turned red with embarrassment.

"Sorry 'bout that," he said sheepishly.

He then looked down at the British Astronomical Association star chart Epoch 1950.0. Near the red-giant star Betelgeuse, near the prominent constellation Orion, he pointed to another constellation marked Cetus.

"Somewhere in here," he told her. "At least, that's where my Alpha satellite dish is pointed."

Suddenly, the louder, much clearer raspy white noise and even louder warbling tone filled the room. The original message now scrolled off the screen from its position under the graph.

"Here we go."

Lisa was wide-eyed and flushed with excitement. "My God, I don't believe this. Is this another civilization talking to Earth? My God, oh, my God, I can't stand it!" she said.

Letters began to form along the bottom third of the screen.

"Here we go," Sam announced.

The tone fluctuated in pitch as the message began.

HELLO CONTINUATION.
SOURCE IN CETUS CONSTELLATION FROM
PLANET ORBITING STAR DESIGNATE AS

*** TAU CETI ***
RIGHT ASCENSION AT:
1 HOUR . . . 44 MINUTES . . . 4 SECONDS
DECLINATION AT:
-15 DEGREES . . . 56 MINUTES . . . 15 SECONDS
AS VIEWED FROM PLANETESIMAL DESIG-
NATE EARTH OUR SIG DIRECTED TO PLANE-
TESIMAL   EARTH   ORBITING   STAR
PLANETESIMAL AS SUN

Lisa turned to Sam. "I don't understand, Sam. What does all of that mean?"

Sam picked up the star chart and looked closely at the constellation Cetus again. He moved his finger along the white chart covered with minute black dots, precisely placed and identified, until he found the star Tau Ceti.

"It means this message is being transmitted—or, I should say, was transmitted—from an intelligent civilization on a planet circling the Sunlike star Tau Ceti, eleven-point-eight light years from Earth."

Sam looked at the screen again. "I am familiar with this star, Lisa. It was considered a good candidate twenty-eight years ago."

The warbling sound stopped for a few moments, and the message held. Sam looked at his disk drive, which instantaneously began saving the data from the incoming message on the screen. He looked at his reel-to-reel recorder and his cassette recorder. The VU meters bounced across their scales as the audio from the transmission was faithfully recorded. "Thank the Lord all this is saving onto disk and tape," Sam thought, heaving a sigh of relief.

The warbling tone began again.

"What's this? Are we repeating again, or is this new stuff?" Sam asked rhetorically.

New information began to flow on the screen.

DESIGNATE AS CIPHER CODE
K . . . 6 . . . Z . . . D . . . Q

The blood drained from Sam's face. Lisa looked at Sam, then up at a large plaque containing Sam's call letters and his FCC amateur-radio license. It read, "K6ZDQ."

"Sam?"

Sam held up his hand. He bit his lip.

The message continued:

    NAME DESIGNATE SAM

Sam gasped. He began to shiver. "My God, my God . . . what is this?"

FROM HIS SIG ATTAINED AT TAU CETI PLANET MONITOR RELAY SLAVE
SIGNAL RECEIVED AT OUR TERMINUS REPEATER
MESSAGE RECEIVED AS FOLLOWS

Sam's and Lisa's attention jumped from the computer screen to the receiver speaker. They heard a crash of static, then the background noise that is always there between signals or when signals are transmitted—hash and noise. Then, garbled and filtered and weak, as if being received from a station very far away, Sam and Lisa heard human voices, muffled, then suddenly clear:

"So back to you in New Zealand, Mac. Again, the name here is Sam. I am six years old and I live in Pasadena, California. Zed . . . L . . . 1 . . . W . . . K. This is K . . . 6 . . . Z . . . D . . . Q."

Sam violently rolled his chair away from his equipment, jumped up, and flung the chair aside. Lisa was scared, but not terrified.

"Sam, what was that? That little boy. Was that you, Sam?"

Sam stared at the monitor again. He was ashen, shaken, and shaking. His eyes were large and fixed. His voice was weak.

"Lisa, my God—I sent that transmission in 1976. They know who I am. Maybe they know where I live. What do they want with me?"

"I don't understand, Sam."

"What the hell is going on?" Sam screamed.

CHAPTER 16

"**C**an you see it?'' the filtered voice inquired. "Can you hear it? It's there, but just barely. It's there."

Richard Redden sat at one of the controller positions at JPL Mission Control. The room was large. It had a high ceiling with separate control stations, painted lime green, in front of large projection screens. The controllers were bathed in the light of their VDTs (video data terminals). The atmosphere was hushed, and the room was filled with low-level ambient light.

When planetary encounters were in progress and press and public interest was high, Mission Control would be abuzz with scientists, journalists, and politicians. Interest in these encounters waxed and waned, and at that moment, no spacecraft were near solar systems, planetary bodies, or approaching comets. The relative peace and quiet was what Richard desired.

He leaned back, arms folded, as he stared at one of the four monitors in front of him. A baseline graph was interrupted by a miniscule vertical spike. He reached for a volume control and turned it slightly. Richard heard the weak raspy white noise and warbling tone, which were strong and loud at Sam Alexander's "Master Control." Relayed to JPL from the desert receiving site at Goldstone, the signal was attenuated to an almost undetectable level.

"Yes, I hear it," Richard said softly.

A distant voice blurted out of a console speaker.

"Richard, what is this gibberish you're having me monitor on fourteen-twenty megs?"

Richard either didn't hear the question or didn't want to answer. He just considered the signal source and, more important, its intended target.

CHAPTER 17

Even at tremendous speeds, movement in space is difficult to detect. There are no close-proximity reference points to indicate even the faintest illusion of speed. It is not like sitting in the back seat of an automobile and watching a row of trees flash by. Looking beyond the treeline toward the mountains on the horizon, the back-seat rider would see less movement. Objects farther away would have even less relative movement. Stars light years away from the point of observation would reveal no relative change in position.

But the flat magenta disk with its radiating circles was moving at faster-than-tremendous speed. Beneath it, in relation to direction and closing position on the looming Earth, the Moon receded quickly away from the spacecraft. The disk then suddenly held its position after stopping dead in space in a nanosecond. G-forces that would have torn Earth-hewn men and machines to shreds had no effect on the magenta disk.

Inside the complex mechanical–biological structure, the signal being sent to Earth and Sam Alexander was being generated and was still audible.

But then, there was a lower, heavier noise.

A larger, segmented spacecraft moved into position. It looked more like cubic modern art than like a piece of biological machinery. The craft had form and line, perspective and shape. It was large but not lumbering. It moved closer to the disk with smooth and unrestrained motions, as quickly as the disk that had just traveled hundreds of thousands of miles in a manner of seconds.

The spacecraft was a darker shade of magenta than the disk. Its surface was covered by small antennalike devices, placed at exact distances from one another. The protuberances looked like flagella, but they remained stationary.

The large spacecraft and the small disk joined, reforming into a sleek but still irregular shape. The low-frequency hum component of the spacecraft joined the disk's noise component; they combined and changed to a variation on a theme.

Then the movement stopped. The hum stopped. The signal generation stopped. The spacecraft and the disk held their position above the Moon.

CHAPTER 18

Kenneth Wood scanned his department heads, seated on both sides of the long conference table—five men and one woman slowly coming to order. Computer printouts were spread out in the middle of the table, and various bound reports were being opened and readied for presentation. Kenneth looked toward the long wall of windows and squinted as the morning sun blasted the room. He turned to Richard, seated at his right.

"Richard, would you mind pulling those blinds a bit?"

Richard obediently stood and performed the task in silence. The others chattered softly to themselves.

Wood had been director of JPL for a short time. He had taken over a program that was relatively quiet, with only one or two major missions to planets, asteroids, and comets planned. He was determined to push unmanned space exploration and found resistance almost every step of the way in the NASA administration. NASA was married to manned missions, to the shuttle and the space station. That was fine with Kenneth Wood, as long as he could get cargo space and preference for his experiments over Department of Defense packages. But during the current administration, those "civilian" scientific loads took a back seat to DOD requirements.

Every night, Wood said a private prayer that one day, maybe soon, the American public would once again fall in love with the thrill, excitement, and adventure of reaching out into space on either manned or unmanned missions to explore the space around Earth and the universe beyond. It was important to him and to mankind, he felt. It was a goal that stirred the imaginations of the Earth's people. There was so much to do, so many exciting places to explore.

He looked around the table at his people. "If I could just get them the funding they needed to expand that adventure," he thought. "Damn it, if the DOD dropped just one weapon system, there'd be enough for us to do the job. All we need are the tools and. . . . Wishful thinking. He'd have to grind away hard and long. He'd fight every inch of the way. Maybe this possible discovery will . . . no, let's see what we have here first."

Kenneth Wood was a tall, lean man in his early sixties who held a doctorate in physics. He had spent most of the latter part of his career in the scientific administration of either major corporations or science foundations. His hair was gray, and his lean, weathered features reflected maturity and experience. He had a winning smile and a strong voice with good timbre. He was the voice of authority and carried himself and the JPL mantle well. He was cast for the job—a good man for a hard job. The scientists' and engineers' egos sometimes got in the way of their judgment. But what a team—the greatest space scientists in the world.

Richard had finished closing the blinds. Charlie Williams, a young, bearded radio-frequency engineer, knew it was a task that Richard could handle well—maybe the only job the asshole could handle. The loathing between them was mutual, but Richard was his boss. The other department heads at the table were ambivalent toward Richard; they could take him or leave him. Richard finally sat next to Wood.

"So where are we? What the hell is going on?" Kenneth Wood asked.

He turned to Charlie. "Charlie, does RF or Goldstone have anything for me?"

Charlie looked over at Richard. Richard, studying a report, ignored the RF engineer.

"We've been pushed pretty hard to come up with some quick answers," Charlie said. "The audio-analysis people are still working on Richard's tape. But so far, I think it is safe to assume that it is not an artificial terrestrial source. Both signals detected by Goldstone are from the same area of the sky, the same source. The Very Large Array dishes in New Mexico, by the way, did not get any of the signal. Very strange that it is so finely focused.''

Will Webster, the somewhat portly, bald scientist sitting next to Charlie, poked Charlie's arm. ''Any strong carrier component? What's the frequency of this thing?''

Charlie shook his head. ''It was weak, and the freq was at the water hole we all know and love. The hydrogen line.''

''And have abandoned as being too apparent,'' Kenneth Wood added.

At the end of the table, physicist Vicki Crane chimed in, ''And Richard was right, Ken. This definitely is simple radio teletype. But unlike the first message we received, the message last night was totally encrypted. Why? We don't know.''

Richard smiled at Vicki. He liked her open support. He always thought that she was a looker, but too skinny, and besides, she was an employee. Getting involved wouldn't look good for the deputy director. He always thought it was fine for the peons but not for him, especially under that stiff of a boss Kenneth Wood. Richard looked down at his meaningless report again.

Wood took off his glasses. ''Just great. It could take about a hundred years or so to break. Can you please tell me, Vicki, why the signal attenuates and falls off at Goldstone and is undetectable everywhere else—hopefully for the Russians and everyone else—and is strongest near San Diego?''

''I don't know,'' she replied.

''The Russians have an active program. I sure as hell hope they haven't picked this up,'' Wood said. There was silence at the table. ''Has anyone heard from Life Sciences on this yet? What's their opinion?'' Again, silence at the table.

Wood turned toward Richard. ''Richard, I want you to work on decoding the second message. Too bad it wasn't in the clear like the first one. Why it's not doesn't make sense to me.''

"I'll start on that today.''

"Fine,'' Wood replied.

He liked the fact that Richard gave him little argument whenever he gave him a directive or a job to do. He thought his deputy was too quiet at times, and strange, with no personality. Perhaps Richard thought he would get the job of director when the position was available. Wood sensed the jealousy and tried to ignore it.

"By the way, I want everyone to know that your initial discovery, Richard, from the Goldstone reports was . . .''

"Lucky,'' said Richard, looking at Wood.

"No, more than that,'' Wood responded. Then he turned his attention to the rest of the table. "It's fantastic—the astronomical discovery of a lifetime, or a century. But listen, everyone; absolute silence on this. We don't want to look like fools on this one. Let's be sure, OK?''

The meeting participants nodded in agreement.

Wood turned his attention to Charlie again. "Charlie, I want round-the-clock monitoring of fourteen-twenty megs at Goldstone and everywhere else on the Deep Space Net.''

"What about our ongoing non-SETI observations?'' Charlie asked with some annoyance.

Wood's demeanor chilled. "Charlie, work it out. And send Will Chatam and a crew down to San Diego to find out where the signal strength is greatest, and why.''

Richard smiled, cheered by the fact that his "friend'' Charles just had a dart thrown at him.

Wood continued, "Ladies and gentlemen, do you realize the impact of all this? What it means? I talked with Phil Morrison about this this morning, and he does. And if one of this country's most eminent scientists understands the import of this discovery, we'd better get out of our parochial shells here and pull together to crack this one. For this institution and this country, I want us to be the group of people to discover whether this event is real or some elaborate, sophisticated hoax. If it isn't, we'll know for sure that we're not alone in this universe.''

CHAPTER 19

Gorki was a closed city. No foreign journalists or tourists were allowed in this large city at the fork of the Oka and Volga rivers, approximately 265 miles east of Moscow. It was a large city, and Evegeny Romanov preferred it to the desolate valleys that cradled his country's astronomical radio telescopes. The days of remote data transfer by satellite back to the central offices of the USSR's CETI program made travel nearly unnecessary now.

He looked down on the city from his twelfth-story office window onto the wet late-night streets of Gorki. Few cars were on the road after the passing of an explosive thunderstorm. The lightning, thunder, and heavy rains had moved south, leaving behind a cold blast of fall air. Winter was surely on its way.

Romanov was head of CETI, or Communication with Extraterrestrial Intelligence. His sixty-eight years of studying the far-flung galaxies and the radio noise they produced had convinced him of the possibility that life, intelligent life, existed elsewhere in the universe. His search had now become a personal quest, even though he was obliged on many occasions to praise the Central Committee and the state apparatus for allowing the search to prove the brilliance of Soviet scientists and their desire to be pioneers in every scientific endeavor. That praise validated the Soviet system that allowed and paid for the CETI search.

He often thought that such political posturing was nonsense. To him, it really didn't matter whether his group, the British, the Japanese, or even the Americans were the first to discover some faint signal aimed at Earth. The discovery would verify his lifelong beliefs and answer the questions he asked even as a young boy as he stared into the brilliant night sky.

Romanov, a regal-looking man with a regal name, rubbed his tired eyes, pulled his glasses down from his forehead, and rested them again on his nose. He brushed back his white-gray hair and turned to his three research assistants.

"So what you are saying, lady and gentlemen, is that until the *Provideniya* reaches its destination, there are no radio telescopes available to us to catch this anomolous signal. Correct?"

The lead assistant, a middle-aged man with a wild shock of hair, answered reluctantly. "Yes, sir, I am afraid so."

Romanov released a long sigh and sat at his huge desk. To his right was another long desk on which books, maps, and reports were piled several feet high. Behind that desk was a wall-length bookcase full of books and reference materials. Around the large high-ceilinged office were pictures of the Earth taken by Soyuz spacecraft and by the cosmonauts in the Mir space station.

Romanov rubbed his hands, a common nervous habit, and looked at his assistant Ledakov. "You must also be afraid to tell me that the Defense Ministry will not allow us to move any of their precious satellite time for this, right?"

"Correct, comrade Romanov," Ledakov answered.

A young female graduate student sitting next to Ledakov, Myra Pemin, leaned forward.

"Myra?" Romanov asked.

"Do you dare ask the KGB or the GRU if any of their operatives on station near San Diego can help us?"

Her older male counterparts, Ledakov and Chelkar, laughed. Romanov didn't. He thought for a moment, then responded, "Not a bad idea." The men's chuckling stopped. But Romanov knew that it would take too much time to obtain the necessary equipment and relay the information back to Gorki, Moscow, or wherever.

Chelkar added, "Also, Myra, those goons are trained for other purposes. They wouldn't have the faintest idea of what to look for, what to listen for. Impossible."

Ledakov said, "Comrade Romanov."

Evegeny held up his hand. "Please, Vasily, stop calling me comrade—comrade this, comrade that. You've been here for over six months, and still you insist. We're informal here, believe me, very informal. I call you Vasily, and you call me . . . Czar Evegeny of the Romanov dynasty." They all laughed.

"Yes, Vasily, have you got another suggestion?"

"Yes, your highness," Ledakov said playfully. "Have you considered contacting your friend Professor Sagan at Cornell? Or possibly Professor Morrison or Professor Stephen Hawking? How about Kenneth Wood at JPL in California?"

Romanov leaned back in his chair and thought carefully before he answered. "Oh, how I would love to. But no, I can't. Moscow won't let me. They want us to see what we can get on our own. That's why they are pulling the *Provideniya* off its assignment near the Alaskan coast."

"You know, of course," Chelkar added, "it will be damn near impossible to get a lock on the signal on a ship that does not remain stationary."

"The bright engineers have assured me that with proper isolation and gimbling, it can be accomplished," Evegeny said. "And they have one of their own—their best, the navy has assured me—working on the problem as they steam down the American Pacific Coast."

"They'll never do it," Myra Pemin said.

"Perhaps, Myra, but we'll let them give it a try. Meanwhile, I want all our dishes pointed in the direction of the signal. I want our best linguists to try to break the code, in conjunction with our best radio-detection people, and I want everything recorded and shipped here. And Vasily, see if our team in Australia can delay their departure from Canberra to secure more information, after giving the Australians several ales or whatever they drink down there."

"Yes, sir," the three assistants said in chorus.

"And I . . . well . . ."

Romanov stood again and made his way toward the window. He saw sheets of green and blue lightning on the horizon, moving farther away from Gorki.

"And I will try to convince those blockheads in Moscow that we must be able to cooperate with the NASA SETI people. This is too important to let jingoism and bureaucracy get in the way. This is too important for the politicians or the press."

He turned to his assistants. With a mischievous grin, he said, "After all, it is the philosophers and poets and scientists who should be in charge of an event with such import as this. Philosophers, poets, scientists, and, of course, me." They all laughed again, Romanov the loudest.

CHAPTER 20

Mountain View Road curved sharply to the right about one hundred feet from the Alexander home and Stu's nearby auto-repair garage at Mountain View and Palmyra, a busy commercial intersection. The deeper the drive into the residential section and away from Palmyra, the quieter the surroundings.

At the curve, under a large ash tree, Richard Redden sat in his dark-blue government-issue sedan. The windows were up and his sun visors were down as the late-afternoon sun blazed on the horizon. The dark tint of the car windows made it difficult for anyone to see him sitting behind the steering wheel. He reached for his binoculars, then looked through them down the street to 6607.

Stu walked out the front door and shuffled toward the family Ford Bronco, parked in the driveway. He was followed quickly by Marion, Cindy, Mindy, and Sara. The twins darted around Stu and climbed into the Bronco as Stu continued to drag his exhausted body down the walkway. Marion grabbed his arm.

"Honey, I just don't feel like cooking tonight. Is it OK?" Marion asked.

"Yeah, sure. I'm so dog-tired tonight, I don't even feel like eating."

Sara grabbed her father's other arm. "Dad, once we get to Bob's and smell the greasy burgers you like so much, you'll be hungry."

Marion looked at the street and back toward the curve. She didn't notice the dark sedan.

"I left a note for Sam," she said. "He's late again, and . . ."

Richard could not hear what the family was saying, nor did he care. As he watched Stu get into the vehicle, he waited for Sam. He wondered where the boy could be. He looked up at the antennas on top of the garage and through an unshaded open window. From his narrow view into the room, he correctly surmised that the top floor of the garage was where Sam kept his equipment. Was Sam there? Why didn't he leave with the rest of the family? When was he going to be home?

Richard couldn't be bothered by details. He knew that he had to get into that radio room and get out quickly. The darkening sky would cover the work he would have to accomplish on the roof.

He started his car and put the transmission into drive. He looked to his left and started to roll. Suddenly, he slammed on the brakes as another vehicle flew by him. He cursed under his breath. His displeasure, however, quickly turned into relief; Sam was now parking in the driveway. Richard turned off the ignition. He would wait for however long it took for Sam to leave again—if Sam would leave.

Richard put the transmission into reverse and pulled back against the curb. He watched Sam bound up the exterior staircase to his door. Daylight was quickly fading, and Richard had to use his binoculars again to follow Sam's movements.

As Richard settled back and watched Sam's open window, he began to formulate a plan to draw Sam out. Maybe a phone call, asking Sam to meet him somewhere. Maybe an emergency call from the police. "There's been an accident. Go to the Escondido hospital. Your uncle has a problem."

But Richard didn't have to think long. Sam's door opened, and Sam bounded down the staircase to his Jeep.

He started the vehicle quickly and roared away, making a left on Palmyra.

Richard started his car again. He had a short drive to make to the Alexander house.

What idiot made the decision to put a public telephone next to a toilet stall and across from a sink? Sam shook his head, trying to understand the reason why. He held the handset to his ear and waited. And waited. He could hear the hold equipment clicking on and off. At least JPL didn't have music on hold—the worst abomination ever devised by man, Sam thought. It was particularly revolting when sleepy elevator music was used.

He could hear movement in the toilet stall next to him. A groan and grunt, the sound of toilet paper being pulled off the roll, then the sound of a glob of spit, explosively ejected and landing in the stool with a splat. Sam bowed his head. His stomach turned. If the call he was making had not been so important, he would have left immediately.

The toilet stall opened, and a large, scruffy-looking man stepped out. He seemed surprised to see Sam.

"Oh, gwarsh, sorry 'bout that. Didn't know you were on the phone."

"That's OK."

The man moved around Sam and toward the washbasin. Sam turned away and faced the wall. He heard a click on the line. "I'm sorry, sir, Mr. Redden doesn't seem to be in his office now. It is after six, you know."

Sam was about to answer when his large restroom partner turned on the the water and spit into the sink with a raucous splat. The man turned toward Sam and smiled.

"Sorry again. I don't know why in the hell they put phones in bathrooms. Do you?"

"I was just wondering the same thing. By the way, is it all out now?"

The man laughed. "Yeah, son, I think I got 'er. There may be a wad or two left in me yet. But for the most part, I'm dry."

* * *

Sam walked out of the restroom and around the counter toward the main seating section of Bob's Big Boy. He slipped into the booth, where his family had already started eating. He looked down at his plate. He stared at the food. Marion looked up from her salad.

"Sam, are you all right?" she asked.

"I lost my appetite. I don't think I can eat."

Cindy looked up from her hamburger. "Sammy, can I have your fries if you don't want 'em?"

Sam looked sternly at his cousin. "Don't call me Sammy."

"Did you make your call?" Marion asked. She continued to pick at her salad as she waited for Sam to reply. Everyone at the table was eating, except Sam.

"No. There wasn't an answer. No one was there."

Sam finally lifted his hamburger, but parts began to fall out onto his plate—a tomato slice, a bit of salad.

Stu looked over at Sam. "Tell me how your search project on the radio is coming along, Sam."

Mindy spoke before Sam could answer. "Daddy, is Sammy looking for space monsters?"

Sam flashed with anger. "They're not space monsters, and don't call me 'Sammy'!" he shouted.

Mindy froze for a moment, then began to cry. Sam put down his hamburger.

"Mindy, I'm sorry. I didn't mean to." Sam sighed. He pushed away his food and walked away from the table.

Sam sat on the curb outside the restaurant. The parking lot was full, with several cars circling in front of him, looking for open spots. He cursed at himself for taking out his anxiety on Mindy and his adoptive family. He looked to his right at the garish, smiling statue of Bob, holding a burger high in the air. Sam considered the stupid look on the statue's face—always smiling. "Who came up with that shit, anyway? And who chose his clothes?" he wondered.

He heard Sara walk up behind him; he knew her step. She leaned against Bob. They exchanged a glance, and he looked away.

Sam said, ''Don't tell me. They sent you out here to find out what's bugging me.''

''Yeah. But *I* wanted to come out here to find out what's bugging you.''

He turned toward Sara. He trusted her. She was close to his age. She may have been in her own world, but at least she was closer to his. They didn't talk much, but when they did there was no game-playing, and he liked that.

''Sara, I discovered something. Or something has discovered me. It's developing and expanding. It's something I don't understand. It's the signal I found. I went to a guy that Dad knew at JPL, and he won't return my call. I don't know what to do about that or the discovery.''

''Do nothing,'' Sara said. She sat down next to Sam.

''What?''

''Well, almost nothing. Just figure out a plan of action, and stop worrying about it. Just do something.'' She looked up at the statue and put her hand on his shoulder. ''Just be happy, like Bob here.''

''Yeah, and he's a dummy.''

She moved closer and looked into his eyes. ''And so are you.''

CHAPTER 21

The sky was dark and moonless as Sam turned onto Mountain View Road from Palmyra. He stopped in front of the garage and his room. Slowly emerging from his Jeep, he looked up but could see only a thick blanket of light from the nearby mercury-vapor street lamp, which obscured all but the brightest stars. Sam turned away and, running his hand along the warm hood of his vehicle, started toward his staircase.

From the moment he took the first step and looked up at the landing, he felt uneasy. Something was wrong. He continued up the stairs step by step until he saw that his door was ajar. He heard sounds coming from inside his room. He balled his fist and hesitated five steps from the landing, looking toward the house for something he could use as a weapon. Nothing.

Sam quietly climbed the next five steps and stopped at his doorway, carefully and deliberately putting his right foot just in front of the door. He saw the yellow glow of the incandescent lights spilling out through the door. As he put weight on his right foot, the board underfoot squeaked. He froze. The interior noise suddenly stopped.

In an instant, he jumped into the room, ready to confront whoever or whatever was in his sanctuary. He heard his heart pounding, ready to explode.

In another instant, his mind and eyes assessed the scene. The empty tape-recorder reels were spinning wildly. Drawers were open and tapes were scattered. His precious collection of computer disks was spread out over his long workbench. Equipment was twisted at odd angles, with broken pieces littering the floor. The cables entering the room were separated, cut, and frayed. And standing before Sam was Richard Redden. Richard's expression was wild. His tie was askew and his shirttail was out. He was sweating profusely. He stared blankly at Sam. He was holding Sam's META box—the priceless translator that allowed Sam to detect and decipher the SETI signal and the messages he had been receiving.

"Mr. Redden, what are you . . . ?" Sam asked weakly.

Sam didn't have to wait for an answer. He already knew it.

Richard tilted his head to one side. A sinister grin began to form on his face.

Sam's fist balled even tighter. Anger spread from his toes to the top of his head. The sudden rush of heat and strength permeated every muscle in his body. He tensed. He coiled. He sprang.

The lunge caught Richard off guard. He instinctively stepped back, and the META box flew into the air. Sam caught it, then tumbled to the ground, stunned for a moment—but long enough for Richard to snatch the box out of his hand.

Richard stepped over Sam and attempted to rush for the door. Sam rolled over and lunged again for Richard, catching his lower leg. Richard tripped and fell just short of the door.

Richard screamed, "Yeeoowww! You little bastard!"

They began to wrestle for control of the box. Sam was furious. His mind raced. This respected and responsible man was a thief—a thief not only of his translator box, but also of his signal discovery. This was the true purpose of this intrusion.

Sam and Richard grunted and groaned as they rolled on the floor, each trying to gain a superior position over the other. Richard managed to break free, but Sam pushed the META box under his bed with a free arm.

Richard jerked up and kicked Sam in the stomach. "You fucking little creep."

The words coming out of Richard's mouth and the

twisted look of hate scrawled across Richard's face shocked Sam. He lay on the floor and looked up, ignoring the dull pain in his stomach. Who was this man? Was this the same Richard Redden he'd met with at JPL just several days before? The same man? Impossible.

Richard grabbed Sam by the shoulders and threw him across the room. He landed on top of the worktable. Miraculously, it didn't collapse. But Sam's SETI receivers were damaged even more. Sam screamed in anger and fear. In that moment, Richard reached under the bed, grabbed the META box, and raced out of the room.

Sam rolled off the table and crumpled to the floor. He raised himself to his hands and knees and moaned as he heard Richard bounding down the stairs. The entire room and garage shook. Through his pain and shock, Sam knew that he would have to pull himself together quickly and chase Richard, or he would never see his META box again. He knew that Richard would use it for his own purposes before he could build another box and put his receiving equipment back in order again. He heard the roar of Richard's car engine.

Sam struggled to his feet, ran to the landing, and saw Richard screeching away toward Palmyra. "Redden, come back here with my box, you son of a bitch!" Sam screamed at the top of his lungs.

Whether he stepped on only one or two of the twenty steps as he jumped down the staircase, Sam didn't know or care. Running to his Jeep and sticking in the ignition key, he whispered a quick prayer to the gods and Chrysler that his Jeep Cherokee would start. It did, jumping into gear without hesitation.

Sam was no more than five seconds behind Richard as they raced eastward on Palmyra. Their speed was extraordinary for even that forty-five-miles-per-hour thoroughfare, and luckily, traffic was light. Sam hoped that Richard would be captured by the Escondido Police Department or the California Highway Patrol. He wanted to catch and strangle Richard, wanted it with an intensity and ferocity that he had never before imagined he possessed. Now, in his Jeep, he felt that he had the upper hand. At least now he could combat Richard on an even footing; the man's size and weight would not be an advantage now. It was Sam Alexander against Richard Redden, with only eight miles to go to the freeway on ramp.

Sam's mind raced as he weaved in and out of traffic. Through yellow lights, around corners on red lights, Sam tried to keep up. Richard would make his turns, then loop back around toward the main road to the freeway. Sam had the advantage of knowing the streets, so Richard would have to stay close to the only safe route he knew would lead him to the freeway.

Suddenly, Sam realized that he had another advantage over Richard.

He picked up the microphone of his two-meter amateur radio and punched in his first memory frequency, a frequency he and his ham radio buddies always monitored. It was where they initially called one another before they moved off frequency.

"JER, this is ZDQ. Pick up the mike quick, Efrim!" Sam shouted into the microphone. "Hurry! This is an emergency."

Richard was now lost in the residential streets just off Palmyra. In and out and around corners, he raced on, trying to keep his sense of direction straight. Sam smiled. This would give him time to call up the posse.

"Hurry up, Efrim! Where the hell are you?" Sam screamed.

Finally, the reply came through the speaker. "OK, OK. What's up?"

Sam had to drop the microphone to put both hands on the wheel as he rounded a sharp corner. He nearly hit an oncoming car. As he flew by the car, he heard a loud honk and an even louder string of curses.

Richard looked frantically for any sign of the main drag as he stopped in the middle of an intersection. Several blocks ahead, he saw a heavy stream of cars and a stoplight. A major intersection? He glanced in the rearview mirror and saw Sam approaching quickly. Richard slammed on the accelerator and sped toward the busy intersection. He didn't see Sam holding the microphone.

Under his breath, Richard said, "You gonna follow me all the way to LA?" Suddenly, he screamed, "You little maggot!"

Sam put down his microphone and concentrated on Richard, who was pulling away. He listened to the sudden transmission activity on the frequency.

"Sam says he's on Jordan now, Mitch. I'm rolling near Sanborn," Efrim said breathlessly.

Sam could hear Mitch's excited reply through the speaker. "Yahoooo! All right! Some real heavy-duty action. Let's do it!"

Mitch simultaneously pulled open the bathroom door, tried to button his jeans, and juggled his hand-held radio. He sailed down the stairs and bolted through the front door of his home. His mother cautiously walked out of her bedroom, only to see her son's fleeting image.

"Mitch, did you flush? I told you, I am not going to flush the toilet for you anymore!"

She stepped into the restroom and turned quickly. From the top of the stairs, she shouted, "Mitchell! Did you hear me tell you I wasn't going to flush anymore? And there's paper all over the floor. You have to be gentle with the roller. Mitchell? Mitchell?"

There were only three miles or so to go before Richard would reach the entrance to the San Diego Freeway. Sam knew it would be impossible to keep up with him in heavy traffic on the freeway. He looked down at his gas gauge. He realized that he would have to stop for gas even if he could keep up with Richard. About a quarter of a tank remained—enough for this chase, but not enough for a trip to Los Angeles.

Richard was weaving in and out of traffic ahead of Sam.

Sam shouted, "Where the hell are the police when you need them?"

He looked in his rearview and side mirrors. He picked up the microphone again.

"This is K6ZDQ. Where are you guys? I need your help now."

Before he could release the microphone key switch, he looked to his right and left. Then he smiled broadly and raised his fist in the air. His ham radio buddies were with him.

"All right, guys!" Sam said triumphantly.

Mitch responded immediately. "Sam? Mitch here, to your right."

Sam looked to his right and gave him a thumbs-up sign.

Mitch continued, "What's the plan of action?"

"Does everyone see that dark sedan in front of me, weaving in and out of traffic?"

There was a quadruple transmission. "Box the guy in. Stop him. We have to get my META box back. He's got it. He stole it."

Rollo quick-keyed. "What if he won't stop? He'll wreck us all."

Sam replied, "With all four of us working together on the radio, he'll stop, believe me. We'll scare the shit out of him."

"Or us," Efrim said warily.

Richard looked in the rearview mirror. He saw Sam holding a microphone. Then he saw three cars with Sam's, following Sam closely, maneuvering around the traffic. The other drivers were Sam's age, and they held microphones as well. He suddenly saw the four vehicles surge forward. Two of the cars raced to Richard's rear bumper.

"All right, boys, you want to play? I'll play with you," Richard said. He jammed on the accelerator and made a quick right turn. Mitch and Efrim missed the opportunity to turn and kept rolling straight on Palmyra. Behind them, Rollo and Sam turned and followed Richard onto another residential street.

In, around, and through the streets, the three vehicles raced past astonished pedestrians, finally heading back onto Palmyra. The freeway was no more than a mile away. Richard pulled away from Sam, Mitch, and Rollo.

All four vehicles sped faster. Radios squawked with quick commands. "Move up!" "To your right!" "Parked car; watch your left!'' Sudden turns into neighborhood streets, near-collisions with bicyclists and other cars pulling out of driveways, racing through gas stations, people scrambling to avoid being hit. ''Break away!'' ''Close in!'' ''Watch the next light coming up!''

The caravan moved faster. Sam slammed on the brakes to avoid a collision. Efrim almost caught Richard in a box with Rollo. The freeway ramp was in sight. ''San Diego, North, Los Angeles.''

In synchronization, all five drivers saw the ramp across the intersection in front of them and up one hundred feet. Richard was in the lead as he jammed on the gas, pushing his foot through the firewall. Sam panicked. He was directly behind Richard. He had to make a move now, around and in front of Richard, to stop him from reaching the uphill ramp.

Sam jerked his steering wheel to the left and pressed the accelerator as hard as he could. He finally pulled up next to Richard. He looked over and saw Richard look at him. Richard smirked—the same evil smirk Sam saw as Richard held Sam's META box a million years ago back in his room.

Eighty feet . . . Sixty feet . . . Forty feet—Sam was running out of room. He started to cut in front of Richard where the ramp entrance turned to the right. Sam pulled in front of Richard; he was too late. Richard jerked his steering wheel hard to the right and raced up the ramp.

A concrete right-hand bridge abutment loomed in front of Sam. In an exploding flash of time, Sam confronted death and decision. If he turned right, there was no guarantee that he would make it to the ramp. If he turned left, he would lose Richard but miss the abutment. Time would run out in less than a heartbeat.

Sam flipped the steering wheel to the left and saw Rollo next to him. He turned to the right again. The freeway ramp was behind him, and death loomed half a second ahead. With both feet, Sam stood on the brake pedal. His tires screamed and smoked, but held. The jeep spun 360 degrees and skidded to a stop twenty feet from the four-foot-diameter column of concrete.

Sam was immobile and in shock. His hands squeezed the steering wheel so tightly that all color drained from them. His breathing was quick and shallow. He stared into space. Sweat trickled from every pore in his body. He felt as though he were in the hottest, most humid rain forest he could imagine. He didn't hear the calls of concern on the radio.

"Sam, are you OK? Sam? Sam? Sam?"

CHAPTER 22

The Revilla Gigedo Islands are situated south of Baja California on nearly the same latitude as Mexico City. The string of small islands lie approximately four hundred miles from the western coast of Mexico, off Manzanillo. It is in the waters of the eastern Pacific Ocean that cyclonic storms are born. The warm waters and humid atmosphere feed these sometime monsters, which threaten Baja California, Southern California, and the Hawaiian Islands. The spiral arms of these tropical storms spew out streams of moisture and humidity that flow across Mexico and into the southwestern United States.

And in the early fall, that moisture feeds errant tropical thunderstorms that make their way across the Mexican border or up from the Pacific into Los Angeles, San Diego, and Escondido. These storms bring with them, at times, high winds, lightning, thunder, and torrential rain. They produce nothing like what the Gulf of Mexico or the U.S. East Coast can experience with west Atlantic and Caribbean hurricanes, but strong thunderstorms can occur none the less.

Sam lay, exhausted, on the chaise lounge on top of his roof and watched the low but building wall of cumulonimbus clouds marching northward, accompanied by phosphorescent green, blue, and yellow lightning illuminating the southern horizon. Pulsating low thunder followed seconds later. The air felt heavy.

At the bottom of the nearby antenna tower, Sam could see a one-foot piece of electrical tape slowly fluttering in the breeze. He closed his eyes after a particularly bright flash of lightning shot through the clouds and crashed into the ground. Booming thunder followed. Sam knew that within an hour, the tropical thunderstorm would march in from the sea and begin to drench the summer-parched land with the moisture it so badly needed.

Sam loved to watch storms move in. Their power, majesty, and beauty were as entertaining as any movie, sporting event, or fireworks display. It was entertainment that he could enjoy by himself. He preferred it that way. It was lonely, sometimes exciting, sometimes scary. He had seen several violent summer-afternoon thunderstorms in the desert and watched flat plains, cracked and parched, suddenly turn into raging rivers that swept away anything in their paths. All around him, the character of the desert would change after such a storm. Life would spring from lifeless sand and bricklike earth. The freshness was glorious, as sweet and pleasant as any smell Sam could imagine. The pungent odor of sage permeated the air, which had been washed clean and bright. The range of vision was limitless, with resolution enhanced to infinity.

Sam watched the spectacular light show, but his usual enthusiasm was not there. He felt disconnected and passive about the storm, the sounds of the street below, and his family inside the house. He felt apathetic and listless—and nauseous as he looked over the destruction in his room and on his roof.

Both satellite dishes pointed to the ground, their edges bent and their low-noise amplifiers smashed. The suspension rods that precisely placed them at their peak node reception points were twisted like pretzels. It had taken a great deal of anger and strength to contort them into those positions. The thin metal tubing of various amateur-radio antennas was grotesquely bent, rendered useless.

Sam stood and took several difficult steps to the bundle of cables that snaked across the roof and into an inlet box. He bent over and picked up the frayed remains of copper center conductors and black plastic insulation. Every cable had been cut. Connectors had been squeezed flat. Sam could not understand the anger and jealousy that led his father's old workmate to wreak such destruction. What was he so angry about? So scared about? What did he think Sam would do to him? Why did Richard take this so personally? What in God's name had Sam ever done to Richard?

All he wanted was Richard's help. All he got was Richard's hate.

Sam was more perplexed by WHY than he was by WHAT had happened. Richard obviously wanted Sam's META box to make the connection with the SETI signal emanating from the Tau Ceti planetary system. But why did he destroy Sam's equipment and antennas? Sam concluded that it was fear that ruled Richard at the moment—fear that somehow, Sam could make the contact even without the translator/detection equipment; fear that Sam would be credited with the discovery of not only the century, but also of human history. Sam knew that Richard desperately wanted to be the one associated with that discovery.

How foolish he had been, Sam thought, not to have detected Richard's jealousy and interest when he visited him several days before at JPL. How could Sam ever again trust anybody? He knew it was unnatural to live that way, but he would be more cautious and watchful in the future, carefully analyzing any move.

"But the hell with the future. What am I going to do now?" Sam thought. The signal could continue, the information could grow and become more precise, and the transmission of data could be even more critical, perhaps calling on Sam for some type of action. He would never know.

Sam put his head in his hands. A sharp flash made him look up. He saw a latticework of brilliant lightning etch across the sky and felt deep within his body the low frequency of the thunder.

Sam sat hunched over his workbench. He and the META prototype he had built months ago were illuminated by a gooseneck lamp. Surrounding him in the shadows were the devastation and disarray that used to be his amateur-radio station and his SETI receiving equipment. He knew it would take days, or even weeks, to put the major components back together. But he could fashion another META box quickly from the initial model. Schematic diagrams were taped to his equipment, facing him. He would refer to them periodically as he soldered one small electronic piece after another. The resistors, diodes, and transistors would be easy. The integrated-circuit chips would have to be burned in separately with outside help, but he had friends who could do that quickly as a favor. The cost would be minimal, compared with the sum that would be needed to rehabilitate his reception and transmission gear, the antenna system, and the cabling.

It was too much to even think about at once. Sam leaned back in his chair and looked out the window. He heard the wind howling and the rain pummeling the street and the roof. He stood and walked to the window. He was blinded by a flash of lightning and jumped at the immediate report of thunder. It had been months since the area last received rain. And this rain was not the cold, steady rain of a winter cold front from the north; this was a violent tropical storm from the south. At any other time, he would have enjoyed the awesome power.

Tonight it was a miracle for him just to concentrate on the reconstruction of the box. "If I could just finish that element," he thought. If he could just finish that element, he knew that somehow, he could jury-rig a transmitting/receiving station with Efrim's or Rollo's or Mitch's gear. With his small hand-held transceiver? Where would he get access to a large satellite dish? He had to find a way quickly. Somehow.

Sam rubbed his heavy eyes and stumbled back to the workbench. He looked down at the partially completed motherboard. He gently held a small bundle of hair-fine wires that cross-connected disparate sections of the board. He tried to regain some modicum of concentration as he collapsed in the chair. He watched a thin stream of smoke float upward, away from the tip of the hot soldering gun. He was transfixed by the smoke, which curled and shimmered as gentle interior wind currents made it waver and dance.

There was another flash of lightning and a smaller thunderclap. The rain slackened a bit as the storm moved northward.

As if in slow motion, he picked up the soldering gun and began fumbling with the minute wire harness, placing the wires in position on the board, in and around the empty IC chip bases. He worked quietly and slowly. In the past, a precise wiring mistake would have caused him to curse, would have raised his level of nervousness. But now his movements were so calculated that any mistake would be corrected without fuss and fury.

Sam did not hear the heavy steps of his Uncle Stu climbing the staircase. Stu walked into Sam's room and shook the rain off his coat. Sam didn't look up from his work.

Stu stood in the dark entryway and looked around the room. He had never seen such a mess. He walked up slowly behind Sam and waited for Sam to say something. Sam didn't.

Stu looked around and found a folding chair leaning against the wall. He grabbed it and opened it next to Sam. He sat down with a moan.

He watched Sam work for a moment or two, then asked, "Sam, how long you gonna be workin' here tonight?"

Sam hesitated, then quietly said, "As long as it takes."

Stu looked down at the floor and thought. Then he said, "You have school tomorrow, you know."

Sam suspended his soldering gun in midair and looked at Stu plaintively. Stu knew what it meant: here comes a favor request.

"Uncle Stu, can't I just straighten up here later and get my thoughts together? I don't think I'd be any good in English or biology, or even P.E. Please, lemme stay home?"

Stu shook his head. "Ya know, of course, your aunt is gonna kill me if I say yes." Stu looked around at the devastated room again, then back at Sam, who was still staring at him. "But OK."

Sam turned away and continued his work on the shiny aluminum chassis and the wiring harness. "I may even take a drive out to Anza, just to think."

Stu looked toward the window. "I don't know if this is gonna be finished by tomorrow. There's a flash-flood watch out there."

"Only if it's not raining, Uncle Stu."

"Why don't you wait till after the detectives come by to interview you tomorrow morning?"

Sam appeared to be distracted. The damage had been done. His META box was gone. He would have to spend all his energy on putting a new META together and considering how he would tie it into some means of reception and transmission on the cheap. He didn't feel like talking to detectives. That evening's interview with the investigating officers had been enough. He had more important work to do. But he would do as his uncle asked. He liked Stu—he loved Stu—and responded to his uncle's confidence in him and the freedom and independence he gave him.

Stu pushed himself to his feet and pulled back the folding chair. He looked over Sam's shoulder and shook his head. He was amazed by the accuracy and precision it took to work the way Sam worked with the circuitry in front of him. Then he looked at the back of Sam's head and stroked his disheveled hair once. He reached around Sam's chest and gave him a hug. Sam held his soldering gun in place. He closed his eyes for a moment and enjoyed the warmth and love of Stu's embrace.

Stu released his nephew and walked toward the door. He tightened his jacket and opened the door. A gust of wind blew in and filled the room. Sam breathed deeply, inhaling the sweet smell of the rain, and listened to the dripping water rolling off the roof and hitting the landing. An overwhelming sense of exhaustion grabbed him from head to toe.

Stu looked at Sam. "Not too late, Sam. Not too late."

Sam nodded without looking back toward Stu. He heard

the door close. He stared straight ahead at the schematic but did not see it. He heard another crash of more distant thunder.

Sam whispered, ''I hope it's not too late.''

CHAPTER 23

The magenta satellite had not changed position. It had remained silent. Nothing was being transmitted. It was still hovering over the Moon, motionless.

Then the numerous protuberances quivered and began to flatten against the irregular, sharp-angled spacecraft surface. A low hum sounded deep inside the craft. The craft slowly rotated on its axis in a complete circle, then made another 360-degree rotation. Then it stopped.

Suddenly, an even larger spacecraft appeared, stopping twenty-five feet from the satellite. It was ten times the size of the smaller craft. Its hum was louder than the smaller ship's. Sound does not travel in a vacuum, but the smaller craft was buffeted by a force peculiar to the propulsion system of both spacecrafts.

Steadily the large craft moved in, then finally joined with the smaller craft. A slow mutation began to take place. The forms of both became rounded, then the lines straightened. Finally, an equilateral triangle was formed. Gone was any hint of the protuberances; gone were the concentric grooves and markings.

The interior mechanical-biological structure was intricate and seemingly endless. The formations were more in the realm of the surgeon than of the engineer. The craft was an amalgam of the best that nature and thinking creatures could fashion through evolution, construction, and manipulation of natural resources. The best designs were employed to create this space-transport system.

It rotated. It was no longer a triangle. Now it was a

pyramid of perfect proportions, and it was about ready to move closer to Earth.

It moved. The distance from the Moon to 1,000 miles above the Earth's surface was covered in a matter of seconds. The shape did not change with the rapid acceleration and deceleration. The craft stopped above the Western Hemisphere, above the West Coast of the United States, above the southern portion of the state of California. The blunt end was pointed toward the Earth's surface.

The magenta coloring of the spacecraft darkened. Deep within the confines of the ship, the low hum began, accompanied by the raspy white noise and the buried warbling tone. Another signal was again being directed toward Earth.

The spacecraft was in perfect alignment with the Tau Ceti planetary system behind it. The spacecraft was between 6607 Mountain View Road, Escondido, California, United States of America, planet Earth—and Tau Ceti. The shaft of transmission was even narrower now because of the proximity of the spacecraft to Earth. But the signal spillover still reached out within 225 miles of the primary focus point . . . Sam Alexander, K6ZDQ.

That night, Sam would be unable to receive the transmission. One thousand miles below the spacecraft, Sam was busily soldering, occasionally distracted by a continuing tropical thunderstorm.

CHAPTER 24

Anaktuvuk Ridge Radar Site, Alaska

The large radar dome was clearly visible from the tiny outpost town of Anaktuvuk Pass, just south of the dominating Brooks Range in northern Alaska. The lonely hilltop U.S. government installation was one of several such sites in remote, hard-to-reach Alaskan locations. Tours of duty were generally short because of the ever-present boredom factor. Military personnel might as well have been posted on the far side of the Moon; they had no other human contact, no access to local civilization and entertainment. But that aided the twofold purpose of protecting secrecy and keeping personnel down on the farm, concentrating on their duties, and away from distractions.

The small control room could have been mistaken for the NASA Manned Mission Control Center in Houston. Rows of terminals, and men and women wearing lightweight Plantronics headsets, filled the facility. Large status boards towered over the front rows of terminals, detailing current Soviet military activity near each radar site. The Anaktuvuk site was much larger than most of the other sites in Alaska because of the additional search radar units on that bleak, snow-packed ridge. One of those radar units had the capability to look up as well as out.

Air Force Lieutenant Carolton gazed blankly at his round twelve-inch radar scope. His mind tended to drift more and more lately. He was nearing the end of his tour at Anaktuvuk, and he was eager to get back home to

Florida. He often wondered how in God's name he had managed to survive his tour of duty in the frigid Brooks Range foothills. The rugged wilderness and the never-ending views fascinated him. But what he wouldn't give for just a few hours on the fine white sands of Daytona Beach, especially in spring, with all the college girls in their tight, small bikinis with those tight . . . Carolton blinked. He saw something on the SSR, the Sky Scanning Radar. The sweep passed again, and again, and again. It was still there.

He sat up in his chair and adjusted his headset. His months and months of training began to dominate his thoughts and actions. He pressed several command and control buttons to manipulate the radar pulse and change the view. He rolled his chair several inches to his right and rested his hands on a computer keyboard. In a few quick strokes, he inserted an entry to correlate the screen data with the memory data, determining whether they matched. They didn't.

Carolton turned to see whether the colonel was seated in the on-watch command position. He wasn't. Carolton turned back to the screen. The large triangular blip held its position. The lineal readout on frame right determined that the object was approximately one thousand miles over California. Triangulation calculation determined that it was above Southern California.

Underneath the string of data, a warning pulsated: "NONCONFIRMED OBJECT."

Carolton could feel his blood pressure rising. He took a deep breath to calm himself and to steady his voice, which in a few moments might sound the alarm. He said softly to himself, "No false alarms this time. Be cool, Carolton. Be very cool."

He reached for a telephone touch-tone pad, threw a switch next to the pad, and began punching in digits. He waited several seconds for the call to beam up to a synchronous-orbit military satellite 23,500 miles above Earth, then down to Cheyenne Mountain, NORAD's headquarters in Colorado. The connection with the control center was made.

"Cheyenne, this is Anaktuvuk Ridge. Can you verify the anomaly on field I'm sending now?"

Carolton punched a few switches next to the radar monitor. The five seconds it took for the transmission to reach Colorado seemed interminably long. There was no noise on the telephone line, none of the pops, cracks, and hisses associated with civilian long-distance lines. The connection was direct, with no intervening stations to add noise or to interfere with or steal the transmission—or so it was believed.

Cheyenne replied, "I have no idea. Is this Mark?"

"Yeah. Is that you, Jeff? What the hell is that?"

Jeff Capler replied, "Hey, man, I have no idea. Lemme get the OIC on this. Standby one."

At fourteen thousand feet above sea level, the Mauna Kea Observatory was thought to occupy the best astronomical-observation location in the world. The extinct volcano rose high above the tropical maritime air of the big island of Hawaii. Civilization was sparse, so light pollution did not present a problem. Scientists from around the world tended to their studies in all sections of the electromagnetic spectrum, observing objects as close as the Sun and as distant as galaxies tens of thousands of light years away. Mauna Kea was a viewing platform from which one could almost reach out and touch the heavens.

Astronomers working at Mauna Kea had to make a slow adjustment to the altitude; the air there held 60 percent fewer oxygen molecules than it did at sea level, less than three miles below. But bearing the hardships—the altitude, the cold, and the sometimes-scary drive to the top of "the White Mountain"—was worth it. The "seeing" couldn't be better, and the camaraderie with the scores of fellow enthusiasts about the universe created a bond.

The scientists had to battle for time on any of the numerous instruments on the peak, so they could waste little time on frivolous searches. Every moment using the facilities, from the 120-inch Infrared Telescope or the new

Keck telescope, was to be cherished. Each moment of telescope time was scheduled carefully.

Surprises? There were few. But one night came the biggest surprise of all.

That night, Lee Keeling, a graduate student at the University of California, sat at the control panel, setting the parameters for the night's study. The eighty-eight-inch Ritchey-Chretien cassegrain-focus reflecting telescope was badly out of tune, and it took Lee extra minutes to set it up. She checked to make sure that the charge-couple device detector was up and running and that the magnetic tape recorder was ready to store the target images.

Both the telescope chamber and the control room were bathed in dim reddish light. Lee Keeling had already spent thirty minutes in the near-dark setting and tweaking knobs and switches.

She looked out the control room's large window at the towering telescope. Through the slit opening of the dome, she saw a small swath of twinkling stars. She glanced at them for a moment and considered how much she loved her work.

Pulling her chair to the nearby computer keyboard, she turned down the image intensity on her monitor. She ran through a string of commands. She typed in a set of aiming instructions. The entire building began to rotate into position with a grinding and creaking that had scared her the first time she heard it. But after many solo nights, she was used to the sound.

The building stopped moving. After another computer instruction, the large telescope began to tilt down with a light sound of meshing gears.

Lee reached into her purse and pulled out an oatmeal granola bar. As she busily tried to bite open the package, she halted and didn't move for ten seconds. She squinted at the monitor. She put down the granola bar and leaned over to the monitor.

"What in the hell is that?" she whispered.

She stood quickly and walked over to the large viewing window. Looking up, craning her neck, she viewed the top of the scope. Sitting down again quickly, she stared at the monitor, extended her index finger, and touched an intensely bright magenta blur covering one-quarter of the viewing field.

She was perplexed and excited. "What the shit is this?"

Lee engaged the intercom button. "Professor Warshaw, could I see you for a moment? It's an emergency."

She heard grumbling in the background. She shook it off.

A short, balding professor walked into the room. He leaned over Lee's shoulder and stared at the screen.

"What's so damn important that I should stop my work, Lee? What is this you have here? What is this?"

He looked over the control panel and studied the settings as quickly as possible. He looked down at Lee again. "What's dangling in front of the aperture?"

Lee continued to stare at the screen. "Nothing."

"Well, what is that? Refocus."

She initiated several commands and threw a series of switches. The focus became marginally clearer, and a rough triangular shape emerged. The magenta coloring was deep and exceptionally bright. The Earth position of the observatory, three thousand miles from California, made the viewing more angular. The Mauna Kea site looked at the object from the side, so its true shape was evident.

"What were you going to do tonight?" Warshaw asked.

"I was going to do some close-in work. Jupiter."

The professor shook his head. "I don't get it. Have you checked the catalog to see if it's ours or the Russians'? Maybe it's some newly launched piece of gear that's not listed."

He straightened up and put his hands on his hips. "Have you seen this before?"

Lee looked up at her beloved mentor. "Professor, it wasn't here last night, and I dunno what this is."

"Damn strange. The tape from this is going to have to give us some answers, because I can't explain this. What the hell is it?"

CHAPTER 25

There was nothing more Sam could do. His new ICs wouldn't be ready for several more days. He still hadn't determined how he would receive and process the data from the Tau Ceti signal source. Richard Redden? There were no reports from the police or JPL. Richard had simply vanished. Sam would have to think about the immediate future.

He drove to where he could think best, the Anza-Borrego Desert. It was a refuge for him, a place where he could be alone and prowl the parched hills in search of whatever it was he sought, be it peace or contentment or understanding.

Sam drove slowly through the small mountain community of Julian, the gateway to the Anza-Borrego. Every time he passed through the quaint town, which looked more like a sparsely populated Rocky Mountain community than like an outpost on the edge of the Mojave Desert, he felt as though a great weight had been lifted off his shoulders. The crush of people and events were far behind him. It was just him and the coyotes, the antelopes, the cougars, the deer, and the great horned owl. Stretched out before him that bright, crisp midweek morning were rugged mountains and 1,000 square miles of protected wilderness that contained countless species of birds, mammals, insects, and reptiles.

To most people, the desert was silent and desolate. But Sam heard the sounds of life in the desert and was able to distinguish species that were invisible to the untrained eye. Even at the Indian Sand Dunes, which he and his father frequently visited, Sam would find an area teeming with life.

Sam stayed on Highway 78, the main route into the park, as he looked for the turnoff that would lead him north past the Tamarisk Grove campground and past the crowded visitor center and Borrego Palm Canyon campground.

The thunderstorm had washed the air clean of dust and debris. The chaparral was etched sharply against the clear blue sky, and the winding canyons displayed their grotesque rock formations with particular clarity. Sam was in another world, as far away as the far side of the Moon, trying to suppress his dilemma. He didn't know who or what was trying to contact him from deep space.

He turned sharply onto State Road S3. S22 wouldn't be far . . . but how would he reestablish the contact without equipment?

He turned his view to the edge of the road. A large roadrunner and her small baby dashed across his path, running with their long tails stretched parallel to the ground. What odd creatures, Sam thought—birds that feed on geckos and small snakes, and rarely fly.

The narrow asphalt road intersected with S22. He turned right. His goal was not that far away. There were few cars passing him or in going the other direction, and he saw no other humans on the desert floor, in the canyons, or in the hills. A midweek day in the fall was the best time to go to the desert, Sam thought. He could be alone. He would be undisturbed.

The elevation began to rise. Sam thought of Lisa as the road took him around one mountain outcropping, then another. He looked down to his right and saw the Borrego Badlands. The rising high-angle sun began to obscure the shadows, which made it easier to see features in the maze of ravines and flat creek beds below.

Finally, Sam reached the turnoff to Font's Point, which was well marked and featured in almost every park publication as a point of interest. Sam hoped that on that day, however, he could explore the narrow ledge and mesa by himself.

He parked at the side of the road and, reaching behind his seat, pulled out a backpack filled with the essential gear that experienced backpackers and hikers carried. A bite of lunch, an adequate supply of water, and a small pair of binoculars would keep him happy and occupied for some time.

A twisted path beckoned upward. Sam walked up it one careful step at a time, avoiding the nearby boulders and brush, the hiding places of the rattlesnake and the scorpion. His steps were measured but confident. He'd had years of experience in exploring the Anza-Borrego hills.

He finally reached the plateau and stepped forward to the edge and the sharp dropoff. There was no need for guardrails; if a hiker or backpacker knew enough about his craft to reach that point, he had sense enough to know how close to the edge he could go. Sam could go to the limit. He caught his breath and scanned the undulating hills below, their shapes carved by wind, rain, and erosion over thousands of years. No sculptor could copy the features of the ravines that plummeted from unnamed hills.

Sam found the flat rock that he had claimed as his and sat on it. He easily slipped off his worn leather backpack and put it behind him. Then he wrapped his arms around his raised knee and surveyed the creek beds, almost devoid of vegetation. He turned to his left and scanned the rising, then falling outline of the arid Santa Rosa Mountains to the north.

He sniffed the air. It smelled of sage. He heard the fluctuating buzzing of a bee. Looking to the south, he noticed a broad band of cumulonimbus clouds moving in. Another tropical storm from the waters off Mexico? Perhaps, but not until later, much later. Maybe tonight. Maybe not at all, if it slipped up the coast and to Los Angeles or Santa Barbara, or even turned away and died in the colder northern waters.

Sam tried to concentrate on his environment. He leaned

back against his backpack and gazed into the sky. The humidity, fueled by the thermal columns of heat rising from the desert floor, was causing the formation of cumulo clouds—sure signs of heavy amounts of moisture still in the air. He watched several large formations expand and mushroom. They were pure white and shaped like balls of cotton, but thicker, firmer. One section of the formation would grow; then a different section would suddenly blossom.

He tried to concentrate on the beauty around him, but his thoughts always went back to the signal, to Richard, and to Lisa. He wished she were lying next to him. He wanted to hold her. He closed his eyes and imagined what it would be like to touch her soft skin and smell her delicate perfume.

Again, however, his thoughts were interrupted by thoughts of the signal.

Sam began to think about the improbable. He had heard the television interviews and read the books about the "visitors," the abductions, and the sometimes-painful medical experiments. He speculated about how he would handle abduction, confinement, and experimentation. He would fight back. No, he would question the aliens. Who? What? Why? Where? How? He would want to know as much as possible as quickly as possible.

Parallel universes, mirror realities, and astral planes—good God, what can one believe to be real, or unreal? The line between reality and fantasy was as fuzzy as the line between wakefulness and sleep.

Openings in time and reality, slits in the universal fabric of time and space, where alien beings could slip in and out? C'mon. But what if?

But Sam was certain of one thing: the signal he had received was no hallucination, no fantasy. The hard proof was there on disk and tape. He had heard the signal. Sam knew that he had been fully awake and alert when he heard those signals. And with him to confirm his discovery were his best friend, Efrim, and his new friend, Lisa. For them, the experience was just as real.

He had been contacted for a specific reason. He did

not know what that reason was, but he could not and would not let Richard Redden's jealousy and hate interfere. He would find a way to reestablish contact and assert his role in the unfolding drama of which he was an integral part. It was *his* SETI signal and his alone. It was directed at him and meant for him. It was his, and he would solve its mysteries.

Sam took a deep breath, then sat up. The sun had reached its zenith, and the growling in his stomach reminded him that he had skipped breakfast.

He enjoyed his chicken sandwich, chips, and apple, then spent the next several hours exploring the escarpments in and around Font's Point. Sam could hear rustling in the creosote bushes and the white burroweed. He suspected that the source was a kangaroo or black-footed mice. Perhaps a gambel quail was scratching for seeds. He had seen the desert sparrow and a lone scott oriole earlier in the day. The variety of life diverted his attention from his problems.

Late in the afternoon, Sam drove south, past Ocotillo Wells, to view the sunset among the elephant trees. Among those puffy-looking squat trees along a rocky hillside trail, he gave ample room to Ocotillo, Beaver Tail, and Deerhorn cacti. A cactus thorn was painful, but the fruit from the purple bud of the prickly-pear cactus was sweet and juicy. The bulb tasted like kiwifruit, only more tart, more like raspberry.

Sam was getting hungry again as darkness began to cover the Anza-Borrego. He knew that the Moon would be new that night. There would be only the light of the stars and the small flashlight he always carried in his backpack to help him find his way back to the parking lot at the head of Elephant Trees Nature Trail several miles away.

He wanted to continue on toward Split Mountain. He looked ahead and saw its outline against a nearly black sky. It would be invisible soon, and he had no intention of adding the venomous bite of *Crotalus cerastes*, the sidewinder, to his troubles. He knew that the small but hot-tempered, quick-to-strike snake hunted at night, and

Sam did not want to stand between the sidewinder and his prey.

It was time to go home. He turned and glanced southward at what he thought was lightning on the horizon. There was no thunder yet. But judging by the rapid buildup of the clouds marching northward, his earlier suspicion that another tropical storm was moving into California had been correct. Sam took quicker steps along the familiar trail. He looked over his shoulder and saw the first star of the evening. He didn't know why he had turned to see that particular star, but he closed his eyes and made the most fervent wish he could imagine. He smiled, turned away, and concentrated on the rocky path.

A short walk to his Jeep and a long drive home would lead him to his bed and sleep. He craved both.

From one thousand miles straight up, the view of the squall line approaching the California coast from the south was much clearer. Nearly continuous blue-green lightning deep in the cloud mass was visible.

Also evident were the sounds of data streams being sent from the magenta spacecraft to Earth. The magenta hue was even brighter. Life was coursing through the spacecraft. It was active; it searched and listened, asked questions and awaited answers.

There was no reply from the intended recipient. How long could unanswered queries be tolerated?

CHAPTER 26

The radioman aboard the Navy P-3 Orion submarine hunter squeezed between the pilot's and copilot's seats. He pulled down his heavy David Clark headphones and put a map in front of Capt. Mark Stephens. The veteran Navy pilot listened to his radioman over the din of the four screaming turbo-prop engines. No amount of insulation could adequately quiet the noisy cockpit.

"Captain, you wanted me to tell you when we were there," the radioman shouted.

"And lemme guess, Miller—we're there," Stephens said.

Miller pointed to the map. "Yes sir. The navigator wanted me to tell you personally. We are at 33 and 120 degrees exactly. We should be over the *Provideniya* any minute."

Stephens looked over at his copilot, who was busily looking for the Russian "fishing trawler." "I hope we have enough daylight to spot Ivan and take a couple of shots," Stephens said.

The copilot strained his eyes, trying to find the small spy ship against the vast dark expanse of the Pacific Ocean. The last rays of sunlight were quickly vanishing. The copilot could see only whitecaps and the outlines of some of the heavier waves that were building in front of the thunderstorms pushing in from the south.

The copilot turned back to Captain Stephens. "Mark, I can't see shit or shinola down there. It is getting black as peat. Why in the hell didn't they get us out sooner?"

"Paperwork, my good friend. What else? Orders are on paperwork, and paperwork has to be typed, slowly and carefully at times. Therein lurks the delay—paperwork and orders."

Stephens grabbed the radioman's sleeve. "What was the last condition report?"

The radioman thumbed through several pieces of paper on his clipboard. He began to read from one narrow slip, "Sky is fifteen-hundred, scattered. Ceiling eight thousand. Altimeter is twenty-niner seven-niner. Temperature is seven-six. Winds out of one-eight-zero at one-eight, gusting two-six."

Stephens looked out the windshield. "That's nice. We're gonna be in a thunderboomer in a short while, and we're trying to find a Russian pimple in the middle of a huge black ocean. Who thought this one up? Where's the *Nathaniel* now?"

The radioman answered, "The frigate *Nathaniel* is steaming north now off Leucadia at two four knots."

Stephens thought for a moment. "Well, Ivan is in a seam and will be for a short while until we get a radar fix . . ."

He was interrupted in midsentence by the intercom. "Captain, we have a radar fix at three-zero-five, twenty-five or twenty-six from our present position."

Stephens turned to the radioman. "Mr. Miller, ask and ye shall receive."

Genady Mirotshinov was wedged between the greasy gearbox at his right and the equally dirty bulkhead at his left. He watched and listened intently as Chief Engineer Edouard Perchora went through his litany of difficulties in repositioning the transmission and gearing controls for the giant forward satellite dish. Perchora's flashlight bounced from one oil-stained lever to another, resting occasionally on an oil-bathed gear as large as a man.

Mirotshinov furrowed his brow, then shook his head in disgust. "Chief Engineer Perchora, I hate to stop this dissertation on the engineering complexities of your task, but you lost me long ago. All I need to know is, can you be up and ready within three hours? That's when we'll be on station.''

Perchora looked around from his position on a ledge just under the massive gearbox.

''My friend, I have been working thirty-three hours straight just on the gimble frame, which may or may not be able to hold the dish on target in these heavy, building seas. The gear mechanism must be adjusted to handle the wide swings it was not designed to dampen. I can only work so fast, and there is much to do.''

Mirotshinov's patience was at an end. ''Yes or no, chief engineer? I must tell Moscow. Can we be ready?''

''Yes, comrade captain, but I can't guarantee that we'll be able to hold on target in these seas. The system was designed to intercept transmissions from American terrestrial and satellite communications sources, not from extraterrestrial communications sources deep in the cosmos, comrade captain.''

Mirotshinov pulled himself away from the confining gearbox crawl space and walked toward the ladder that led to fresh air and the upper deck. He tried to brush a smudge off his lightweight yellow rain gear but succeeded only in rubbing grease farther into the fabric.

He looked back at Perchora. ''Just try to finish, chief engineer.'' The captain took his first step up the ladder. His old bones twinged with pain from the fatigue of staying in a cramped position too long. He stopped and called to Perchora. ''And stop calling me 'comrade captain,' comrade chief engineer. Captain Mirotshinov is sufficient.''

The chief engineer watched his captain climb the stairs. He mentally noted the remark for the crew political-fitness log he periodically submitted.

Mirotshinov quickly closed the forward hatch and walked along the deck toward the bridge. Young seaman Inaiyev, who was finally warm, his color back to normal, ran up to the captain and saluted.

''Captain, radar has just picked up an American P-3,

coming in at approximately two hundred and fifty knots. They will be here any moment.''

Mirotshinov looked up at the moonless sky, covered with a layer of clouds. He stepped to the rail, nearly losing his balance on the pitching deck. The seas were higher than they had been in Alaska and much, much rougher.

"They will see us, but with this dark, cloudy sky they will not see much. And their frigate—where is it?''

"IP in one hour near our station, sir.''

"Wonderful. Then we will have company,'' Mirotshinov held up his forefinger, "in international waters, thank God, to watch us make fools of ourselves as we try to hold a bead on some wild, imaginary transmissions from the deepest parts of the cosmos.''

"Thank who, sir?''

CHAPTER 27

The second storm had moved onshore. It was not as strong as the previous one. The rain was steadier, not as violent, but there was still an occasional burst of natural fireworks.

Late at night, a small figure was outlined against the wall of Sam's garage. The figure began to ascend the slippery staircase, its steps interrupted only by a distant boom of thunder. The figure continued to the top of the staircase and the unlocked door to Sam's room.

Sam was sound asleep. A bit of rearranging had cleaned up the room sufficiently for Sam to walk from his bed to the workbench or bathroom without crashing over a piece of radio hardware or pile of papers. There were no pilot lights to illuminate Sam's completed prototype META box. It was unpainted and rough-looking. It was labeled like his stolen, neatly designed META box, covered with decals and carefully placed input/output plugs. The new box was on the floor next to his leather backpack.

Sam's chest was moving up and down gently and evenly. His arm was wrapped around his foam pillow. He had been asleep for only a short while.

The slight figure pushed open the door. It squeaked, but Sam didn't move. The rain pounded on the landing. The figure closed the door and stepped lightly to Sam's bed. With each step, the swish of rain gear and the squeak of boots was audible. The hood came off, and Lisa looked down at Sam. The light from the streetlight in front of the Alexander house was just strong enough to illuminate Sam's room.

Lisa sat on the edge of the bed and watched Sam sleep. She thought he looked young and helpless, sleeping with his arm clutching his pillow as if he were trying not to fall off the bed. She listened to him inhale and exhale. The steady, deep breaths indicated to Lisa that he was out completely. She leaned over, touched his shoulder softly, and kissed him on the cheek. He stirred, mumbled some incoherent words, and settled back down. She shook him.

"Hey, Sam. C'mon. We gotta take a ride," Lisa whispered. He didn't move, but his breathing became shallower and somewhat erratic. She knew he was starting to waken. She shook him again, this time a bit harder.

"Sam. C'mon, sleepyhead. I wanna take you someplace."

Sam turned over on his back and swallowed hard. He mumbled again, then slowly opened his eyes.

It took at least thirty seconds for him to become fully conscious and for his eyes to focus. He looked up and saw Lisa. He could sense that she was there but didn't fully comprehend. But once he saw the broad smile, the wet bright-red hair, and the beautiful piercing green eyes, he knew. The clincher was the smell of her perfume. He wondered whether he was dreaming. He verbalized his thoughts.

"If this is a dream, I hope I never wake up," Sam said softly. He rose slightly, putting his weight on both elbows. "What is going on?"

Sam yawned and looked at the digital clock, next to the picture of his parents, on the nightstand. "Good Lord, it's twelve-thirty."

Lisa stood and looked around the room. She spotted what she was looking for—Sam's pants, draped over a nearby chair. She picked them up and returned to her seat next to the still-groggy Sam.

"I know, Sam. I can read a clock, too, ya know."

She handed him his pants. "Here. Put your jeans on. We're going for a ride."

"What the hell are you talking about?"

"Just put your pants on and we'll talk as we ride."

"What are you doing here, and what are you talking about?"

She folded her arms. "You weren't in school today, but I covered for you . . . again. So the least you can do is get dressed and come with me. You'll need the new box and your laptop computer."

"Why?"

She stood and looked around for a shirt, a sweater, anything to keep him warm and dry. She found a sweater dangling out of his dresser, moved toward Sam, and threw it on the bed.

Sam sat up and started to get out of bed. Then he stopped and quickly pulled the blanket and sheet over himself.

Lisa tilted her head and smiled. "Not bad, Sam Alexander. Not bad at all."

Even in the near-darkness of Sam's room, illuminated by a flash of lightning or two, Lisa could see that Sam was turning a deep shade of red from embarrassment. She sat on the edge of the bed again.

"Where the hell are we going with my gear in the middle of the friggin' night?"

Lisa moved toward him and put her warm, soft hand on his arm. Sam was beginning to get excited. At that moment, he would believe anything that she was about to tell him. With the rhythmic beat of the rain, the smell of her perfume, and the gentleness of her touch, Sam was having difficulty keeping himself from grabbing her and taking her under the covers.

" 'Member how you were carrying on and on earlier tonight on the phone about how your equipment and antennas were wasted, and wondering how you could give . . . whoever they are that we heard the other night a password to prevent that dude from JPL from impersonating you with your META thing, or whatever you call it?"

"Yeah. So?"

"Soooo, it just so happens that my father is a director

of technical operations and installation for the phone company. My interest in what you're doing, Sam, is because I've been exposed to that type of technical stuff all my life. I'm interested in that sorta thing, and I just began to think about how I can help you.''

Sam grinned from ear to ear. He couldn't believe what he was hearing. He couldn't believe that for all this time, seeing Lisa in the hall, admiring her from afar, he didn't know that her interests were so similar to his. He was now truly falling in love with her. If there was such a thing as soul mates, males and females who are meant for only each other, this beauty sitting in front of him must be the match that was ordained for him.

''I never knew all that. Why didn't you tell me when we went out before?''

''Because I was interested in hearing what you had to say. I wanted to know more about you. I didn't want to talk about myself.''

Sam listened raptly as Lisa continued. ''Anyway, Daddy's been talking about this new, modern transmission site they're finishing up in Ramone Valley, just over the hill from here.''

''I know that place. But you have to go down this private road to get there. I've seen the Pacific Bell signs, but I never knew what was down there.''

''Sam, will your other META box and your laptop computer work? And that portable hand-held transmitter you were converting tonight—is it finished? You could. . . .''

He finished the sentence for her. ''. . . use the hand-held transmitter; hook it up to the input of the dish; go through its high-gain amplifiers; point the dish with the right coordinates, if they will rotate that far; and transmit the password code. I hope I'll have enough power to . . .''

Sam slapped his forehead. ''Lisa, this is crazy. The Tau Ceti system is eleven-point-seven years away. It'll be twenty-four years until I get a reply. Wait a minute. Maybe they've figured out a way to beat the speed of light. But that's impossible.''

Sam's mind raced. Two-way conversations with a planet that far away would take twenty-three and a quarter years. The search for extraterrestrial civilizations' stray signals, then, was necessarily a one-way proposition. He considered the possibility that maybe the aliens had found some means of overcoming the rule of nature that nothing, absolutely nothing, travels faster than light.

For man in the latter half of the twentieth century, that was an immutable law. But Sam did not rule out any possibility. If it could be imagined, it just might be possible. Sam shook his head.

"Crazy. But at least they will know in eleven-point-seven years that it was me who received their message. And if they want to send me a reply when I'm an old fart at twenty-seven or twenty-eight, they'll know I'm still here. They'll know I got their message and sent the password they can use to reestablish contact."

Sam turned serious as he looked at Lisa. "But it has to be me they contact again, Lisa, not Richard Redden." He was rejuvenated. "Let's do it. What the hell? Let's give 'er a shot."

"But there is one very important thing you gotta do first."

"What's that?"

"Put your pants on."

Sam stared through the rain pounding on the windshield. The wipers of Lisa's Honda Civic tried, with only partial success, to poke a hole through the steady stream of water. The streets were deserted, and Lisa was nudging the speed limit with gusto.

Sam adjusted the hood of his raincoat. He suddenly thought of, and asked, a simple but pertinent question that to that point had not been raised.

"How we gonna get in?"

Lisa looked over to Sam and smiled. "Get my purse. It's in the back seat."

Sam obeyed.

"Hand me the yellow wallet in there," she said.

While struggling with the wheel and the narrow, hilly

road, Lisa reached for the wallet and pulled out a plastic card with a magnetic stripe on one side.

"Card key." Lisa began to sing an old Eddie Money song. " 'I got two tickets to paradise. Pack your bag, we'll leave tonight.' "

Sam looked at her with a half-smile.

"OK, smarty-pants. Those places usually have some type of Gestapo or gendarmes."

"Guards? Don't worry. They're rent-a-cops. Give 'em a dry guard shack and a space heater, let 'em eat on the job and bring a portable TV, and they're happy."

"And occupied." Sam chuckled.

The rain started to ease as Lisa and Sam drove out from a mountain pass and onto fairly flat terrain. A distant flash of lightning was just bright enough to illuminate three forty-foot satellite dishes straight ahead.

Sam was usually intrigued by these facilities, but now he looked at the looming installation with twinges of foreboding. He certainly did not relish the idea of breaking and entering, or having his name and picture in a police record, but this would probably be his only opportunity to receive the signal again and transmit a reply.

His fear was ameliorated by the fact that Lisa was sitting next to him. She seemed fearless and looked upon the adventure as a challenge, an exciting diversion. In fact, he felt somewhat inferior to her courage. She could get into even more trouble than he could. It was her father who worked for Pacific Bell, and she and her father would have some difficult questions to answer if she and Sam got caught or somehow damaged the equipment. But with what was at stake, and not knowing what Redden might do with his original META box, Sam had to take the chance, regardless of the ramifications for all concerned. He had to become crafty, cunning, and daring, because now he was desperate.

He looked at her soft profile. She noticed him staring and stared back. Almost too long. She swerved around a downed palm frond in the narrow country road that led to the satellite transmission/reception facility. It was no more than one mile away.

"What?" Lisa asked quietly.

"Nothing. I was just looking."

"You like what you see?" Lisa asked coyly.

"Oh, yeah."

"That's good."

Lisa strained to see the outer gate. She slowed her car and turned off her headlights. She looked in the rearview mirror and around the car for other traffic. There was none. She made a quick, quiet left turn to the swing-arm barrier and the card-entry island. She pushed the card into the receptacle. A moment later, the barrier was raised.

She drove slowly over the treadle that closed the gate, toward the far side of the main facility-control building. In the distance, she could see the single guard gate underneath one of the large dishes, near the employees' and visitors' entrance. She parked behind a large emergency generator. The car was hidden from the view of the guard at the brightly lighted gate. Through a slow, steady drizzle, they could see an elderly guard moving from one side of the small building to the other. He was eating a sandwich and watching television. Lisa was correct. He had all the comforts of home and was as comfortable as if he were at home. After all, the guard must have thought, who would try to vandalize this remote transmission site in a pouring rain in the middle of the night? Who in their right mind would be out in weather like this?

Sam and Lisa emerged from the car as silently as possible and walked half a dozen steps toward a service entrance in a heavy chain-link fence. They were now within view of the guard, about two hundred yards away, but the light of the guard shack coupled with the steady sheet of light rain, made it difficult for him to detect Lisa and Sam. Lisa removed the plastic card key from her purse again and inserted it in the control lockbox. There was a loud click and a soft buzz as the catch released the door.

Lisa stepped in quickly, but stopped short as she saw Sam staring at the gleaming white disks. He was transfixed by the brilliantly lighted bowls and the large low-noise amplifiers that hovered over the satellite dishes.

"Sam, c'mon. This way," Lisa whispered.

Sam continued to stare at the three dishes. He considered the fact that these monster antennas did not exist forty years ago. Their capability to receive and transmit information reached far beyond the Earth's surface. "If I could control just one of those mammoth dishes someday," Sam thought, "or the 205-foot monster at Goldstone, or the multiple dishes at the Very Large Array, what wonders I could discover!"

To Sam, his signal search and exploration was no less exciting than Magellan's journey around the world, no less daring than the Viking expeditions to North America, no less triumphant than the journey to the Moon in 1969, when Neil Armstrong took the first human step on a nonterrestrial object floating in free space.

He heard but didn't respond to Lisa until he realized the danger of his mission. He could be easily spotted. He had to move on. But what beauties those dishes were! Brand-new, with the latest state-of-the art equipment on line and in the loop. Sam sighed and turned toward his friend. He looked into her eyes. He was back from his journey, reaching for the stars. He was in the here and now.

Sam said, determinedly, "Let's do it."

The building also had a card-key lock system. Not only did the key have to be inserted, but also the correct four numbers had to be entered on an attached touch-tone pad. The four tones echoed down the dark, empty hallway. The two adventurers stepped inside that hallway and closed the door.

Lisa and Sam stood in silence as they looked down the hall. Light trickled toward them from the end of the hall, barely lighting the long, wide corridor. The light originated from their goal: the main control room for the entire satellite facility.

Lisa grabbed Sam's arm and whispered, "Did you bring a flashlight?"

"Not here. I don't want to be caught flashing a beam of light around the place."

As they walked down the hall, Sam looked straight ahead. Then Sam gasped and stopped short.

"What?" Lisa asked.

Sam was staring at the joint between the ceiling and the wall at a small box with a semicircular plastic probe pointed down at the hallway. Sam nodded toward the device.

"Motion-detection alarm."

Sam looked around, then looked carefully at the device and its inoperative red LED warning light.

"Did it go off?" Lisa looked frightened.

Sam shook his head. "I don't think so. I didn't think it is activated."

Lisa gave a sigh of relief. "Sam, you scared me." She put her head on his shoulder and squeezed his arm. He looked down at her and flashed a warm, reassuring smile.

"Don't worry. We're OK so far."

When they finally reached the glass wall of the control room, they could see that some large component equipment had not been installed. The large, unlighted room had several rows of low consoles that faced the high windows, which presented an unobstructed view of the three gleaming satellite dishes, the scrub-brush hills, and the well-lighted guard gate. The island of light glowed brightly through the steady drizzle.

Much of the smaller control-panel equipment seemed to be installed. Pilot lights cast an eerie red, green, and yellow glow. On either side of the room were nineteen-inch equipment racks covered with sheets of heavy plastic. Cables, some with connectors and others bare, dangled from the ceiling and snaked along the floor. Tools, soldering guns, and test equipment were scattered throughout the room. Ceiling panels were not fully in place. Wire trays and air-conditioning ducts crisscrossed the room just below the exposed high ceiling.

Sam approached the double glass doors. He checked to see whether the door was locked. It wasn't.

"Lisa, this is it. We gotta stay low so the guard doesn't spot us. He's got a perfect view into this room." She nodded.

"Let's hope there aren't any magnetic or infrared alarms on this door," he added.

Sam carefully pushed open the door, and they entered the room, crouching below the level of the window ledges approximately twenty-five feet away. Sam duckwalked around a cart of tools. As Lisa followed, the tip of a cold soldering gun hooked her coat. As she moved forward, it hit the floor with a crash. They both abruptly halted.

"Sorry."

"That's OK," Sam replied softly, patting her back. "Help me find the dish-movement control panel."

Sam and Lisa squatted around the first, then the second row of connected control stations. Not until they went to the third row, nearest the window, did they find the panel switches that Sam wanted. Lisa peered over the edge of the desk, then grabbed Sam's wet raincoat.

"Is that it?"

Sam turned, stood slightly higher, and looked down at a series of switches, levers, and cable connection inputs. He nodded and studied the panel for several seconds, then crouched back down to Lisa's level.

"I don't believe what they did," he said, smiling. "Everything can be coupled from right here. The connections between the transmitter and receivers are connected from this room directly to the dishes out there."

He looked at the freestanding equipment racks.

"Look at what these nice, smart phone people did."

He pulled Lisa up and over the counter ledge and pointed to several protruding connectors. "They installed remote nipples so they can plug other components directly into the cable that runs out to the dishes. Wasn't that thoughtful?"

Lisa was excited for Sam. She sensed that his happiness meant that the job he had to do would be much easier and that both of them could take care of business and get out fast.

Sam began pulling his equipment out from under his raincoat. First, the computer, a small Heith-Zenith 286 laptop; then connecting cables and connectors, his hand-held radio, and finally the new META box. Sam grabbed the radio and showed it to Lisa.

"Lisa, this is my one-point-two-gigahertz hand-held radio. It only puts out two-and-a-half watts, but its frequency is close to the one-point-four-two-five gigs I've been receiving the signal on."

"Is it going to be powerful enough to talk to them?"

Sam looked over the console and at the dishes. He took a long breath, letting it out slowly.

"With the size and the amplification of those babies, I hope so." Sam looked over her shoulder at an imbedded equipment box of some kind on the far wall. The box was plainly marked "Main Power."

Sam instructed Lisa to throw the main switch, if she could determine the proper switch. Lisa scooted to the panel, quickly found the largest switch in the box, and flipped it.

Bright-blue fluorescent satellite-dish position numbers popped on. The several rows of marked panel switches also came to life. Lisa crawled back next to Sam as he continued to stare at the panel.

"Sam, do you know what to do here?"

"I guess I can figure out what is happening. I gotta connect everything up, 'cause once I initiate the dish move, the noise may alert the guard."

Sam concentrated again on his equipment on the floor. He attached the patch cords between the computer and radio and finally to his new META box. Then he attached a twelve-foot antenna cable to the box. After another quick glance at the antenna-input nipple, he found the proper connector among the connectors in one of his raincoat pockets and attached it.

A flash of lightning and a report of thunder made both of them jump. Their nerves were on edge, but they managed smiles that recognized that anxiety.

Sam attached the antenna connection to the input connector on the panel. He threw three switches marked "LNA," "AMP," and "POWER."

"I don't know how those dishes are numbered, so I'm gonna fire up all three," he said.

Sam stood over the control panel, pulled out a notebook, and looked at his watch. Then he bent down to his computer and turned it on. He tapped a few keys.

"OK, I've got the position readings."

He stood again and turned the thumbwheel knobs next to the display. Sam put his index finger on the "INITIATE" switch. He looked out at the satellite dishes and the guard shack, then at Lisa.

"Here we go. This is gonna make some noise out there, and I hope the guard's TV and the storm will mask it. Let's move the dish," Sam whispered.

Erwin Frankmeyer always used to tell his security-officer friends that Midwesterners make the best guards. Living out in the plains attuned them to unnatural noises and events. They could tell immediately when something was amiss or awry. They knew when things just weren't right.

Officer Frankmeyer was in his late fifties and had a paunch that at times made his belt disappear into his uniform. He could see his shoes, but not his belt, and he had to trust his hands when it came to finding his fly. He loved to eat. That night, his wife had fixed a ham on white with a little mustard and mayonnaise, topped with a slice of Monterey jack cheese. She also gave him a bag of fritos and an orange crush. Frankmeyer was in heaven.

He leaned back on his stool, engrossed in a Jean Harlow classic, an early drawing-room comedy. It was perfect to cut through the loneliness of a dark, stormy night. Behind the television and the counter it rested on were sliding glass windows. Beyond the windows were the three satellite dishes.

Frankmeyer was staring at the television set and munching on his sandwich when he thought he heard a grinding noise. He put down his sandwich and turned the television volume down, then off. He looked out at the empty parking lot, then back at the satellite dishes. He was still chewing his food when he noticed that the number-three dish, directly overhead, was moving, turning very slowly on its base.

He bolted out of the guard shack, tipped his head back and craned his neck to view the top of the huge dish, moving slowly in the rain. Then he whipped his head around and looked toward the control building, into the large window. He saw something—a shadow, a form, a movement. He wasn't sure what.

The guard grabbed his yellow rain slicker and a large black aluminum flashlight and walked toward the Technical Control Facility Building.

Sam released the dish-movement activation switch and checked the program and readout position setting numbers to ensure that they matched. He glanced at the dish and the guard shack. Then he took a closer look at the shack. He grabbed Lisa's arm.

"Quick—kill the master switch and get back here fast," Sam said.

Frankmeyer's master key opened the gate in the chain-link fence and the door to the building. He slammed the door behind him and flashed the 17,500-candlepower beam down the hall and toward master control. He crept down the hall with the flashlight in one hand and a nightstick in the other.

Sam and Lisa squeezed through the back panel opening underneath the second control counter. Sam finally swung his right leg inside the cramped space as he reached for his computer, META box, and hand-held radio. He could see the beam of light dancing in the hallway and into the control room. He moved quickly. He knew that he had only seconds. He splayed the connecting cable flat on the floor and carefully replaced the panel cover. The light was now just outside the room. He put his finger to his lips.

"He's coming in," Sam whispered to Lisa.

He tried to show no fear, only determination and resolve. Lisa held his arm so tight that she almost cut off his circulation. He grabbed her hand and loosened her grip. "It's OK."

He could hear footsteps just outside the room. Cables were swinging from the control panel under which Lisa and Sam sat, smacking both of them in the face. Sam paid no attention. His fingers flew over the keyboard of his computer as he entered a seemingly endless stream of simple data lines.

As Sam hit the last key, Frankmeyer stepped inside the master control room.

Lisa stared at Sam, then down at Sam's forefinger, which was resting on the return key. The guard's steps were coming closer to their hiding place. Frankmeyer was moving down the first row of control consoles.

Sam and Lisa looked into each other's eyes, their fear mixed with excitement. Then Sam pressed the return key.

Silently, the red "transmit" LED light on the hand-held transceiver flicked on. In the dark, Sam's message was scrolling at 1200 baud, over and over, through the computer to the hand-held transceiver, through the META box, through the coaxial cable, through the satellite transmission line from the Tech Facility Building to the satellite dish. It finally hurtled toward Tau Ceti at 186,282 miles per second.

The guard was five feet away from their cramped hiding place. Closer and closer, brighter and brighter, the beam of light edged toward Lisa and Sam. The intensity of the light made them grimace.

Sam's jubilation at getting his message out quickly turned to fear. He and Lisa held their breath and each other's hand. The guard was three steps away. Two steps away.

Through the ventilation holes in the panel cover, Sam could see Frankmeyer's yellow rain slicker. He could hear the drops of rain hitting the carpeted computer-floor tiles. He heard the guard's heavy breathing.

Sam and Lisa stared at each other. Immobile with fear, they looked as though they were frozen. Their heartbeats pounded in their ears. Sam thought he could hear the blood rushing through his veins.

Frankmeyer was next to the panel. He stopped. Sam closed his eyes. Lisa could see Frankmeyer's foot resting on the connecting cable.

Frankmeyer also froze. He listened but heard nothing. He had no idea that just two feet away, two humans were sending a message that would eventually be relayed and retransmitted by unknown means to a highly technological society more than eleven light years from Earth.

Time stood still. Lisa and Sam remained motionless. Frankmeyer remained motionless. Lisa prayed that the guard would disappear. She prayed as she never had in her life. She even promised God that she would never leave her room dirty again.

Sam opened his eyes and looked out through the ventilation holes. He saw Frankmeyer lift his foot off of the cable. He heard the guard step quickly around the end of the console. The room became dark as the flashlight pointed out into the hallway. Several seconds more, and they heard the exterior door slam shut.

A minute passed. Sam slid off the panel cover and peered around the corner. He saw and heard nothing. He stood and looked out the large window toward the guard shack. He saw Erwin Frankmeyer, Midwestern guard extraordinaire, hang up his yellow rain slicker and sit down again to his sandwich and the Jean Harlow movie. The shack became harder to see as heavy rain engulfed the valley.

Sam looked at the still-frightened Lisa huddled in the corner, her big green eyes staring at him. He glanced down at his computer. It was scrolling the same message over and over. He looked at his transceiver and saw the tiny, glowing transmission light.

He leaned down toward Lisa, pulled her close, and kissed her gently on the lips. Her frightened eyes closed. The fear melted, replaced by love, longing, and peace.

Sam pushed her away slowly. "Ya know, I think I love you."

Lisa nodded. "I think I love *you*."

Sam whispered, "Good. We have something in common. Let's get the hell out of here."

CHAPTER 28

A magenta glow filled Sam's room.

The showers had intensified as another band of strong thunderstorms moved in from the Pacific Ocean. Next to Sam's bed, his laptop computer sat on top of his damp raincoat. Sam was sleeping peacefully.

Suddenly, he jerked up violently to a sitting position. His eyes were wild and wide.

"Aaaaaaahhhhhhh!"

There was a blinding bolt of lightning. Immediately, thunder rocked the garage and Sam's room.

The magenta glow disappeared.

Sam's pulse raced. His breathing became shallow. His eyes were riveted on the rain pounding on his window.

With both hands, he wiped the sweat from his face. He scanned his room. Then he closed his eyes and flopped back down. His breathing gradually slowed, and sleep quickly returned. The noise and light faded and disappeared, but the magenta glow bathed his fading consciousness.

CHAPTER 29

GEO Tech Industries had decided to build its world headquarters building in downtown San Diego. Los Angeles and San Francisco were ruled out because of the traffic and congestion that Chairman of the Board Warren Alsop couldn't handle. But lately, Interstate 8 and Interstate 5 were becoming more like their cousins to the north in LA. Commuters' drive times created gridlock near the downtown loops and access roads. But at 3:45 in the morning during a driving rainstorm, only one moving vehicle could be seen.

A blue panel van bearing the proud logo of Signal Specialty of San Clemente slowed and parked in the red zone in front of the building. There was little to no chance of being ticketed under such adverse conditions in the early morning. Two men stepped out of the van, both dressed in white work suits with the company logo on the breast pockets. The two men were middle-aged and looked rugged, healthy, and strong.

The well-lighted foyer was wide as it was tall, a cavernous space with an electronic directory and an enormous reception desk/security station. The night security guard straightened in his chair as the two men approached. The guard did not hear them exchange quick words in Russian as they entered the lobby. They switched to English as they approached the reception desk.

". . . and if the Chargers don't bring back Fouts, they're shit out of luck for the season," Jim said.

"What the hell do you know, goofball?" Bob asked.

Jim, known in Moscow as Andrei Bonolov, and Bob, listed in the personnel files of the KGB as Joseph Teshkin, approached the guard.

"Yes, gentlemen. May I help you?"

Jim chuckled. "Yeah, you can tell me why in the hell I was called in on this job smack-dab in the middle of the night. We're here to service one of your satellite dishes on top of the building."

Bob pulled out a Satellite Specialist work order. The bogus document was professionally printed, with all the familiar boxes, lines, and warranty disclaimers in place. GEO Tech's name and location were plainly printed in the customer box. The guard reached for the work order.

"We been told the big boys have got a big meetin' up in the conference room at around nine and need to raise a com link with some biggies in New York, and the link is down. We gotta tweak a few knobs and look at the hardware."

The guard read the document carefully. He seemed satisfied. He talked with the two men as he walked toward the bank of elevators. He fumbled with his keys.

"This is typical. I wasn't informed but I'll get you men going. I sure don't want to stop a workin' man from workin'," the guard said.

Jim and Bob laughed, tensely.

The guard inserted his master elevator key, and the service elevator doors opened. Jim and Bob stepped inside.

"Say, while you guys are up there, why don't you see if you can stop this rain? Man, can you believe it? We've had one sou'wester after another."

"I tell ya what, officer, since we'll be up there, I'll talk to the big man upstairs—I mean, way upstairs—and see if I can shut this shit off."

The guard reached in and pushed the button marked "PH."

"I'd appreciate it. When you get off, just go down the hallway to your right. There's a door that leads up to the roof and the microwave room. I'll buzz it open for you."

Jim replied, as the door started to close, "Much obliged."

Bob stopped the door and opened it again. Jim gave him an "if looks could kill" look.

"Say, we'll be shutting the juice off for a while to check the power supply, so your security cameras may go off for a couple of moments," Bob said with a broad smile.

"Thanks for warning me," the guard said. "Otherwise, I would've had to track the problem down. Don't get too wet, and be careful. It's slippery up there on that platform. And watch out for that damn wind on the roof."

Out of the guard's view, Jim was furiously pushing the door-close button.

The door finally did close. Jim softly but fiercely started to curse Bob in Russian.

Bob replied, "In English, comrade. And what the hell is the matter with you? You forgot about the damn camera. The idiot can see every move we make."

Jim was quiet. Then he said, "Warn me first, comrade, before you jabber on about a key element of the plan."

"Listen, Andrei—Jim—it's late and cold, and I'm wet. I'm senior on this mission, so just do as you are told, and let's get this fucking Mighty Mouse job done and get the fuck away from this stupid assignment."

" 'Mickey,' not 'Mighty'."

"What?" Bob was perturbed.

" 'Mickey Mouse job.' "

Bob turned away and looked up at the floor-indication lights. They blinked off and on as the elevator went past 39 to the next stop, the penthouse. The door opened and Bob stepped out, but not before delivering a parting line to his KGB partner.

"Fuck Mickey Mouse."

Jim muttered to himself, "I like Disneyland. There's nothing wrong with Mickey, or Minnie, or Goofy."

CHAPTER 30

Condon Ranch was still in a state of limbo. The 2,800-acre dormant ranch adjacent to the city limits of Escondido was set for multipurpose development. The Repco Development Company wanted to drop in 1,100 homes, 8 commercial buildings, and a 150-store shopping center. But the plan was being fiercely contested; the environmental-impact study showed that a species of fox and hundreds of oak trees would be devastated in the process. So the prime property, which once was the working ranch of a Chicago publishing magnate, remained idle. It had inevitably returned to its pristine state. The ranch house, long since boarded up, sat silently, surrounded by overgrown chaparral in a beautiful valley.

Foreman O. B. Temeier's job—his only job—was to keep away poachers and ensure that the main gate was securely locked at all times. The long-since-retired railroad man from Joplin, Missouri, was intrigued by all the activity on Hunter Hill that morning. It used to be a favorite vantage point for the deceased Midwestern publisher, who could gaze across an expanse of land toward a small town at the bottom of the hill. But Escondido had grown, and the publisher would not recognize it if he could view it once more.

O. B. sat on the front porch of the guest cottage and rocked back and forth, peering through binoculars at the four large white vans he had escorted to the top of Hunter Hill. He had seen dim lights glowing in the vans the night before. In the dark, through the rain, he occasionally saw slender beams of light darting around the encampment. The men and women who were on top of the hill were probably up and working on whatever they were working on all night long.

Prompted by a sudden thought, he stood, tossed the binoculars on the rocking chair, and tightened the belt around his corduroy jeans. He was going to be neighborly and bring those people a treat—and maybe find out what they were up to on "his" hill on "his" ranch.

Charlie Williams had been up all night, and he was glad to see the early-morning sun finally clearing the horizon. He stepped out of NASA command vehicle TC/283-2, a forty-five-foot-long converted recreational vehicle, and onto the soggy plateau overlooking Escondido. To the west, he could see San Diego and the ocean. Three other white trailers of various sizes were parked in a semicircle near the command vehicle. Off to the side, the eighteen technicians had positioned a conglomeration of antennas and satellite dishes. The men and women had been working since their arrival, and they were suffering great lethargy on that chilly, brilliant morning.

A steaming cup of black coffee was the only thing that prevented Charlie from falling over with exhaustion. He weaved toward the edge of the plateau and looked back at the NASA contingent. The equipment was now quiet, and the slow movements of the technicians—some sitting on lawn furniture; others curled up inside the trailers, sleeping next to banks of warm reception and transmission equipment—belied their frantic activity of the night before.

Charlie turned back toward the west and pulled his North Face windbreaker a bit tighter around his neck. The dampness of the ground and the clammy air made him feel even colder. He felt the warming sun on his back and looked forward to the day's heat. He hoped that a comfortable bed awaited him at his La Canada home near the JPL facility. He closed his eyes and imagined his head hitting the soft down pillow nestled on creamy cotton sheets. He opened his eyes again, took another sip of the stinging coffee, and tried to shake off the drowsiness that was beginning to cloud his thinking. Then he heard quick footsteps and turned to see who was approaching.

Larry had been with his group only a few months, and his enthusiasm was intense. But early in the morning, after no sleep, it was hard for even-tempered Charlie to take.

"Oh, shit. Now what?" Charlie whispered, turning back around.

Larry walked around in front of Charlie, blocking his view. Larry was wide awake and fully charged. "I heard that," he said.

Charlie moved a few steps left and continued to gaze into the distance. He took another sip of coffee and warmed his hands on his mug.

"Good. I hoped you would. Whaddya have, Larry?"

Larry stood next to his boss and looked out at the same view.

"I just got on the horn with JPL, and there's no word yet on Redden. They don't know where the devil he is."

Charlie looked at Larry and smiled. He said, "Gee, that's too bad. Now tell me something really important."

"There's a lot of shit pouring in this morning from all over the place. It's all being pieced together now. But the most important thing"—he paused and handed Charlie a computer-generated map—"is this."

Charlie squinted at the map. His incisive scientific mind suddenly awoke.

Larry continued, "I did some number-crunching with all the positioning data we processed last night and merged it with a mapping program of the target area I got at Software City."

"You mean that chain of stores that sells software to civilians in every shopping center in the Southland?"

Charlie was intense now. The adrenaline was flowing. He tried to compare the map with the city below.

"Is this map current?"

"Yes."

"Are all the streets listed?"

"Yes."

"Does this look right to you?"

Charlie held the map out. He glanced from the map to Escondido, then back to the map.

"Yes," Larry answered quickly.

O. B.'s battered pickup truck crested the plateau road and stopped behind the two NASA scientists.

O. B. stuck his head out the window. "Good mornin', Mr. Williams," he shouted in a friendly voice. The ranch foreman opened the door and reached back inside the truck.

Charlie ignored him. "Larry, get me my binoculars."

Larry had another surprise: he was hiding them behind his back. He held them out for Charlie. Charlie grabbed them and stepped even closer to the edge of the plateau.

Charlie looked at the map and got his bearings on the streets. The rain had washed away any smog or dust. The "seeing" was perfect, with little heat to distort the view through his binoculars.

Charlie pulled the binoculars to his eyes. He scanned the streets below, looked down at the map, then pulled up the binoculars again. Again he switched views until he found Mountain View Road, until he found the Alexander Automotive Garage, until he found the Alexander house, and until he found Sam's roof. He saw the twisted antennas reflecting the brilliant sun. He clearly saw the Alpha and Beta satellite dishes pointed, at what Charlie thought was an impossible angle, toward the Tau Ceti system, which moved in an endless arc across the sky.

He lowered the binoculars and stared down at Escondido. Even without the aid of his powerful 20x80 binoculars, Charlie saw the reflection of the sun on Sam's antennas—the antennas that had failed to receive the previous night's transmission, the jumbled transmission that Charlie's people had detected and recorded in the pouring rain on top of Hunter Hill at the edge of Condon Ranch.

O. B. stepped up to Charlie and held out four pink bakery boxes.

"How'd you boys like some pie?"

CHAPTER 31

The air was clean and clear in the La Canada–Flintridge foothills above the Jet Propulsion Laboratory.

Kenneth Wood tucked his copy of the *Los Angeles Times* under his arm and swung his briefcase from one hand to the other. He looked up and saw the wide fronds of several Mexican Fan palms waving in the breeze against the clear blue sky.

The door of the reception building closed behind him, and he took a leisurely walk into the quadrangle, a walk that he loved to take early in the morning. He could hear the wind through the trees and watch the gardeners laboring over their precious beds of marigolds and daisies. He could get a small touch of nature before battling the bureaucratic wars at JPL "central," listening to complaints from department heads about not having enough money to complete projects, hearing about slow deliveries by vendors, and fielding requests for interviews.

As he crossed the quad, Kenneth saw a group of ten to twelve engineers and PIO officers. He knew their faces and their jobs, but not their names. They were running down the wide concrete staircase of the administration building toward him. His happy countenance suddenly became defensive. He knew they weren't running toward him to give him the cheerful morning greeting "Have a nice day!" He abruptly stopped walking.

"My God, what is it now?" he whispered.

He watched the thundering herd approach. The first wild-eyed JPL employee to reach him was short, stubby

Will Webster. Will was out of breath and hyper compared with the last time Wood saw him, in the staff meeting. He stared down at Will.

"What, Will? What the hell is it?"

Another engineer, sensing that Will wasn't able to reply quickly enough, pulled Will away. "Ken, all hell is breaking loose."

A barrage of requests and shouts poured over Kenneth Wood. His attention darted from man to man. He couldn't understand anyone in the shouting and screaming.

"What? What?" he asked.

"I must talk to you," Will said breathlessly.

Will was pulled away again, this time by Brian Small, manager of the Public Information Office. "Ken, we gotta talk. Should we release the pictures?"

An assistant of Brian's leaned into the group surrounding Kenneth.

"Mr. Wood, the *National Enquirer* wants to know what color the aliens are. Green, purple, or blue?"

Kenneth was overwhelmed by questions and comments by engineers he did not recognize.

"We know the target of the SETI signals."

"Should we continue a spectrometry scan?"

"What should I tell the Deep Space Network people to do?"

"Washington wants you to call immediately."

"Charlie Williams wants to know what to do next. He's in Escondido, and . . ."

"The police are looking for Richard Redden. LAPD Detective Turner wants you to call down to Parker Center immediately. They say he's nowhere to . . ."

Wood cut off the questions with the wave of his hand and stepped close to Brian Small. "Mr. Small, don't you think that the director of the Jet Propulsion Laboratory should see any pictures first, before anyone else?"

"Well, yes."

"Including the *National Enquirer*?"

"Well, yes."

"Are these the Mauna Kea photos I got a call about in the middle of the night?"

"Well, yes."

Kenneth turned to Will Webster.

"Will, tell the imaging people to bring whatever they have up to my office right away."

Will dutifully nodded. Kenneth marched forward and began to climb the stairs quickly and with purpose. He stopped suddenly and turned toward Brian Small again.

"Where has Richard been lately, and why in the hell are the police looking for him?"

Kenneth Wood turned the corner and walked into his outer office. As soon as his secretary saw him, she sprang out of her chair and ran over to him. He tried to avoid her by racing to his office door, but she stepped in front of him. Her excitement was running high, consistent with the excitement of every employee at JPL. The large multibutton telephone on her desk was constantly ringing; all the lights were blinking.

"Here, Mr. Wood." She handed him a stack of messages. "Sir, these things have been coming in so fast and furious, I've had an awful time just trying to keep up."

His shoulders drooped. "OK, Peggy. Thanks. I need some tea."

He grabbed the messages. "Which is the hottest?"

She thought for a minute, then said, "Well, the president called about thirty minutes ago."

"Which one, Peggy? Rockwell? McDonnell Douglas? Lockheed?"

"No. The United States."

Kenneth looked away, then back at his secretary. "Yeah. That probably should be the first call, wouldn't you say?"

"I'd advise it. But you also have Evegeny Romanov calling from Gorki."

Kenneth turned quickly and bolted into his large, mahogany-paneled office. He threw his briefcase and newspaper on a nearby coffee table and collapsed in his tall chair behind a cherrywood desk.

"I knew it! I knew it!" he shouted.

Peggy entered the office and walked to the front of his

desk. He ripped open the top button of his shirt and opened the knot on his tie.

"Knew what, sir?"

"The Russians. The fucking Russians. I knew they'd pick up on this."

He put his hands over his face. "Christ, now what?" he asked through his hands. Then he sat up quickly and leaned on his desk.

"I wonder how much they know," he said quietly. "Which line, Peggy?"

"Three-four."

He reached for the phone. Peggy left the office, closing the door behind her.

Kenneth grabbed the handset and put the phone to his ear. He contemplated his approach toward an old colleague of sorts. He pushed the line button.

"Evegeny, is that you? How are you?"

Kenneth heard the deep, slow Russian accent he had heard many times before. Cooperation in the unmanned exploration of space had become an intimate pledge between Soviet and American scientists and administrators. There had been unusual cooperation in the use of the Deep Space Network during the recent pass of Halley's Comet, and there was more to come.

Wood knew just how far to go with Romanov. There had been quiet moments over Smirnoff or Jack Daniels when they dreamed together about what great things could be accomplished with the Russian heavy-lift capability and the American genius for technology and engineering. In a perfect world, in a perfect time, much could be done toward reaching into the depths of space, exploring the nearby planets, and cooperating on Earth-science studies in space.

Although the climate was improving, these still were not perfect times. Wood knew that his responses would have to be measured and carefully structured, especially since he was talking to the Russian before he had a chance to call the president of the United States. But such was the nature of this SETI signal discovery, he thought. Maybe he could glean some morsel of information or tidbit of data that would help him and his people determine the origin and content of the supposed message from another civilized society before he talked to the president.

But he had to be careful. Pleasantries first, a little naïveté second. Third, probe for information, and finally try to pick up for any overlooked shards of information.

"So tell me, Evegeny, it's the middle of the night in Gorki? Right?"

"Yes, my friend. And it is the first thing in the morning in Pasadena," Romanov replied.

"It's not that early."

"I tried to call you at home earlier, but your line was busy."

"Oh, really?" Kenneth thought of playing dumb. But after rapid reflection, he realized that would be a bad idea.

"Yes, Kenneth. When a possible Earthbound signal has been sent by an extraterrestrial civilization, directed specifically at your neighborhood near San Diego, I think that requires a call to you in the middle of the night."

Kenneth took a deep breath and exhaled into the mouthpiece.

Romanov continued, "Yes, my friend, we know. Even the confused old men in the Politburo know. Of course, they don't know what it means or what should be done. But we do, don't we?"

"Yes, Evegeny. We most certainly do. You know, of course, that the story has hit the news wires?"

"So I have been told."

"And you can bet that the leak was on our side."

"These days, Kenneth, I wouldn't bet on it. We have a group of people down in Australia, and they like to sit and drink with the Australians."

"To get information?"

"And because they like to drink."

"OK. Do you want to data-dump me first, or should I give you the privilege? I should talk to Washington first, however."

"That won't tell you any more about the signal, I can tell you that. You'll get the same response I got from

Moscow. Give us more information, and make sure it is not a hoax.''

Kenneth thought for a moment, considering his next line of questioning. ''Which it is not, Evegeny, which it is not.''

''I believe you're right.''

''So?'' Kenneth asked.

''So?'' Romanov replied.

There was silence.

Romanov finally broke the silence. ''Enough games. We still haven't cracked the signal text. We, of course, have military surveillance satellites in the area. Which ones, I won't tell you, of course.''

''Of course.''

''But that won't do us any good because they are pointed down at you, not up toward Tau Ceti. And the gout-ridden generals won't let me touch them.''

Kenneth pulled over his yellow legal pad and wrote down his first note. The Russians knew the origins of the signal. That probably would be one of the first questions the president would ask.

Romanov continued through a crash of static on the line. Kenneth thought that the recording analysts at CIA were probably cursing from the sharp pain caused by that volume spike.

''We have a, shall I say, research vessel nearby, just off the coast of San Diego.''

''Obviously studying the gray-whale migration,'' Wood said, laughing.

''Obviously. But the sea conditions have made getting a lock on the signal nearly impossible. Data is only sketchy, because the signal keeps popping in and out. We can't keep a firm lock with our tracking dishes in twelve- to fifteen-foot seas.''

Kenneth scribbled that down as well. Did that mean that in heavy seas they couldn't track American surveillance satellites?

''We even had some . . . tourists who are visiting your country and enjoying the sights of the California coast, trying to get us some data. But you know it takes a lot of equipment, and with what they got, it was not of any use.''

"Aw, gee, that's too bad. Why don't you have your 'tourist' friends stop by for a chat? We can get to meet them and maybe see what they did get.''

"No. Not possible. They are traveling today. The idiots locked onto Epsilon Eridani. These tourists are not astronomers, Kenneth, and they rarely look up at the sky. Mostly down at the ground.'' There was a long pause. "Your turn.''

Kenneth let out a long sigh.

"Oh, c'mon, Kenneth. We will find out anyway soon enough.''

"We know the signal strength is greatest in the San Diego area,'' Wood said reluctantly. "Precisely where, we are still working on.'' He bit his tongue. "Why that area, we don't know. How they, or it, or whatever can focus the beam so narrowly is a mystery. You know, of course, about the triangular purplish object approximately one thousand miles above the California coast. It is obviously involved with this phenomenon.''

"Yes,'' Romanov answered. Wood immediately sensed the tentative nature of the answer. But what the hell, he thought. He was pleased that the *National Enquirer* had scooped the KGB, the largest spy organization in the world.

"A fuzzy picture was made from the observatory at Mauna Kea.''

"You know, I'm jealous of that spot. When are you going to take to Washington that proposal for a joint instrument?''

"Evegeny, it's on the list in Washington.''

"Probably at the bottom. Can you fax me a copy of the picture?''

"That's no problem. But by the time you get it, it'll probably be on every evening newscast in this country.''

"That's fine, but maybe it would be more significant if a copy came directly from you. Politics, Kenneth.''

"I'll have to get clearance on that one, too, but I see no problem. So now what?''

Kenneth knew that volume switches were now being

turned up in some dark recording facility in McLean, Virginia, and in the bowels of the Kremlin.

"I think that it is important that we form a scientific alliance of our CETI program and your SETI program," the Russian said. "Working together, we can verify the authenticity of this signal, decode its hidden message, and determine why it is being directed so accurately to one spot on the North American continent. As you know, we have an active and very-well-funded CETI program here in the Soviet Union, and it would be good for our two programs and for all of mankind if we worked together on this momentous discovery. Well, what do you say?"

"I say it sounds great. But I will have . . ."

Romanov quickly completed the sentence. ". . . to check with Washington."

"Right."

"By the way, has your deputy Richard Redden been found yet?"

Wood sat straight up in his chair. "How in the hell did you know that?"

"When a high executive is sought for a petty burglary in the town of Escondido, it makes a little noise. These kinds of things do appear in police journals, no?"

"Your guys are everywhere."

"So are yours. But we are both lost when it comes to intelligently handling this historic moment. We cannot let this pass. We cannot let it slip through our fingers because of the stupidity of the politicians. If we cannot respond to this, even though a reply aimed at the Tau Ceti system won't be received for more than eleven years, we will have committed a sacrilege."

"A sacrilege? Are you getting religion now, Evegeny?"

"Kenneth, how can you look up into the beauty and majesty of the heavens above our tiny blue globe and not have religion?"

"Quite true, my friend. Quite true."

CHAPTER 32

Alarm clocks were usually not necessary at the Alexander house. The sounds of high-power pressure nut drivers, clanging tools being thrown to the concrete floor, revving car engines, and screaming auto mechanics filled the house starting at precisely seven every morning except Sunday.

Stu's auto-repair shop had never been busier. His friendly, caring nature spilled over into his business practice. Having a car repaired there was like visiting a friendly country doctor. Fine workmanship went hand in hand with courtesy and customer satisfaction. Business was good, and Marion and the kids and Sam were taken care of nicely. There was always enough money for them to take vacations and keep the house in top shape.

But that meant long hours for Stu. He was usually in the shop before opening and well after closing. The saving grace was that he had to walk only one hundred feet to work. That also meant that he could have lunch with Marion at noon, his favorite time of the day, when the kids were in school and the house was quiet. No matter how crazy it was in the shop or how busy the schedule was, he always took time for those precious calm moments with Marion.

The office area of the shop was on the same level as the eight service bays. A long, double-thick glass wall separated the office from the service area, but the glass doors always seemed to be open, and flies and noise traveled freely between the two sections.

The aluminum garage doors had just swung open, but Stu was already in his office just inside the glass wall. The morning schedule needed to be reviewed and matched with work orders. Stu looked up and saw several of his mechanics sipping that last bit of coffee before plunging into someone's transmission or clogged air-conditioning drain tube. He saw Sam turn the corner of the building and stumble in. The sun was intense, even that early in the morning, and Stu had to squint to check the condition of his nephew that morning. Sam had looked washed-out lately, and his lethargy worried Stu. Sam looked particularly pale and drawn as he shuffled into his uncle's office, bumping into the edge of the door and then bouncing into a file cabinet.

Stu returned to scribbling on the schedule sheet.

"Good morning, Sam."

He heard what he thought was a grunt. He looked up at Sam.

"Sam, I wanna tell you, you look like a truck hit you. Did you get any sleep last night?"

Sam took a few cautious steps toward a nearby coffee station. He grabbed a foam cup and poured in a liquid that resembled the thick, gooey oil reclaimed from countless crankcases not far from where he was standing.

"Not really. I was too busy." Sam looked at Stu and collapsed in a chair. "Doing things."

"Things? What kind of things?"

"You know. Just things."

Stu concentrated on his work again. "Maybe you're sick. Are you feelin' OK?"

"Yeah, I'm just fine."

Sam took a sip of coffee and glanced through the window at the quiet garage. There was still very little activity, but Sam was paying attention to one particular part of the shop, the storage alcove. Supplies were kept in that area. It was easily accessible from the service floor, but from the office and Sam's vantage point, it was difficult to see clearly because of the sun reflecting off the concrete floor.

Sam held his steaming cup of coffee as he walked

through the long garage toward that dark corner. He heard a few obligatory greetings from several of the mechanics. They knew him well, and he knew them. Sam's silence that morning was a signal, however, that said "leave me alone." His usual curiosity about the intricacy of a transmission or engine computer was not of interest to him. He continued to walk.

The stacked cases of oil, the racks of parts, and the neat piles of new tires softened the sound in the rest of the shop. Two high windows brought in some light, but they were smudged and dirty from years of neglect. The space was quiet and dark. The most prominent fixture sat in the middle of the garage on blocks, covered by a greasy, graying tarp.

Sam moved slowly to the tarp and pulled back the heavy cloth to reveal a cross-member support rod of a vehicle. A strange vehicle. The name "Glamorous Gertie" was stenciled on the pipe. The paint was faded and chipped.

Sam set his coffee on a nearby carton of oil cans, pulled off the tarp in one sweeping motion, and saw his father's sand-rail dune buggy. Sam's heart jumped when he saw it. Years had passed since he had seen the bright red dune buggy. Even with the covering tarp, dust had found its way in; it covered the entire vehicle in a thin film.

Sam could have cared less. His mind was suddenly sharpened; he sprang out of the thick fog he had been under since waking. He stepped closer and gently wiped the dust from the name decal. He looked down at the powdery dust covering his fingers. He walked around the vehicle and let his fingers glide over the tires, the bright chrome engine parts, and the cool rubber steering wheel. He lovingly took in every turn and bend of the strong metal frame and the gleaming light fixtures.

He gingerly swung his leg over the side and slid into the driver's seat. He grabbed the steering wheel with both hands and stared straight ahead at a tall column of new tires. But he didn't see the tires; he saw the desert stretched out endlessly before him. He was perched on the crest of a high dune; all around him were other dunes and the ridge of chocolate-colored mountains on the horizon. The air smelled sweet. A gentle, cool wind swept away the searing heat of the sun, and there was no sound but an occasional sigh of the wind and the slow, steady thumping of his heart.

Sam leaned back in the driver's seat as his imagination let him fly over the dunes. The raw horsepower slammed him against the seat. He was at peace, yet thrilled.

The prize for the winner of the Messiest Office contest was a gourmet dinner, so to speak, at the studio commissary. It was not known whether the other networks had similar contests, but studio management had tried various methods of engaging employees and infusing them with heightened company morale. Success had been moderate. But the Messiest Office contest was always a highlight. The grand tour of judges was a nervous time for contestants and a dreaded time for secretaries, who generally had the task of cleaning up their bosses' mess after the judges left. But the vice president of operations always promoted the event as being more important than the annual Christmas parties at the International Broadcasting Network. It was great fun to watch the ingenuity of normally conservative managers and directors as they trashed their offices in the gray atmosphere of the IBC.

The winner was invariably Burton R. Dunlap, director of network news operations, West Coast. His ingenuity was unique. This year, he had a simple method of winning. He decorated his office, floor to ceiling, with toilet paper. He was the instant and unanimous winner. The only down side to the contest was the clean-up. He saddled his secretary with that chore. He was magnanimous in victory, sending conciliatory memos to the losing department heads.

Several feet of toilet-paper debris still cluttered his office as he decided to take a break and go over the latest news wires.

He negotiated the narrow hallway and stepped into the "pit," the open, high-ceilinged newsroom that served as set and working space for the writers, reporters, producers, and news anchor. He walked around the large studio toward the bank of computer printers. The pit was usually quiet this early in the morning, and his demeanor reflected that calm.

Burton Dunlap was in his early fifties and had been through the local news wars in cities around the country at various network-owned and -operated stations. Finally, he got the assignment he had hoped for in an area of the country that he dreamed about—Southern California. He'd had it with the numbing winter wind off Lake Michigan knifing through Chicago, with the sweltering humidity pumping up from the Gulf of Mexico to suffocate Houston, and with the vituperative environment of the New York news scene. He wanted peace and quiet and the ability to still stay connected with a network news operation. So when he was offered his current job—head of the West Coast operations of a new network, with unlimited funds pumped in from Australia—the opportunity was too good to pass up.

Burt finally reached the row of high speed news printers in the far corner of the studio. He scanned the local printer and then went past several others, scanning as he moved. He stopped when the alarm started buzzing on the AP wire. He grabbed the copy and read it as it fed off the rollers.

He ripped it out and turned back toward the row of offices on the opposite side of the studio. As he walked, he surveyed the anchor position and the newly installed chrome-and-oak desk. Thirty thousand dollars for a desk and some simple electronics. Burt shook his head. Half the cost was in the design, which his college-bound son could have designed for a hundred dollars. His son was a good enough artist to come up with the original rendering, but of course he wasn't an art director, so the work stayed in-house and cost the news department a small fortune. Burt wondered whether the audience would appreciate the cost and effort. "I doubt it," he thought.

The agitated, unkempt assignment director, Joseph Atlas, passed him. Burt grabbed him and pulled him along. "C'mon, Joe."

Joseph's thankless job was giving assignments to minicam crews and reporters. He wished that he were as strong as his namesake. He always seemed to be in a rush and fatigued.

"Boss man, I got things to do," he protested.

"Yeah. Like seeing me. Now," Burt replied.

Burt reached his office, Joe following him. They carefully stepped over the toilet paper on his office floor. Burt flopped into his chair, finding a spot on his cluttered desk to rest his feet. He pulled off his glasses and looked at his door.

"Maria, when you have a chance, help me clean up this mess you made in my office!" he shouted to his secretary. Then he looked at his panting assignment editor, sitting uncomfortably in a guest chair.

"Hard to get good help these days," Burt said facetiously. "So whaddya want?"

Joe gave him a dirty look. "Burt, I have things to do."

Burt handed him the wire copy. "Look at this."

Joe grabbed the copy and read it quickly. He shook his head. "Yeah, yeah, yeah. Another UFO report. Different, but the same."

Burt held out his hand and reached for the copy. He glanced at it again and put it on his desk.

"When it comes from the JPL? Something is afoot here, my friend." Burt began to nibble on the end of his glasses.

"So I should divert a crew there? Is that what you're saying?"

"No, that is what *you* are saying, and I agree."

Joe stood and began to walk out.

"Hey, Joseph," Burt yelled.

Joe turned. He was perturbed, but listened politely.

"Yes, boss?"

Burt pointed with his glasses at Joe.

"This is no ordinary UFO report." Burt looked at the wire copy. "Something is happening over there. So get a crew there. Code 3. Go past the public-information office and directly to the head honcho there. OK?"

Joe nodded. He began to sense that maybe his boss

was correct. Maybe there was something of substance in this wire report.

"OK, great. You wanna put it on, and what segment? How shall we slug it? With video or not?"

"Let's see what we get. Let's see what's going on first."

Joe turned and walked out of the office. Burt read the copy one more time. With his experience and innate ability to smell news, he knew that this story was going to dominate all others. There was substance to the wire copy, and the story just might be a big one. And it was in his backyard, in his jurisdiction. But radio signals from outer space? He would have to be careful and cautious, but not overly careful and cautious. That wasn't his nature.

Burt smiled. This one might be fun, especially if he was first with it.

CHAPTER 33

"I have to use the toilet, Mr. Eberle. I gotta dump real bad. Like it's ready to start squirting out."

The skinny, middle-aged mathematics teacher looked up from his *Time* magazine and pulled down his glasses.

"Matthew, there is no need for vivid detail. All I need to hear is, 'May I go to the restroom, Mr. Eberle?' I do not need to know the present position of the feces you need to deposit or the speed at which the excrement is moving through your bowels."

Matthew was rocking back and forth on the balls of his feet. His face was twisted with discomfort, and the length of the study-hall teacher's response was prolonging the agony. Eberle knew that. He was enjoying poor Matthew's predicament.

"Go ahead."

Eberle pulled out a small yellow hall-pass pad and checked off the box marked "restroom." He dated, signed, and timed the pass and handed it to Matthew, who ran out of the room.

Eberle looked over the thirty-three students under his command that hour. Rows of desks and chairs were occupied by students bent over books, magazines, and notepads. Some had their heads down and were sleeping. Eberle didn't care. At least they were quiet.

Eberle's voice carried to where Sam was sitting toward the back of the room, trying to absorb another boring chemistry formula. He stared at Eberle and wondered why some teachers seemed to take great joy in control-

189

ling and manipulating their students. Sam rested his head in his hand and tried to think of any teacher, just one, who truly loved what he was doing and really liked the students he taught. Sam thought of Mr. Reese, his English teacher. He smiled when he thought of the tall, slightly chubby man, who was always smiling, always joking with his students. Mr. Reese was lenient on tests and made life bearable under sometimes unbearable conditions.

Sam's countenance suddenly turned sour again. He was brought back to the reality of his personal circumstances. Richard Redden crossed his mind. Sam stared down at his notepad and looked at the list of ways he could get his hands on transmission and receiving gear. Time was short, whatever the alternatives. It might take weeks to put a station together again. No time. So what else is new in life?

The more Sam thought about the possibilities, the angrier he became. He couldn't just sit back and wait for someone to tap him on the shoulder and say, ''Ah, yes, Mr. Alexander, we have equipment you can use, as much as you want and whenever you want. Do what you want with it.''

He was going to make something happen.

Sam scooped up his books and book bag and jumped up from his seat. The squeak of the metal desk leg against the vinyl tile echoed through the room. Everyone looked up, including the teacher–monitor for that day.

''Mr. Alexander?''

Sam marched up to the front desk and stood over Eberle. Sam had fire in his eyes and in his belly.

''Mr. Eberle, don't give me any long-winded bullshit about the necessity for study-hall time. Half the people in this room are either asleep or dreaming, and the other half are reading *Road and Track, Sports Illustrated,* or *People* magazine. I'm a busy man, and I have things to do and people to see. I am going to be active from now on, not reactive. So give me a hall pass to get outta here so I can get some real work done.''

Lisa had been concentrating on some bit of innocuous

schoolwork and was stunned to hear the words pouring out of Sam's mouth. She had been trying for the past thirty minutes to get his attention and could see why she had been unsuccessful. Sam was coming unglued in front of her and the study-hall teacher.

The schoolyard was empty as Sam strode angrily away from the study hall. Lisa raced after him.

"Sam, wait up! Sam!" she shouted.

Sam didn't stop. He continued his brisk pace past the school office and toward the parking lot.

Lisa almost lost her books, juggling them from one arm to the other, as she ran after Sam. Finally, she grabbed his arm and pulled him to a stop.

"Sam, hold up, will ya?" she asked furiously.

Sam was breathing hard and glaring down at her. As he looked into her face, he calmed, but not much.

"Where are you going? What's gotten into you?"

He looked over toward the office. "I can tell you one place I'm not going, and that's Jackson's office."

"Sam, if you don't go in there, Eberle is really gonna be pissed off. They could suspend you."

"Lisa, the planet Earth and Sam Alexander are being contacted by an extraterrestrial civilization, and I should worry about being suspended for talking back to that blockhead Eberle?"

Sam turned and began walking swiftly again toward the parking lot. Lisa followed.

"But where are you going?"

He stopped again. "We sent a password. Redden still has my META box. What if he figures it out? Changes the password?"

"What if they won't let him? They are looking for you, Sam. They want to communicate with you—no one else."

"I have to be sure, and I have to receive and transmit somehow. And I have to stop Redden from doing whatever he plans to do with my translator."

He put down his bag and gently held Lisa's shoulders.

"Can we get into the Pac Tel satellite facility again tonight?"

She shook her head. "No way. I overheard my father on the phone this morning. They discovered the settings and equipment moved around. They have extra guards in there now."

Sam turned away. The vast schoolyard was empty and quiet. He considered his alternatives.

He grabbed his book bag and looked into Lisa's eyes. "Let's take a ride to LA."

CHAPTER 34

Driving on Interstate 15 north from Los Angeles would be taking a great risk for Richard Redden, so he decided to take the less-traveled State Route 247 north from Lucerne Valley to Barstow. Barstow is where he would have jumped off the interstate, saving time, but Richard could not take the chance of being spotted on the heavily patrolled route to Las Vegas. The few exits in that area would surely increase the chance of his vehicle's being identified. And the sedan he was driving, with the large NASA logo stenciled on the door, was a necessity. Without it and his ID, it would be impossible to get through the guard gate at the Goldstone Deep Space Tracking Network. And once he got through the gate . . . but even if he had to crash the gate, he had a better-than-even chance of getting into the control room, his goal. Right? If, if, if.

As Richard drove northward in the midday heat of the Mojave Desert, he paid no attention to the sharp mountains and the clear air. He watched the road and sat erect every time he spotted a car passing him or coming toward him. He kept his speed at sixty miles per hour. In the desert he could have gone the speed limit, sixty-five, or even seventy or seventy-five, and the odds of being stopped would have been low. But Richard couldn't take that chance, either. He knew that the CHP, the sheriff's department, NASA, the FBI, and probably the secret government types in the National Security Agency were probably looking for him. He wasn't sure whether they had pegged him for the break-in at Sam's or would be looking for him just because he was missing. No one would possibly believe Sam. The deputy director a thief? No way. Impossible.

At that moment, he would have loved to know what was going on at JPL.

Richard's mind raced. Why should he be scared? He was a damn hero. He discovered the SETI transmission. Yeah, a bona-fide hero. But what was he doing with this strange black box? It's his, that's why. Sam Alexander—who's he? No, my secretary is mistaken; I've never seen him.

Thinking, just stop thinking. Just go to Goldstone. Tell 'em that the big boss from HQ in Pasadena is at the gate, and let me in right away. It's an emergency. Use your key to get in. They can't stop you. Thinking, you're thinking again.

Richard glanced in his rear-view mirror. He leaned forward and squinted. His body prickled from heat and fear. He turned up the air-conditioning fan to high. He was sweating too much. A black-and-white California Highway Patrol car was gaining on him. Its red lights were flashing; its headlights were rapidly blinking off and on, alternating from one side to the other. Richard snapped his head from side to side, looking for a turnoff. But there, in that landscape of parched earth and no green cities, no side roads existed. Could he outrun the CHP? No way. A lousy four-cylinder sedan would never be able to stay in front of or lose an eight-cylinder supercharged engine built for pursuit speeds.

The highway-patrol car was coming up behind him. He slowed down. He gripped the steering wheel tighter and watched the patrolcar inch closer and closer.

Richard closed his eyes. The CHP car was on his tail. It swerved to the left, passed Richard, and raced ahead. Richard opened his eyes and saw the CHP patrol car become smaller and smaller on the road ahead.

"Shit! Goodbye, you fucking asshole!" Richard screamed. He threw his head back and laughed and yelled at the same time.

Barstow was no more than twenty miles ahead. Richard looked at his watch. 5:30 in the afternoon. He looked to the west, to his left, and saw the sun edging closer to the horizon. He decided to go into Barstow, have dinner in some obscure restaurant, and wait for darkness. He would not risk moving closer to Goldstone until the blanket of night could hide his movements. The only people who would be moving along the road had business with government installations north of Barstow.

Richard let out another yell. He was ecstatic. Tonight would be his night. He would be the one to contact whoever was trying to contact Earth from deep space. They would be looking for him from now on. He would be the liaison between their civilization and ours.

He relaxed and slowed down to fifty-five miles per hour. He extended his right hand and rested it on Sam's META box, now his.

The unfamiliar knock at the door was that of someone she didn't know. It was late in the afternoon, and Marion had an uneasy feeling as she opened the door. Standing in front of her was a slight man with glasses and a beard. She became fearful when she saw two other men behind him. They wore some type of identification badge. With her poor eyesight, it was difficult for her to make out the logo printed on the badges. Her attention switched to the bearded man as he began to speak. She stood partially hidden behind the door, ready to slam it shut at a moment's notice.

"Mrs. Alexander?"

Why did he know her name? Who was this? "Yes," she said hesitantly.

"The aunt of Samuel Alexander?" The man looked down at a ragged piece of paper. "His amateur-radio call is K6ZDQ, I believe?"

Now Marion was truly frightened and worried. Was Sam injured? Dead? Were these people policemen? They certainly did not look like policemen.

"Yes. What about him?" she answered in a higher-pitched voice.

"Mrs. Alexander, my name is Charles Williams. I'm from NASA, from the Jet Propulsion Laboratory in Pasadena. May we talk to you about Sam for a few minutes? We have a few questions to ask."

CHAPTER 35

"May I take your order?'' the squeaky voice asked through a rattling six-inch speaker.

Sam leaned out the window and glanced at the back-lighted menu board. He had to shout over the street noise and the idling of his own engine.

"Yeah, I'll have a six-piece chicken with sweet-and-sour sauce, two hamburgers, a large order of fries, and two Cokes. And can I borrow your telephone book for the Pasadena area?''

Lisa looked over at Sam and tried to hide her face.

"I don't believe this,'' she whispered.

Sam turned to her. "Hey, this way I can kill two birds with one stone. We can eat and save some time trying to get the address.''

"OK, that'll be $5.24 at the first window. Your food and phone book will be at the second window,'' came the reply through the speaker.

"Thank you,'' Sam said. He put the Jeep in gear and pulled forward. "Stick with me, kid; we're goin' places. Do ya think she thought I was weird?''

Lisa shrugged. "I don't see why, Sam.''

Sam's Jeep turned down Markham Avenue, slowed in the middle of the block, and stopped in front of a modest tract home. It was well lighted, and some money had been spent on landscaping. But it was no different from any of the other houses on the street, except for the color and the fact that the director of the Jet Propulsion Laboratory lived there.

"Well, this is it," Sam said.

He shut off the engine and put his hand on Lisa's shoulder. They both stared up at the house on the elevated pad.

"Sam, is this gonna do any good?"

Sam pulled his hand back and considered his response carefully. "I don't know. I don't know what Redden has been telling him. If this guy can be made to believe me, then I can get the help of NASA. It's either that, or I go to the newspapers or television. And they'll think I'm some kind of nut. They'll never believe that I was the one who picked up the signal. It's not like discovering a new comet or star or supernova, where you can call or telex the discovery to a central logging authority that verifies the event so proper credit can be given."

Sam took a deep breath. "Who knows how many more times the signal has been sent, or who has picked it up, or even who else has figured out a way to decode the message?"

He opened the door of his vehicle. "C'mon. Let's do it and get it over with."

Kenneth Wood had had an impossible day. The phone was still ringing off the hook, and he had to eat dinner at the kitchen table while taking messages and giving orders. His wife had given up on conversation and gone up to the bedroom to watch TV.

He was stretched out on a long leather couch in the living room/library with his eyes closed. The FM tuner was playing Mozart. Nearby, a glass of Scotch was almost gone. A few feet away was his desk, littered with reports and pictures.

Wood was not surprised to hear a knock at the door. He sat up quickly and stumbled to his feet. He grabbed his glass and finished his drink. He suspected that it was a zealous reporter who was eager for a story.

Reluctantly he walked to the door, asking himself, "What do you think they want? Where are they from? Is this a precursor to an all-out invasion? Was Orson Welles right? Will our viruses and bacteria kill them, too?''

He grabbed the door and swung it open quickly. He was only somewhat surprised.

He looked down through the screen door. ''Lemme take a guess. You must be Sam, and you . . .''

''Lisa. My name is Lisa.''

Wood opened the screen door and held out his hand to Sam. He shook it briskly.

''C'mon, kids. Let's talk.''

Sam thought that Kenneth Wood looked the way a director of the JPL should look. Tall, stately, an air of authority, older but not too old.

''You two want something to eat? It was a long drive from Escondido, right, Sam?''

They followed Wood down a short hallway and into the library, somewhat put at ease by Wood's easy manner and honest concern.

''No, thank you. We stopped and got something before we came here,'' Sam said.

Wood loosened his tie a bit more and gestured for Sam and Lisa to sit on the couch. He leaned against his desk, then sat on the edge. He was now wide awake.

There was a long, uneasy silence. Lisa leaned back and waited for the show to begin. Sam sat on the edge of the couch.

Kenneth knew that Sam was nervous and distrustful. That he should show up at all, especially at his front door, was nothing short of a miracle. At that point, Wood could trust Sam's veracity. Sam was desperate. The other way around—well, that was something Sam would have to test.

The first thought that popped into Sam's mind was, ''What am I doing here? How could I trust this guy? What if Redden is in the other room, taking notes?'' That, he guessed, seemed impossible. He had to trust Wood at that point. He had no alternative.

Wood did not have to be a mind reader to know what was going through the boy's mind. He would have to gain his confidence, and quickly, if he was to get any information about the whereabouts of Redden and data on the signal.

"Sam, I'm glad to finally meet you. I really am."

"How so?" Sam replied carefully.

Wood stood and moved to an overstuffed leather chair across from Sam and a glass coffee table.

"I want to tell ya, I have had one helluva day. Have you been watching the TV news or listening to the radio on your way up?"

"We have. They're going crazy," Lisa said.

"And most of it, Lisa, is just knee-deep bullshit. As usual, these guys don't know what they're talking about. They've got crews out talking to anyone who can give them a reasonably intelligent answer about the authenticity of this signal. I seriously doubt that there is a human alive who won't think by tomorrow that this is an invasion from outer space or the second coming of Christ."

"Maybe it is, Mr. Wood," Sam replied jokingly.

"I doubt that either applies. But let me tell you what I do know."

Sam settled in and waited. He decided that he would know in the first twenty seconds whether the man was going to lie to him.

"I know you were the one who discovered the signal."

Lisa grabbed Sam's arm. Sam looked over at her, smiling and half-tearful at the same time.

"I also know that your black box, or whatever you want to call it, has been purloined by my 'ex' deputy director, who is still at large. His secretary, by the way, is a very sweet lady who came forward and gave us a wealth of detail about your first meeting with Richard. Sound does carry well in our administration building offices."

"Thank God," Sam said softly.

"No, Sam, thank you. The nation thanks you for what may very well be the single most important discovery in human history. The future will determine what it means." He rose, his furrowed brow showing his concern. "But now we have to worry about the present."

Sam carefully followed Wood's movements. Sam's trust was growing; he was hearing what he wanted and expected to hear.

Wood walked over to his desk and leaned back in his high-back desk chair.

"Sam, do you have any idea where that asshole Redden might be with your equipment? Did he say anything or indicate in any way where he might be going with it, or what the hell he would be doing with it?"

"Mr. Wood, when we were struggling in my room, there was no time for an intellectual chat. He was cursing at me and kicking me, and flew out the door when I was momentarily stunned."

Kenneth shook his head in disgust. At that moment, had Richard been in the room, Wood might have attempted murder.

"Did you get any info from the signal source as to where they're from or what they want or what they want to tell us?"

Sam tensed at the probing questions. He wondered how much Kenneth knew. It was obvious that Richard was not working with him; Richard was still acting alone.

"So the man is the Lone Ranger," Sam said.

"Sam, we're not all megalomaniacs. We at JPL have the same dreams you do. I hope that someday you'll believe that and will come to work with us. What I wouldn't give to have you as my deputy director instead of that cretin Richard Redden! I know your father would have been proud of what you've accomplished so far."

Sam's reaction told Wood that he had hit a nerve. Sam lowered his head, then sat up quickly. Lisa scooted closer to Sam and wrapped her arm around his.

Wood stood, grabbed a stack of eight-by-ten photos, and handed them to Sam.

"These have been computer-enhanced," Wood said. "That's the best we can do, considering the distance and the unstable—intentional or not—wobbling of the orbit of this . . . vehicle, I guess you'd call it. We'll need some time to compute the wobble and vibration rate so we can take it out and digitally take out the fuzz. The damn thing won't sit still, so we can't take a sharp image.''

Sam's eyes opened wide as he looked at the pictures. The magenta blur of the triangular object was not familiar, but it was what he had expected.

Then suddenly, he looked straight ahead. He was catatonic. The magenta color. He flashed back to the night he was awakened suddenly. The crash of thunder. No, it was the glow of the nearby lightning strike. But it was the same color.

Sam started to sweat. His eyes began to tear. His pulse began to race. He felt waves of nausea pass through his body.

Lisa noticed the redness of his cheeks. Wood asked, ''Sam, are you OK?''

Sam came back to reality and steadied himself. ''Can I have some water?''

Wood stepped over to a small refrigerator and handed Sam a plastic container of bottled water.

Sam asked weakly, ''Is this what's been trying to contact me?''

Wood, still slightly concerned about his young guest, sat next to Sam and put a reassuring hand on his knee.

''Are you sure you're OK?''

Sam nodded.

''I guess that's the source of the signals,'' Wood continued, pointing at the picture. ''But we are not sure. You see, when the signal was transmitted last night . . .''

''Last night?'' Sam asked quickly.

''Yes.''

Sam turned and exchanged a worried glance with Lisa. He then looked at Kenneth. ''I hope you recorded it.''

''Sam, we record everything,'' he said. ''Well, almost everything, but this signal for sure. Anyway, it stayed in a direct line between Tau Ceti and the precise longitude and latitude of your home in Escondido.''

''So does the signal originate from the Tau Ceti solar system or the satellite?'' Sam asked.

Wood answered, ''Or both? We just don't know. And

of course, we had a study group last night attacking the biggest question of all.''

Sam posed the question. ''Is this a real-time transmission or a programmed transmission from the satellite?''

''Correct,'' Wood said. ''We think it's the latter. I mean, if it is real time, they, out there, have figured out how to break the ultimate speed barrier, the speed of light. And from everything we know . . .''

''. . . and Mr. Einstein has taught us,'' Lisa added.

Wood nodded. ''. . . that that is impossible. It seems to be one law of nature that is unchanging, immutable, intractable, unwavering, fixed, rigid.''

Sam's eyes were clear once again; his voice was strong. ''From what *we* know,'' he said.

Kenneth stared at him. ''Yes, Sam, from what we know. What they know, who knows? The simple fact is that they must have picked up your ham radio signals long ago, and they must think that you are the contact for the entire planet Earth.''

''They couldn't have chosen better,'' Lisa said.

Wood smiled and nodded. ''Lisa, I think you couldn't be more right.''

''Then, will you help me reestablish contact with them before it is too late? Before Richard . . .''

''Sam, you discovered this signal,'' Kenneth said, ''You are the key to the entire operation that is just getting underway. We will do everything we can to reestablish this contact for you. Whatever it takes. The administration is fully behind this operation.''

Kenneth had difficulty delivering the last statement. He was saved by the raucous ring of his telephone. He picked up the handset.

''What? What's he doing there now? Don't tell him anything. I'll be there as fast as I can. Don't let him leave.''

Wood was obviously agitated. He began to pace. Then he stopped and turned to Sam and Lisa.

''Let's take a helicopter ride.''

CHAPTER 36

Richard nervously tapped the steering wheel as he watched the armed main-gate guard talk on the telephone. Richard's was the only vehicle in sight on State Route 247.

Out of Barstow, the road led to Fort Irwin, then ended. The main gate was situated at the entrance to three major government installations: the Fort Irwin National Training Center, the highly restricted Naval Weapons Center, and the equally restricted Goldstone Deep Space Tracking Station.

Richard's goal was a few hundred feet beyond the main gate, then left down NASA Road for four-point-nine miles to another gate that led to the headquarters of the Goldstone facility, Echo Station.

The lights at the guard outpost made it hard for Richard to see the buildings ahead. Darkness had obscured most of the nearby unlighted buildings, and beyond, twinkling lights were the only evidence of human activity. The surrounding mountains were invisible.

The Moon had not yet crossed over the eastern horizon, so the night sky was filled with pinpoints of light. Richard noticed that he could see stars just above the mountains. It was a sight he could never see in Los Angeles. The glow of millions of city lights had long ago obliterated stars and other astronomical phenomena near the horizon. That, of course, was the reasoning behind the placement of the dishes and the listening outpost in the Mojave Desert just south of Death Valley. Light and radio pollution were negligible there.

Because of military restrictions, the area was one of the most desolate places in the continental United States. Considering the heat and the lack of rain and facilities, it was a wonder that anyone would want to live or work in the area. The U.S. government expended substantial funds to maintain life at that location, which was much less like the planet Earth than like the planet Mars. Unbearably hot days were often followed by intolerably cold nights. The animals that lived in that environment rarely appeared during the day, but the night was filled with the sounds of animals, large and small, scooting across the desert in search of one another, looking for a meal and something to drink.

Trees and cover were rare, so Richard did not contemplate sneaking into the facility. He hoped that he could show his credentials and get into the control room. That was all he needed to do. He needed just a few minutes at the main control desk. History would judge him kindly for his daring and cunning.

The guard was a tall, muscular man. There were usually two men working the main gate at all times. Richard knew the schedule well. He had helped create many of the new security procedures. The second guard was required to check the work of the first and to dissuade anyone from trying to trick a guard into letting him on the grounds. The second guard was also supposed to keep both guards awake and alert. It was comforting to know that another human being was with you in the middle of a hostile environment that was a target for terrorist acts.

Richard glanced as nonchalantly as possible at the guard, who was now looking directly at him while talking on the phone. Richard suspected that this oaf did not need another guard's help; he probably ate live wild game just to 'keep his edge'.

The guard hung up the phone and approached Richard's NASA sedan. Richard could not tell by looking at the man's face whether he was going to be allowed on the premises or not. The emotionless guard leaned against the driver's-side door.

In a deep but quiet, restrained voice, the officer said, "Yes sir, Mr. Redden. I am sorry for the delay. But I had to make a call to specially clear you. We've been getting a few phone threats lately, and I just wanted to be sure."

"I understand, officer. I designed your job-posting responsibilities, so I understand the enormous pressure you must be under."

The guard pulled his six-foot, five-inch frame erect and held out Richard's photo ID badge.

"Here you are, sir," the guard said, returning the badge to Richard.

"Thank you, I appreciate your . . ."

The guard ignored him. He pointed toward the intersection of 247 and NASA Road. "I'm sure you know the way—down to NASA Road and turn left. Go down approximately five miles."

"It's less than five miles, you blithering idiot," Richard muttered to himself. He didn't gladly suffer fools and security guards.

"The guard at Echo Gate will ask for ID, then clear you for Echo Station. You are to wait there for . . ."

The guard stopped talking in midsentence. He realized that he had already said too much. Richard noticed. What did that mean "you are to wait"?

Then he realized what was happening. The big boys at NASA, and probably the FBI or some other goon-squad organization, knew that he was on the premises. Wait? For what? For them to arrive by car or helicopter to pick him up and haul him away?

He smirked at the guard. The guard still did not think that Richard knew what was about to occur—that Richard would be nabbed inside Echo Station. But he guessed that Richard would not become violent. It wasn't his nature—at least, he didn't think so, judging by his past encounters with the deputy director of JPL.

The guard thought that the best course of action would

be to merely shut up and wave the man through the gate. He did just that.

Richard slipped his ID into his shirt pocket and waved as he drove away.

In his rearview mirror, Richard watched the guard turn and run to the telephone. He was humorously amazed by the guard's lack of discretion and by the way he handled his job. The guard never gave away his position, right? Richard laughed.

He knew that once he got inside the headquarters building, it would be very easy to slip into the main transmitting/receiving control room. But he also knew that the farther he drove along NASA Road, the deeper he was going into government property and the more difficult it would be to escape.

But soon, very soon, he would be a hero. He reached over for Sam's META box and placed it on his lap.

"Do you wanna go? Or maybe I should," Eugene said.

"You're bigger. You go, just in case the guy tries to pull something," Eddie replied.

The two men at Echo Gate were ready for Richard Redden. Richard knew them both.

Richard slowed his vehicle to a crawl as he approached the small guard gate. He drove into a pool of light in the darkness of the two-lane road. Approximately one hundred yards past the gate were the main HQ and control buildings; beyond HQ, Richard could see the giant dishes pointed skyward.

Eugene stepped out of the guard shack and leaned toward Richard's car.

"Good evening, Mr. Redden."

"Good evening . . . uh . . . Eugene. Right?"

Eugene straightened and smiled nervously. "Yes, sir."

"Eugene, I'll be here for about an hour or so."

Richard released the brake and started to roll forward. Eugene grabbed the door handle and held up his hand.

"Uh, OK. But I've got some expanded procedures that I'd like to show you first."

Richard looked straight ahead at the headquarters

building. The last thing he wanted or needed was to be held up by a guard, looking at security cameras or card-entry systems. He needed to get into that control room alone and unencumbered. He dropped his pleasant demeanor.

"Look, Eugene, I have some important work to do, and I don't . . ."

Eugene glowered at Richard. "It will only take a second. I want to show you the sign-in sheets for the reception counter."

"All right. Get in," Richard barked.

Eugene was not much taller than Richard, but his bulkiness made him seem to loom over Richard. But Richard knew that the man ultimately reported to him through vendors that provided service to JPL and NASA, so he could decide the man's fate. At least he had that edge.

The light in the small reception and holding area was intense. Richard squinted. Eugene closed the door behind them, and they approached another guard, sitting at a small Steelcase desk. To the right of the guard were a card-key lock and a heavy door that led into the office suites and control room.

"Mr. Redden, can I ask you to wait here while I get together my, uh, security suggestions?"

Richard knew that he was being detained. He looked at the hallway entry and gripped his briefcase. The small bulge of the META box in the canvas briefcase did not arouse the suspicion of the guards.

"Eugene, lemme use the head, and I'll spend as much time as you like. I do have to take a leak."

The guards stared at each other. Eugene looked down at Richard's briefcase. He knew that two guards could restrain Richard if necessary. Eddie was at Echo Gate, and another guard was at the main gate. His orders were to detain Richard, not to arrest him or place manacles on him. All Eugene knew was that the man was to be detained for some unknown reason. At least Richard was in the building and could do no harm. And while Richard was in the restroom, Eugene had a good opportunity to call Pasadena.

"Sure, go ahead, Mr. Redden. I'll wait here for you."

"OK. great."

Richard relaxed, pulled his card key from his suit pocket, and jammed it into the receptacle. There was a buzz, and the door opened.

Eugene watched him walk down the narrow hallway toward the restrooms at the far end of the hall. The heavy security door closed with a bang.

Eugene leaned over to the guard seated at the desk.

"Quick—call Bettman at JPL and tell him the guy is in the building. I'll try to talk Redden silly. But tell them to get here quick and do whatever they are gonna do, 'cause I can't hold him here forever."

Richard stepped out of the restroom and past an office. The night supervisor of the facility saw a form dart past his office door.

Short, nervous, somewhat chubby Byron Irtysh jumped up from his chair and stuck his head into the hallway just in time to see Richard step into the control room. He heard the click of the door lock, the dragging of a chair inside master control, and a thump against the door.

Irtysh turned and saw Eugene step cautiously into the hallway.

"Who is that, Eugene, and what is he doing in control?"

CHAPTER 37

The 137th Reserve Airlift Command was tucked away at the northwest end of Van Nuys Airport. The private aircraft that jammed the twin north–south runways on any given Saturday or Sunday were few during the middle of the week and especially at night. But that night, the activity several hundred feet beyond Operational Headquarters was intense. One Army and two white NASA Huey choppers were already turning their blades in anticipation of a police-escorted convoy that was rapidly approaching.

Three white NASA vans pulled up to the choppers and their waiting crews.

Kenneth Wood, Lisa, and Sam had driven to JPL and were transferred to the vans for the fifteen-minute high-speed drive to the airport in the middle of the San Fernando Valley, northwest of downtown Los Angeles. A phalanx of LAPD motorcycle-escort patrolmen whisked them down the San Diego Freeway and onto the tarmac of the airport.

All flight activity was halted that night. The control tower had closed the airport during the estimated departure time for the three government helicopters. Of course, this only raised speculation among the ground crew still working at various flight facilities and hangers at Van Nuys Airport. In an attempt to suppress speculation and curiosity and keep uninformed people from viewing what was going on, just the opposite had occurred. Within minutes word had spread through the airport about the nature of the flight, who was flying, and why the unusual security was necessary.

Wood scrambled out of the van, with Lisa and Sam following. It was impossible to converse over the din of the helicopters. Everything moved as if it had been choreographed. The other vans unloaded gray-suited NASA security officers, who boarded the second and third choppers.

Sam and Lisa instinctively moved to the rear of the comfortably appointed number-one NASA chopper and strapped themselves firmly into the plush seats. Sam took all the noise and excitement in stride. He put on a pair of heavy David Clark headphones as though he had flown this way many times before. He helped Lisa secure her two-point seat-belt restraints. Directly across from them, Kenneth Wood also made himself ready as ground personnel slammed the sliding door.

With a quick lurch, the helicopter was airborne.

Wood tapped Sam and Lisa on their legs. His voice was compressed through the intercom system. The noise-canceling headset microphone only marginally took out the percussive *s* and *p* sounds popping from their mouths.

"You two ever been up in a helicopter before?"

Lisa and Sam shook their heads.

"Ya know, Sam, in all the hurry and excitement, I guess we forgot to get permission from your mom and dad to take this quick trip with us. You, too, Lisa," Wood said. He then turned toward the front of the chopper to look at the view.

Lisa studied Sam's reaction.

"That's OK, Mr. Wood. I'm sure they wouldn't mind," Sam said.

As the helicopter moved higher it angled toward the northwest. To the right of the steadily vibrating chopper, Sam could see the carpet of city lights stretching to infinity. He had been in commercial jets before and had landed at Los Angeles International Airport at night, but it never ceased to amaze him how many lights sprouted beneath the plane. As far as he could see in every direction, the ground was a sea of light, a universe of earth-bound stars seen only at night.

The choppers were now past the spine of the San Bernadino Mountains and over the dark southern Mojave Desert. There was little conversation on board. Sam and Lisa clung to each other as they stared at the view below and beyond. Wood glanced at them occasionally, enjoying their excitement. It made him think of his first trip aboard the chopper. He had long ago become jaded to that thrill and buzz. That night he felt a tingle of the old excitement, but it quickly evaporated at the thought of that evening's destination.

Sam twisted his neck to look at the view south and the bright lights radiating from the other side of the mountains, then looked forward again, The desert below revealed only scattered patches of civilization, which soon became less and less visible. His view then was naturally directed skyward. The interior cabin lights were turned off.

Wood leaned toward Sam. "We'll be there in just a short while. You'll see Barstow below us. Then it's just a couple of minutes past there to Goldstone."

Sam nodded. Again, he was drawn to the window and the night sky above. He quickly orientated himself relative to Polaris, the North Star, and from there scanned the sky for familiar star groupings, for constellations that he knew by heart and that were only slightly easier to pick out on the ground.

He saw Orion, the most distinctive constellation, with the cool red supergiant Betelgeuse at its apex. The pulsating monster, whose diameter is 800 million miles, was clearly visible to Sam; its color was bright and clear high above the ground haze of Los Angeles.

He saw Canis Major at Orion's heel, not far from the "diamond of the sky," Sirius. Sirius was ranked number-one in brightness and, for Sam, beauty as well. The sparkling beauty did twinkle like a diamond in white, blue, red. It was only 8.7 light years away. Sam knew that its color and temperature made it an unlikely candidate to have planets with life. But it was beautiful.

Sam's gaze shifted toward the constellation Taurus, the mighty Bull. He knew the myth: Zeus changed himself into the white bull to win the hand of Europa, the princess of Phonecia. Within Taurus was the nursery of young stars, the Pleiades. Sam often tested his eyesight before viewing the sky through his telescope by looking at this tight cluster of young, hot white stars. The more he counted—six, then seven, then eight—the better his eyes were adjusting to the dark.

But it was the constellation Cetus that drew Sam's attention at that moment. The vibrating of the helicopter and the faintness of the stars made it difficult to discern. But he found it. It was there, within the constellation named for the whale, that the star Tau Ceti resided. And somewhere in the ecliptic plane of that star was a planet whose inhabitants were calling him. Who were . . .

"There—Goldstone is just over that ridge," Wood shouted into his headset microphone as he struggled to get his first glimpse of the dishes. Wood turned toward the pilot.

"Captain, land this thing right on the road next to the Echo building. Don't worry about blocking the road."

The pilot nodded.

Sam's stomach began to tighten.

Lisa held on to him even tighter. "Sam, are you OK?"

He nodded unconvincingly, "Yeah. Just fine."

Within a few minutes, the chopper was slowly settling down on the road in front of the Echo control building. Sam was so focused on the building that he got only a fleeting look at the huge radio-telescope dish not far away.

The chopper landed, and the high-pitched whine of the engine began to dip in frequency and strength. Sam could see a husky uniformed guard, Eugene, run to the chopper door, wrench the handle, and pull the door open in a quick single move. Wood immediately jumped out and ducked to avoid the rotor blade, now almost stopped. He turned and looked at Sam.

Sam hesitated for a moment. He knew that Richard was in the building. He knew that Richard had his META box, and now he was going to get it back. The adrenaline started pumping through his body. Sam would have the opportunity in the next few minutes to get his hands on Richard and . . .

"What did you say?" Lisa asked.

Sam turned to Lisa. His face was red with anger.

"I'm gonna punch his heart out through his back."

He jumped out of the chopper and held his hand out to Lisa. She hesitated, then jumped out next to Sam. They turned and followed Kenneth Wood and Eugene into the building as the other two helicopters landed. The plainclothes security men scrambled out and moved toward Echo.

CHAPTER 38

"I told them there was something strange about the guy, but no one ever believed me," Byron Irtysh said. "If I told 'em once, I told 'em twice that he fit the profile—a loner, an underachiever, probably a mama's boy. I told 'em." He paced four or five steps to one side of the small reception vestibule, turned, then paced back to the other side. Eugene was standing, arms folded, beside the open door to the narrow main hallway. The reception guard was quietly talking on the phone to the Echo gate guard.

The door flew open, and Kenneth Wood, Lisa, Sam, and several of the NASA security men filled the small area. Eugene stood at attention, and Irtysh rushed over to the top JPL official. The short, rotund scientist put his hands on his hips.

"I never trusted your deputy director, Mr. Wood. Please forgive me for being so blunt. But you know me. I am blunt. I say what is on my mind. I don't hold back. Everyone who knows me . . ."

Wood was perturbed and in no mood to hear Irtysh carry on. Sam glanced over at Lisa and shook his head in disbelief.

"Mr. Irtysh, that's fine. Just tell me what is happening now in Master Control. What is Richard Redden doing in there?"

Irtysh turned and pointed down the hallway.

"I explained to the man that those readings from NGC twenty-nine, ninety-seven are what we're looking at tonight. That is what was on the schedule. By God, if I told people once, I told 'em a hundred times—the schedule is the schedule. This isn't Griffith Observatory or some Omnimax theater. We got important work here, a busy schedule to keep.''

Wood looked over at Eugene. ''Is the man in Master Control now, officer? That's really all I want to know.''

Eugene nodded. ''Yes, sir. With the door locked and a chair propped up against the handle.''

''Where is he?'' Sam asked angrily.

Wood put his hand on Sam's shoulder, then turned his attention back to Irtysh. ''Is there any way of cutting off power or command control to the dishes other than Master Control?''

''No, sir,'' Irtysh replied quickly. ''The cables are channeled through a damn near impregnable conduit. Not that you would dare do that—I mean, cut the cables. No, you're not going to do that. Tell me you're not.''

''No, Irtysh. How 'bout circuit breakers?''

''Another security feature. The breaker box for power and control are all inside the room to prevent exterior penetration and to protect from the elements. No. Everything is in there.''

''C'mon, let's go,'' Wood said as he rushed past Eugene and toward the Master Control door near the end of the hallway. Irtysh was directly behind, with everyone else trying to keep up.

''Mr. Wood, I didn't know you'd be so upset about the change in the schedule.''

''I'm not. I couldn't care less,'' he said. A look of shock and surprise registered on Irtysh's face.

Wood finally stopped at the door, which had small signs reading ''AUTHORIZED PERSONNEL ONLY'' and ''NO THROUGH ACCESS.'' He began pounding on the door and trying to turn the heavy knob. ''Richard, open this goddamn door right now,'' Wood shouted.

Irtysh suddenly noticed Sam and Lisa.

''Who are the kids?''

''They're friends of JPL,'' Wood said quickly. He

turned to Eugene and pointed at the door. "Bust it," he commanded.

Eugene aligned himself perpendicular to the door. With a great lunge and a loud grunt, he smashed the doorknob. The "NO THROUGH ACCESS" sign flew off the door, which swung open wildly and bounced back. Eugene pushed the door open again. Sam and Wood were the first to rush into the room, followed by Irtysh, Lisa, and two plainclothes NASA security men.

The predominantly light-yellow consoles crammed into the living-room-size control room, made Richard's dark-blue suit easy to spot. Richard's tie was undone, and so was he. His fingers rested on a computer keyboard. In front of and on either side of him, large color monitors displayed data that Sam could not comprehend in that moment of confrontation.

Everyone froze. Cooling fans and the light hum of equipment power supplies were the only noises.

Richard raised his hands slowly from the keyboard. His eyes fixed on Sam, then on Wood. His features softened. He was frightened. He was drenched with sweat. His appearance and manner were pathetic. The chair that had secured the door was now resting against his leg. Splinters of wood from the door frame were spread around his feet.

Suddenly resigned, he tilted his head and stared almost pleadingly at his boss, Kenneth Wood.

"I was . . . ," he moaned.

Richard then focused on Sam. He turned sullen and angry. "You get outta here, you little twerp. This find is mine. I've been waiting all my life for this, and you . . ."

Wood snapped back, "You didn't find shit. Sam discovered the signal, Richard Redden, ex-deputy director."

Wood turned to his security men. "Drag his lying smelly ass out of here before he stinks up the equipment."

Richard lunged at Sam. Lisa screamed, and Sam recoiled, waiting for a blow. But the security men and Eugene grabbed Richard by the arms and shoulders and dragged him, kicking and screaming, through the busted doorway, into the hallway, and to one of the waiting helicopters.

Wood turned to Sam. "He won't be bothering you again," he said.

Sam wasn't listening. His attention was on the primary control board. He was fascinated by the amount of equipment needed to control the movement of the 230-foot-diameter dish, the twin 112-foot-diameter dishes, and the 85-foot-diameter dish. Large digital readouts were at eye level at the controller positions; several racks of equipment with myriad switches were nearby. Potentiometers and blinking LED lights dominated the end of the long monitor row.

More important to Sam, his META box was connected through a patching jack directly into the transmitter pre-amplifier module on one of the racks. He stepped up to the black box with orange lettering, gently grasping the box and the connecting cable. His thin fingers moved along the gray cable to the BNC connector post, marked "AUX INPUT."

Irtysh's eyes widened when he saw the box. He swiftly moved up to it and grasped it roughly with his stubby fingers.

"What the hell is this crap he's got connected?" Irtysh asked.

Sam grabbed Irtysh's wrist and squeezed it until Irtysh was forced by pain to release the box. His daggerlike stare pierced Irtysh and made the small man step back in surprise. "Don't touch that," Sam said quietly through gritted teeth.

Kenneth walked up to the primary monitor. He watched the movement of the text across the screen.

"Sam?"

Sam turned away from Irtysh and moved toward Wood. Lisa moved between Irtysh and Sam to get a good look at the monitor. Sam turned the chair that Richard had occupied and sat down in it. He rolled up to the monitor. He looked down at the keyboard to familiarize himself with the layout. He then looked around the monitor at the parameter controls and above the monitor at the digital readout for the dish positions relative to the Earth's ecliptic plane.

Behind the control plane, readouts and pictures of the planets taken by the two Voyager spacecraft were posted on the wall. Hanging from the ceiling was a black-and-white monitor, showing the video image of the huge dish outside the building.

Irtysh was hovering over Sam. Wood noticed Irtysh's look of concern and apprehension.

"Mr. Irtysh, Sam has my permission, so just cool your jets."

"All right by me, Mr. Wood. I just work here."

Sam leaned forward to look at the confusing series of numbers and letters scrolling upward on the screen. They occasionally paused, then moved on.

"Mr. Irtysh, what is the beaming heading on the dish? What are we looking at?" Sam asked.

Irtysh looked at the numbers, glowing an intense blue-green on the digital readout. "Well, I don't know. I mean, rest assured it is not NGC 2997." He then looked up at the monitor picture of the large dish. "I can just look at the altitude and azimuth pitch of the dish and tell you it's not NGC 2997. I mean, it may be nothing. It's not even programmed or linked with anything, for all I know."

Wood was now losing his patience. He said sharply, "Damn it, Irtysh, just tell us."

Irtysh reached down to a numerical touch pad adjacent to the keyboard and punched in a short command.

"OK. I know when to shut up. I know Momma didn't raise no dummy. I work here all the time, and no one bugs me. You guys come swooping in here with helicopters and security and cart away the damn deputy director. But it's fine by me. OK."

"Irtysh!" Wood screamed.

The correct dish-position setting flashed on the display.

"Right ascension one, forty-four, four. Declination, minus fifteen, fifty-six, fifteen." Irtysh took a deep breath, then exhaled. "Tau Ceti. So what else is new?"

Sam whispered to himself, "The fucking spacecraft is aligned with the planet. It's gotta be."

Kenneth leaned close to the screen and put his finger on the glass tube. He gently tapped it as the text flew up from the bottom of the field.

"Sam, what is that on the screen? I thought your box could decode it."

Eugene charged into the room. He was breathless and agitated.

"Mr. Wood, sorry to bother you."

Wood stood and turned. "Yes?"

"Sir, Mr. Redden got out of hand. He tore away, and we had to chase him down. He tripped and fell and ripped open his forehead. I mean, there's blood all over the place." Eugene looked down at his white polyester shirt, splattered with blood.

Sam's attention was on the screen but he couldn't help but reply, "Gee, that's tough."

Lisa added, "Damn awful shame."

Irtysh was taken aback, not knowing the damage that Richard had caused Sam, NASA, and Wood to that point.

"Who are you two? That's Mr. Wood's deputy you're talking about."

Wood said to Eugene, "Officer, put a bandage on his head, throw him back on the helicopter, and turn him over to the LAPD when the chopper lands back at Van Nuys. Handle it personally. Please."

Wood turned back to Irtysh. "Mr. Irtysh, Richard Redden is no friend of JPL or me. He's caused us grief and loss of time."

Irtysh shook his head in confusion. "I don't get it."

Sam jerked his head toward the META box. "I know what's wrong. The dip switches are not set correctly," he said.

Sam rolled the chair over Irtysh's toes and toward his META box. He turned the box 180 degrees and flipped open the small hinged cover to expose seven micro-switches. With assured flicks of his forefinger, he reset the switches to their proper configuration, then rolled back to his position in front of the monitor. Irtysh moved out of the way this time and shook his foot, trying to ignore the pain.

The scrambled text was immediately transformed into readable English.

"Bingo," Sam said, then jerked his head around toward Irtysh. "Quick—turn on the audio for this incoming signal."

Irtysh reached for an unmarked switch near the monitor and flipped it. Through a flush-mounted speaker Sam heard a familiar sound: the raspy white noise and the fluctuating and warbling tone. And on the screen:

INPUT INCORRECT.
RETRANSMIT DATA MARK.

Sam sat up in his chair. "What data mark?"

Lisa added, "What does that mean?"

Wood pulled another chair next to Sam and leaned toward the screen. "Sam, is this it? Is that box of yours translating the signal, the same one I hear now? The same one we got before? Is this them?"

Irtysh furrowed his brow. "Them. Who's 'them'?"

Sam cocked his head and listened to the signal. "It doesn't sound quite as strong, but that's it. That's the signal I've heard from the outset."

"That's what I heard, too, Mr. Wood," Lisa said.

The message repeated over and over. The tone repeated, the frequency deviation congruent to the text data continually flowing up the screen.

Kenneth said, "Sam, ask them . . . or it . . . to repeat the data request. Just punch it on the keyboard. Redden has this thing set up for direct transmission. Right, Irtysh?"

Irtysh leaned in and looked at the bottom strip of data overlayed on the repeating text.

"Yes. But what is going on here?"

Sam rested his hands on the keyboard. "OK, folks, here goes."

Sam complied with Wood's request, typing in a request

for a repeat transmission of the data. He looked down at the keyboard and saw an unusually large button marked "SEND." Sam looked up at Irtysh. "Is this the . . ."

Perturbed, Irtysh replied, "Yes, that's it."

Sam sent his reply on its way at the speed of light. The data packet of information was received even before the light spring underneath the "SEND" button had fully retracted to its resting position. The slight change of tone frequency startled Sam.

Lisa noticed. "Sam, what does that mean?"

"I guess they got my reply and are digesting it."

"Sam, please tell me—who are 'they'?" Irtysh asked. "What is going on here, Mr. Wood? I'm really confused."

Wood looked up at Irtysh and sarcastically replied, "I was worried, Mr. Irtysh, for a brief moment that you just might be the only one to understand what was going on here. We—you—are hearing a SETI signal. You know, like the faint signal you have been recording for us."

Irtysh's mouth dropped open. "But is this the same one? I mean, it is louder and doesn't sound the same. We haven't initiated our SETI program yet."

"This signal didn't wait for our program to start."

A broad smile crept across Irtysh's face. "This is unbelievable."

Sam held up his hand. "Wait a minute. Here comes the reply."

The tone returned to its original pitch and timbre, and a new message appeared on the large black screen in the pale-yellow frame:

ORIG SOURCE FROM PLANET
TAU CETI START SYSTEM TO
MONITOR RELAY SLAVE NOW IN PROGRESS***

***DESIGNATE PLANETESIMAL EARTH
ORBITING SUN STAR SYSTEM TO DESIG-
NATE***

***K6ZDQ

Sam snapped his fingers. "That's it." He turned to Lisa. "The message is coming from Tau Ceti to an Earth-orbiting satellite of theirs to us."

Wood added, "To you."

Sam nodded. "To me."

Irtysh looked down at Sam with new respect and some awe.

"This is wonderful beyond belief. It's, it's—I don't know, it's . . ."

"There's more coming," Sam said.

K6ZDQ
PLEASE TRANSMIT PRIMARY AND SECONDARY
EARTH IDENTIFICATION DESIGNATION***

Sam studied the screen and shook his head. "I don't . . ."

Lisa pushed his shoulder. "Your name, silly. They wanna know what your name is."

Sam looked up at Lisa and smiled. "Thanks."

His hands descended on the keyboard and quickly typed the requested information, "SAMUEL ALEXANDER." He pushed "SEND." He leaned back in the chair.

The screen began to move again.

ABBREVIATED SAM SUFFICIENT FOR CONTIN-
UATION
FOR CONFIRMATION
***PLEASE DESIGNATE GLAMOROUS GER-
TIE??????***

"What?" Wood asked.

Sam smiled broadly.

Wood said, "I sure hope to hell you know who Glamorous Gertie is. I wonder if they mean Yaeger's *Glamorous Glennis*, the first plane to break the sound barrier."

"No, Mr. Wood, they mean something that was named after Yaeger's *Glamorous Glennis*."

As Sam's fingers flew over the keys, he read aloud what was being input into the buffer, staged for transmission.

DESIGNATE GLAMOROUS GERTIE, A 185 HORSEPOWER BLOWN DUAL-CARB WEBBER FORTY-FOURS VW ENGINE CHERRY-RED WITH PADDLE-TREAD REARS AND THREE MILLION-CANDLEPOWER LIGHT BAR 110-POUND SAND-RAIL DUNE BUGGY.''

He paused and considered his next insertion, "SAM . . . DESIGNATE . . . K6ZDQ.''

"A text password. Very clever. But how did you get it to them, Sam, without your . . .'' Kenneth said, nodding toward the META box.

"He is very resourceful, Mr. Wood,'' Lisa responded.

A new message began.

RESPONSE CONFIRMED
PLEASE COPY FOLLOWING***

Sam turned to Irtysh. In a clipped voice he said, "Somebody better write this down. Do you have a recorder going on this?''

Irtysh reached for a pad and pencil on a nearby desk.

"No. I wasn't ready.''

Before Irtysh returned to his original position, he stepped over to the nearby equipment rack and threw a switch. In some adjacent room a bank of audio and digital recorders began their task.

Irtysh was once again in position next to Sam. "OK. Ready, ready, ready.''

"Here it comes,'' Sam said loudly.

And so it did.

DESIGNATE SAM K6ZDQ
AND DESIGNATE GLAMOROUS GERTIE
VECTOR TO DESIGNATE DESERT AREA
LOCATION TANK TARGET

Wood scratched his head. "Tank target? What and where is that?"

Sam looked at him blankly but did not answer. He knew that Wood didn't know. Good. Just in case.

SATURDAY***NEXT***1988
TIME 0800 UTC
PHYSICAL DATA TRANSFER FOR
PLANTESIMAL EARTH
TO BE DELIVERED FOR EARTH USE & STUDY
***
VOLUME, NATURE & PIXEL OF DATA
TRANSMISSION IMPOSSIBLE
ADDITIONAL DATA AS REPLY TO
DRAKE AERICIBO INTERSTELLAR MESSAGE
SENT NOVEMBER 1974

Wood leaped from his chair, shouted, and clapped as though his college football team had just won the deciding touchdown of the homecoming game. "They got it! I don't believe it!"

"They got what?" Lisa inquired.

"A blind message, sent to anyone out there who would or could listen, from our thousand-foot radio telescope at Aericibo in Puerto Rico. It was a greeting. A hello message that says where we are from and what we look like. It was a very primitive message."

"But effective," Sam added.

"I was there," said Irtysh. "It's a tremendous facility. You know, they have this beautiful valley. It is very green there. Not much man-made interference. Of course, we are in the desert, and the environment . . ."

Wood held up his hand. "Please, Byron, please."

"Wait a minute. Wait a minute."

"What, Sam? What is it?" Lisa asked.

Sam turned white as he looked up at Wood.

"They wanna land here."

The previous text was just starting to sink in. Only the signal noise flowing from the small control-panel speaker broke the silence. Kenneth Wood stared at the message.

"Oh, my God, you're right."

"Who wants to land?" Irtysh asked in a high, tense voice.

"They do," Sam said weakly as he pointed at the screen. The text moved up, replaced by a new message.

"Now what?" Sam asked.

DESIGNATE TO BE ALONE AT VECTOR POINT
NO CURRENT CONFIRMATION REQUIRED
****
NO REPEAT
****
END MESSAGE

The last message moved up and off the screen. The screen field went black. The raspy noise and imbedded tone were gone. Background hiss replaced the signs of life and intelligence and reason.

Wood grabbed Sam's shoulders, his eyes boring into Sam's. "I want you to know something, Sam. JPL, NASA, and the U.S. government will do everything we can to make sure you have all the help and support you need."

Wood then looked up at Irtysh. "C'mere. I wanna talk to you a second. Let's leave these two alone for a while."

Without a word, Irtysh pulled himself away from the screen. Wood and Irtysh left the room.

Sam and Lisa stared at each other, searching for emotion. Fear and joy—neither was there. Sam was excited and at the same time relieved. He couldn't believe that he had gotten his META box back and had reestablished contact.

His reverie was disturbed by the lights that blinked on as Wood and Irtysh stepped into the adjacent equipment room, separated from the control room by a glass wall. Inside the equipment room, several racks of electronic gear stretched from floor to ceiling. The room contained nothing else, no desks or chairs. It looked much like a telephone-company central office that Sam once saw.

Wood closed the door in the equipment room and winked at Sam. Sam then turned back to Lisa.

"Can you believe this? The way it's turned out?"

"I am so happy for you. Are you gonna be ready for the crush of attention? It will be . . ."

Lisa was interrupted by faint voices coming from another panel-mounted speaker. Sam flicked his eyes down to the speaker and a small volume control marked "INTERCOM." Trying not to attract the attention of Wood and Irtysh, who could clearly see him and Lisa, he gently turned up the volume.

Through clenched teeth and a false grin, Sam spoke softly to Lisa. "Ssshhh. Just keep looking at me. Smile occasionally. Nod occasionally."

The voices in the other room were clear and distinct.

". . . is that understood? I don't want Sam to know what we are up to. So just act normal, as normal as you can, when we go back out. We'll hustle both of them out of here, and you'll be out of it as soon as we leave here. Keep this quiet after that, OK?" Wood said.

Irtysh protested, "I know, sir, but you read the message. They want him."

"They'll get him, but for his safety we have to cover the area with sensors, cameras, and manpower. It's too much of a chance for him and us to take. Radiation, heat, exhaust. God alone knows what he would be facing. He'll just tell us where the place is. We follow. That's all."

Kenneth looked through the glass at Sam. Sam returned the stare and nodded.

Kenneth continued, "I can't take any chances when it comes to his welfare. He'll understand why he was taken out of the loop after it's over."

Sam tried to keep a firm grip on his emotions. He knew that if they thought he was ignorant of their plans, he would have the advantage. He looked into Lisa's eyes and saw anger and hurt. Her face was flushed.

Kenneth Wood stood in the doorway of the helicopter. Sam looked down at him. Lisa was sitting directly across from Sam.

"Mr. Wood, aren't you joining us?"

Wood looked around back toward the Echo control

complex. "Uh, no, Sam. I have a few things to wrap up here. You go on back. I'll take the third helicopter back. It's getting late, and I'm sure your people are getting worried. OK, captain, take 'em back. Bye, kids, and thanks."

Wood closed the sliding door of the Huey chopper with a bang. Sam could see Wood waving as he walked away.

Sam whispered, "Yeah. Thanks."

CHAPTER 39

Marvin Himmelstein pushed his chair away from the conference table and poured more decaffeinated coffee into his china cup. The long mahogany server was covered with a white tablecloth, and all the supplies required for the morning coffee break in the basement conference room at the White House were in place. Several hundred feet away sat the president of the United States, who awaited Marvin's report.

The conference room was soundproof and, according to the FBI agents assigned to the White House, bugproof. The room was simple, dominated by a long, highly polished walnut conference table. The fifteen chairs, conference table, server, and several other tables along the walls were all Early American in design. A beautifully carved chair rail lined the room, and several pictures of early American forefathers were hanging elegantly lighted, at strategic points. But one wall was dominated by a projection screen. Numerous rolled maps hung from the ceiling directly in front of the screen, ready as needed to pinpoint any coordinate in the world.

The conference room was used much more than the Cabinet room and at times was the scene of crisis meetings. This morning's meeting, with Kenneth Wood and his group in California participating by telephone, was almost considered to be a nuisance by Marvin Himmelstein, the president's science adviser.

The president's upcoming visit to Canada required that a detailed study of the acid-rain problem in the Northeast be completed. Marvin's report was already two days late, and here he was waiting for a telephone call to discuss extraterrestrials.

Himmelstein sipped his coffee as he scanned a tray of danish and looked for his favorite. It had already been taken, naturally.

He considered the possibility that Kenneth Wood was exaggerating the reports, coming in from various government and university facilities, about the strange radio signals and a purple satellite hovering over California. Maybe the Russians were up to something. Perhaps it was a natural phenomenon of unknown origin, with an impossibly hidden explanation. Maybe it was a rare plasma cloud. But extraterrestrials?

Himmelstein turned and looked at his fellow participants. Air Force General Tatum was chatting quietly with Navy Admiral Smith. Himmelstein's assistant, Terry O'Neil, sat quietly, giving his boss an exasperated "I want outta here" look.

Himmelstein combed back his graying hair as he sat at the head of the table. He had been at the White House for two years after being plucked from his tenure position at MIT.

At least, he thought, this meeting would give him a short break from the all-night conference that surely would be required to finish the acid-rain report the president had been pressing him to turn in.

The two military representatives at the meeting had been assigned by the Joint Chiefs of Staff office. They were required to observe and to report to the Joint Chiefs any plan of action or request for support by the administration. General Tatum and Admiral Smith were highly suspicious of the reports and suspected that some terrestrial political or military mission was unfolding. The recent appearance of the *Provideniya* off the coast near San Diego may have been linked to the low-orbiting purple satellite and the unusual signal it was emitting.

The admiral turned to Himmelstein. "Ya know, Marvin, General Tatum and I have been considering the possibility that this is some type of missile-defense or detection system. It makes much more sense than the explanation we have been studying and hearing during these last hours.''

Himmelstein put his coffee cup down and pulled the telephone and speaker attachment closer. ''Admiral, that is a distinct possibility that you and the Air Force must continue to follow up. The president does not want any surprises. But let's see what Wood and NASA have to say.''

''And when will that be?'' Terry O'Neil asked.

''We'll give Wood''—Himmelstein glanced at his Omega Chronograph watch—''two minutes. Then we'll call him.''

General Tatum pushed his coffee cup to the center of the table. With his experienced blue eyes he gave Himmelstein a stare that could cut through concrete.

Tatum said quietly but firmly, ''Marvin, my people and I are highly skeptical of the SETI theory. We think it is of land-based origin. But whatever means they are using to cloak the construction and configuration of that craft is making any detailed ground-based photography, or airborne photography, damn near impossible. It just won't hold still. This anomalous movement is very effective and puzzling. We all need some answers.''

''General Tatum, that is why we are here. Maybe we can get some answers,'' Himmelstein said.

The phone buzzed. O'Neil jumped. ''Good God, Marvin.''

Himmelstein grabbed the handset and put it to his ear. There was a pause.

''OK. Put him through,'' Himmelstein said.

He punched the speakerphone switch and replaced the handset in its cradle.

After a few pops, the hiss of a long-distance call poured from the speaker.

Three thousand miles away in a bright JPL conference room, Kenneth Wood pulled his speakerphone microphone closer to his two assistants, Charlie Williams and Will Webster.

Webster pushed the "mute" button on the speaker-phone and pointed his chubby finger at Wood. Webster was always known to speak his mind, and now was no exception.

"Listen, Kenny, don't take any crap from those military types. We'll handle this, and they can stay the hell out. They'll botch it for sure if they get control."

Wood waved his hand. "Quiet, Will. Lemme handle this."

In the White House basement conference room, Marvin Himmelstein leaned toward the speakerphone. The telephone conversation began slowly and haltingly.

"Kenneth, how are you? This is Marvin."

"Marvin, how are you?" Wood replied.

Himmelstein leaned back and grabbed a pencil and a yellow legal pad.

"Could be better, Ken. I gotta report due by six A.M. tomorrow that'll take thirty-six hours to complete, and I have only sixteen hours left, and here we are talking about *War of the Worlds.*"

Wood's nervous laughter rattled the speakerphone and echoed through the basement conference room. Himmelstein turned the volume down a bit.

"Ken, as I told you in my fax, I have some company joining us here this morning—Terry O'Neil, my assistant, and Air Force General Tatum and Admiral Smith from the Chiefs' office."

There was a moan at the other end of the line. The military representatives shouted hello. Introductions were exchanged on the other end. Wood introduced his RF expert, Charles Williams, and his science services administrator, Will Webster, who gave the Washington end of the conversation a less-than-enthusiastic hello.

In a more formal tone, Himmelstein said, "OK, let's start. We are conferenced here for two reasons, Ken. First and foremost, the president wants to know what is going on, and I need you to fill in some details on the report that came along with your fax last night. Second, you included some requests for support and assistance in your report. How's all this sound so far?''

"Fine, Marvin. First tell me about the president's reaction.''

"Uh, let's see. Astonished, amazed, and predominantly incredulous.''

"He doesn't believe us?'' Will chimed in sarcastically.

"No, uh, I think that was you, Will.''

"It was,'' Tatum said.

Himmelstein continued, "But let's just say he is highly skeptical.''

Himmelstein heard Wood sigh. Then Wood said, "Fine. That's understandable. But will I get the manpower, equipment, facilities, and military backup I requested to prove or disprove what has occurred or what will occur in the desert on Saturday? Maybe?''

Smith said quickly, "We have to dig up the funds somewhere for this, Kenneth, so as far as the military is concerned. If the president orders us to help out, we will do so and worry about the money later on.''

O'Neil leaned into Himmelstein and showed him a large dollar sign written on his pad. Beside it were a question mark and the words "WHERE FROM?''

Himmelstein shrugged. "OK. We will proceed with your list of needs and set up the liaison requirements. Who is going to head up your end?''

"Will Webster. That's why he is here.''

Tatum and Smith shook their heads. Their brief exposure to the loudmouth from JPL made them realize that this was not going to be a smooth task.

"Mr. Himmelstein, this is Charlie Williams. Is our request to quarantine the area, on land and in the air, still a viable possibility?'' Charlie asked.

Himmelstein turned to the two military representatives. "Gentlemen?''

"Mr. Williams, just shoot us the approximate parameters for the areas you want secured on the ground and in the air, and we'll see what equipment and manpower resources will be needed. We'll get back to you this afternoon.''

᠔᠁at agreed, details of the operation were discussed. Will Webster's distrust of military involvement spilled out with almost each sentence he uttered. Wood had to control Webster, and Himmelstein had to control the equally confrontational general and admiral.

But the biggest and most controversial point was saved for the final portion of the telephone meeting. Wood was insistent about the participation of Evegeny Romanov and a small team of observers, and the military was equally insistent about keeping him and the other Russians out. Himmelstein already knew the president's decision; nevertheless, he wanted to hear both sides of the argument.

"No way, Mr. Wood," Tatum said vehemently. "There are no treaties allowing them on military property and JPL/NASA secured areas, other than the recent INF treaties and the other space-cooperation agreements."

Wood answered, "General, we don't have the time to negotiate a treaty with the Russians on this."

Webster added, "General, there are no state secrets to be compromised here. I mean, we are going out to the middle of the friggin' northern Mojave Desert . . ."

Tatum jumped in. ". . . which just so happens to be within spitting distance of the Naval Weapons Center and the Fort Irwin Training Center. Webster, you may not know—or at least I hope you don't know—that we have a lot of classified shit going on there."

"I know that, general. I mean, Goldstone is just south of there. I know what's going on there."

"No, you don't, my good man."

"Yes, I do, my good man."

Himmelstein held up his hand and tried to gain control.

Wood said, "All right, Will. Enough already. Listen, Marvin, this event has worldwide impact. This deep-space signal is not a secret anymore. I mean, turn on 'Good Morning America' or the 'Today' show or CNN. It's all over the place."

"We know," said the perturbed presidential science adviser.

Wood continued, "This event has worldwide impact.

It just so happens to be in our backyard. The Russians are far ahead of us in deep-space signal searches, and they may have something important to add to our knowledge so we can handle this thing with some degree of intelligence. Romanov is a friend. He has given us immense help in the past. To have him with us follows well with our current state of political thaw, and besides, it is the right thing to do, Marvin. We are all in this together on this planet. We don't know what we are dealing with here, and the ripple effect of the discovery of this signal touches many levels of human existence.''

"Yes, Kenneth, but this is also a military operation,'' Smith added.

Webster started to speak but was silenced by Wood.

"Yes, admiral, this is very true. But your organization is a partner in this operation. And from our viewpoint a small Russian contingent, as well as representatives of the technologically advanced countries elsewhere on the globe, would help to defray any criticism the president might have to endure if he locked the rest of the world out of what is essentially a boon for mankind, advancing our understanding of our place in the universe.''

Himmelstein sat up in his chair. "Enough discussion. Gentlemen, the president has made up his mind to allow the Russian contingent and representatives from other countries to journey to the desert.''

The two military men leaned back in their chairs in disgust.

"Well, that's something else we have to worry about out there,'' the general said. "But we will do what the president wants, and we are going to treat these people first-class. I don't want to hear any grumbling. They will be escorted, though, wherever they go.''

The admiral reached for the microphone. "And tell your Russian friend to tell his navy buddies to get that fucking spy trawler, the *Provideniya,* the hell out of U.S. waters.''

Himmelstein agreed. "Yes, Ken, that is a strict requirement. That ship is making us tie up our resources just to watch it. We want to reallocate those resources to help you. So they've gotta move that ship out of our area before Romanov will be allowed on site.''

"OK. I'll pass that along. From what Romanov has told me from a scientific perspective—and I think he's telling the truth—the ship has not been able to lock on the signal anyway and can't perform any credible function when it's out at sea like that.''

"Except spy on us.''

"You're right, admiral. I agree entirely,'' Wood said.

There was a long silence as the participants gathered their thoughts and mulled over the conversation.

Wood asked the final question. ''How 'bout the press?''

"The president,'' Himmelstein said, ''wants it limited to pool coverage and from a distance—a great distance.''

O'Neil chuckled. ''Good luck.''

Himmelstein looked around the room. ''Anything else?''

The admiral looked at Himmelstein. ''Yes. The *Provideniya*. Get rid of the son of a bitch.''

CHAPTER 40

"They watch us, we watch them. They listen to us, we listen to them."

Capt. Genady Mirotshinov stood at the bow of the *Provideniya*. He refocused his powerful watertight binoculars on the bridge of the United States frigate *Nathaniel*. He could see a U.S. Navy officer peering back at him through binoculars. Mirotshinov waved with one hand and steadied his binoculars again. He saw an equally vigorous wave. He lowered the glasses and roared with laughter.

"Isn't the comradeship of the sea marvelous?"

Mirotshinov turned his view to the east. The day was clear and crisp. And through his binoculars, he swore, he could see the prominent red dome of the Hotel del Coronado. He nudged a seaman standing watch next to him. The seaman scanned the horizon with his own binoculars.

"See there—a reddish-brown roof. That is the Hotel del Coronado. I actually had dinner there once, long ago, as a young sailor, a trainee loaned to the Americans during the war. What a marvelous hotel. Old, stately."

"It looks much like those hotels I have seen pictures of on the Black Sea, comrade captain."

"Yes, my young friend. But I bet the wine list is much more complete at the Coronado." Mirotshinov laughed out loud again.

Both men were still chuckling as the ship's chief radioman approached. The young Russian sailor handed the captain a dispatch in a red envelope. The color of the envelope had a clear meaning for Mirotshinov. This was a top-priority message, probably directly from the Ministry of Defense in Moscow.

Before opening the envelope, he turned to the sailor standing watch. "Seaman Bitushev, please walk to the stern and see if it is as beautiful a day at that end of our ship as it is here."

The sailor needed a few moments to digest the meeting. "Yes, sir." He saluted quickly and then was gone.

Mirotshinov began to tear open the envelope. "So tell me, Danov, should I laugh or cry when I am finished reading this message? Huh?"

Radioman Danov looked at the nearby *Nathanial,* then up at the cloudless sky. He felt the warm sun caressing his face and a cool zephyr freshening the air.

"Captain, I think the entire ship will be crying. Even the political proctor will be sad to hear the news. That is the one problem with being the chief radioman, sir. The bad news comes to you first, as well as the good news."

Mirotshinov finished reading the short dispatch. His laughter was now forgotten.

"You're right, chief radioman." The captain patted the man on the arm and handed him the short note typed on bright-red paper. "But who knows? Perhaps now we will be home sooner. Correct?"

"I hope so, sir."

Mirotshinov turned and grabbed the railing of the starboard ladder, which led to the exterior hatch entry to the bridge.

Once there, Mirotshinov strolled around the compass and the small bridge plotting board. He moved slowly to the forward control panel, standing between two young sailors who warily looked through binoculars at their American escort, now no more than 300 yards away.

One of the young sailors turned to Mirotshinov. "Comrade captain, do you believe that they will be with us throughout?"

"Only for a short while now," Mirotshinov answered.

He turned to the helmsman and the officer of the deck.

"Comrades, come about to two-eight-five. All ahead two-thirds. Set a new course from where we just came in the Bering Sea, and tell Chief Engineer Perchora to start rigging again for cold weather."

The look on his executive officer's face told the captain all he needed to know about what the reaction of the men would be. His face sagged with disappointment. Perhaps even the fanatical KGB interpretative unit, sitting in front of sophisticated radio equipment in the dark bowels of the ship, would be sad to leave the calm seas and warm weather.

Mirotshinov looked around at the several men on the bridge. There were no smiling faces looking at him, for sure. He was slightly angered. "What do you all want me to do? Say no? Perhaps request that the Americans give us shore leave? Maybe we can even take a tourist bus down to . . . what is that Mexican slum town called? . . . Tijuana, so we can watch the bullfights? Huh?"

He slammed his binoculars on the nearby captain's chair and stormed off the bridge, but not before barking another order. "Get under way immediately."

Mirotshinov grabbed the slippery brass rail with his calloused, snarled hands. He had been at sea most of his life; he knew what warm, calm waters meant to him and to the men he had commanded on so many ships before the *Provideniya*. He truly wished that he could order shore leave. Perhaps he would have visited a seaside restaurant and enjoyed a bucket of steaming clams, a hot loaf of bread, cakes, and thick black coffee.

He strode quickly toward the stern of the ship. He heard the rumbling engines start below. The creaking and groaning of the drive shaft would begin very soon.

The young Russian sailor whom he had commanded to the rear of the ship was now making his way back to his station at the bow. The sailor saluted. Mirotshinov grabbed his arm, startling the young man.

"So what's the verdict?"

"The verdict, comrade captain?" The sailor looked

around, hoping that something within view would help remind him of what he was supposed to say.

"Yes, the verdict. Was it as nice at the stern as it was at the bow?"

The fresh-faced Georgian smiled, revealing crooked teeth. "Maybe even nicer."

Mirotshinov grunted and released his grip. He smiled back and gave the man a quick salute. "Carry on, comrade."

"Yes, sir."

Mirotshinov walked slowly to the stern railing. He grabbed the chain to steady himself as the ship lurched into its turn. He looked down and saw froth beginning to bubble up as the twin screw propellers began to speed the *Provideniya* away from the coast of the United States. He looked up as the wind began to blow harder at his back. Across the short stretch of Pacific Ocean, he heard the call to quarters on the frigate *Nathanial.* He saw men scrambling to their stations. He was amused that his sudden departure had obviously caught the Americans off guard. They would follow for mile after mile.

But it was comforting, in a way, to have company on the open sea. To view another ship, even an adversary, on an otherwise featureless ocean was a soothing point of human reference. You would know that you weren't the only civilized creatures floating on the universe of water stretching as far as the eye could see and the mind could imagine.

He watched the *Nathanial* recede in the distance. He turned his view to the east. Perhaps he saw, for an instant, the red-brown roof of the Hotel del Coronado. Maybe one day he would visit again.

CHAPTER 41

The trailer was double-decked. Two shiny, bright-red Honda Odyssey off-road vehicles were stacked in the trailer. With their fat paddle tires, they worked equally well on the hard desert floor and on dunes. Their specifications were noisy 350cc engine, variable-speed Salisbury clutch, point seat-belt harness, wrist-strap restraints, and one-person capacity. The frame of the small open vehicle provided enough protection to enable a helmeted driver to walk away from a rollover. It was built for speed and abuse. It was a mini version of the sand-rail desert dune buggy.

In the hands of an experienced driver, such a vehicle provided a fun, exciting way to traverse rough desert floor or rolling dunes at speeds of thirty or forty miles per hour. The screaming engine and roller-coaster ride provided a challenge and diversion from the day-in-and-day-out grind of life in the city, where the most exciting drive could be getting off the freeway onto an off ramp.

But in the hands of an inexperienced driver, the vehicle would have limited potential. It could be downright dangerous for a beginner.

The KGB's American field agents, Jim and Bob, were novice drivers. Driving a Volga sedan on streets covered with ice and snow was the extent of their dangerous driving experience. So Moscow Center had correctly advised them to test the new vehicles in an inconspicuous location where they could get the feel of the ''wasteful and decadent'' equipment—equipment that they would have to use in the desert on Saturday. Perhaps they could even be field-tested for possible use in the great stretches of the Kara Kum and Kyzyl Kum deserts.

Jim and Bob had been chastised severely for botching their caper at GEO Tech Industries, and they were determined to make this operation work to perfection.

Bob was once again lead man on this mission. He was only slightly taller than Jim. Although both men were strongly built, it took all of their strength to pull the top vehicle out of the stacked trailer.

They had pulled the new trailer and Odyssey vehicles to Pismo Beach with a rented Chevrolet van. Pismo Beach was the only beach in California where average citizens could drive any vehicle that they preferred. It was designated a national park and controlled by the U.S. Park Service. A short sandy drive off the main road, through a gate where a few dollars were relinquished, down a ramp, and onto the sand was all that was required to get on the beach.

During the summer and holidays, the several-mile stretch of beach was clogged with vehicles of every make, size, and description. There were areas for overnight camping on the adjacent low dunes, but day use of the park caused the worst traffic. But today, in the middle of the day in the middle of the week in the fall, there were no beach traffic jams.

Jim looked around at the beach as it curved to the south. It was shrouded in dense fog. The ocean looked cold and gray, and only a few hardy souls ventured out into the chilly water. The beach was grooved with tire tracks, but only a few odd-looking dune buggies and motorcycles could be seen. The remainder of the traffic consisted of three-wheel vehicles, most of them driven by teenagers.

To his right Jim saw a huge sign marked "15 MILES PER HOUR—STRICTLY ENFORCED."

"Bob, look," said Jim, pointing to the sign.

Bob opened a red gas can and began to carefully fill the tanks. "To hell with that. There are no police on the beach."

"OK. I'll follow you, then. You get one more ticket and they'll send us both home."

"Stop worrying and help me out," Bob ordered.

Jim cinched up his nylon windbreaker against the cold, wet wind moving off the ocean.

They pulled the lower vehicle from the trailer and continued to prepare the Odyssey vehicles for their test run. Several young men driving all-terrain vehicles stopped to admire the new equipment and equally new trailers. They were amazed that Jim and Bob, average-looking schmos, had enough money to buy two Odysseys and a trailer. The young men roared off.

Bob turned to Jim and asked quietly, "What's a 'schmo'?"

"You, comrade," Jim said, laughing.

Bob chided him for saying the word "comrade" and reminded his more cheerful partner not to slip back into Russian. "English. Always English. Nothing else."

After another glance at the instruction manual, they were ready to roll.

The first several miles were uneventful. The engines sputtered and spat, but after warming up they came to life and began to hum smoothly, if not peacefully.

The two men observed the 15-miles-per-hour speed limit and stayed on the right side of the beach, nearest the water. They periodically had to dodge a wave or other inexperienced Pismo Beach drivers. They both laughed and ridiculed a fool who drove his two-wheel-drive passenger car onto the sand, only to have it bog down in a depression. The tow-truck drivers were making a fortune, charging fifty dollars for each retrieval from the sand.

As they drove down the beach, Jim staying behind Bob, they gained confidence and speed. At one point, Bob began to push twenty-five miles per hour. Though no police or beach-patrol jeeps were in sight, Jim pulled alongside Bob and screamed at him to slow down. Bob merely stuck up his middle finger and raced ahead.

"This is great fun!" Bob screamed.

Jim shook his head, sensing disaster.

After another mile, Jim spotted an open section of small dunes to his left. The dunes were no more than twenty or thirty feet tall. He sped next to Bob and pointed to the dune field.

"We'd better get used to them! Let's give it a try!" Jim screamed above the noise of the engine.

They swerved toward the dunes and found themselves alone on undulating dunes that were perfect for their present needs. For twenty minutes they practiced climbing, turning, and speed-shifting, never once coming close to turning over. They stopped to discuss how easy it was to use the vehicles; they were proud of their quick learning curve. After another quick turn on the dunes, they knew that they could handle whatever would face them in the Mojave. Then they turned back onto the level beach for the two-mile drive to their trailer and van.

On the final leg, Bob pulled alongside Jim. "I'll race you to the van," he said.

"No, you idiot. That's where the police will be."

"Wrong. They're looking for the hooligans at the end of the road, where it's more isolated."

Bob secured the top button of his coat and pulled down his knit hat. He grasped the wheel tightly, revved the engine up to full throttle, and zoomed ahead. Jim could only watch as his partner tore up the beach, nearly running over an all-terrain vehicle driver.

Ten seconds after Bob raced ahead, a yellow beach-patrol jeep was pursuing him.

The armed deputy sheriff made Bob sign for the ticket. After a quick "Thank you, and have a nice day," the officer drove off.

Jim unbuckled his seat belt, got out of his vehicle, and strutted over to the downcast Bob. Jim grabbed the top bar of the vehicle and leaned toward his friend.

"Now do you know what a schmo is?"

CHAPTER 42

Sam's Jeep Cherokee turned down another residential street. He looked at the Thomas Brothers map book on his lap and then from one side of the street to the other. The sun was bright, and it was difficult to spot the small numbers above the doors.

Efrim slumped down in the passenger seat. "Oh, God, please protect and save me."

Sam paid little attention to his friend. "It's too little and too late for you, Efrim. You're already a lost soul. Hey, did I turn down the right street? I mean, the numbers on Cactus Avenue are supposed to be higher than this."

"Sam?"

"What?"

"This is crazy. We're gonna die for sure. Why are we doing this?"

"Because it is absolutely essential, that's why."

Efrim had no inclination to help Sam find the address he was looking for. His fear turned to anger. "Damn it, you tricked me," he said.

Efrim reached down to one of Sam's scanner radios and tuned it to the local airport control tower. Small private planes radioed landing instructions and wind conditions on a regular basis. Efrim wanted to listen to anything at that point to divert his building fear of seeing the house of the punk Lynn Dozier. It would be there, Efrim concluded, that he would surely die.

"No, I didn't trick you. This isn't right. Damn it, Ef-

rim, you are confusing me.'' Sam reached down to the
scanner and turned it off. ''Can you forget about this
thing? I can't concentrate.''

Sam pulled to the side of the road and parked under a
giant oak tree. The Jeep's engine idled as he tried to
reconcile the map with his intended destination.

''So where is the 5100 block of Cactus?'' Sam asked.
He ran his finger along Cactus Avenue to a break on the
map. ''Here we go. The son of a bitch doesn't cut
through.''

''Good. Let's go home.''

''Not on your life.''

''Which won't be worth much.''

Sam threw the book behind his seat and rotated toward
Efrim. He was beginning to lose his patience.

''Efrim, you promised you would help me, and I absolutely need you to carry out my plan. Unless we go to
Dozier's house and convince him to help out, I'm up shit
creek without a paddle. Please stop bellyaching and help
me. Please.''

Efrim looked into Sam's pleading eyes. He was a sucker
for Sam's begging and liked being in a position of advantage over Sam, although he knew that he wasn't.

He played coy. ''I just don't know.''

''Efrim!'' Sam shouted.

''OK, OK, already. Gimme a break.''

As Sam turned down Cactus Street, Efrim began to
tense again.

''This is . . . I don't know what to call it.''

''Crazy,'' Sam said. He began to feel uneasy as well.

As he drove closer to Dozier's house, he saw the young
tough in the front yard with his slow-of-thought friend
Craig. Two other lowlife types were leaning against a
beat-up '56 Chevy. Dozier was bending over the rear engine of his all-chrome sand-rail dune buggy.

Sam pulled into the driveway and admired the buggy.
A faint smile crossed his face. He could hear Efrim
whimpering a fervent prayer over and over.

One thing was sure: Sam did admire the work that Do-

zier had done in constructing his picture-perfect sand vehicle. He remembered seeing a picture of the vehicle in
some obscure off-road magazine the previous year. It was
the centerfold of the magazine, listed as the vehicle of
the month. Dozier had won a cash prize of five hundred
dollars.

Considering the exquisite condition of the buggy, it
had probably cost Dozier twelve thousand dollars to build
the vehicle and hundreds more to maintain it. Five hundred dollars would pay for only the gas-filled shock absorbers.

The sand-rail buggy was a nearly perfect machine. The
welds at each joint were smooth, and the design of the
vehicle flowed. Almost every exposed engine part had
been chromed. Even the cable linkage connecting the gas
pedal and the engine throttle had been coated with
chrome. The buggy sparkled in the sun; not a dent could
be found. The vehicle was a mechanical work of art.

But Dozier was still Dozier.

Sam shut down the engine of his Jeep, stepped out of
his vehicle, and walked toward the group of ne'er-do-
wells. Craig pushed himself away from the old Chevy,
and the other two punks started to chuckle. Craig slapped
Dozier's buttocks.

"Hey, man, what the fuck you doin'?" Dozier asked.

His frown turned to a grin as he grabbed a greasy rag
and sauntered up to Sam, who was standing ramrod-
straight and confident. Dozier looked Sam up and down,
then turned back to his friends. "Hey, dudes, lookie what
we have here."

Dozier turned back to Sam. "So, chump, what? Huh?
You want somethin', or did you just come by for some
tea and crumpets?" Dozier looked over Sam's shoulder
and saw Efrim peering over the passenger-door window.

"Hey, toad face, aren't you comin' out to join us for a
nice friendly chat?" he asked. Dozier's eyes narrowed as
he turned back to Sam.

The rest of Dozier's slimy friends strutted over and
surrounded him. This gave Sam only more resolve.

"I need to talk to you," he said in a strong voice.

"Oh, yeah, shit for brains? What about?"

Sam nodded at Dozier's prized sand buggy. "Your sand rail. I wanna borrow it."

Craig and the other two punks laughed with gusto. "Oh, man, this guy's got his head up his ass. What a dweeb," Craig said.

But Dozier wasn't laughing. That vehicle was his prize possession. "What did you say, motherfucker?" he asked through clenched teeth.

Sam stepped up to within six inches of Dozier.

"I said," Sam said quietly, "I want to borrow your sand rail Saturday. Let's go inside, talk about it . . . and have some tea and crumpets."

CHAPTER 43

Sam was sitting up in bed. The lights were out, and his room was dark. He was leaning against the headboard, staring out the open window behind his equipment.

The transceivers were quiet; all the pilot lights were off. No sound emerged from any of his radios. He had disconnected the remaining antenna stubs. He was in no mood to rewire all the cables with new connectors. But that would have been useless, because most of his equipment had been smashed beyond repair by a crazed, enraged Richard Redden.

Sam was looking beyond the equipment, however. He could see several of the brighter stars through the window, but he was looking beyond those as well.

He recalled the plan that he had nearly been pummeled for earlier in the day. Sam smiled when he thought of the finesse he'd used earlier in the day on Dozier and the dimwitted Craig. Now both of them were his buddies. It never ceased to amaze Sam that if an individual just showed a miniscule amount of interest in the other person's interests, that person suddenly became a friend or at least did not remain an enemy. Of course, it didn't happen all the time; some people were unreachable. But others become very close friends. Sam considered one in particular.

He pulled over his standard desk telephone and placed it on his lap, picked up the handset and dialed.

"Hello, this is Sam Alexander. Is Lisa there, please?"

He heard Lisa's mother whisper the caller's name and ask why the late call. Lisa picked up the telephone in her room and waited for her mother to hang up the extension.

Sam sank down in his bed. As he exchanged pleasantries with Lisa, he relaxed. The sound of her voice made his pulse rise. He wished that her warm body was next to his. He wanted more than ever to hold her and love her.

"I know it's late, but I just had this irresistible urge to call," Sam said.

"Try not to call so late again, OK?"

"OK. Listen, I went out to Dozier's place today."

"Oh, my God. You really did speak to that clod?"

"Well, I spoke. He just kinda grunted."

Lisa laughed. "And?"

Sam took a deep breath and became serious again. "Everything is set with him. But I've changed my mind about something, Lisa."

"What is it?"

"Efrim can't handle what I want him to do. And if you're game, I need your help."

Lisa purred, "You know you have it, Sam. I'm all yours."

Sam liked the sound of that. It had several meanings. And that was what intrigued him; she kept him off-balance.

"Oh, yeah? What does that mean?" he asked.

"Whatever you want it to."

"For the moment, I need you to do something on your own on Saturday, rather than stay with me."

"Oh, Sam." Lisa's voice revealed her disappointment.

"Yeah. You're gonna have to handle this assignment by yourself."

CHAPTER 44

Attorney Paul Porter leaned against the front fender of his Porsche 928 and raised the collar of his Armani suit around his neck. Fall in Los Angeles usually meant late-evening fog. That night, in front of the jail holding facility in Van Nuys, the fog was especially thick. He was parked in the red curb zone and knew that if his client, Richard Redden, wasn't released soon, he would surely get a ticket from one of the traffic officers who cruised that street. It was a shortcut to the "barn" where LAPD patrol cars were stored and serviced, and nothing would give a police officer more pleasure than to give a ticket to a defense attorney, particularly one that they all knew and hated.

Counsel Porter's loud mouth in court was infamous. Sometimes he was thrown in jail faster than his clients were. If he wasn't talking back to the judge, he was screaming at his clients to shut up or tell the truth or lie through their teeth. Unfortunately, the prosecutor usually heard his instructions to his clients and informed the judge. Judges did not take kindly to officers of the court who instructed their clients to lie when they had just taken oaths to "tell the truth, the whole truth, and nothing but the truth."

As cold as it was, Porter could not turn down Richard's plea for help—or the fat fee he was paying. He had known Richard for only a short while. Porter's former employer was a large firm in downtown LA that handled Richard's various scrapes with the IRS, and Porter was usually assigned to the case. Richard approved of the rough tactics Porter employed on the tax collectors. Some IRS attorneys could be bullied; most couldn't. Porter was usually lucky.

Richard pushed open the courthouse door and pulled his suit coat around his neck. He looked up and down the deserted street below, then at the thick fog beginning to obscure an intersection several hundred feet away. Richard seemed to be in a jubilant mood, even though he had spent a night, a day, and part of another night in jail. A large gauze bandage covered his forehead.

"Beautiful night, Porter, huh?" Richard shouted from the top of the stairs.

Porter pushed himself away from his car. "Get your ass down here, Richard. I'm freezing my butt down here, and it's late, and I'm tired."

Richard bounded down the stairs, smiled broadly, and slapped his attorney on the back. Porter moved around to the driver's side of the Porsche.

"Yeah, just wonderful. You owe me twenty-five hundred bucks bail money, buddy."

"No problem, mi amigo."

"How's your head?" Porter asked.

"Oh, I got twenty-six stitches in there. We'll sue 'em for fifty grand for each stitch. Police brutality."

"Sure." Porter chuckled.

Porter accelerated away from the curb and into the empty streets surrounding the complex of municipal buildings. Several blocks later, he turned onto the Ventura Freeway and headed east, toward Pasadena and Richard's home.

"Will you please tell me what the hell is going on?" Porter asked. "I mean, the rap on this one is long and hairy—breaking and entering, assault, trespassing, burglary, assault on a federal officer, assault on an LAPD officer, not to mention malicious mischief on federal property. What's happening here, Richard?"

Richard smirked at his lawyer. "You wouldn't understand if I told you."

"Try me."

Porter was now pushing eighty-five miles per hour in a fifty-five zone on the still somewhat busy freeway. Richard glanced down at the speedometer.

"Hey, buddy, you better slow down. You wouldn't want to get a ticket."

"Smart ass."

Richard looked ahead at the road again and nodded. "Yeah, you're right. I am," he said defiantly.

CHAPTER 45

"It's not my fault they're sending you back. I warned you. This is what you get. Since they put me in charge of this mission now, you do the dirty work and heavy lifting."

Jim bit off another large piece of his bear-claw sweet roll and looked across the quiet intersection and down the cross street at Richard Redden's small house. The Russian agent was standing in front of a neighborhood convenience store and talking on the telephone with his forlorn partner, Bob, who was packing and preparing for the next step of their mission.

The fog was even thicker now, and Richard's house at times vanished behind it.

Jim put the sweet roll on a napkin and grabbed his coffee. "Listen, comrade, just get everything ready. Now that he is out, he's gonna make a move, I tell ya, and he knows what is happening. I can feel it."

Jim pulled the phone away from his ear. Bob's screaming and yelling in Russian wasn't making his job of surveillance on a cold, foggy night any easier. "Look, Teshkin, just be ready when I call. I'll use the portable phone and give you specific directions." There was more screaming at the other end of the telephone. "Because, dummy, you know as well as I do that every goddam channel is monitored. Right, comrade. Just be ready. Goodbye."

Jim slammed down the handset and muttered,

"Ukrainian asshole. I'm glad you're leaving, son of bitch. I hope they send you to Siberia."

He turned and casually walked back to his rented Ford Thunderbird. Many times he had told Bob that he would love to pack that car in a suitcase so he could drive around Moscow in the only decent car near the Kremlin.

He shoved the rest of the bear claw in his mouth, set his Styrofoam coffee cup on the roof of the car, and grabbed the door handle. He stopped when he saw a red Porsche run a red light and screech around the corner, stopping in front of Richard Redden's house.

Jim swallowed the wad of bear claw and squinted at what was happening in front of Richard's house. A fog curtain moved in, momentarily blocking his view. As it cleared, he saw the Porsche drive away and the dark figure of a man opening the front door of the house.

Jim scrambled into his car. He started it quickly and backed out of the parking stall, spilling his coffee on the windshield. Jim unloaded a string of Russian curse words that continued for a solid minute.

The silence of the streets and the cocooning fog surrounding the car had nearly put Jim to sleep. His eyes were heavy, and the effect of several cups of coffee had long since worn off. Through a shroud of haze, he tried to concentrate on the digital clock on his dashboard. It read 3:10 A.M.

His arms went limp, and his head sagged to the right. A jolt of noise from a racing car engine and the blinding light of a pair of auto headlights zapped him back into the world of the living and awake. He saw Richard pull away from his house in his NASA sedan. Jim was frantic and disoriented for five seconds. He finally jammed his foot down on the accelerator and started the engine of his rented Thunderbird. He made a screaming U-turn in the middle of the street and raced off in pursuit of Richard.

The freeway loops of downtown Los Angeles had little traffic, but Richard was keeping a steady even speed under fifty-five. Jim tried to hang back as far as possible and still keep Richard in sight. He reached for the control head of his portable cellular telephone and pushed one of the memory buttons. Within seconds Bob was on the line.

"So where are you? I'm just passing the San Pedro exit, and he's continuing to head east."

The connection was excellent. Bob was talking to Jim on his portable phone in the rented van. Behind the van, Bob was pulling the new trailer carrying the two Honda Odyssey buggies.

"I'll intersect with you in about ten minutes if he continues going east on Interstate 10."

"OK. Then in five, go to the com route, OK?"

"Fine."

Jim heard the line go dead. He replaced the control head on its cradle and moved the portable phone to the passenger floor. Then he reached inside his heavy raincoat and pulled out a commercial-channel walkie-talkie. He squinted through another patch of fog and watched Richard's taillights disappear.

Jim pushed the gas pedal to the floor and tried to catch up. Once he did, he eased off and changed lanes. He thought it best to move to either the right or left two lanes so that he would not always be in the same spot in Richard's rear-view mirror. Jim was satisfied with his cleverness.

"OK, you fuck, where are you taking us?" he asked.

CHAPTER 46

Most production meetings on Stage 55 at the International Broadcasting Network were the same. Heaven help the poor unit manager assigned to coordinate the meeting who forgot to order the coffee, tea, milk, danish, and bagels.

The news-pool-coverage meeting was set for nine A.M. sharp, but by the time everyone arrived, grabbed refreshments, and chatted with old friends, it was nine-twenty. The meeting was finally called to order by Burt Dunlap.

NASA had chosen IBN and Dunlap to coordinate pool coverage for the electronic media. It probably was Dunlap's experience, his friendship with Kenneth Wood, and the proximity of the Burbank studio to JPL in Pasadena that swayed the decision.

The large production studio where the meeting was being held was guarded by the tallest, toughest, meanest studio guards Dunlap could muster. Everyone coming in had to go through a strict screening procedure; the guards had a list of names, and they issued ID badges only to people who were on that list. Besides the studio guards, a small platoon of NASA and JPL security personnel logged in all those in attendance.

For some of the most hardened, experienced field producers, technicians, and reporters, the extraordinary security precautions were unnerving. After all, the studio was their turf, well protected by crack guards who protected them against interlopers. The studio was where they lived and worked, so they felt at home, comfortable, and safe. The unusual security measures cast a nervous edge on what would become a contentious meeting.

Burt Dunlap was sitting behind a ten-foot studio cafeteria table with several members of the JPL logistical liaison staff and Will Webster. Webster was not thrilled at having to attend. He thought that he had more important duties to perform than to sit down with a group of vipers and snoops.

Dunlap finished speaking quietly to Webster, rose to his feet, and looked out at the crowd of about two hundred people. They were seated in an audience section that only the day before had been used by the screaming, shouting audience of the game show "Winner Loses."

Dunlap looked right of the audience section and saw some of the show's set graphics partially hidden in the shadows. He hoped that the title of the show had no significance for the responsibilities he had assumed.

Dunlap turned quickly and saw that a tall orange curtain had been drawn across the stage behind him, hiding the gaudy $200,000 set. Someone had mercifully thought to use the curtain to prevent the attention of the news audience from being divided between Burt Dunlap and the set.

Burt looked back out at the crowd, which was now starting to quiet. He nodded and smiled to old friends from NBC, CBS, and CNN. He didn't know anyone at ABC. He saw representatives of various national and regional networks and a large contingent from shortwave-broadcast-band organizations such as Voice of America, the BBC, Swiss Radio International, Deutsche-Welle, and even Radio Moscow. He took a deep breath. It would be an interesting meeting.

"Ladies and gentlemen, perhaps we should start to discuss this . . . uh . . . event—or, as some think, pseudoevent—which may be the greatest story or the greatest hoax . . ."

From the back, a voice rang out, "Or maybe both at the same time."

General nervous laughter spread through the jaded group.

Dunlap continued, "I trust that you all picked up the rundowns as you walked in here. Sorry for the slowup in getting in, but the government and NASA felt it was required."

"It made me feel at home," someone called. There was another round of laughter. Dunlap smiled and nodded at a stocky gentleman in the front row. "Thank you, Sergei. I was waiting for that. So anyway," he continued, "I'm sure you have questions, but maybe we should do a short presentation and run over what NASA's security people will and will not let us cover. And of course, we'll go over logistics and other important details, like where we eat and where we pee."

"To hell with that, Burt," said a tall, dour-looking gentleman at the back of the audience section. Burton slumped and shifted his weight onto one foot. So it's starting, he thought.

"Yes, Herman, what is it?" Dunlap asked sourly. "By the way, for those of you who don't know, Herman Downey is an independent supplier of equipment systems for several news organizations. SatelStat is the name of his company."

"Can I just bring up a few points, now that I've read this poop sheet you gave us? Which is what the information is—poop."

A few more chuckles bounced around the studio.

Dunlap threw up his hands. "Go ahead, Herman. I can't stop you anyway."

Downey used his handout packet like a weapon, punctuating key thoughts by using the rolled-up paper much like a club or blackjack. He went over disagreeable point after disagreeable point. Finally, he wrapped up his long-winded speech.

"The simple fact of the matter is we might as well all go home and not even be in this meeting. These restrictions are so stifling. I mean, what is the use of spending one damn dime on coverage? Here we are, going to the middle of the goddamn desert with no food or water or proper toilet facilities. We can't get our satellite transmission trucks within twenty-five miles of the command site because of the fear of RF interference in the microwave range. All tapes shot by our minicam crews have to be scanned by NASA to prevent leaks of sensitive material that might panic the public—which is outright censorship and bullshit.

"And NASA and the feds don't even know the precise impact or selection point. They are trusting an unnamed source, which, I predict, will by the end of the day be named by one of the astute reporters in this room, or by some editorial assistant who will accidentally dig it up when a loudmouth at JPL, NASA, or the NSA feels he can't keep a secret anymore.

"And to top it all off, the main video and audio feed is going to be provided not by us. We'll have to use what the government gives us through their Signal Corps or communications people. No telephones, no two-way radio. All this bullshit because of safety concerns.

"Hell, I was crouched next to a reporter from Australian Channel 9 during Nam and saw the guy's torso blown in two by a VC grenade launcher. His viscera were flying all over the place. And now we're talking about a remote in the middle of the fucking Mojave Desert, where the only goddamn danger comes from the motherfucking government and their motherfucking paranoia."

The room was silent except for Downey's heavy breathing. Dunlap stared at Downey, then at Will Webster, sitting at his right. Webster was smiling at Downey.

Dunlap looked back at Downey. "Herman, you really should show a little more passion for your work."

Downey screamed back, "Fuck you, Dunlap! Don't give me any of your arrogant condescension."

And so the meeting went. For several hours, there was more screaming and less screaming. There was screaming until the very end, when the meeting was adjourned.

The meeting broke up with people bloodied and battered, but no egos were broken or even fractured. For that group of high-strung individuals, that was as impossible as impossible could be. In the end, of course, everyone knew that they would do the best with what they had; still, it would look good and sound good. A tough set of restrictions had been placed on them, but they would overcome these difficulties to bring to the world words about and pictures of this momentous event. It couldn't be any worse than a war, they thought.

Dunlap asked his secretary, who had been taking notes in the audience, to transcribe the audience's ''want'' list within thirty minutes. Will Webster quietly agreed to present the demands to Kenneth Wood, who would forward them to Washington for consideration.

Dunlap said his last goodbyes and turned away from the group that was making its way toward the visitor parking lot. He rolled his head and stretched his back, trying to relax after being pilloried time after time during the meeting. His frantic assignment editor ran up to him and stopped him cold.

Joe Atlas was breathing fast. He tried to control the volume of his voice.

''We're OK, Burt. The vehicle can be ready by midnight.''

''Will all the transmission equipment be installed?''

''Every bit of it. Video, audio, VTR, cellular phone, two-way radios, satellite dish, light pack—the whole nine yards.''

Dunlap moved closer to him and whispered, ''And the satellite time. Is it reserved?''

Atlas was still trying to catch his breath. ''You bet. We've locked out everyone on Vidcom four. No one else can get it. And we're listed as Revival Ministries. No one will know who bought it until we are on the air.''

Dunlap smiled broadly. ''How do the vehicles look?''

''Those half-tracks are ready to go to battle, boss.'' Now Atlas smiled broadly.

Dunlap replied softly, ''Fucking-A great. We're gonna beat 'em all, whichever location it lands. Tell that editor, Marko, that for giving us that choice bit of geographical and historical data, he gets a raise. We're so damn good!''

CHAPTER 47

Myra Pemin was standing in line behind her beloved boss, Evegeny Romanov. But of course, she was a citizen of the Union of Soviet Socialist Republics, so she was used to standing in line. But this line was the line to disembark from the lengthy Pan American flight arriving in Los Angeles from Helsinki, Finland. She and Evegeny were tired and somewhat disoriented, their bodily functions and biological clocks disturbed by crossing so many time zones.

The door of the plane still had not opened, and the plane had been sitting in front of the gate for at least ten minutes. Evegeny turned to Myra and said, "Just like home, eh?"

"Yes, Evegeny. But at least we are not waiting for toilet paper."

"Or vodka."

The line finally proceeded through the forward fuselage opening. When Evegeny and Myra emerged, loaded down with carry-on luggage and briefcases, they were met by a tall, handsome NASA security agent. Myra took quick notice.

"Dr. Romanov, could you and Miss Pemin please follow me for transportation?" the agent asked.

Myra asked firmly in a thick Russian accent, "And just who might you be, sir?"

"Oh, I'm sorry." The man held out his hand. "My name is Mark Stevens; I'm with NASA. I'm your driver and escort. Mr. Wood is waiting for you at the bottom of the ramp with a transportation van.''

Myra and Evegeny had to put down their briefcases to shake Stevens's hand.

"Nice to meet you, Mr. Stevens," Myra said with a smile.

"Mr. Stevens. Now let's proceed," Romanov said.

At the bottom of the ramp, Kenneth Wood held out his arms and showed honest excitement at seeing an old acquaintance. As the two men hugged, Myra looked on in quiet amazement. She glanced over at the handsome young man who had greeted them as he carefully placed their baggage in the plushly appointed VIP stretch van.

"It is great to see you again, Evegeny. I can tell you now, it wasn't easy to get you over here on such short notice," Wood said.

"Not because of any reluctance on our end, Kenneth, I can assure you. My people were so happy to kick out this old troublemaker to see what is going on here that I didn't have a chance to pick up that taffy you like so well."

"Come, let's get in. We have a short drive and a long helicopter ride ahead of us."

"We are going directly to the site?" Romanov asked, surprised.

Kenneth Wood helped herd Romanov and Myra inside the van. All three of them collapsed in heavily upholstered captain's chairs. Stevens slammed the passenger door shut and moved to the driver's seat. In a second, the van rolled away from the ground crew swarming around the 747 passenger jet. The whine of the jet's air compressors faded as they drove away from the terminal.

"We're going to the other side of the airport to grab one of our choppers. From there it's about an hour or so in a beeline to the desert location, at a place called Dumont Dunes. I'll tell ya, Evegeny, I've been told the place looks like the surface of Mars."

"I wish it were."

"Tall, jagged peaks. Barren. Unbelievably hot." Wood looked at his watch, then looked out at the sky. "It should be daybreak soon, and there is a lot to do in just a short time. I have a lot to show you and tell you about. What has been cleared for me to tell you, of course.''

Romanov looked quizzically at Myra, then back at Wood realizing that he had forgotten to make introductions. ''Oh, how stupid of me. This is my assistant, Myra Pemin. Myra, Kenneth Wood.''

Wood shook her hand. He had been admiring her clear blue eyes and creamy complexion. She was a beautiful young girl with a nice figure and softly styled dark blond hair. Stevens occasionally glanced at her in the rear-view mirror.

''I'm sure you've met our driver today. He's one of my people in administration at JPL,'' Wood said. ''He'll join us at the site at Dumont and be assigned to you.''

Romanov smiled. ''To watch us.''

Wood shot back, ''To assist you.''

The van twisted and turned around the access road, skirting the main taxiway and runway at LAX. The aircraft traffic was light. Plane after plane was fueled, and the gates were ready for the crush of early-morning traffic that would soon engulf the airport. By that time the NASA chopper would be long gone, flying to a stark environment only a short distance from civilization and its restaurants, business parks, and traffic. Civilization at Dumont consisted of the lizard, cactus, and scorpion.

Romanov leaned forward and grabbed Wood's forearm. ''My friend, it is good to see you. When was it last?''

''It was either the second or third shuttle launch. Remember?''

''Absolutely. What a thrill that was. And what do you think about our little shuttle beauty?''

Wood leaned back, folded his arms, and smirked. ''It looks a helluva like our shuttle, Evegeny. How did you manage that?''

With a knowing twist of his head, Romanov said, ''Kenneth, it may look like your shuttle on the outside, but believe me, on the inside it is not your shuttle.''

There was a brief silence. Wood looked out toward the

plainly marked hangar and the white NASA chopper sitting in front of it. A small military ground crew was waiting, pacing. Stevens pulled the van just beyond the reach of the rotor blades and shut off the engine. He stepped around to the door and pulled it open.

Romanov turned to Myra. "Why don't you help young Mr. Stevens with the baggage, Myra? I want to talk to Kenneth for a moment." Stevens shot a look at Kenneth. Wood nodded. The luggage was removed, and Romanov and Wood were left alone in the van. The ground crew and flight crew began to load the baggage and finished topping off the fuel tank. Chocks were pulled from the landing framework, and several service vehicles were moved away from the chopper.

"So, Kenneth, is this for real? And what about this young man who stumbled onto the signal? Is he playing a game with us?"

Kenneth took a deep breath and looked deeply into Romanov's eyes. Wood wanted to spill his guts, to reveal his innermost thoughts to the man he had come to respect and like so long ago. Their dreams were similar, and their battles with bureaucracy were similar. He felt kinship with the Russian, more than with some of his most trusted aides, especially Richard Redden. But he also knew that Romanov was on the other side. He would have to weigh his words carefully.

"I'll tell you, Evegeny, we think it is an authentic beacon signal with attached data. And we think the purple satellite, if that is what you want to call it, is some type of repeater that is relaying the signal. The young man, Sam Alexander, discovered the signal. His father worked for us at one time long ago, but he was killed or lost in a plane accident. So the boy has felt it necessary to pick up the baton. The kid is smart and inventive. He put together a signal discriminator that equals or surpasses our own. It is limited in bandwidth and some sensitivity, but it works."

Romanov interjected, "But the signal seems to be directed at him."

"Yes, this is true. Why? Who knows? We may find out when the next acquisition or data transfer occurs."

"Why in the middle of the desert?"

Wood shook his head, feeling goose bumps pop up all over his body. "Because it will be a physical transfer of information. We guess they don't want a circus surrounding their arrival."

"Arrival? Impossible. Tau Ceti is over eleven light years away. Impossible."

"Evegeny, my friend, how many naysayers told the greatest scientific minds and inventors that radio transmission was impossible, or that the transmission of pictures was impossible, or that man would never fly in long aluminum cylinders carrying over four hundred passengers?"

Romanov continued the thought. "Or that we would set foot on another celestial body, or take close-up pictures of Saturn or Jupiter or Uranus. But light speed is an impossible barrier to cross, whether we talk about electromagnetic signals or the transfer of matter from one location to another."

Wood put a hand on his old friend's shoulder. "Well, we might find out whether that is true within the next twenty-four hours."

As the final data segments were being analyzed and compiled, the council moved closer to a vote. The Sovereign would poll each continental representative for his decision: initiate or terminate.

Such extraordinary processing of a relatively simple exchange of data had wide and lasting ramifications. Consideration revolved around the possible effects on both the Tau Ceti planet and the target, solar planetesimal Earth.

Electromagnetic transmissions from the planet had been reviewed, and it was determined that difficulties in dealing with on-planet primitive cultures had occurred there as well. The contact had caused great disruption in the view the isolated culture had of itself relative to the outside world. The discovered peoples displayed a strange combination of fear, hope, and longing.

When the more advanced culture had carefully considered its actions, the toll on the less advanced culture was considerable; harm was irreparable and widespread. Not only had increased virulent diseases been manifested in people who had no built-in immunity, but also, the sweeping adjustment to the other culture had been difficult and, at times, deadly for both. How much information should be kept from the original culture? What should be introduced was as important for the survival of the primitive culture as were their environment and their food supply.

Despite the fact that a million millennia had passed during the evolution of the Tau Ceti system, the emotional component of all creatures was part of their thought process. Among the higher beings within the system, emotions were controlled.

During the discussion, however, emotion was being used to press arguments and influence others. There were those within the Sovereign body who felt that the final phase of data transfer, which would enlarge contact to the entire population of the planetesimal Earth, would be a serious mistake. The purpose stated in the beginning was to study and explore only, with absolutely no disturbance of the indigenous plant and animal life. The Earth was a laboratory, the galaxy a school, and the universe a university.

Concern about the unpredictable bipedal life forms was expressed. Their numbers and ingenuity were formidable; they were potentially dangerous to small groups of explorers. Current technological and social dictums transferred to a semideveloped culture could have an adverse affect on continuing exploration of Earth. It might make future data collection impossible.

Examples from previous debacles were presented, and the disturbing results were reviewed. To repeat those mistakes would be an additional mistake and a lost opportunity, considering the wealth of information to be gained on the planetesimal Earth. The argument was convincing, and those presenting it were strident in expressing their fears and hopes.

Opposing Sovereign members postulated, as they had before, that the change in the basic experiment strategy was in and of itself part of the experiment. Only so much could be gleaned without grand-scale interaction of the creatures through large study groups. Beyond the cold clinical arguments, however, were the possibilities of advancing the development of thinking, reasoning, resourceful subjects. Acting as catalysts, the explorers would be able to determine whether the data transmitted would be used or abused by the subjects. It would be interesting to see how the technical and cultural data would be applied.

The effects would go far beyond the decision of the Sovereign. Experience and knowledge might help them cope with the effects in their own society, but it would take all their knowledge to control them.

All elements of the decision were implemented. A low-level transfer of pictures and text would be made. The presentation messengers were selected. The "initiate" command was given.

Recognizable, applicable Earth-playback-format engineering began.

CHAPTER 48

Richard Redden stood at the edge of the sidewalk on Main Street in Brawley. He had his arms folded and rocked back and forth, from one foot to the other, as though he were waiting for a bus. He looked straight up at the noon sun, beating mercilessly on his head. Richard could not believe how hot it still could be in the fall in California. It must have been ninety-five or more, he surmised. He turned his attention to the traffic on Main Street. He looked at the faces of the residents. If anyone had any doubt that Brawley was an agricultural town, Richard could prove it merely by describing the people.

At JPL, he had always been suspected of being intolerant toward minorities and women. As he looked up and down the street, at the pickup trucks and the chopped Chevys and beat-up flatbed trucks, he had disdain for where he was and what he was seeing. A man of limited vision, such as he was, sees the world only in his own image of perfection. Richard's perfect view of himself and his omnipotent intelligence and judgment did not include spending time with the decent folk in that hard-working town.

Richard was told by the gas-station attendant at a Shell outlet on Main, the primary road from the west that ran east toward Glamis, that cattle ranching was the mainstay of Brawley. It was known, the attendant said proudly, as the cattle capital of California.

Richard sniffed the air and could tell why.

He initially drove the five or so minutes it took to get

from one side of the town to the other and noticed how different the western section of Main was from the eastern section. The west end was modern, comparatively, with fast-food hamburger and chicken stands, gas stations and mini-malls. The entire business district in that end of town catered to the incoming tourist traffic; Brawley was the last stop before the desert resorts of Glamis and the Sand Hills.

The other end of Main catered to the needs of the community, with clothing stores, movie houses, and grain and feed outlets. That stretch revealed the age and the wild-west aura of the town. Shabby buildings that needed paint and a ragtag combination of liquor stores and bars that should have been renovated years before extended for only two blocks, but they made lasting impressions. But Richard thought that maybe the townsfolk liked it that way. He couldn't care less about the blight.

He turned and watched the salesman at Desert Motorcycle finish installing of a small trailer behind Richard's NASA sedan. He had to do some fast thinking when the salesman asked whether he worked for NASA and what the hell NASA wanted with a desert motorbike, anyway. Richard told the young Mexican–American that he had purchased the car from the government, used. But Richard's suit pants and white shirt didn't convince the young man of that. Again, Richard didn't care.

Richard put his hands in his pockets and slowly walked toward the salesman.

"Say, son, about how far did you say that Glamis and the Boardmanville general store are out on 78?"

The salesman cinched the last chain link on the bumper mount and stood up. He reached into his back pocket and pulled out a rag. He looked down Main Street.

In a soft accent, the young man said, "Oh, go 'bout twenty miles or so, but don't forget that quick left I told you about, down there about fifteen miles or so. Just keep going and you'll see Boardmanville." The salesman stepped forward and looked Richard over. "You sure you don't want me to find some riding clothes? At least a helmet and goggles and definitely a bandanna, at least. Man, that sand gets everywhere.''

"No. I brought some of my own.''

"OK. It's your body. Lemme get your bike.''

In less than a minute, Richard's new desert motorcycle was wheeled out of the store and onto the small trailer. The salesman danced around the cycle as though he had mounted numerous bikes before, securing the mounting straps and clips. The high fenders and spiked tires immediately identified the motorcycle as an off-road desert screamer. It was a machine engineered to be abused. The question in the salesman's mind was whether the new owner knew how to operate the powerful engine and cope with the wild ride that the cycle and the environment would provide.

Richard leaned against his car and wiped the sweat around the bandage on his forehead. The heat reopened the wound slightly. A brown discoloration began to show around the deepest part of his cut forehead, where most of the stitches were.

Without looking up, the young salesman asked, "Say, do you know how to ride this thing? I mean, have you ever ridden a sand scooter like this before?''

Richard tried to be cool. "Oh, yeah. I've come out here often. I just had some work in the office and couldn't buy the new machine I wanted in LA. It would've been a lot cheaper there, I'll tell ya that.''

The salesman used all his strength to tighten the last buckle. The motorcycle was standing vertical and rigid on the trailer. A center guardrail kept the wheels from turning and the bike from lurching forward.

"Yeah, but you wouldn't have gotten service with a smile like you do here at Desert Motorcycle.''

Richard replied unemotionally, "Yeah, sure.'' He pushed himself away from his car and stepped up to the cycle. He walked around the trailer and shook the bike to make sure that it was firmly in place.

"Not bad. You got my receipt?'' he asked.

"Oh, shit.''

The salesman ran into the shop and returned with the

yellow paper, handing it to Richard. Richard rudely snatched it, turned away, and got into his car. He slammed the door in the salesman's face as the young man said goodbye.

"Thank you, sir. Be careful out there on those dunes. There's some monster drops and holes. The sand's been soft, with all the wind we've been having."

The warning fell on deaf ears. Richard didn't look at him or thank him. He just started the car, backed away, and pulled away, leaving the store and the salesman in a cloud of dust.

"Thank you for your patronage!" the salesman shouted. "Hope you break your fucking neck, gringo. *Pendejo* . . . asshole. Hope your head opens back up and you bleed to death." He then gave him the one-armed salute that did not translate into affection.

The salesman watched Richard till he passed the Plaza Park Municipal Center several blocks away. The salesman turned as a dark van carrying two brand-new Oddyssey vehicles, and Jim and Bob, whizzed by.

Jim and Bob entered Plaza Park, and two dark-blue FBI sedans flew past Desert Motorcycle.

The FBI sedans passed Plaza Park, and a long flatbed tractor–trailer carrying a half-track truck, topped with a small microwave transmission dish mounted on a long push-up extension pipe, roared past Desert Motorcycle.

The Sand Hills were going to be very crowded very soon.

CHAPTER 49

The eastern Mojave Desert and the southwestern corner of Nevada are full of restricted stretches of parched land. The areas are used as practice sites by American land and air forces. The deserts of Libya, Iran, and the Soviet Union are much like those areas in and around the China Lake Naval Weapons Center, Fort Irwin National Training Center, and Nellis Air Force Testing Range just northwest of Las Vegas. In the heart of the battered and scarred landscape, southeast of Death Valley National Monument, sits Dumont Sand Dunes.

The NASA helicopter began to descend toward Dumont Dunes. Myra Pemin, Evegeny Romanov, Mark Stevens, and Kenneth Wood were awed by the stark beauty of the craggy mountains and the steel-hard desert plain.

Two A-10 tank-killer planes, with their moaning twin jet engines mounted on either side of their tails, zigzagged around the helicopter and around a razor-sharp peak. Romanov looked at the feared airplanes and smiled. It was a view he was not supposed to see. But one plane, he was sure, would be photographed from several hundred miles above his head when the brain trust in Moscow decided to retarget the aiming computers of several spy satellites floating in low Earth orbit.

Romanov leaned toward Wood and shouted, ''Do you think I can next see a Stealth fighter or bomber? I would love to take a picture.'' He laughed. So did Wood. Stevens turned toward the Russian from his position in the front navigator's seat and frowned at him.

Wood answered, "I seriously doubt you will have the opportunity. They fly out of Edwards, which I'm sure you know. And only at night, which I am also sure you know."

Romanov waved his hand. "Who cares, Kenneth?"

"I'm sure you do, Evegeny."

Far in the distance, Myra Pemin saw the two A-10s curl around the peaks and flip-flop like darting hummingbirds. They flew behind a dark-brown mountain ridge and disappeared.

The helicopter made a hard right turn and angled downward.

At eight points equidistant from the confined dune-field perimeter, NASA had set up monitoring stations not unlike the one that Charlie Williams had put together on the hills above Escondido at the Condon Ranch. This time, however, NASA was sharing the space with military communications trailers and Signal Corps photographic detachments. A wide array of still and television cameras were placed at each location. Long lenses and wide-angle lenses were mounted on half a dozen still cameras and three video cameras at each site.

Tents and toilet facilities had been helicoptered to the site, as had tall antennas and monitoring towers. Radio, TV, fax, and data links were interconnected and ran down to the headquarters compound. That nerve center had been erected in an open sand field at the center of the dunes.

Hundreds of men had been assigned to this special event. From the security guards at various checkpoints to the highly skilled equipment operators and scientists, nothing it would take to monitor and record this event had been spared.

Helicopters dashed to and fro overhead, and an occasional high-speed pass by small formations of F-16s increased the level of noise and excitement.

It was truly a massive effort, all based on the short bursts of signals directed to Sam Alexander and finally recorded at Goldstone with Kenneth Wood witnessing the event. All that remained was for Sam to finally tell Wood and the assembled masses where the landing would take place and the promised information would be transferred. Like the tablets bearing the Ten Commandments, written by the hand of God, the hoped-for words and pictures of another species, whose biology and appearance were unknown, would be awaited eagerly by the scientists and the world's people.

To bring the story to the people of the world, the press would have to rely on those eight government installations to provide sound and picture. No "up close and personal" segments would be allowed.

The airspace above and the interior dune field below were strictly off limits. Only the periphery of the site and the interior command post would be open to the hordes of reporters and electronic-media crews. The government was fairly confident that no fool would attempt to go in alone. It wasn't so much that anyone who tried would be easily spotted on the barren plate of ground; the elements were too harsh for news crews and reporters to venture out into the threatening terrain. The guards knew that some maverick wild man with an Ikegami video camera would attempt to penetrate the ring of security nevertheless.

A large number of reporters and civilians without credentials were camped out in front of the newly erected main gate on the two-lane highway that led into the command post. Arguments and fist fights broke out over who could and could not enter the military-controlled area. Several dozen rough-looking bikers and off-road-vehicle enthusiasts were furious that their favorite weekend playground had been commandeered by the military. Tempers flared and insults flew. But human beings are curious animals, and the crowd stayed and grew, waiting for something to happen. They were unsure what was about to take place, but sure that if something big was happening at Dumont, they didn't want to miss any of it.

The frantic setup continued; the food trucks and toilet wagons and giant generators joined the tons of other equipment. A huge effort was under way, and many in the group of experts and not-so experts wondered whether this would turn out to be just an overnight campout in the desert or an affirmation of the life process, repeated in other worlds.

Each helicopter that landed on a nearby steel-mesh landing zone brought in observers from around the world or clutches of scientists carrying sophisticated detection and monitoring equipment. It was a scene out of a movie, or an electronic gadgeteer's nightmare gone wild.

As Wood stepped away from his just-arrived helicopter, he looked around at the chaos in and around the several dozen trailers and tents. He shook his head in disbelief. He shuddered when he considered that all the expense and activity could be for naught if nothing happened or if Sam didn't show. No, that couldn't happen. He'd seen the last message, commanding Sam to be in the desert that night, and Wood had made sure that there was enough close-in security to escort Sam to this location.

Stevens stepped out of the helicopter and held his hand out to Myra as she stepped off the high first step onto the temporary landing pad.

Romanov surveyed the men and women running back and forth, struggling with equipment, shouting orders, and sweating under the hot desert sun. He saw every convenience from the city brought out to the middle of the wilderness.

He turned to Wood. "I must say, Kenneth, when you Americans do something, you do it in a big way."

"Let's just hope it's all worth it. All we're missing now is the young man, Sam Alexander."

CHAPTER 50

Sam stood to the side of his window and looked down at the mob scene outside his Uncle Stu's garage. An area in front of the wide driveway had been cordoned off by Escondido police to restrain the hundreds of people. Sam shook his head and wondered how a small, quiet operation could get out of hand so quickly.

The minicam news trucks were parked three deep along Mountain View Road, stretching back toward the main thoroughfare, Palmyra. Reporters were interviewing anybody and everybody. The male field reporters adjusted their ties and the female reporters smoothed stray strands of hair as they stood in front of the ring of NASA security men and Escondido police officers. The line was there to protect Sam's Jeep and the covered sand-rail dune buggy inside Stu's garage.

Any movement in and around the Alexander house was photographed. Marion stepped out to look toward the garage, and reporters shouted dozens of questions at her from a distance. She scurried back inside the house to avoid them.

Inside the garage, Stu secured an elastic tether on the corner eyelet of a dull-green canvas tarp that covered the dune buggy. The buggy was on a trailer attached to Sam's prized Jeep. For a moment, Stu accidentally exposed a bright chrome cross member of the frame, but he quickly covered it and the rest of the buggy. Only the fat, knobby rear tires were exposed.

In the shadows of the garage, several mechanics were

straightening toolboxes and workbenches. Their uniforms identified them as Stu's mechanics. Two of the mechanics were Dozier and Craig.

Sam turned away from the window and pulled a bright-orange helmet and black goggles out of his closet. He set them on top of his jeans and his black leather jacket, laid out neatly on the bed. Next to the jeans were two bright bandannas, one red and one blue. On the floor, a pair of black boots, stuffed with a pair of heavy wool socks, stood at the ready.

He stared down at his clothes, put his hands on his hips, and wondered whether he had everything he needed. He turned and looked at his book bag, then bent down and opened it. He fumbled with a cassette tape recorder, three cameras, several rolls of film, and a radiation-detection badge, all provided by NASA. He had been given the equipment earlier in the day so that he could become familiar with it. The technician who explained to Sam how to use the recorder and load the camera talked to Sam as though he were an idiot. But Sam had expected that.

He stripped off his shorts and undershirt and stepped into the shower. He turned on the water and adjusted the temperature balance. The warm velvety water poured over his body and relaxed him immediately. He leaned against the cool white tiles and let the water hypnotize him. It helped turn off the world and forced him to think of nothing. But that could be for only a moment.

He jerked upright suddenly. He thought he had heard his exterior door open. He looked out through the frosted glass shower door. He thought he saw a shadow, heard a noise. He wondered whether one of the reporters or NASA people had sneaked into his room again.

"Aunt Marion, is that you? I'll be out in a second."

Sam listened carefully and heard no reply. Then the shadow came closer. Who was it?

The shower door opened. Lisa.

Sam's mouth opened and his eyes widened. Lisa stepped into the shower with Sam. They were both naked, wet, and now very close. Sam looked at her well-formed breasts, then down along the gentle curve of her side and her small, tight buttocks. He saw her small clump of pubic hair. He looked back into her eyes. They made not one sound.

They moved closer, smoothly and carefully. He put his arms around her back and held her close. Slowly and deliberately, he gently kissed her lips. They were cool, but they warmed quickly. The water continued to beat on both of their bodies as they entwined closer and tighter.

With both hands, he lightly held both sides of her head. Her red hair had turned darker in the soaking flow of warm shower water. They looked into each other's eyes and fell into each other's souls as if for the first time. It was a view of love that they wanted to linger, that they wanted to last forever. They could not turn away as flesh melted into flesh.

Sam moved his lips to her neck and gently caressed the small of her back. His hands moved over her back, suspended at times, pressuring at times. He felt as though they were one. She felt as though they were one. They were one.

Sam stared at his reflection in the mirror and looked deeply into his own brown-green eyes. A smile crept across his face. He turned toward his window.

Within seconds, an orange-helmeted figure moved from Stu's office into the driver's seat of the Jeep. The driver's-side door closed.

Inside, Lisa made sure that the black one-way visor was shut so that no one would know she was driving instead of Sam. She started the Jeep and began to slowly back up.

Behind her, bedlam broke out. The unprepared security force immediately threw back the barriers behind the dune-buggy trailer and forced away the screaming, nearly riotous crowd of journalists, neighbors, and other onlookers. The screaming, shouting, pushing, and shoving were intense, almost overwhelming the police. The NASA convoy of white sedans and vans began to spin around and assemble into a line, leaving a hole open for Sam's Jeep and trailer.

Lisa looked out through the rear window and stopped suddenly. She pulled a pair of leather gloves out of her leather jacket and hastily put them on. Her hands certainly did not look like Sam's hands.

Once the gloves were on, she continued to jockey the trailer into position. She heaved a sigh of relief and silently thanked Sam for allowing her to practice backing up with an attached trailer. She'd had to learn moves of the steering wheel that were totally against all her driving instincts in order to move confidently out of the garage. Lisa and Sam did not want any suspicions to be raised, nor did they want Lisa to scramble out of the Jeep if she couldn't back up the trailer.

But she did. Swiftly and surely, through the path made for her by the dozens of police and security officers, she moved the trailer back. Finally, she placed the transmission into drive and moved forward, ignoring the continual flash of photo strobe lights and the dozens of minicams pointed at her. With the visor of her helmet down, her jacket zipped to the top, and her gloves on her hands, she was confident that she would not be mistaken for anyone other than Sam.

So far, the ruse had worked.

As the caravan pulled away, so did the crush of people. It took only five minutes for most of the crowd and security people to disperse from the Alexander house and the street. Several reporters did their story wrap-ups, using the house and garage as a backdrop. They finally packed up and drove away.

Dozier, Craig, and Stu stood in front of the garage, watching the stragglers leave. With a toothy grin, Craig turned to his buddy and jabbed him in the side. "Man, tell me that wasn't bitchin'."

Dozier was not smiling; he was more concerned than excited. "Man, I just hope Lisa brings back my buggy in one piece." He took a deep breath. "She will, I think. She's a pretty cool chick. Sam's lucky."

"Hey, man, he's a cool dude himself. Ya know what I mean?" Craig asked.

Stu looked at Craig. "Yeah, I know what you mean." Dozier nodded.

Stu put his arms around the shoulders of his two new mechanics. "OK, gentlemen, it's a ritual around here. All new employees get to be taken out to lunch by the boss for some burgers and a couple of brews on their first day of work so we can talk universal joints, electronic ignitions, and valve covers."

"All right, man, all right," Craig said happily.

Stu had found two new dedicated, experienced mechanics; Craig and Dozier had found a new friend, Sam.

It had been half an hour since the last police cruiser had left the Alexander house. The neighbors had all gone back to their homes, and Mountain View Road was quiet again. Sam cracked open his door and looked down the long stairway. He saw no one. He held on tightly to his orange helmet and goggles. He checked to make sure that his gloves and bandannas were in his pockets. He zipped his leather jacket, bounded down the stairs, and rushed into the house garage through an unlocked side door.

Inside the garage, he paused to look at Glamorous Gertie sitting on top of her black trailer, hitched to the back of Stu's Ford Bronco. He walked to the driver's side of the Bronco and placed his helmet and goggles on the seat. He turned when he heard the kitchen door open. Marion, Sara, Cindy, and Mindy were standing in the doorway, staring at him. He looked across the long garage at their apprehensive faces.

He approached them silently. Then, at the doorway, he gave them each a hug. First Sara, then Marion.

"You be careful, OK?" she said tearfully. "I'll lie my ass off, Sam, if we get any calls from the news people for the rest of the day or night."

"Thanks, Aunt Marion."

Sam looked down at the twins. They were very restrained, not like squealing and active girls. They didn't quite understand what was going on, but they sensed that it was serious and possibly dangerous. They had been huddled together all morning, whispering and wondering about the madness outside and the family-imposed secrecy inside.

Sam kneeled; both of them hugged him as they had never before hugged him. Mindy, in a quiet and soft voice, spoke first. "Sammy, they aren't going to hurt you or steal you, are they?"

Sam tried to comfort her with a reassuring smile. "Absolutely not. I wouldn't let them take me away from you." He gave her a big kiss on the cheek. "Goodbye, Mindy. I'll see you tomorrow when you wake up."

Cindy started to get teary. Her lower lip quivered. "I love you, Sammy."

Then Sam began to get teary. He had never heard those words spoken so sweetly or with so much meaning. "I love you, too, Cindy."

He hugged both of them, then stood.

Once inside the Bronco, he secured his helmet and flipped down the visor. He pressed the button of the garage-door opener and started the Bronco. He looked in the rear-view mirror. The door to the kitchen was closed. He was on his own.

He pulled away from the house quickly and was on Highway 78 in a matter of minutes. He looked in his rear-view mirror and on either side of the Bronco through his hot helmet. The helmet came off, and Sam continued to look around and back at the trailer and the gleaming red dune buggy.

Finally, he settled into the seat and relaxed. He thought of Cindy and Mindy. He thought of Lisa. He thought of Sand Hills. He thought of the raspy white noise and the warbling tone of the signal, which grew louder in his mind and erased all other thoughts.

CHAPTER 51

Richard slowed his sedan as he passed the narrow road that led to the Gecko campground. Ahead he saw several motor homes, pulling trailers loaded with three- and four-wheel ATCs, pull into the campground. His destination was farther down the road. To his right he could see the beginning of the sand dunes. The blanched color of the sand reminded him of the clean beaches he had seen north of Los Angeles, but in a flash, a dune buggy or ATC would fly over the top of one dune, then disappear down another, reminding him that he was no-where near the beach. To his left he heard a boom and saw two needle-point F-16 fighters skimming over the deck. They were quite a distance away; he determined that they were flying very fast. As he drove on, he knew that in a few minutes he would be away from the center of the U. S. Naval Aerial Gunnery Range.

Richard forgot about the noise and the campground and focused ahead and to the left, concentrating on the sign that would lead him to the bump in the road called Glamis, a town that consisted of several buildings. The one he really wanted to locate was the Boardmanville Trading Post. He had memorized the map and knew that he must be only minutes away. If his calculations were correct, it would be around the bend. And there it was.

Richard turned right off Highway 78 and moved about one-half mile down a bumpy dirt road, past a gate that was permanently left open, and onto a gigantic gravel parking lot. Richard pulled as close as possible to the main building. He was surrounded by vans, trucks, RVs, and an odd assortment of off-road vehicles pulling in from the dunes about a hundred feet away.

Boardmanville was the destination to which buggy drivers traveled from across the dune field and the campground that Redden had just passed.

The compound contained several attached and several detached buildings. All were constructed of wood, and none was in the greatest condition. The main structure was a large two-story building with a large grocery and general supply store on the first floor and a window-lined restaurant covering the entire second story.

The facility was not for highway travelers or tourists. It existed solely for the people who came to the desert to cruise up and down the Sand Hills in off-road vehicles.

Nearby, a flea-market city had been set up by sellers of trinkets and swap-meet items that were considered necessary for existence in that environment: motorcycle parts; refreshments of all kinds; useless gadgets and souvenir T-shirts portraying the area, splashed with images of wild-eyed buggy drivers soaring through the air, the wind blowing back their hair and clothes.

The market was open only during the peak fall and winter season, and mainly during the weekends. It was Saturday afternoon, and the flea market and the main Boardmanville facility were booming with traffic and people.

Dust and noise were everywhere. Only when Richard finally shut off his engine did he notice the cacophony of roaring engines that surrounded him. Dozens of people were moving in and around the main building; hundreds were walking around the nearby flea market. Everyone wore jeans or shorts or leather riding clothes. The dust that was kicked up coated everything and everybody. The air was filled with screaming engines, shouts, laughter, curses, threats. Richard looked at the madness and wondered how he would ever be able to pick out Sam at this main launching point. Richard knew that he would have to blend in and keep his eyes open. He knew that Sam would start from here. It was where, he was told, most day riders off-loaded. So this spot, when the afternoon crowd cleared, was where he would find and follow Sam.

Richard stepped out of his car and grabbed a small overnight bag from the back seat. He locked the door and made sure that his motorcycle was locked and securely fastened to the trailer. He looked out of place in his dark suit pants and white shirt—the same clothes he had been wearing since he was arrested. The blood-stained bandage covering his forehead was turning a sickening brown and gray.

He was obviously not dressed for the conditions or the place, and people stared at this strange duck as he entered the second-floor restaurant. Richard was oblivious to the attention. He was single-minded in his pursuit of his goal, and public disapproval would not deter him.

The open dining room had the atmosphere of a rustic hunting lodge's dining hall. Faded pictures, mostly of ancient versions of dune buggies, and amateur paintings interpreting the barren desert terrain, attributing nonindigenous animals and plants to the locale, were hung haphazardly around the room. Great artistic license had been taken in portraying the southern Mojave Desert.

There were enough open tables around the room that Richard had no problem finding a place to sit. Half of the fifty-five tables were occupied by sand crazies, male and female, who all looked as though they had just stepped out of a severe sand-and-dust storm. Helmets, gloves, face masks, and boots cluttered each table. Most of the patrons had driven directly from the desert to the Boardmanville Trading Post Restaurant.

Richard found an empty table next to a corner window that gave him an excellent view of the dune field to his left and the crowded parking lot straight ahead. He put his small luggage bag on the empty seat next to him as the waitress walked over.

The teenage girl was wearing cut-off jeans and a halter top. A greasy white apron was wrapped around her waist, and a wad of gum lumped one cheek. She looked Richard over and stared at his stained bandage.

Richard stared at the pimply teenager. He thought that

she looked like a disaster. She thought the same about him.

The girl leaned over to get a closer look at Richard's forehead. She twisted her mouth and made a face as she stared at the caked blood in the center of the bandage.

"Wow, that sure is a nasty bump you got there. How'd you do it? You turn over on Competition Hill or something?"

He looked at her as though she were speaking another language. "What? Did I what?"

"Did you flip on your head charging up Competition Hill?" She looked around the room, then pulled her pad and pencil from a back pocket. "Most of these guys here, right in this room, are gonna eat it later on tonight over on Competition Hill. They go chargin' up there a million miles an hour, racing with other guys."

The waitress turned back to Richard. "And they're just weekenders. Ya know what I'm talkin' about? Ya know what I'm sayin'? Ya know what I mean?"

Richard picked up the dog-eared menu from the corner of the table. "Yeah, I get your drift, honey."

She smiled. "You ain't lookin' like you'll be doin' much ridin' in them duds, mister."

"Oh, yeah? Where's the restroom, by the way? I have to change."

She nodded to her right. "The head's over there."

Richard looked down at the menu. The fare was sparse and simple. "OK, let's see what we have here."

The waitress leaned toward him again. The crash of plates in the kitchen and the screams of other waitresses didn't seem to bother her in the least.

Richard looked toward the kitchen. "What the hell is going on in there?"

"Ya know, if I'm not mistaken, I'd say you got some pus oozing from that mess on your forehead."

She put pencil to pad and finally got to work. "OK, what'll it be? The special today is fried chicken with all the trimmings, and we may have some of that roast turkey left."

Richard touched his bandage and saw moisture on his

fingers. "I'll tell ya, sweetie, just bring a hamburger, well-done, some french fries and a Coke."

The waitress grabbed the menu and stuffed it between the sugar dispenser and the wall. "OK," she said, walking away. But she couldn't help delivering a parting remark. "I'd check my bandage if I were you. You got something leaking up there."

Richard suddenly lost his appetite. He turned and stared out at the setting sun. He looked back at the parking lot. The cars were beginning to thin out, so it might be easier to spot Sam now.

He looked down at his watch. It was almost six P.M. He knew he had a long wait before Sam would show. Sam had to be there before midnight—at least, that was what his inside source at JPL had mentioned as the time set for contact.

Richard leaned back. He decided to take his time and enjoy the delicious meal that was about to arrive. He looked around at the early dinner crowd. He occasionally received a stare back from someone in the surly crowd.

There was one table at the end of the room that he couldn't see clearly. It was occupied by two men who were keenly interested in Richard Redden. Jim and Bob sipped their Cokes and ate their fried-chicken dinners while they took turns keeping an eye on their prey.

Richard did not notice or sense their interest in him, nor did he notice the two dark-blue FBI sedans, one in the parking lot and the other behind the building. The agents' ties were off, but their clean white dress shirts immediately identified them as not being part of the desert scene.

Richard sipped his Coke and casually scanned the parking lot. His eyes followed a flatbed truck, carrying a half-track truck with a microwave dish on its roof, as it rolled to a stop at the edge of the lot. He whispered to himself, "What money people throw into this shit out here. A half-track with a goddamn TVRO satellite dish."

His hamburger finally made its way to the table. The waitress set it down, then brought ketchup and mustard from a nearby empty table. She was still intrigued by

Richard's injury, staring at the bandage again. She started to speak as Richard grabbed his hamburger. He raised one hand and held it up.

"Please, miss, don't talk about my cut and what's oozing out. I'm getting ready to eat."

She shrugged and turned to walk away. "OK by me. I was just trying to keep an eye on it for you."

"Thank you. I appreciate your concern. Now, please?"

The waitress was not alone in her observation of Richard. But the important quarry that everyone was waiting for was still several hours away.

CHAPTER 52

Night. In the excitement of the moment and the thrill of the challenge, Lisa and Sam forgot two very important logistical matters: gasoline refills and bladder relief. As Lisa squirmed in her seat, sweating profusely under her hot helmet, she considered both. She turned up the volume on one of Sam's scanners that was tuned to the NASA convoy frequency. She heard the conversation about those mechanical and biological needs. But knowing that other people were having similar problems that had to be solved didn't help her situation; it complicated matters. She was supposed to be Sam. If she stopped along with everyone else, she couldn't very well stroll into a men's restroom and stand at the urinal.

The thought of just relieving herself in Sam's black-leather riding pants didn't seem to be a viable solution, either. But the pressure on her bladder was such that soon, the forces of nature would make the decision for her.

The caravan was well beyond Victorville, north of Los Angeles, and heading deep into the Mojave Desert. Cities, services, and Interstate 15 exits were becoming rare, the distances between them greater.

The scanner told Lisa that a stop was planned in Barstow, so her stop at a gas station for a tank of gas and an unloading of urine would have to be made before Barstow. Letting the rest of the caravan turn off at Barstow and just staying on the interstate would not have worked. The several security sedans would just hop right back on the interstate.

Another problem Lisa had to deal with was the time—too much time. The caravan was ahead of schedule. Lisa had to arrive at the Dumont Dunes site no earlier than 11 P.M. She had to give Sam enough time to make the contact point by midnight and not give the alerted government officials enough time to reach the Sand Hills with helicopters flying at top speed. Lisa feared that too many factors were working against their carefully thought-out plan. She had to make some kind of move that would take care of all the negative factors, including her throbbing bladder.

Lisa turned her attention to the rear view mirror. The security sedan's high beams began flashing off and on. Suddenly the car zoomed next to the Jeep, and one of the plainclothes security officers motioned for Lisa—or Sam, as they thought—to roll down the window. Reluctantly, she rolled the window halfway down and secured her visor.

Rolling at forty-five miles per hour on the busy interstate from Los Angeles to Las Vegas, Lisa would have to fake a conversation with the people she was trying to delude.

"Sam, we are getting off at Barstow for food and fuel," the security officer screamed through a wall of howling wind.

Lisa nodded and rapidly rolled up her window. The sedan then sped ahead of her. Both NASA vehicles were in front of her; behind her were several station wagons loaded with news personnel.

She reached for a California road map and lifted her visor. The cool blast of air from the air-conditioning vent was a relief. The black sky and the lack of moonlight made the slow ride through the Mojave a tedious task, even with the heavy weekend traffic on the busy interstate. Lisa unzipped her leather coat and let the cool air flow down her chest. She began to think again about her ever-more-painful bladder. Something would have to be done about that, and quickly.

Lisa flipped on the small map light that Sam had installed in his cigarette lighter. It directed a narrow col-

umn of light at the map, not her face. She located her
position on the map and guessed that it was another half-
hour to Barstow. But no more than three or four miles
ahead, she located a turnoff for a paved road that led
northward toward Baker, Death Valley, and Dumont
Dunes. She looked away from the map and strained to
see the exit. She didn't know whether she could hold on
any longer without urinating in her pants.

As she was about to open the spigot to her urethra, she
spotted a single street lamp off the interstate at the head
of Stoddard Mountain Road. She flipped off the map light
and began to slow from forty-five to thirty-five to thirty.
The security cars ahead of her began to pull away, reaching and passing the Stoddard exit. Lisa slammed on the
accelerator and sped up steadily to almost seventy. Even
with the weight of the trailer, Sam's Jeep easily transferred smooth, steady power down the drive shaft.

The station wagons behind Lisa began to speed up as
well. She was several hundred feet from the narrow exit.
She knew that the news vehicles behind her had been
alerted by her erratic speed. She only hoped that they
thought Sam was trying to catch up with the NASA security vehicles.

Now almost on top of the exit, she took her foot off
the gas and turned hard into the short turnoff. The news
station wagons flew past her, still accelerating, racing
northward on the interstate. When the drivers of those
station wagons realized what had happened, it was too
late. They missed the turnoff that Sam's Jeep was taking;
the next turnoff was miles ahead. The deep, impassable
median strip formed a natural barrier, making a U-turn
virtually impossible. Finally, Lisa was alone, even if for
a brief time.

Before the era of the interstate system, the desert coun-
tryside was crisscrossed by narrow and not-always-
passable two-lane roads that served as transportation
lifelines in the harsh landscape. There were no modern
franchised gas outlets with brightly lighted pumping stations, protective canopies, secure pay windows, and

well-stocked food counters. The early filling stations were small shacks with one or two working pumps, maybe one trashy-looking service bay, and an office that usually displayed a faded, cracking twenty-year-old calendar with a picture of a scantily clad model in an advertisement for shock absorbers or piston heads. The attendant was nearly always asleep. Awake or asleep, his movements were usually slow and unaffected by the travelers' need for a quick fill-up and a clean restroom. The attendant was usually so excited to see another human being that he carried on conversations that continued long after the gas tank was filled and the windows were cleaned.

Such was the kind of filling station that Lisa had to settle for when she steamrollered off the interstate.

Several miles down Stoddard Road at the intersection of Kiowa and Stoddard, she pulled into the dimly lighted station. The owner was leaning against the wall of a small office that was littered with trash. He was watching a semi-clear TV picture, beamed from San Bernadino, on a black-and-white set that was at least twenty years old.

Lisa quickly pulled to a stop and jumped out of the Jeep. She popped open the gas cap and reached for the pump hose. She fumbled to get the nozzle down the neck of the fill pipe. The old man jumped out of his chair and waddled through the door of the small concrete-block office toward Lisa.

"Hold on there, sonny, just a minute," the old man said.

Lisa pulled off her helmet and put the gas-dispensing lock on the handle.

"I mean, missie. I do the pumpin' around here."

Lisa ran up to him and handed him a twenty-dollar bill.

She said in a flash, "Here's twenty bucks. Put in ten bucks' worth of gas as fast as you can, and you can keep the change."

Lisa ran toward the office. "Where's the john? I have to go bad."

The man was confused at the sudden excitement. "Uh . . . it's uh . . ."

Lisa stopped and squeezed her legs together.

"In back. Go 'round back," the man finally said.

She opened the door of the restroom and couldn't believe the filth and corrosion around the toilet. She stepped inside and held her breath. With her buttocks just inches off the seat, she managed to urinate into the stained, cracked porcelain toilet.

The owner was just putting the handle back into the ancient pump when Lisa ran up and kissed him on the cheek.

"Thanks," she said breathlessly.

Lisa started Sam's Jeep and sped away, leaving the station and the old man in a cloud of dust and flying trash. She had moved through the gas station like a whirlwind or like one of the dust devils the man had so often seen through his dirty office windows. Of all the customers who had passed through his out-of-the-way establishment, Lisa was the one he would remember. He watched the red trailer lights grow smaller in the distance.

The convoy suddenly appeared and raced into his station. A fusillade of questions bombarded the poor confused soul. He answered them slowly.

After all the newsmen, security officers, and NASA officials had used the funky toilet facilities, they raced off to catch up with Sam's Jeep and the dune-buggy trailer.

Eventually, they would catch up with Lisa but would not be able to pull her over. She continued northward toward Dumont Dunes, albeit much more slowly, over a rough, narrow, somewhat graded desert road.

CHAPTER 53

"**H**ey, buddy, how would you like it if I smashed your fucking face in?" the bulky tough guy asked.

His equally rough-looking friend added, "And when he's finished with your head, I'll punch your fucking heart out through your back."

"Look, guys," Richard stammered. "Here. I have an idea."

He reached into his pocket and pulled out a wad of cash. He peeled off several fifties and some twenties. "Here. I'll give you each a hundred bucks if you let me go ahead of you. I gotta get my bike fixed before midnight, and . . ."

"And just why is that, dickhead?"

Richard looked blankly into the evil eyes boring into him. "I gotta make it back over to Gecko campground, or I'll miss my ride back to LA."

The friend snatched away Richard's money.

Richard then stepped back, picked up his bike, and rolled it under the brilliantly lighted canopy. He rushed up to Malcolm Libby.

Malcolm had been living in the desert for almost twenty-eight years. He owned a repair shop and parts store that serviced thousands of off-road vehicles each season. His large open garage was several hundred yards from the trading post.

From six in the morning till nearly twelve at night, beneath a bank of fluorescent fixtures, Malcolm would fix crankshafts and replace blown headers, but mostly he spot-welded. And usually, it was the newcomers who had to see Malcolm. They would foolishly charge up a sand dune and find themselves careening out of control. Repairing busted axles and cross members took ninety percent of the crusty man's time.

His sixty years didn't show as much as his tremendous beer belly did. He was loved by the regulars and worshiped by the newcomers. Since everyone was stuck in the middle of the desert and the nearest fully stocked auto-repair shop was many miles away, everyone who had a dune buggy, all terrain cycle, or motorcycle was at Malcolm's mercy. He sold parts for do-it-yourselfers and spent the rest of his time either showing them how to do it or welding on pieces himself.

His prices were fair and his work was top-notch, but he wasn't speedy. A beer break would occur once an hour, more frequently on especially hot days or on nights like this.

His only pet peeve was pushy newcomers, smart-ass know-it-all newcomers, or drunken bums who thought they could push him around.

Standing in front of him was Richard Redden, who was either one or the other. Malcolm was ready for a beer break and his nightly meal sent over from the restaurant: a plate of fried chicken, mashed potatoes with gravy, canned green beans, and a slab of apple pie topped with a scoop of vanilla ice cream. He was about to enjoy it.

He turned away from the last customer before his dinner break and headed through the pitch dark for the parts shack across the driveway. He took a quick slug of beer and let out a tremendous belch. Richard followed him. Richard was finally wearing his new jeans and Western shirt; a red bandanna and Army-surplus tank goggles were wrapped around his neck. He looked and sounded as though he were near hyperventilation as he approached Malcolm.

"Malcolm, wait a minute! I gotta talk to you!" he shouted.

Malcolm turned to see who was calling him, then walked on toward the parts shack.

"Sorry, buddy. I'm eatin'."

"But I got a repair—an easy one that you gotta do right away."

Malcolm stopped sharply and turned toward Richard. "Listen, mister, I ain't *gotta* do nothin'. I been workin' since six this morning, and I haven't et yet. Whatever it is, it'll hold." Malcolm continued walking. "C'mon, settle down. Join me for a beer, have some chicken with me, and tell me all about yourself."

Richard stopped and watched Malcolm walk away. "It's just a busted chain."

Malcolm's booming voice echoed against the nearby buildings and the restaurant. "Great. Easy job. But it'll wait. *Sabe?*"

Richard turned and saw the two men he had bribed laughing as they moved toward the restaurant. He was at Malcolm's mercy.

He followed Malcolm into the parts shack and saw him sit down at a steel-legged table with a well-worn formica top.

"C'mon, whatever your name is—bring your butt over here and tell me what you do and what the hell is going on in Smog Central, LA or wherever you're from. We're gonna have some food brought. C'mon." Malcolm waved him to the table.

Richard looked down at his watch, then back out at the parking lot. It was 10:30 P.M. Sam would be arriving any minute. If Sam were to make it to the Sand Hills contact point on time, he would have to arrive by eleven.

"Shit. A lousy chain link," Richard cursed quietly. He had to acquiesce to Malcolm's demands, or he would never get the chain fixed in time.

Malcolm threw his feet up on the table and took a swig of beer. "Hey, how'd you bang up your head?"

Richard couldn't wait to get as far away from this place as possible.

CHAPTER 54

The final evening briefing sessions were over. The press contingent—more than one hundred carefully selected reporters, mostly science reporters—had been shown maps and aerial photographs. They had been given the specifications of the personnel carriers that would take them to the still-unknown contact location.

The barrage of questions and complaints centered on the site itself and on how to get out instantaneous print, sound, and picture reports. The television linkup, designed and manned by the Army Signal Corps, was discussed; line connections to satellite-transmission trucks, which had been under way all day, were complete.

Very few of the press representatives were happy about relying on the government to transmit all video and audio, but they had no choice. A representative of NASA's public-information office had warned them to avoid any independent action because of one West German news organization's futile attempt to lease a high-speed Bell jet helicopter. The clandestine refueling pad and temporary heliport had been discovered deep in Death Valley and quickly dismantled. The press was warned that Army Apache attack helicopters with night-vision devices and targeting radar units would be constantly in the air, scanning the perimeter of Dumont. Whether any stray aircraft would be shot down was a question that was left unanswered.

Video and audio tests were under way; every available satellite channel was locked up for this event. The squabbling and fighting over access priority was long over. Now chief engineers sweated from the still-potent heat and nervous tension, praying that their equipment would hold out under the harsh conditions.

Power was provided by a long row of portable generators, set up in an adjacent canyon to shield the command compound from the exhaust fumes of the engines. Long electrical lines snaked along several miles of guarded cable racks mounted above the desert floor.

On the other side of the compound, filled with trailers, tents, and Army desert vehicles of every shape and size, a final briefing for the foreign scientists was breaking up. Goggles and long coats were passed out in preparation for the journey into the heart of the Dumont Dunes. Last-minute refreshments were served in a dimly lighted, open-sided cafeteria tent; the astrophysicists, anthropologists, engineers, and astronomers took the opportunity to make a last pit stop in the portable toilet station, set up in an obscure corner of the command compound.

Kenneth Wood, wearing twill pants and a bush jacket, was being hounded by several NASA engineers as he walked toward Evegeny Romanov and his assistant. They were sitting at a picnic table with Mark Stevens and several elderly scientists, drinking tea and eating sugar-coated doughnuts.

Wood ducked under the lip of the dark canvas tent and into the meager light. "Ah, Kenneth, so what is the news?" Romanov asked. "Where is our young friend?"

Wood motioned to the two men next to him to stop talking. "Just a minute, guys." He nodded to everyone sitting at the table. "Oh, a typical screwup," he said. "Sam took a turn off the interstate and is coming up here using side roads. It's slowed the convoy up considerably, but I understand that they should be here any minute."

Romanov looked at his watch. "Isn't that cutting it rather close? It's ten hours and fifty minutes now."

"I know. But there is nothing we can do about it. I mean, they want him and we need him, and he's not telling us much." Wood shrugged.

Myra asked coldly, "Why don't you just pressure him,

force him, to tell you what he knows, and take over from there?''

Wood was taken aback by the abruptness of the question. ''We don't do things like that here, Miss Pemin. We are well prepared for whatever happens. All our equipment and measuring devices are portable and lightweight. They are easy to move, set up, and run. Our eight observation posts are ready. I can't force anybody to do anything.''

He leaned on the table. ''And besides, the area isn't that big. I mean, if something or someone comes floating down from the sky, we will detect and track its trajectory long before the thing lands.''

''Yes, but you have a boy in charge of your mission, Mr. Wood.''

He was preparing a caustic reply when he was interrupted by an emergency page on his two-way radio. He brought the radio up to his mouth.

''Go ahead, main gate.''

The entire table heard the reply over the tremendous background noise.

''Sir, the convoy has arrived. We are directing it to the compound. Is that a roger?''

''Yes, it is. We want him offloading and disembarking from here so we can track him. Send him through. Now.''

The mob scene at the temporary main gate to Dumont looked like a riot. Inside Sam's Jeep, Lisa struggled to drive through the pathway made by a phalanx of security forces, who were being shoved, pushed, and in some cases overrun by photographers and minicam crews. Behind them were hundreds of ordinary citizens who had thought they were coming to Dumont for a quiet weekend of fun and relaxation.

Lisa saw faces pressed against the closed windows of the Jeep and a continual flash of photographic strobe lights. Shouted questions and screams of ''Roll down the windows!'' culminated when the passenger door opened and a NASA security officer hopped into the seat next to her. She cursed herself for not locking the door, but she remained silent and continued the charade. She knew that every minute counted now.

She glanced down at the large digital clock on the dashboard. It was almost eleven P.M. Just a few more minutes of subterfuge, and she would finally reveal her identity to a shocked Kenneth Wood.

The breathless officer pointed straight ahead. "Sam, head straight for that bank of lights down the road about four or five hundred yards. We're taking you to the command compound. OK?"

Lisa looked straight ahead and nodded.

"OK?" the guard repeated. He stared at the helmeted driver and waited for a reply. He furrowed his brow and put a hand-held radio up to his mouth.

"Dumont Control, this is Main."

"Go ahead, Main," came the reply from an unseen radio operator.

"Yeah. I'm with Alexander now. We're pushing through this crowd, and we'll be on site in two minutes. Two minutes. Copy?"

"Copy."

Lisa steered around a group of minicam operators who would not move off the road. She honked the horn and flashed her headlights as she slowed to only one or two miles per hour.

The officer furiously rolled down his window, leaned halfway out, and waved angrily at the camera crews. "Get the hell off the road, you bastards, before we run your asses over!" he screamed.

He pulled himself back inside and turned to Lisa. "Sam, put it in neutral, gun the engine, put it back in drive, and punch it. If they're still in the way, run 'em over. OK?"

Lisa nodded. She still hadn't uttered a word. The officer stared at what he thought was Sam. His training and instincts told him that something was amiss. But he was more concerned about getting through the crowd and depositing Sam and his desert dune buggy in the middle of the command center. His superiors would handle it from there.

Lisa did as she was told and jerked ahead, scattering guards and cameramen as she lunged forward. The path finally cleared, and she sped up to a reasonable forty miles per hour.

The security officer turned and watched the madhouse recede. It was quiet again inside Sam's vehicle.

"Man, those leeches just won't leave you alone. How was your trip up?"

Lisa lifted her right hand off the steering wheel and made an "OK" signal.

The officer continued to stare at the driver. His suspicion was increasing. "Don't wanna talk much, I guess," he said.

Lisa shook her head.

The compound was just ahead. Lisa had caught up with one of the convoy sedans, which slowed as it veered around several tractor–trailers and onto the hard desert floor.

A small crowd of workers paused to watch Sam's Jeep and the trailer carrying Dozier's dune buggy proceed to the center of the compound.

Lisa took a deep breath. She knew that within seconds she would be discovered. Again, she glanced at the digital clock. It was a minute or two past 11 P.M. She had done her job.

Kenneth Wood handed his two-way radio to Mark Stevens, who stood at his right. Romanov and Myra trotted up with several other scientists. They were eager to meet the young man who had made the discovery of a lifetime. Wood was eager to secretly and quickly put a small tracking device on Sam's buggy.

Lisa pulled up to the group and stopped. Even before she shut off the engine, the officer was out of the front seat, helping several technicians unstrap and pull the tarp off the dune buggy.

As the tarp was pulled away, the chrome frame gleamed like a diamond under the bank of brilliant white lights. The technicians rolled the dune buggy onto the ground as Wood approached the driver's side of

Sam's Jeep. Lisa was still sitting inside, holding the wheel tightly.

Wood leaned toward the closed window. "Sam, you wanna come out now? We have a lot to do and not very much time to do it."

The door of the Jeep Cherokee opened, and Lisa stepped out. The guard moved closer to Wood. His curiosity was so great that he wanted to rip the helmet off Lisa's head.

Wood smiled. "So, how was your trip? And how the hell did you find yourself off the main road?"

There was no answer.

Wood's face dropped.

The security officer mumbled, loud enough for Wood to hear, "Something is wrong here."

"Sam, take your helmet off," Wood said. "I want to talk to you, and I can't if you've got that thing on. Sam?"

Lisa had to make her move. Everyone standing around her sensed that something was wrong, as the security officer had said.

Lisa released the strap and methodically rocked the helmet from side to side until it came off. Her red hair fell to her shoulders, and a big smile crossed her face.

Wood was thunderstruck. He began to turn beet-red.

Myra Pemin stepped forward and coldly looked at Lisa. In her thick Russian accent, she said, "This doesn't look like a Samuel Alexander to me, Kenneth Wood."

Romanov rubbed his eyes, shook his head, and moaned.

The security guard balled his fist.

Then Wood stepped back and screamed at the top of his lungs, "Shiiiiiit!"

He bounced back in front of Lisa. "All right, young lady, do you want to tell me what is going on? Where the hell is Sam?" Wood asked angrily.

Lisa put her hands on her hips. "Where you'll never to able to get to him and push him aside, like you were planning to do."

Romanov let out another moan.

Wood grabbed a two-way radio from the security guard

and put it up to his mouth. "Control, this is Wood. Copy this fast and good."

"Ready, Mr. Wood."

Wood's voice was strained. "Get every single chopper you can back to the heliport. Bring up all transport to the command post. Organize groups to be taken to the heliport. Call the CHP and any other police agency down in Brawley, and tell 'em we're coming. Get immediate flight clearance all along a route south. Tell . . . get . . . find . . ." Wood stumbled and fumbled. He released the transmit button.

He grabbed the officer's arm. "Get down to the main gate. Try to find one of the local desert types who knows something about that other location, someone who knows something about the tank target. Fast!"

Wood pushed him toward the gate. The officer broke into a dead run.

Wood glared at Lisa. She glared back at him.

CHAPTER 55

The traffic in the Boardmanville Trading Post parking lot had cleared away.

Sam climbed out of his uncle's Bronco, stretching and twisting to relieve his stiffness after the long drive. He looked up. Sirius and Jupiter were just clearing the eastern horizon; most of the other star groups and constellations were obscured by the light flooding from the general store. A gas attendant strolled toward Sam and squeezed between two of the four battered pumps on the gasoline island not far from the trading-post entrance.

Sam looked at his watch. He had to start driving to the tank target soon and could not waste time. "Uh, fill the buggy tank and the Bronco."

The sleepy young man moved slowly—too slowly for Sam.

"And I wanna get outta here, so . . ."

The attendant had had a busy night, with sand-rail dune buggies, all terrain cycles, cars, and trucks waiting their turns at the pumps.

"Yeah, I know. Right away. As soon as possible."

Sam cinched his belt tighter and pulled the bandannas from his pocket as he walked toward the general store.

It was quiet inside the store, a combination convenience shop and small grocery store offering all the snacks and sundries necessary for survival in the desert. The aisles were narrow. The merchandise had been fairly well handled throughout the day; boxes and containers were scattered around, and the enormous vertical cooler was fairly empty. The amount of soft drinks, beer and wine sold by that small general store was equal to the amount sold by any major grocery story in Los Angeles or Phoenix.

Behind the cluttered checkout counter, the night-shift crew was waiting impatiently for midnight. Closing time was the best time of the day for the two young men, but also the most dangerous; it was a time when the threat of theft was greatest. Every customer who walked in at that hour was a potential felon.

Sam, however, did not look or sound like a felon. He innocently walked up to the counter and threw down a single-serving pecan pie and a cola. There was no conversation. He received his change and turned to walk out.

Once he crossed the threshold, he was spotted by his nemesis, Richard, who was leaning against the canopy supporting post attached to Malcolm's garage. The talkative mechanic had given Richard some chicken, a beer, and unending conversation about the pit called Los Angeles. Only now was Malcolm finally working on Richard's busted chain, and Richard knew that any minute, Sam would arrive at Boardmanville.

Malcolm was still droning on about LA's crime and smog as Richard stared at Sam. Adrenaline poured into his system. He turned to Malcolm.

"Malcolm, how much longer? I gotta leave."

Malcolm looked up slowly. "Hey, Dick, don't worry. I'll have this clamped on in one minute. See what I mean about LA? You people are pushy, always pushy."

"I know. It's terrible. But please . . ."

Malcolm secured the new link. He began to place the chain in position as Richard pulled out his money.

Jim and Bob watched Sam and Richard from a hidden vantage point at the rear of the general store, the Odyssey vehicles side by side, both drivers in their seats. The small but powerful high-torque engines were ready to be started. With a flip of a switch, they could roll. The Russian agents watched Sam as he paid the pump attendant.

Also in position were the two FBI sedans. The two agents in each vehicle watched the Russians, Sam, and

Richard. Their attempts to call for backup on their two-way radios were futile; they were well out of radio repeater range. Finally, one of the agents got out of the car and strolled as nonchalantly as possible to the telephone outside the general store.

Sam started the Bronco and moved it and the trailer to the middle of the dark parking lot. He parked and got out of the Bronco, unhooked the retaining straps on Glamorous Gertie, and carefully rolled her off the ramp. He fiddled with the carburetor covers and, using a small flashlight, checked every connection, line, and hose he could see. The buggy had been given a thorough overhaul in Stu's garage, but Sam felt that one more check was necessary.

He glanced at his watch and realized that he had only forty-five minutes to reach the tank target. He stepped to the driver's seat and grabbed his helmet and goggles. He turned to look at the distant dune field. He noticed a nearby dark sedan and two shadowy figures seated inside, watching him. He thought that was strange. But he knew that if the sedan was going to tail him, it wouldn't get very far on the hard-packed earth around Boardmanville.

Sam wrapped one bandanna around his neck and the other around his mouth. It had been some time since he had last played at Glamis with his father, but the impressions were deep. The contour of the land had changed somewhat, constantly shifting, shaped by the sculpturing winds, but the underlying form of the dune field remained the same. Sam knew where the tank target was located; he knew the bends, twists, and turns he would encounter on his way there. The route to his goal was as familiar to him as the drive from Los Robles High School to his home on Mountain View Road.

He put on his goggles, then his bright-orange helmet. He eased inside the driving cage of the silent dune buggy. It felt comfortable and safe. The seat wrapped around his torso and held him in place. If he had been sitting in the cockpit of a multimillion-dollar single-seat fighter jet, he would have felt the same sense of power, control, and excitement.

He engaged the clutch and exercised the gearbox. He turned on the ignition switch and flipped on the light bar. Roll-bar halogen beams and the front-end lights blasted out a wall of light, three million candlepower strong. The buggy was facing the dune field, lighting a path to the soft sand tracks beyond.

Sam nestled into his seat and took a deep breath. He placed his left hand on the steering wheel and grabbed the ignition switch. He was about to turn the key and engage the electric starter when he heard the roar of a motorcycle engine starting up in Malcolm's garage. He turned to look behind him but could not see who was sitting on the desert cycle. Only the front tire was visible from his vantage point.

He turned back and heard the almost simultaneous start of two other engines, muffled but still audible, behind the general store. Then he saw the headlights of the dark sedan. Another dark sedan appeared around the corner of the general store.

Sam pulled the goggles off for a better view. His hearing was impaired by the padding of the helmet, though he had clearly heard the sounds of several idling engines. Sam wondered whether it was a coincidence that all those engines had started at the same time, at the exact moment he was ready to start the engine of Glamorous Gertie.

An overwhelming sense of unease began to creep over Sam, a curious feeling of being observed and measured. He looked at the sedans and said softly, "They'll never make it."

He turned the ignition key. The powerful motor sprang to life with a deep, throaty roar. From the second it kicked over, the engine was smooth and steady. Sam gunned the engine rhythmically and watched the temperature gauge slowly rise. He secured his helmet and goggles. He pulled the restraint straps tight, and plastered himself against the seat. As he did so, he saw the motorcycle pull away from Malcolm's shop. He still couldn't see the driver. The sedans moved closer, and the Odyssey vehicles rolled into view around the side of the general store.

"What is this?" Sam asked.

He eased the transmission into first gear and let out the clutch. He lurched forward. Within seconds he was up to cruising speed and moving away from Boardmanville.

The glowing light of that outpost of civilization vanished almost at once as he rolled along the bumpy desert floor and around clumps of creosote bush and chapparal. He followed a well-worn narrow path that curved around these small islands of vegetation.

The sound and heat of his smoothly performing engine were comforting. He barely had to push on the accelerator pedal to know that if he needed it, the power was there.

He could see in the distance, perhaps one or two miles ahead, the lower mounds. A few miles more beyond them were the towering sand dunes. And a few miles beyond them were the valleys, curves, and bowls that concealed the tank target.

Sam looked around and saw the bouncing lights of the two Odysseys which were just leaving Boardmanville. Jim and Bob were the first to follow Sam from the parking lot.

Richard was dumbstruck when he saw the twin vehicles race after Sam. "Who the hell was that?" he wondered as he kicked his cycle into gear and raced after them and Sam. Now he would have to contend with interlopers as well.

He flipped the cycle around the corner of Malcolm's and raced to catch up with them. It had been a while since he had ridden a motorcycle, but he felt sure that he could handle the rough ride after Sam Alexander. He wanted to stay cool; he didn't relish an out-and-out chase.

As Richard raced off, the two FBI sedans followed. But for them, the hunt would be a short one. The men in the lead sedan saw Richard's taillight race over the berm; the driver gunned the engine and followed. The gravel parking lot gave way to hard pack, then softer sand. The sedan was going no more than thirty miles per hour as it approached the berm, crested the rise, and flipped sideways on the soft sandy bottom.

The second sedan was following too closely. The driver slammed on the brakes, spinning the second sedan out of control as it crested the rise only yards behind the first FBI vehicle. The second sedan rolled on top of the first, with the horn blaring and the agents inside cursing and yelling at one another.

All four agents scrambled out of the crumpled cars, their front wheels spinning wildly. They watched Jim and Bob, Richard, and Sam disappear into the blackness of the dune field. They were gone. The FBI agents were out of the chase.

There was only one way for Sam to determine whether he was being followed. He had to confirm his suspicions. As he dodged the thinning bushes and made a ninety-degree turn, he saw the Odysseys still moving toward him. Behind them was the motorcycle. Sam caught a glimpse of them every time he spun around an obstacle. He saw a fifty-foot hill straight ahead.

He gunned the engine and sprinted to the top of the hill. He stopped short on the crest, using the friction of the sand and his front-wheel hand brake. The engine idled. He was stopped. He turned to his right and saw the Odysseys slow and stop about a hundred feet away. Behind them, the motorcycle moved to a position several hundred feet away on another small hill.

Everyone waited for Sam to make a move.

Sam would test them again. He gunned his engine and slammed the transmission into first gear. He popped the clutch and roared over the hill. The other vehicles were behind him and out of view for the moment.

Sam entered the soft, hilly section of the Sand Hills. From here on, all the dunes would be soft sand, rising higher and steeper.

He began to push the dune buggy to the limits of its capabilities. He did not race the engine, but he had to hold on tight during several high-G turns as he down-shifted, then gunned the engine. He kept flipping the steering wheel right and left on the increasingly difficult turns and banks.

Behind him, Jim and Bob were using all their nerve, skill, and strength in their effort to keep up. They got only fleeting glimpses of the dune buggy's taillights and the glowing exhaust fumes that occasionally flew out of the vertical exhaust pipe.

Richard was having problems controlling his motorcycle, which didn't have the stability of the second set of wheels that Sam's buggy and the Odysseys possessed. He had to struggle to remain upright on the tight turns. He decided to ride along the ridgetops, which formed an irregular spine cutting through the Sand Hills. Sam and the Odysseys would be below him.

He raced up a steep dune and stayed on a path well worn by other off-road sand vehicles. Richard had to make a quick recovery from a nearly disastrous tumble that snapped his helmet strap. The helmet flew off and tumbled into a dark depression below. All he now had for head protection was his goggles.

Sam raced around the smaller sand bowls, catching an occasional glimpse of the piercing lights of the Odysseys. He charged up a sand dune that had a commanding view. He applied the front hand brakes, using the high friction of the sand to help him make a quick stop.

Once Sam knew that the buggy was settled into the sand, he unstrapped and leaned toward the ammunition box that his father had long ago welded to the front of the frame. He popped it open and pulled out a pair of binoculars. The purring engine gave him comfort; he knew that he could move away speedily if he had to. He also knew that if his "friends" were still on his tail, he would have to pour on speed and power to streak away.

He looked toward the horizon and saw the twinkling lights of Boardmanville in the distance. He turned to see illegal magnesium campfires blazing at the Gecko campground. He estimated that he was fifteen minutes away from the tank target. He would have to immediately outdistance whoever was following him.

Sam raised the binoculars to his eyes. He scanned the featureless narrow view and finally spotted the two Odysseys rather close by. Their lights nearly obliterated the outline of their spindly frames. They had stopped moving as well. Jim was looking back at Sam through a pair of binoculars. He saw Sam looking at him, and waved.

Sam could not make out the man's face in the dark, but he was now sure that the two Odysseys were following him.

He turned his attention to the motorcycle, which was moving above and around the Odysseys. It was coming closer.

Sam refocused as the cycle moved steadily closer. When he finally got a clear view of the driver, he nearly dropped his binoculars. He reached for one of his powerful roll-bar lights and turned it toward the motorcycle and its driver. Richard Redden was fully illuminated as he kept coming closer. He was only one hundred feet away.

"Richard Redden! Damn it!" Sam muttered.

The chase began anew and in earnest.

Once strapped into his dune buggy, Sam jammed the accelerator to the floor and zoomed down the back side of the dune. He would have to race at top speed on a moonless night over steep terrain made of soft sand. And he would have to race at top speed in a vehicle that could reach speeds of fifty or sixty miles per hour, yielding multi-G turns.

Sam headed for a small plain near a large impassable dune. It was there that he hoped to gain enough speed to lose his pursuers. If he could outrace them there, he would have a chance to hide in the series of sharp, pointed dunes ahead—The Towers. The Towers' slopes were slanted near the maximum angle of inclination—thirty-two degrees—at which sand could hold together in a hill rather than tumbling downward.

He flew off the base of a large dune and over the short flat at top speed. Glancing over his shoulder, he saw the Oydsseys right behind him. Whoever they were, the drivers were good, Sam thought. But not that good.

In and out of The Towers, Glamorous Gertie didn't miss a shift or slip a wheel. After at least half a dozen rocking turns, Sam stopped again. Unbelievably, the Odysseys were still behind, and so was Richard Redden. Sam looked at his watch. He had now less than ten minutes.

His mind raced. "How can I escape from them?" he asked himself. He looked up at the night sky, filled from horizon to horizon with a brilliant canopy of stars. But Sam was not looking at them; he was looking through them, considering his next move.

He once again looked straight ahead and punched the accelerator. He would venture into the Pits of Hell.

Even in full daylight and at moderate to slow speed, the perfectly formed sand bowl known as the Pits of Hell was treacherous. The terrain formed a series of natural velodromes. The sides of the smooth sand bowls were uniformly canted. An error in judgment by the driver of an off-road vehicle or a misreading of the slope could result in a vehicle's being thrown over the lip of the bowl, or, more likely, in a driver's being flipped out of his vehicle to tumble into the narrow funnel at the bottom of the bowl.

The sides of the hills were extremely steep and soft. A lookout was usually required and no one dared go in alone. Too many injured drivers, and more than a few body bags, had been airlifted out by medivac helicopters.

At night, it was nearly impossible to calculate the angle of the slope. Sam hoped that the contours he remembered had not changed.

He drove up and over several more dunes into the first of a daisy chain of bowls, traveling around each one as fast as possible in an effort to disorient his pursuers. He hoped that he could flip his buggy up, over, and out of the "sand traps," leaving the other drivers hopelessly lost in a maze of sand where each hill and bend looked like every other hill and bend.

Sam exited the first bowl and flew to the next one, then the next one. Finally, he reached the most dangerous of the bunch. Jim and Bob were directly behind him. As the two Russian agents got more used to the style of driving required, the bolder they became. But they did not have the experience to handle the dizzying turns.

Sam made several hard, fast revolutions around the tight bowl. He was driving so fast that he almost caught Bob, who was now in front of him. Sam started to turn and crest the hill but was hit in the face by a flash of light.

Richard Redden had stopped at the top of the dune to watch the chase below. He had purposely turned his bright headlamp into Sam's face.

Sam was blinded for only a second, but that was long enough for him to lose his sense of direction. He veered up and over the dune and sailed through the air. His engine screamed and roared as the fat paddle tires spun wildly; they had nothing to grip but air, which forced the engine to rev up to extremely high RPMs.

Sam had enough presence of mind to see his landing position and turned his wheel hard to the right. The buggy hit the ground with a bang. Sam gunned the engine and swept down the face of a very high dune.

He stopped with a jolt. He was stunned and struck. His back tires were buried in a small depression at the base of the dune. He saw a wide plain and another set of dunes straight ahead. He knew exactly where he was. Over those dunes was a gently sloping series of mounds that led down to the Pits. But his tires were buried up to the middle of the rim, and he wasn't going anywhere.

Rocking the tires was not helping. If he gunned the engine he might get out—or, more than likely, bury the bugger deeper. He looked up at the top of the dune and saw the light of Richard's motorcycle.

From his high vantage point, Richard saw that Sam was stuck in the sand. On the other side of the dune, he saw catastrophe striking Jim and Bob. The two KGB agents were caught in the vortex of the downward-sloping bowl and couldn't get out. Finally, Jim tried to race up to the top of the sand trap, but his angle was too steep. Bob was on his tail and did not see Jim slowing. Bob barely hit the rear end of Jim's Odyssey, but hard enough to nose it into the side of the dune. Both vehicles tumbled and cartwheeled toward the bottom of the deep pit. End over end, they twisted and spun. With a loud crunch of metal against metal, they crashed at the bottom.

Bruised and battered, they struggled with their harnesses and extricated themselves from the twisted wrecks. They frantically tumbled out and began to run up the side of the dune, but were knocked flat by the explosions of the Odysseys. They rolled to the bottom next to their vehicles. They were dazed and blackened, with broken bones, lacerations, and charred clothing, but they were still alive. Their burning vehicles would serve as beacons for their rescue and capture.

Richard looked down at their predicament and laughed. "Fuck you, boys, whoever you are." He then turned his attention to Sam below. "OK, sonny, time to talk again," he snarled.

Sam gunned the engine, without luck. He was hopelessly stuck. That realization, along with the countdown in his head, told him that he was running out of time. And to further exasperate and frustrate him, Richard glided down the slope of the dune and stopped a few feet away.

Richard shut off the engine of his bike. He tried to rest it on the kickstand, but the sand was too soft, so he laid the bike on its side. He strutted over to Sam, took off his gloves, and loosened his windbreaker with great histrionics. He had Sam where he wanted him. He had the upper hand.

"My, my, my. What do we have here?" Richard asked arrogantly.

Sam put the transmission in neutral and let the engine idle. He slowly lifted his clear visor. He still held the steering wheel with his left hand and the gearshift knob with his right. The engine rumbled smoothly.

Richard grabbed the roll-bar cross member above Sam's head, turned his head to the right, and peered at the stuck rear tire.

"If I'm not mistaken, you're gonna be here for the duration, my little man."

Sam was boiling over with rage. "You filthy pile of snot, how come you're not in jail?"

"Jail? No jail. Bail."

Richard laughed at his poor attempt at alliteration.

"How'd you know the landing was gonna be here instead of Dumont?"

"How'd you know the landing was gonna be here . . ." Richard mimicked. "Because, Samuel, unlike you, I have basically an untrusting nature and attitude. I did a little more research than my pals at the space factory."

"Maybe, but you don't know the exact . . ."

Richard interrupted. "Oh, yes, I do, Samuel. That Irtysh—a piece of work, he is. He'll believe damn near anything. Hell, even now he still thinks I am his boss. What an idiot."

"You're the idiot. You don't know where it is."

Richard leaned away from Sam's Glamorous Gertie. "You mean, the tank target? Oh, yes, I do, my good man. I studied the topographic map"—he pulled the map out of his pocket and waved it in Sam's face—"and another dumb cluck, Malcolm, showed me exactly where it is. I'm not stupid, Samuel."

Richard looked around at the dunes. "And I'd say we are very close. Just where exactly?"

"Go fuck yourself, Redden. The only thing I'm gonna do is rip off your head and shit down your neck."

Richard displayed mock terror. "Oh, please don't hurt me! Please show mercy!"

But he quickly dropped the act. With one hand, he grabbed the bar above Sam's head. With the other hand, he held one of the support beams by the idling engine. "OK, enough with the pleasantries. I've got a spaceship to meet, and it's gonna be here at oh-eight-hundred. So get out of the rig, punk. I have to hog-tie you so you don't go anywhere."

Sam just glared at him.

Richard screamed, "Get out, punk!"

Sam replied quietly and slowly, "Fuck you."

Swiftly and simultaneously, Sam jammed down the accelerator, popped the clutch, and shoved the transmission into first gear. A long tongue of flame belched out of the three-foot vertical exhaust pipe at the rear of the engine.

The dune buggy lunged forward and was out of its trap in a split-second, its engine thundering and screaming.

Richard lost his grip on the roll bar but managed to hold onto the rear bar. Sam raced his buggy forward; the wind and the inertia pushed Richard almost horizontal. Faster and faster the buggy raced across that short stretch of flat desert. Sam went through first gear into second and gained even more speed.

Richard was flopping around the rear of the engine cage like a limp rag doll. Each time he was flailed to the right, he would bounce off the white-hot exhaust pipe. The heat began to burn through his nylon windbreaker. He would smash against the pipe again, and another piece of his jacket would burn away.

As Sam made a sharp right turn, Richard was thrown hard against the blazing tailpipe. He screamed as the heat penetrated his jacket. He bounced on the ground, but still held on.

Sam accelerated again and headed back to where he had been stuck, racing again, taking the bumps hard. He slowed and dragged Richard through a clump of creosote bushes. Richard nearly let go.

Again, Sam hit the accelerator and aimed for Richard's motorcycle. Driving faster, then even faster, he ran over the cycle. The impact flipped the motorbike in the air; it landed in a twisted, crumpled pile of rubble.

Sam turned hard again. This time Richard was wedged against the white-hot chrome exhaust pipe. The heat burned through his jacket and shirt and seared his upper arm, cauterized his flesh and exposing the humerus.

Richard screamed at the top of his voice as the excruciating pain raced through his body. He immediately loosened his grip.

Sam turned back and circled around Richard, who was rolled on the ground in agony. The roaring engine of the dune buggy drowned out his curses and threats.

Sam was confident that he hadn't killed the man. Still, he was tempted to run over him.

Sam turned away and steered toward the rounded dunes

ahead. He had an important destination and only a few minutes to get there.

He accelerated again and sped across the flat sandy field.

CHAPTER 56

The geosynchronous orbit one thousand miles above
the Earth's surface had remained steady for some time.
No changes in the pyramidal magenta spacecraft had occurred.

But now, it was time for the craft to come to life. It
gradually started rotating on its axis, taking one second
per revolution. The blunt end of the craft tilted away
from the Earth; the apex of the craft moved into position
and aimed at the southern half of California.

A low hum began to radiate from the craft. The hum
ascended in pitch until a steady-frequency tone was es-
tablished.

Then, with no other noise or visible change, the craft
plunged down in an arcing trajectory, passing quickly
through the upper atmosphere, through 450,000 feet. The
target point was the southern Mojave Desert of California, fourteen miles north of the Mexican border.

Maj. Peggy Wiley rested her chin in her right hand as
she stared at the large green radar scope deep inside
Cheyenne Mountain at NORAD, located in the Rocky
Mountains of Colorado. Her shift had been extended and
her duties altered for one job only. She was to monitor
the movement of the anomalous object hovering over the
North American continent.

Wiley's orders were precise and clear: track and follow
the object, and give accurate reports on its altitude, trajectory, speed, and angle configuration in all axes. She

barely had enough time to activate the intercom switch and transmit a warning about what she saw on her radar screen. She was astonished by the movement of the object.

She dropped her arm and straightened her back. She leaned toward the monitor so that it filled her vision.

Wiley fumbled for the push-to-talk switch on her headset microphone. "Turkey Gulch, Turkey Gulch, this is Lookout."

The immediate response was too slow for her.

"Turkey Gulch, this is . . . Turkey Gulch, target descent has begun and has been completed. Speed off the peg. Course-transition insertion . . . unable to calculate. There wasn't enough time for the pulse to track or lock. It's there with you, somewhere."

CHAPTER 57

Sam tried to clear his mind of Richard Redden and everything else. He had one clear purpose. He had less than five minutes to cover several miles and reach the tank target.

The terrain had now turned into a series of almost-identical fifty-foot dunes that Sam took at faster-than-usual speed. There were no sharp twists or bends; the hard, quick steering required on other sections of the Sand Hills wasn't necessary. It was just as well, because Sam's mind was still racing with the chase, the sounds of the SETI signal, and fear of what he was about to face.

Sand mounds moved up, down, then up again in a hypnotizing repetition that enabled Sam to consider what he was about to experience. The thought crossed his mind that perhaps this was a hoax. A complicated hoax, for sure. Was it possible that all of this was some sick joke? Sam shook his head; he refused to believe that.

He pressed the accelerator even harder as the hills began to grow steeper and higher. He tightened his grip on the wheel as the unevenness of the terrain required his attention. His curiosity pushed him to drive faster and faster. He topped one large dune and flew through the air.

The tank target was near. Driving over several small dunes, Sam looked in every direction. He knew that he was close.

Glamorous Gertie raced down a flat field and climbed a small flat-topped dune. And at the crest of the dune,

Sam finally saw the monster six-hundred-foot dune he was looking for. That was it, straight ahead. Over its crest and in a small valley, in the middle, was the goal. The tank target.

The huge dune looked no less formidable to Sam than Mount Everest had to Edmund Hillary. Sam eased his pressure on the gas pedal as he coasted down the smaller dune. When he reached the bottom, he increased his speed. As he curved upward again, he put all his weight on the gas pedal.

The two-foot-wide paddle tires kicked up a rooster tail of sand thirty feet long. The tires dug into the sand as the engine provided all the horsepower Sam could cajole. The buggy swerved, then slowly but steadily climbed the unrelenting grade. He saw the dune top in the light flowing from the headlamps. "C'mon, baby! Give! Give! Give!" Sam screamed. His forward motion began to slow. He was nearly to the top. His forward motion slowed even more.

Another hundred feet, Sam thought. Now eighty. C'mon. I'm so close. I'll never make it up to the top in time if I roll back. C'mon.

The engine stopped. The headlights went dark. No sound came from any part of the engine or electrical system.

The tires rolled back a foot, then sunk into the sand. Sam was stranded no more than fifty feet from the top of the perilously steep dune.

Sam sat stunned, both feet instinctively jammed on the brake. He turned the front wheels hard to the right and pulled the hand brake with all his strength. He looked back; he couldn't see the bottom of the dune. It was so far away and so dark that it looked like an eternal pit.

He then looked forward again, toward the pinnacle of the dune. He heard, only faintly, a hissing noise, a humming noise. He pulled down his goggles and squinted at what he thought was a magenta sky.

Sam unbuckled his four-point restraints. He pulled off his helmet and goggles and placed them on the passenger seat. He pulled his bandanna down to his neck.

He held onto the steering wheel and stared again at the top of the dune. The hissing continued. His vision began to adjust from the glare of his now-cooling light system to the blackness of the Mojave Desert. His visual acuity was sensitive enough to confirm the magenta glow. Something was on the other side of that peak.

His stomach began to knot. His hands shook.

"C'mon, Alexander, get a hold on yourself," he whispered. But he was having a difficult time. His nervousness made him slightly nauseous. Maybe if he threw up, he would feel better.

He swung his legs over the side of the buggy and tumbled away from Glamorous Gertie. He had to dig his feet into the sand to keep from falling to the base of the dune. Then he was on his hands and knees. The steepness of the dune prevented him from standing erect.

A new wave of nauseousness came over him. He dry-heaved, then spit out some vile-tasting sputum. He began to feel slightly better.

He was ready to make his move to the top. He fought his way inch by inch to the dune peak. He had skipped too many physical-education classes, and he was not in shape, but he continued to scramble to the top. Twenty, ten, five feet. He was at the top.

He fell on his back and struggled to an erect position. Looking back, he saw the lights of Boardmanville. He turned slowly to keep from tumbling down the dune and put one foot over the other side.

A wave of heat flowed over him. He looked down into the sand valley. His mouth dropped open and his breathing became shallow, as he saw a sight that seemed to spring from his fantasies.

"Oh . . . my . . . God," Sam whispered. Then his expression of amazement turned into one of growing joy and contentment.

Below him, nearly filling the valley, was the pyramidal magenta spacecraft. It dwarfed the steel tubing fabricated to resemble a tank that Gen. George S. Patton had used long ago to train his tank corps during World War II.

The smooth surface of the craft glowed in the purist,

deepest color that Sam had ever seen. It was as intense and flawless as the cobalt blue of an optometrist's observation light, yet deeper and clearer. There were no precise features or angular breaks in the surface. It was pointing, apex down, from the bottom of the pit to almost the top of the dune, eye-level with Sam.

Sam squeezed his eyes closed, then opened them again. The craft was still there, filling his view. Nothing was in his mind but the reality of what he was seeing with his eyes and feeling with his body. The heat was gentle, but the humming and hissing were now more evident.

Sam scanned the horizon quickly. Nothing else was in the vicinity. No other human was seeing the sight that was now before him. He looked down at the spacecraft in awe.

He took another step. Both feet were now on the downward slope of the dune. He took several tentative steps down, then stopped suddenly. As the volume of hissing and the higher-pitched hum rose, the huge craft began to turn over.

Sam stumbled and fell on his back as he watched the craft turn 180 degrees. The apex was now pointed up and the base was down. The hum and hiss lowered along with the entire spacecraft. It looked from Sam's vantage point as though the craft were hovering only inches from the ground.

Sam stood again and gathered his courage. "Let's see what's going on here," he whispered.

His steps were firm and purposeful as he descended the dune. The top of the craft loomed higher and higher over him.

When he reached ground level, the base of the craft was fifty or sixty feet away, floating above the small valley.

Sam looked up at the top of the craft high above his head, searching for an opening or entrance or orifice. He waited and looked. What now? he wondered.

"Hello," Sam said weakly. "Hello. Is anyone there?"

The hissing stopped, and the hum lowered in pitch as

the craft settled on the floor of the sand canyon. The hum stopped. Then there was a slight hiss.

Nothing happened for what seemed like an eternity. Sam grew slightly impatient, but that feeling lasted for only a moment.

He took several steps forward, then stopped dead. On the smooth featureless surface, a seam appeared in the form of a trapezoid. It became sharper and formed a door that swung open from bottom to top.

Behind the door was a darker magenta surface.

Sam was frozen with fear. He bent over and peered into the opening. He saw two figures emerge. They had arms and legs and were human in form. They moved in slow gliding steps, arms swinging slightly. One looked male; the other, female. Features began to form. They were dressed in magenta . . . what, Sam thought? What are those—seamless jumpsuits? No buttons. No zippers.

His body suddenly tingled. He felt flushed. His eyes widened and began to tear. He wanted to flee in terror. He couldn't. His arms stiffened. His mouth opened wide. He wanted to scream but couldn't. The figures moved closer, closer still, to within fifteen feet. Sam wanted to scream again. His mouth closed, and he began to weep without expression. His heart ached.

In front of him stood his mother, Ann Alexander, and his father, Peter Alexander.

Sam shook his head. "No," he whispered. "You're supposed to be dead. No. This isn't real."

He tried to close his eyes. He couldn't.

Without moving his lips, Sam's father spoke to him. "Hello, son. It is good and right to see you again."

Sam tried to raise his arm to reach out, but couldn't.

Without moving her lips, Sam's mother spoke to him in the soft, gentle voice that had been imprinted on Sam's mind since before his birth. "We have missed you, and my heart has craved for you."

Sam tried to speak. "Wha . . . wha . . . this can't be."

Ann Alexander moved closer. She moved without walking, floating gently to within ten feet of Sam. He recognized her soft features, her large blue eyes, her soft translucent skin. He began to weaken and melt. His arms ached to hold her; he wanted to touch her cheek and feel the heartbeat he had known while floating in her womb.

"Mother," Sam said softly.

"I am your mother. Do you recognize us, Sam?"

Sam shook his head. "This is impossible. My parents are dead. Who are you? What are you? Are you a manifestation, a vision? Are you imaging my thoughts and memory? Let me go!"

The pure, soft voice of Ann Alexander penetrated Sam's brain. How can this be? Sam wondered. I hear her, but she is not speaking.

"Sam, we can't let you go."

Peter floated forward next to Ann. "Sam, you must stay where you are. We can come closer now."

They both moved to within five feet. Sam did not move. He could not move. As they moved closer, he felt even less control over his body. He felt their strength, or control, or whatever was emanating from their bodies. Sam wondered whether he was feeling some type of holograph or image projection with a surrounding energy field.

"No. Don't. Please."

"Do you recognize your parents?"

Sam nodded, then shook his head. "I don't know," he said.

Sam started to turn ashen, and his eyes began to roll back in his head. His head tipped back; his knees crumpled. Peter raised his hand toward his son. Sam straightened again and revived.

He heard his mother's reassuring voice. "Sam, close your eyes. Now just relax a moment. We want you to relax."

Sam closed his eyes and felt a wave of peace and contentment flow over him. He had goose bumps for a moment, then felt warm and calm again.

"Now open your eyes and look at us."

Sam opened his eyes. His parents glowed and basked in the warm magenta light surrounding everything in the valley. That color was intensified by their own slightly shimmering magenta garments.

Sam felt uncontrollably relaxed and at ease. He felt protected again by his parents' concern and caring. Nothing else around him seemed to be important. He could feel, hear, and sense nothing but the parents who had given him life.

His mother spoke. "Do you still feel faint?"

"No."

Peter said, "Good. Sam, we cannot be seen or heard by others. But what we will tell you and give you, you will retransmit and deliver to those who are waiting for your return and who are approaching at this moment."

Sam looked confused. "What? I don't understand."

Ann replied, "We will tell you now. You are the recipient of a signal transmitted from where we have come. You were not a random selection."

Peter added, "Your early amateur-radio transmissions were traced to this planet and correlated with me and your mother."

Ann continued, in a low, soft voice that reverberated inside Sam's head, "What is known of you has been filtered through us to those on the planetoid in Tau Ceti orbit. An attempt to contact you was made after many such attempts to planets in other Sun-like systems, to other intelligent species whose form and development are familiar in some ways but different in others."

"Millions of which inhabit the sphere of the universe as both you and we know it," Peter added.

Sam began to feel as though he were surrounded by fog that was weighing down his shoulders and clouding his thoughts. He said weakly, "But you're dead. How can you be here?"

His chin dropped to his chest. He was beginning to black out, yet something was holding him up. "Oh, my God, please wake me from this dream."

Peter turned and looked at Ann. Ann continued to direct her attention toward her son. "Sam, we are going to increase your level of consciousness. Be prepared to steady your weight."

Sam lifted his head. His eyes were much more alert,

and his carriage more erect. "What happened to you long ago?" he asked. "What happened?"

Ann answered, "What has happened to others. Against our will then, but with our will now. Our small plane vanished over the ocean, and we were taken to the Tau Ceti solar system."

"That's impossible," Sam said. "How can that be possible?"

Peter said, "We will come back only this one time, for one purpose alone, Sam. The signal you received from the Tau Ceti system was from a planet in a Sun-like star system. Distance makes two-way conversation impossible without our signal-transform capability. But once we leave, you and your science will have this ability."

"We will leave detailed information more readily suited for physical than for electromagnetic radio transmission," Ann said.

With his renewed and somewhat restored strength, Sam stepped forward to his parents. They were within touching distance. He lifted his arm, but it stopped only centimeters from his mother.

"Mother, I feel warmth. Are you alive? An apparition?"

Ann smiled for the first time. "Very much alive."

Peter said, "We have been changed physically and mentally."

"By who? And how?"

"It is in the data information."

Ann said, "Sam, we had no choice in leaving you. We were offered no choice. We could not return, and we would not have been able to return were it not for your efforts—long ago, when you were younger, and more recently."

The fog lifted from Sam's thought process. He looked past his parents at the spacecraft, up to the towering peak of the craft, then back to his parents.

"I can't believe this is happening," he said.

Peter said, "The shock of our landing on the White House lawn, or at Whitehall, or in Red Square, or in Tiananmen Square, or again at Machu Picchu would be too great for your people. It would also be too dangerous for us. But all those who hear you and study the data will finally realize that intelligent civilizations do exist on other planets, just as surely as worlds within worlds exist on your planet.''

Sam shook his head in confusion. ''But this is your world, too. You were born here.''

Ann replied, ''We will not die here.''

Peter added, ''If we *do* die. We are not sure of that.''

Sam stared at his parents as though they were still Earthly flesh and blood. An overwhelming urge to grab and hug them once again surged over him. Then he sensed their growing sadness. He could see it in their eyes.

The hum of the spacecraft suddenly became slightly louder, and Ann and Peter were slowly pulled back several feet. Sam became panicky. ''What's happening? Where are you going? I've got more to ask.''

Ann replied, ''We are leaving now, Sam.''

Peter turned away from Sam and Ann as though there were a presence behind him.

Sam tilted his body to view the trapezoidal opening. The interior magenta light had intensified, blocking his view of a small humanoid figure. Sam squinted and made out some details: leathery skin, slanting black eyes, long fingers. But it was a fleeting glance. The interior light intensified even more, obscuring the figure. The hissing noise increased. A change was occurring, and Sam did not know what it was. He became frightened.

''Don't go! Please don't leave me again!'' Sam said pleadingly to his parents.

Ann said in a cooler tone, ''We have no choice.''

Sam began to weep. ''Not again. Oh, please, Mom, Daddy, don't leave me alone again. I miss you. Take me, please. Let them take me. I'll let them take me.''

Peter replied in a soft, comforting voice, ''We cannot, Sam. They chose.''

''Who are 'they'?''

''They are . . . us now. We have become them.''

Peter and Ann were pulled backward toward the trapezoidal door. Their forms were nearly obscured by the intensity of the magenta glow. A high-pitched whine rose from the spacecraft.

"Please don't go! I miss you!" Sam's eyes were brimming with tears, but he did not cry.

Ann gently said, "We miss you as well. We can feel it when you think of us. We have loved you, Sam, since before you were born. We will love you till the time you die, and beyond. We will always love you."

Sam whispered, "Don't go. Don't leave me."

Peter said, "Sam, I want you to know that I'm proud of you. You've carried on my work well. Don't stop. There is more life in the universe than . . ."

"Dad?"

"Yes, Sam. What is it?"

"How many stars are in the sky?"

Peter smiled. The question that his son had asked so long ago, at a spot not far from where they now stood, was being asked again.

"More than you could possibly imagine."

"How many other stars have planets with people like us on them?"

"More than both of us could possibly imagine."

Sam gave a long, contented sigh. "Good. I hope so."

Ann looked into Sam's eyes. He felt the loving gaze even from so far away.

"Goodbye, my sweet son."

"Goodbye," Sam said softly.

When Sam uttered the last syllable, Ann and Peter Alexander were pulled back into the glowing spacecraft through the trapezoidal door. The small humanoid figure studied Sam, and Sam returned the gaze. Sam tried to talk, but suddenly, he was unable to speak. What had been so easy only moments before was now impossible.

The door suddenly disappeared. The seam outlining the door disappeared.

As if released by an unseen force, Sam stumbled backward and fell on his side. He popped back up and continued to move backward toward the edge of the giant dune.

The hissing increased markedly, with the higher-pitched hum and whine radiating from the spacecraft. Sam looked up in awe as the craft lifted slowly away from the floor of the canyon and rotated 180 degrees. The blunt end of the spacecraft was pointing up again.

The hissing stopped and the whine rose to a pitch too high for Sam to hear. In an arcing trajectory, the spacecraft climbed out of the sand canyon at tremendous speed into the clear night sky.

Sam gaped at the unearthly movement. The craft moved without noise. There was no wind, no sonic boom as the craft broke the sound barrier. It vanished in a flashing magenta blur that stayed on Sam's retinas. If he had blinked, he would have missed it altogether.

He looked at the dark dune walls surrounding him. He shivered as a cool wind plummeted from the top of the dune toward him and the valley floor. He heard the gentle wind once again. He felt alone and helpless and cold, very cold.

Then he directed his view down to the spot where the spacecraft had hovered. In the middle of the canyon, not more than two hundred feet away, Sam saw a slightly glowing metal cylinder about one foot tall. Regaining his strength and control of his body, he walked toward the glowing case. He bent down and studied it carefully.

It looked somewhat like two stacked coffee cans welded together, but the surface was not grooved; it had been machined, much like stainless steel. A strange latching device held down what looked like the top. Sam hesitantly touched the container. It felt cool. His fingers probed the top of the container. He played with the latch until he discovered how it worked. Snapping it open, he lifted the lid.

He peered inside. A ring of miniature lights illuminated a stack of round disks that looked very much like audio compact disks. Sam grinned, then chuckled. "CDs. They're probably in Dolby stereo, too."

As Sam began to close the lid, something underneath it caught his eye. He saw an unfamiliar form of writing. Then, in English, below the Sanskrit-shaped letters:

"TRAVEL PREPARATION INSTRUCTION IN-
CLUDED—TRAVEL TO TAU CETI SUN SYSTEM—
DESIGNATE SAM ALEXANDER."

Sam took the last struggling steps to the sand dune
peak. His right hand held the canister tightly. He hugged
and cradled it as though he were carrying the Bible or
the Koran or the Torah. The writings inside were as valuable.

He turned 360 degrees and took in the entire view as
a fresh cool breeze invigorated his senses and sharpened
his thoughts. He was wide awake and alive with excitement as he saw the lights of Boardmanville, the campfires
of Gecko, and the beckoning glow of some distant Earth
city.

A low thumping bounced off the Sand Hills. Sam heard
the approaching helicopters clearly. He looked down and
beyond to a nearby gully approach to his location and
saw a dozen or more bouncing lights as other buggies
and off-road vehicles vectored toward him.

Sam arched his back and surveyed the colorful canopy
of planets and galaxies and novas and pulsars and quasars.

Sam secured the magenta cylinder and started his dune
buggy. He rapidly drove with his precious cargo to an
eagerly waiting world.

Author's Note

In preparation and research for this book, I used numerous reference sources to verify facts and lend credence to those facts presented.

Half the fun of writing this book was the research. The source material is vast, in some cases easy to understand and in other cases too complicated for the layman to grasp. But many books were invaluable and fascinating and thrilling. I encourage the further study of both astronomy and the search for extraterrestrial intelligence. The following bibliography lists some of the material that helped shape the data base I used to write *SETI*.

The characters and story of *SETI* are fictional. But NASA's Jet Propulsion Laboratory is currently involved in a sky and target-star search for radio signals from deep space. In the early 1990s multichannel receivers and large radiotelescope dishes around the world will begin the search, a search that will change the way man views himself in relation to the universe. It may be that at the turn of the century, in our lifetime, a thin ripple of noise flowing from a small speaker in a remote receiving station will finally answer the question we have all asked as we gazed at the stars above us on a balmy, beautiful summer night: Are we unique and alone in the universe?

Bibliography

Angelo, Joseph A., Jr. *The Extraterrestrial Encyclopedia: Our Search for Life in Outer Space.* New York: Facts on File Publications, Inc., 1985.

Aylesworth, Thomas G. *Who's Out There? The Search for Extraterrestrial Life.* New York: McGraw-Hill, Inc., 1975.

Baird, John C. *The Inner Limits of Outer Space.* Hanover, N.H.: University Press of New England, 1987.

Baugher, Joseph F. *On Civilized Stars: The Search for Intelligent Life in Outer Space.* Englewood Cliffs, N.J.: Prentice-Hall Inc., 1985.

Christian, James L., ed. *Extra-Terrestrial Intelligence: The First Encounter.* Buffalo, N.Y.: Prometheus Books, 1976.

Darling, David J. *Other Worlds: Is There Life Out There?* Minneapolis: Dillon Press, 1985.

Feinberg, Gerald, and Robert Shapiro. *Life Beyond Earth: The Intelligent Earthling's Guide to Life in the Universe.* New York: William Morrow and Company, 1980.

Moore, Patrick, ed. *The International Encyclopedia of Astronomy.* New York: Mitchell Beazley Publishers, 1987.

Morrison, Philip, John Billingham, and John Wolfe, eds. *The Search for Extraterrestrial Intelligence.* Prepared by the National Aeronautics and Space Administration. New York: Dover Publications, Inc., 1979.

Poynter, Margaret, and Michael J. Klein. *Cosmic Quest: Searching for Intelligent Life among the Stars*. New York: Atheneum, 1984.

Press Release from the Public Information Offic JPL, Pasadena, Ca. *SETI: Search for Extraterrestrial Intelligence*. Pasadena, Calif.: NASA–Jet Propulsion Laboratory, 1987.

Regis, Edward, Jr., ed. *Extraterrestrial Science and Alien Intelligence*. London: Cambridge University Press, 1985.

Shields, John Potter. *The Amateur Radio Astronomer's Handbook*. New York: Crown Publishers, Inc., 1986.

Stilley, Frank. *The Search: Our Quest for Intelligent Life in Outer Space*. New York: G.P. Putnam's Sons, 1977.

Tomas, Andrew. *On the Shores of Endless Worlds: The Search for Cosmic Life*. New York: G.P. Putnam's Sons, 1974.